The Hidden Light of Mexico City

CARMEN AMATO

2012 CreateSpace Trade Paperback Edition
Copyright © 2011 by Carmen Amato

Library of Congress Cataloging-in-Publication Data
Amato, Carmen
The Hidden Light of Mexico City/Carmen Amato

ISBN 978-1475200799
Ebook ISBN 978-0-9853256-0-2

Books by Carmen Amato

Detective Emilia Cruz series:

CLIFF DIVER: Detective Emilia Cruz Book 1
HAT DANCE: Detective Emilia Cruz Book 2
DIABLO NIGHTS: Detective Emilia Cruz Book 3
KING PESO: Detective Emilia Cruz Book 4
PACIFIC REAPER: Detective Emilia Cruz Book 5
43 MISSING: Detective Emilia Cruz Book 6
MADE IN ACAPULCO: The Emilia Cruz Stories

Suspense

THE HIDDEN LIGHT OF MEXICO CITY
AWAKENING MACBETH

Non fiction

THE INSIDER'S GUIDE TO THE BEST OF
MEXICO (editor)

The Hidden Light
of
Mexico City

by

Carmen Amato

Stay in this part of the castle, wife, and do not be afraid when you see me fight; with the help of God and His Holy Mother I feel stronger of heart because you are here.

El Cantar de Mio Cid

Note: 10 Mexican pesos = 1 US dollar

◆

Chapter 1

"The next step is to follow the money," said Eduardo "Eddo" Cortez Castillo.

"That's quite some story, Eduardo." Across the table, César Bernal Paz gave his head a bemused shake as if collusion between Mexico's Minister of Public Security and the elusive leader of the country's most notorious drug cartel was a remote and amusing concept.

"There's enough evidence for a warrant." Eddo felt his scalp prickle under the brown hair he kept as short as a general's.

"Really," Bernal Paz said absently. He sliced into the *arrachera* steak on his plate and put a morsel into his mouth.

Eddo reached inside his Brooks Brothers suit jacket, took out a folded document from the inner pocket, and placed it on the starched tablecloth between the two place settings.

Bernal Paz eyed the heavy ivory paper and embossed black border. "*Secreto*, eh?"

The two men were in a private corner of arguably the most exclusive restaurant in Mexico City. The Sanborn's restaurant on the top of the historic Casa de Azulejos near the huge Zocalo square was the lunchtime bastion of Mexico's power elite. The staff was unfailingly discreet, the atmosphere was dim and elegant, and more deals and careers were made and broken there than in the president's office in Los Pinos.

"The warrant is for the central bank to report all of Hugo's financial transactions for the past year, including money transferred out of the country," Eddo said quietly.

Bernal Paz blinked in astonishment, his steak momentarily forgotten. "No. No." He hastily wiped his lips with his napkin. "Honestly, Eduardo. I can see now why you've been telling me all this. But as senior governor, I cannot let the central bank become involved in some petty rivalry between you and your superior."

"This is not personal, Don César," Eddo said in all truth. "I hold Hugo de la Madrid Acosta in very high regard. I hope this investigation proves to be nothing. But we need the truth."

"Yes, of course." Bernal Paz raised white eyebrows. He was an aristocratic man who clung to the elegant manners and rigid societal rules of those few who controlled the country's money and had complete faith in their right to do so. He wore a fitted Italian pinstripe suit and a discreet designer tie with matching pocket square. "But you have to see it from my point of view. You are investigating your own minister. Very awkward."

"The warrant is signed by Judge Arturo Romero," Eddo countered. The problem was that the warrant was Secret. Only a handful of people knew of its existence. Mexico's legal system was so arcane that if Bernal Paz refused to comply there wasn't anybody who had the knowledge and legal authority to compel him, including the president.

"You know him. Not just for this." Bernal Paz made it a statement, not a question.

"My professor in law school."

"Yes. I recall your father saying that." The older man leaned back in his overstuffed chair. "I suppose now you'll tell me that if Judge Romero wins the presidency you're in the administration."

Eddo raised his wine glass in a mock toast. "Attorney General."

"Will you be the youngest?"

"I'm already past 40." Eddo said. "Probably not."

Bernal Paz smiled back magnanimously. "I lose track of the years, Eduardo. To me, you'll always be a boy playing *fútbol*. Running like the wind with the eyes of an angel." He wagged a finger at Eddo. "You should be on television."

Eddo nodded his acceptance of the compliment even as he indicated the document on the table. "Arturo asked that you personally oversee the warrant."

"And when he gets to be president Judge Romero will remember warmly those who were his friends before the election?" Before Eddo could reply, Bernal Paz reached out with a forefinger and slid the warrant toward Eddo's plate of salmon. "But Romero might not even get the party nomination now that Lorena's decided to run."

Eddo suppressed a grimace. Mexico's First Lady Lorena Lopez de Betancourt had tried very hard to upstage her husband ever since Fernando Betancourt had been elected president. Her latest antic was to announce that she wanted to be president when her husband's term expired.

"You don't think she'll get the nomination?" Bernal Paz polished off his steak. The older man's relief that they were no longer talking about the warrant was palpable.

"She has no financial backing." Eddo slid the warrant back to Bernal Paz's side of the table. "Can you get me the information within two weeks?"

"Really, Eduardo." Bernal Paz sounded like a stern schoolmaster speaking to a wayward pupil. "The central bank cannot be involved in dirty politics."

"Ministers of the government cannot be permitted to join the cartels." Eddo kept his voice low, although the effort was nearly killing him. He wanted to jump up and shout, make Bernal Paz see how critical it was that they have the banking records, squeeze the old man by the throat until the numbers popped out of his ears.

"All the evidence you have so far is circumstantial." Bernal Paz made a dismissive gesture with his fork. "The land his son supposedly bought from El Toro--."

"Reynoldo de la Madrid is 14 years old, Don César," Eddo interrupted. The sale of a large tract of desert land from a man using cartel boss El Toro's Christian name to one Reynoldo de la Madrid had been recorded by the town clerk of Anahuac, a small town south of Nuevo Laredo, and reported by a local cop. "Some teenager in the most expensive private Catholic school in the country, with bodyguards around him even at the Santa Fe shopping mall, is not making his own deals with cartels."

"Eduardo, you don't understand." Bernal Paz pursed his lips and pushed the warrant back across the table. "I would like the central bank to help, but getting this type of information is very difficult. It cannot be done and that is final."

"It's all on computers," he countered. "No doubt you have a good systems administrator who can get it done."

Bernal Paz frowned. "Listen to me, Eduardo. Hugo is a powerful man. If he finds out he'll bring down the bank."

"The bank is an institution," Eddo pointed out. "It will survive.

Bernal Paz shifted uncomfortably in his chair. "No. You ask too much."

"So we're too afraid to save our country?" Eddo pressed, leaning forward. "What will you leave your grandchildren? A country that's just a playground of violence for the cartels?"

"Eduardito, that's enough," Bernal Paz scolded.

The childhood nickname was a warning sign and Eddo knew it was time to give Bernal Paz some space. He sat back in his chair and signaled to the waitress. She deftly removed their plates and brought coffee.

"My father always said if I needed anything I should come to you," Eddo said after awhile. He poured some cream into his coffee and stirred it. "That's why he always kept the Marca Cortez money in the Banco de Vieja Puebla."

"Marca Cortez and Banco de Vieja Puebla go back together for more than 200 years." Bernal Paz loaded his coffee with sugar and looked at Eddo meaningfully. "This is what matters in Mexico. Family. History. Tradition. Not your silly secret warrants."

The words were thick with significance. Eddo didn't reply but again let the silence draw out, watching the older man sit impassively across the table, reproof etched on his patrician features. Bernal Paz's refusal to conduct the bank investigation had nothing to do with his fear for the central bank or even, really, of Hugo de la Madrid Acosta. No, it was Eddo's insolence in growing up and attaining a position of power over not only his elders but his peers in Mexico's highest social class, the *criollos* who could still claim a pure Spanish bloodline. Tradition meant preserving the social order and Eddo was threatening to upset it. What he was doing simply wasn't done by one of their own.

"Marca Cortez values the relationship with Banco de Vieja

Puebla, of course." Eddo sipped some coffee. The caffeine hit his stomach and set it alight. "I still sit on the board of directors and Uncle Bernardo and I speak frequently."

"And Octavio oversees Marca Cortez's financial interests just the way I did when I headed the bank."

Eddo carefully centered his cup in its saucer. "I'm just a little concerned that Octavio might be, ah, how shall I say . . . distracted."

Bernal Paz frowned, the white eyebrows dipping toward his nose.

"Three months ago a certain Señorita Vida Sandoval Arnez bore Octavio fine twin boys," Eddo continued softly. "They live in a fine new house in Cuernavaca that Octavio bought at a cost of three times his annual salary from the bank. He's a frequent visitor. Of course, it must be heartbreaking to be away from Elena and the children so much. And his duties at the bank."

Tension hung in the air, stretched by silence. "How do you know this?" Bernal Paz finally asked.

"Octavio's private life is between him and Elena," Eddo replied. "But a bank with a distracted director is not a safe place for Marca Cortez."

To the old man's credit he didn't flinch. They both knew that if Eddo recommended it, his uncle Bernardo Cortez, Marca Cortez's chairman, would move the company's money elsewhere. Banco de Vieja Puebla would collapse and the Bernal family fortunes along with it.

A muscle in Bernal Paz's jaw bunched. "How long have you been director of the Ministry of Public Security's Office of Special Investigations?"

"Over four years," Eddo said. "I was the first official sworn in after the election."

"Four years." Bernal Paz's voice trembled with anger. "In all that time you've been concealed. Lurking in the shadows. Oh, you've caught some people and made a few statements. But even when you were seeing that blonde television woman no one knew who you were."

Eddo nodded once in acknowledgment. For the year they'd dated he'd managed to stay on the periphery of Elsa's fame.

She'd hated his reserve and avoidance of the limelight right up to the day they'd agreed to go their separate ways.

"This is not what your father wanted for you." Bernal Paz jabbed a finger into the air at Eddo. "You were a disappointment. He wanted you to take over Marca Cortez. To be its lifeblood the way he was. Instead you run off to that fancy *norteamericano* college. Let Romero fill your head with crazy ideas in law school and then you threw away all that education by joining up with the police. You were with scum and you've become just the same." Spittle flew from a corner of his mouth. "Never marrying, never carrying on the Cortez name. You wipe your feet on tradition, Eduardito. And now this. You're the man who lifts skirts to see the shit underneath."

Eddo pushed the warrant back to Bernal Paz's side of the table. "Two weeks. Whatever you find send to the office at Marca Cortez."

Bernal Paz snatched up the warrant and stuffed it into the inside pocket of his superbly tailored suit jacket, his face tight with suppressed fury. "I do this only because when I pray for the repose of your father's soul, I can say that when his son asked for help and invoked his name, I gave him the help he asked for."

Eddo nodded.

Bernal Paz pushed out his chair and stood. The man was older, more frail than when he'd entered the restaurant two hours before. Eddo stood up, too, and at that moment their status and power were equal.

"Mark my words, Eduardito." Bernal Paz's voice was so low Eddo had to strain to hear. "Hugo de la Madrid Acosta is a powerful man. He'll learn of this investigation and when he does, you're a dead man. A dead man."

Eddo met Bernal Paz's eyes. "Maybe I already am."

"Two weeks," Bernal Paz spat. "And you will not be welcome in my house again."

The old man stalked out of the restaurant, acknowledging no one although he probably knew most of the patrons.

Eddo sat down. A wave of nausea hit him and he had to lift his chin and gulp air to prevent the searing bile from coming up.

"Señor?"

The waitress in her elaborate pleated paper gown smiled at him inquiringly as she lifted away the remains of the meal. "A *postre,* señor? I could show you the dessert tray."

"No, thank you," Eddo said hoarsely. A sugar rush was the last thing he ever needed. "A brandy, please."

The waitress brought a balloon glass and Eddo sipped the brandy, listening to the hum of unspoken deals and the slick murmur of political wheels being greased. The nausea passed, leaving his body churning with tension and residual adrenaline. The exchange with Bernal Paz had been a hell of a way to end the week, especially given his lack of sleep. He was dealing with the pressure of the investigation with his usual prescription of running and working out, but it was turning him into a chronic insomniac.

At least tomorrow was Saturday, the day when he'd go to La Marquesa, the big area of scrubby parkland between Mexico City and Toluca. He'd played *fútbol* there every Saturday since his earliest police days.

That's when he'd run and run until he was nothing more than two feet and a pair of lungs, until he coughed blood and stank of sweat and forgot for an hour or two everything that he was and what he had to do and the people who'd get hurt along the way.

◆

Chapter 2

Three votive candles burned in front of Our Lady of Guadalupe. There was no one else in the living room to see the tiny flames shiver in the draft as Luz de Maria Alba Mora shut the front door.

In the cheap reproduction painting, prominently displayed in a wrought iron easel on top of a weathered wood cabinet, the Virgin wore a green robe decorated with stars just like when She'd appeared to San Juan Diego in 1531. The picture was draped with rosaries, silk flowers, and a black ribbon marking the day 13 years ago when Luz's father and grandfather had been struck by a bus and the world had changed forever.

"I'm home," Luz called. She put down the backpack containing her sketchpad and the pay-as-you-go *Amigo* cell phone that was just for emergencies.

"In here." Luz's mother's voice filtered through the doorless archway to the kitchen.

Luz peeled off the sweatshirt she wore over a tee shirt and jeans then found her mother behind the ironing board. More than a dozen crisp men's dress shirts hung on a clothes rack wedged between the board and the scrubbed pine kitchen table.

"*Hola, niña.*" Maria Mora was a small, plump woman with tired eyes, a ruddy complexion, and short permed hair. She set the iron on its heel as Luz stretched across the board so the two women could exchange kisses. "Was the bus ride all right? Did anyone bother you?"

"Nobody bothered me, Mama," Luz said. She'd learned how to take care of herself long ago but her mother asked the same question every time she came home. "Everything was fine and the bus even got in a little earlier than usual."

"Good, good," Maria said and took up the iron again. Her

brown polyester dress was as old as the kitchen's chipped yellow and blue tiles. "The children are still at school and your sister's at the church for the ladies craft afternoon."

"Poor Father Santiago," Luz said. She turned on the single cold water tap, found the bar of naphtha soap, and washed her face and hands, getting rid of the stink of diesel fuel, worn vinyl, and unwashed passengers. "I don't know how he stands all their chatter."

"They're planning the *oferta* for the Day of the Dead," Maria said.

"Every woman there is going to have a different plan," Luz said with a wry smile.

Maria chuckled.

Luz dug her pay envelope out of the front pocket of her jeans where it had been safe from the pickpockets that roam bus stations. She opened the jar kept on the counter for household money. Only a few pesos left this week. Working as a *muchacha planta*--a live-in housemaid--earned Luz time off every other weekend and Wednesday afternoons and paid 5000 pesos a month. It was good money but it was never quite enough.

"You keep some to do your hair," Maria said, lifting her chin at the jar even as she kept the iron moving over the cotton shirt on the board. "You should have done it the last time you were home."

"I know," Luz said. "But the weekends go by so fast." Like so many women of *mestizo* heritage--the mix of conquering Spanish and defeated *indio* that made up the majority of café-skinned Mexicans--Luz wore her hair long and permed with bangs curved into a bubble over dark brown eyes. But the perm and the bangs had grown out and lately her head was just a mass of hairpins trying to keep everything in place.

"We have to go to the *mercado*, too," Maria said. "The girls need new shoes. Those two grow out of everything."

Luz put 300 pesos for a new perm in her jeans pocket, dropped the rest of the money in the jar, and opened the cupboard to find an aspirin. The four hour bus ride from Mexico City to the small town of Soledad de Doblado on the outskirts of Veracruz was a huge descent in elevation and she had the usual headache. Of course, everyone had headaches in October when the summer rains gave way to the dry season and sinus pressure fluctuated like crazy. She washed down the aspirin with water from the *garrafon*, the big bottled water dispenser on the counter, and looked at her mother. "I saw the candles," she said leadingly.

Maria pressed the shirt cuffs, the last step in a professional ironing job. "We got some good news."

"Really?" Luz raised her eyebrows. "What sort of good news?"

Maria smiled. "You can wait," she said. "We'll sit and have some coffee and then I'll tell you all about it."

"I'll keep ironing while you make the coffee," Luz offered. The dry cleaner's bag at her mother's feet was still half full; she'd obviously gotten a late start on the 40 shirts she ironed daily for 2 pesos each. Luz took the finished shirt from her mother, hung it on the big rack, flipped a plastic shroud over it and stapled the dry cleaner's coupon to the plastic.

Puffing with exertion, Maria squeezed herself out of the corner between the rack and the ironing board. Luz swiveled her hips and slipped easily into the tight space. Rather than Maria's soft stockiness, Luz had inherited her late father's height and lithe build, along with his high cheekbones and wide mouth. She spread a new shirt over the board.

"I'll make coffee with milk the way you like it." Maria filled the coffee maker's glass carafe with water from the dispenser.

Luz felt her headache lift as her mother bustled around the small kitchen, heating milk in a battered saucepan and finding the right glasses for *café veracruzana*. Obviously a celebration was at hand. Maybe Juan Pablo had won Student of the Quarter again.

The coffeemaker gave a final gurgle as Luz finished her third shirt. She unplugged the iron and sat at the table across from her mother. Maria set a glass of coffee and hot milk in front of her and Luz sipped appreciatively.

"Your sister is pregnant," Maria said and put three heaping spoonfuls of sugar in her own glass.

Luz nearly choked on her coffee. "Lupe?"

"You only have one sister," Maria said.

"She can't be pregnant," Luz sputtered. "She's a widow with two small daughters."

Along with Luz, Lupe had left school when their father died but had been too shy to work as a *muchacha.* She'd married young and been widowed a few years later. Still shy, she crocheted placemats and bowl covers for the tourists at the handicrafts *mercado.*

"She's pregnant," Maria said. "I said I'd tell you before she got home."

"Is she *sure?*" Luz searched for other possibilities. "Maybe she's got the flu. Ate something that upset her stomach."

"She's sure," Maria replied. "She's already been to the clinic. They made her buy some vitamins."

Luz blinked. "That's why there wasn't anything in the money jar."

Maria nodded. "The vitamins cost almost 200 pesos."

Self-pity hit hard as Luz stared into her glass of *café veracruzana.* Lupe was pregnant and soon there would be another mouth to feed and Lupe had two beautiful children already and Luz would never have any.

"I lit the candles," Maria continued. "For her to stay healthy. Twenty-six is old to be having babies."

And 29 is ancient. Tears pricked the back of Luz's eyes as she wrestled with feelings she thought she'd crushed long ago. She'd never married and never had a child in a country where the majority of girls of her social class were mothers before their eighteenth birthday, married or not. "*Madre de Dios,*" Luz said harshly. "This was your good news?"

"Babies are always good news, Luz."

"This is *not* the right time," Luz said. "Juan Pablo graduates from school this year. How are we going to send him to college with all the costs for a baby?"

"You know there's no money for college, Luz." Maria's voice was flat. "There never was. Your brother will get a job."

"No," Luz snapped, although she knew her mother was right. College cost a fortune, but it was one of Luz's dreams that

Juan Pablo would go. He was brilliant. "We haven't scrimped and saved to put him through Colegio Santa Catalina just so he can end up working on the docks in Veracruz."

"He'll be all right," Maria said.

"And I want Martina and Sophia to go to Santa Catalina," Luz said stubbornly. "That neighborhood school isn't teaching them anything."

"The tuition for Santa Catalina is 1800 pesos a month," Maria said. "Double for two. We can't afford to send them and you know it. They can stay where they are for 400 pesos a month. When Juan Pablo graduates and we're not paying his tuition things will be easier."

"There's no room in this house for any more people," Luz went on, unable to stop herself. Maria's bedroom was off the living room. Two other bedrooms and the only bathroom were upstairs. When she came home Luz slept on the floor in the room she'd shared with her sister when they were girls, but which was now used by Lupe and her daughters. "We're cramped enough as it is."

"Luz de Maria." Maria banged her spoon on the table. "What do you expect your sister to do? Get herself cut up by some back street butcher?"

Her mother's words stung. Luz slumped in her chair. Abortions were forbidden by the Catholic Church. And illegal in Mexico. "Of course not," she mumbled. "Does Juan Pablo know?"

"Yes. She told us both last week when she came back from the clinic."

"And Martina and Sophia?" Luz drank some more coffee. An unhappy acceptance settled into her bones. "How is she going to tell the girls they'll be getting a new brother or sister?"

"She said heaven was sending them a new baby."

"*Madre de Dios*," Luz swore softly. "Heaven had nothing to do with this. Who's the father?"

"She won't say."

"What do you mean, she won't say?" Luz looked at her mother in irritated surprise. "Somebody has to provide for this baby, not just Lupe." *And me.*

"She won't say," Maria repeated.

"Did you ask?" Luz asked, appalled that her mother was willing to let Lupe keep such a secret. "Make her say."

Maria shook her head. "She doesn't want to."

The front door creaked. There was a rush of childish chatter and then Lupe and her daughters came into the kitchen. The little girls squealed with delight to see Tía Luz and Luz's heart gave another lurch of self pity as she hugged and kissed both of them. Martina and Sophia were 5- and 7-year-old miniatures of Lupe, short and solid and sweet tempered. They wore their school uniforms; navy jumpers and white blouses. After they climbed all over their aunt, Lupe made them go upstairs and change. They did as they were told without argument, leaving the three women alone in the kitchen.

"Mama?" Lupe's soft brown eyes flickered with nerves.

Maria nodded and poured another glass of coffee and hot milk.

"She told me," Luz said as guilt churned her stomach into slurry. She hugged her sister. "How are you?"

"I'm fine, just fine." Lupe smiled timidly. She took after Maria and was smaller and plumper than Luz. Her hair was short and permed and she wore a plain polyester skirt and blouse. She sat down with her glass and added sugar. "They do this quick little test now at the clinic."

"When are you due?" Luz asked. She went behind the ironing board again and attacked another shirt.

"May," Lupe said happily. "We can have the baptism before Juan Pablo's graduation."

"Won't that be nice," Maria said, watching Luz.

"Nice," Luz agreed, calculating swiftly. She couldn't recall anything significant happening in August. "Early May or late May?"

"May tenth." Lupe smiled. "Maybe it will be a boy this time."

And what will his name be? Mexicans took the names of both parents' fathers. Luz's own name was the combination of Alba, her paternal grandfather's name, and Mora, the name of her mother's father. The paternal name always came first and was always used, although some more progressive Mexicans were dropping the everyday use of the second name. Luz's employer Señora Vega used both names, and added the name of her husband's father as well, preceded by "de," something usually only done by upper class people.

"Who's the father, Lupe?" Luz asked.

Her question was met with silence.

It was truly the first time she could remember that Lupe had hidden anything from her and Luz was suddenly frightened. She slammed down the iron, ran around the table, and grabbed Lupe by the shoulders. "Did he rape you?"

"No, Luz." Lupe shook her head. "He's . . . it's . . . it's good."

"So you have a boyfriend?" Luz asked in surprise.

"It's nice, but it's not like that." Lupe squirmed out of Luz's grasp. "I don't want to talk about it right now."

"Why won't you tell us, Lupe?" Luz pressed.

"Luz," Maria said warningly.

"He should know first," Lupe said.

"Look, Lupe." Luz folded her arms, determined to find out what horny *macho* had done this to her sister. "You can't--."

"I knew you wouldn't be happy about this, Luz," Lupe cut in, her voice still soft and timid. "That's why I asked Mama to tell you. You're the one with the important job. You can draw and paint and remember what you read and make decisions. Juan Pablo's smart and good at everything. But being a mother is what I'm good at." She held up her hands in a gesture of supplication. "I've wanted another baby for so long, Luz."

Luz stared at her sister. She hadn't realized that Lupe wanted anything. Since her husband's death Lupe had seemed content with her daughters and her needlework. And Luz had her own lost dreams to cry over.

Lupe gazed back; untroubled, at peace.

"I'm glad for you," Luz managed. She bent again and hugged Lupe.

"You're the best sister in the world, Luz." Lupe hugged back hard.

"Hardly." Luz closed her eyes and felt unutterably sad.

Lupe sniffed and broke the hug. "Wouldn't trade you for another brother."

The old joke broke the tension. Luz turned back to the ironing board. Lupe got out her crochet basket and lifted out a piece of half-finished lace.

"If the new baby is a boy," Luz said, determined to sound cheerful. "Juan Pablo can teach him how to play *fútbol* and chase girls." She finished the shirt and handed it to Maria who slipped it into a plastic shroud and attached the coupon.

The three women fell into the familiar comfort of each other's company while they worked. They talked about Juan Pablo, on whom they all doted, and Luz described the latest happenings in her employer's house. There was Marisol the cook to talk about, plus Hector the chauffeur, Raul the old gardener, and of course Rosa, the harebrained other maid with whom Luz shared an attic bedroom. Señor Vega and his latest girlfriend always provided good grist for the story mill, as did Señora Vega and the society events she attended and the unbelievable clothes she wore to them. Luz talked, too, about the three Vega children who all went to the bilingual Colegio Americano, the most expensive school in Mexico City.

It was her twice-monthly unfolding of the drama of the Vega household, those people who lived in that other world. Luz usually made it sound like a *telenovela*, but this time she knew her voice was a little flat.

♦

Chapter 3

Watching the news on Saturday night with Juan Pablo was the highlight of Luz's weekends in Soledad de Doblado.

Maria heaved herself off the sofa when *Sabado Gigante*, the popular variety show, ended. "Time for bed," she said to Martina and Sofia. Lupe yawned and followed them all upstairs. Tío grunted something and disappeared into the kitchen. Luz heard the back door open and shut.

Tío was not really anyone's *tío*, or uncle, but they had always called him that. Luz's father and grandfather had taken him in years ago as their young apprentice in the ironworking business. When they died, Tío had simply stayed on, living as before in the small shed in the back yard near the now-abandoned forge. He was handy and fixed things for people, earning money here and there, which he usually turned over to Maria.

"I told Mama he's drinking too much," Juan Pablo said after they heard the door latch. "Sometimes he's gone for days and comes back smelling like a distillery. But she says he doesn't have anywhere else to go."

Luz sighed. Tío had lived on the fringes of the Alba family's life for so long he was like another piece of furniture. Silent and worn, but still marginally useful.

Juan Pablo followed Luz to the kitchen as she went to make tea. He told her about his teachers and his heavy load of science and language classes. Luz listened wistfully as she boiled water from the *garrafon* and got out the mugs. Santa Catalina was the best private school in the small town and Luz had adored her years there. She'd been an outstanding student and artist, expecting to take the medal for the highest grades in French and English and winning regional art prizes, right up to the day she'd been called to the office and Sister Milagros had told her that her father and grandfather were dead. Maybe Luz's future had been crushed by a bus, but things would be different for Juan Pablo.

He took another step toward manhood every time Luz saw him. Juan Pablo was tall like her, and lean from hours spent playing *fútbol* as Santa Catalina's team captain. He looked like her, too, with the same café skin, broad shoulders, high cheekbones, wide mouth, and even white teeth. He kept his hair short so it wouldn't get in his eyes when he ran but it stuck up in front, making him all the more irresistible to high school girls.

They brought their *manzanilla* tea to the living room. The colorful oil paintings Luz had done years ago hid the cracks in the room's concrete walls and made the sofa and chairs, all angled toward the precious color television, seem a little less faded. Maria's candles had burned themselves out, leaving the glass cups sooty from the cheap wax. The shrine was dark.

The big news story that Saturday night was about a group called *Los Hierros*, supposedly a secret brotherhood of police officers sworn to be incorruptible. The group had reportedly infiltrated every police force in the country, both national and local. There was no proof that *Los Hierros*--The Iron Ones-- actually existed, but there was growing speculation.

"Luz, this is going to change things," Juan Pablo exclaimed. He shifted excitedly on the sofa. "Cops won't know who might be in *Los Hierros* so they'll all be looking over their shoulders. Maybe it'll be so strong the dirty cops will be outnumbered."

"If it *is* real, which I'm not saying it is," Luz cautioned. "The dirty cops and their cartel friends will pick off *Los Hierros* faster than they can recruit new members."

The news cut to commercials advertising soap and shampoo while the government subtitle "Cleanliness is Healthy" ran at the bottom for poor people who needed to know why to buy soap and shampoo.

"Whoever started this thing is powerful," Juan Pablo said. "Maybe even the president."

"Betancourt?" Luz nearly laughed. "I doubt it." She'd voted for President Fernando Betancourt, but he had run aground, seemingly helpless as the drug cartels challenged state and local governments in the northern part of the country. The army tried to keep order in the worst areas but the drug-related violence was creeping south. Betancourt's administration from the National Action Party, or PAN, faced daily opposition from the Congress of Deputies dominated by the Institutional Revolutionary Party, known as PRI. The leftist Party of the Democratic Revolution constantly demonstrated in Mexico City's huge Zocalo square. All the parties were jockeying for position as Betancourt's administration struggled on toward the elections in a little over a year. By law Betancourt could not run again and the next presidential election would be pivotal in the fight to save Mexico from the drug cartels.

The show came back on, following up the exposé about *Los Hierros* with a wide ranging discussion about official corruption in the country. The least corrupt state--and eponymous state capital--was deemed to be Oaxaca, mostly due to the tough court system there, led by a law professor-turned-judge named Arturo Romero. Under Romero, Oaxaca's prison system had been reformed, police salaries had risen so that cops were being a paid a decent wage--reducing their incentive to take bribes--and criminal charges against dirty cops had been made to stick.

It was well after midnight when Luz and Juan Pablo turned off the television and went upstairs, both yawning and sleepy.

"Luz, I've been thinking." Juan Pablo paused on the stair landing. "You know, about Lupe being pregnant. I should quit Santa Catalina. It's too expensive."

"No," Luz exclaimed, suddenly wide awake.

"I should get a job," Juan Pablo argued. "Go back to school next year after Lupe's had the baby and things are a little easier around here."

"Nobody ever goes back," Luz said. "You'll graduate this year. Then college."

"Luz, stop it." Juan Pablo rubbed his eyes. "I'm not going to college and watch my family starve."

"We'll manage, sunshine," Luz said firmly. She kissed his cheek then slipped inside Lupe's bedroom before he could say another word.

She stood in the darkness with her back against the door,

her sister and nieces breathing rhythmically, until she heard Juan Pablo finish in the bathroom and close his bedroom door. When his light went out Luz crept back downstairs and dumped the pesos for her new perm into the money jar.

◆

They went to the early Mass. Luz sat and stood and knelt mechanically, lost in thought. Pitted against her own salary and Maria's paltry income from the dry cleaner were school and college tuitions, gas and electric and water bills, clothing and shoes, and diapers for the new baby. No matter how she juggled the amounts, they didn't balance. She barely noticed when Mass ended; Juan Pablo had to elbow her out of the pew after Father Santiago led the processional down the tiny aisle.

The little white church of Santa Clara and Father Santiago were one and the same. He'd baptized Luz, given her First Communion, watched her play Mary in the children's Christmas *posada* pageant, stood by the bishop when she made her Confirmation, blessed her coming-out event when she turned 15, buried her father and grandfather, and gently forgiven her when she'd knelt terrified in the dark confessional booth and admitted for the first time to the sin of sex without benefit of the sacrament of marriage.

"You frowned your way through Mass, Luz de Maria." The gray-haired priest always greeted his congregants in the church's front garden after the service. Father Santiago was shorter than Luz, portly but spry, with kind eyes and the patience of a saint. "Was my sermon that bad or were you thinking of the recent robberies?"

"I heard," Luz said. It was always the same story. Poor, desperate people stealing from other poor, desperate people. "A television stolen just a few blocks from our house."

"Thankfully no one was hurt," Father Santiago said.

"Keep the big light on over your gate, Father," Luz said. She managed to smile. "Someone could steal the entire church if you were busy watching *fútbol*."

"Cruz Azul plays tonight," Father Santiago said with a

wink.

Luz laughed and moved aside to let him speak to the next congregant. She drifted to the gravel path that led to the cemetery where her father and grandparents were buried. She walked to her father's stone and sat on the nearby bench. The church social hummed in the distance. Over the years the cemetery had been both a grateful refuge and a haunting landscape to sketch. Luz wished she'd brought her sketchpad now. It would have been a distraction from her thoughts.

I'm doing the best I can, Papa.

It's not enough.

"You walked right by me."

Luz looked up to see her best friend from the neighborhood. Carmelita Rosales and Luz hadn't gone to the same school but they had been in the church *posadas* together and stood next to each other for their First Communion and Luz was one of the few people who knew that Carmelita had lost her virginity to her father when she was 11.

"Sorry," Luz said and shifted to make room on the bench.

Carmelita sat down. She was thin, with a darker complexion than Luz, and wore her hair in a loose perm that fell to her shoulders. "What's the matter?"

"Have you seen anyone with Lupe lately?" Luz heard herself blurt. "A man, I mean."

"No, but I don't see her very much. Just when the girls play together." Carmelita gave a little shrug. Her two daughters were friends with Martina and Sophia. "Why do you ask?"

"She's pregnant," Luz said. "She's not saying who the father is."

"Oh."

Carmelita didn't say anything else. The two women had talked enough about broken lives to read each other's thoughts. Carmelita had married and left her father's house as soon as she could, and defied *barrio* social conventions by taking her husband's name. When he died she remained in the home of her in-laws instead of moving back with her parents. She did not give her father's name to her daughters, moreover, and never offered any explanation for it. Luz thought Carmelita was the bravest person she'd ever met.

◆

Luz sluiced her hair under the pump in the yard by the old forge. Lupe stared at her anxiously, sewing scissors in hand.

"Just chop it all off about here." Luz gestured to her shoulder.

"You're sure about this, Luz?" Lupe fretted. "It'll be awfully short."

"Yes." Luz set her jaw and closed her eyes.

Lupe sawed at the coarse tangles for a long time. In the end, at least 12 inches went. Luz was left with an even bob of shoulder-length hair, the ends twisting with the last bit of curl.

As she rode the afternoon bus back to Mexico City with her drab new hair, depression settled over Luz, as toxic and pervasive as the unseen sewage on fruits and vegetables that only iodine could soak off. Juan Pablo would end up hefting cargo on the Veracruz waterfront instead of going to college and becoming *licenciado*--a professional with a degree. Martina and Sophia would complete the minimum six years of education, then become maids with no future like Tía Luz. Or unwed and pregnant like their mother.

Depression started to feel like desperation. If Luz asked Señora Vega for a raise she'd surely be fired without the critical recommendation to get another job at a commensurate salary. A second job was impossible; her days started at 6:00 am and lasted until the work was done.

Luz leaned her head against the window. The bus was already on the outskirts of Mexico City and the endless urban landscape had never seemed so gray and or so harsh. Most of the city was nothing like the old money enclave of Lomas Virreyes where the Vegas lived or Polanco where the city's most expensive restaurants and clubs catered to the wealthy.

The bus passed block after block of sooty concrete cut into houses and shops and shanties and parking garages and *mercados* and schools and more shanties where people lived surrounded by hulks of old cars and plastic things no one bothered to throw away. Sometimes there wasn't concrete for homes, just sheets of corrugated metal and big pieces of cardboard that would last until the next rainy season. It was the detritus of millions upon millions of people who had nowhere to go and nothing to do and were angry about it.

The *Reforma* newspaper had reported a few weeks ago that the city's population was in excess of 28 million--more than 25 percent of the country's entire population--and Luz believed it. All of those people were clawing at each other in a huge fishbowl suspended 7500 feet above sea level, where there was never enough oxygen and the air was thin and dirty.

The city was hemmed in by mountains on all sides; mountains like Popocatépetl and Iztaccíhuatl that sometimes spewed smoke and ash and prevented the *contaminatión* from cars and factories and sewers from escaping. Luz privately thought of it as *la sopa*--a white soup that often blotted out the stars and prevented the night sky from getting dark.

The bus slowed in traffic. As they crept along Luz saw a car stopped on the side of the road, pulled over by a *transito* traffic cop. As Luz watched, the driver handed the cop a peso bill from his wallet. The *transito* accepted it but kept talking, gesturing at the car. The motorist handed him another bill. *La mordida*--the bite--of the traffic cop, right under her nose.

Los Hierros was crap.

♦

Chapter 4

"We will not be talking about Judge Romero," Lorena Lopez de Betancourt said crisply. She cocked her head to one side and gave the two journalists what she thought of as her wise yet sincere look.

"He does appear to be your most serious competition for the PAN nomination, señora," the reporter said. He was tall with thick hair worn long and slicked back. Fit; maybe in his mid-thirties. He smiled ingratiatingly.

"There will be no competition," Lorena replied.

"Has there been any discussion of possibly combining forces?" His name might be Garcia. Lorena wasn't sure. She hadn't really paid attention when the introductions had been made. He was supposed to be *HOLA!* magazine's top reporter, which is what her office had demanded, and that was all she needed to know.

"This is my interview," Lorena said, with just enough edge in her voice to put Garcia in his place. "Not Judge Romero's."

"Of course we'll want to hear your views on family life and fashion," the blonde woman next to him interjected.

Lorena smiled frostily at Elsa Caso, the well-known television talk show host. Clips of the interview would be featured on her show.

"Of course." Lorena settled back in her chair and crossed her legs, waiting for Elsa Caso's camera crew to be ready. The interview had been carefully timed to kick off a series of events planned to increase her visibility and portray her as having popular support as well as being someone whose experience set her above any other potential presidential candidate. One way to do that was to remind the populace that as Mexico's First Lady she knew how to conduct business from Los Pinos. The interview was taking place in the main reception room and Lorena knew that she looked as if she belonged there. Her prematurely white hair was caught up in an elegant twist and her beaded blue dress dazzled against the dark antique furniture and satin draperies.

The television people gave a final adjustment to their equipment and signaled that they were ready to start. Garcia and Elsa Caso said some patter, thanking Lorena for the interview, this wonderful chance to meet with the First Lady for a wide ranging chat about the issues facing Mexico today.

"Let's start with reports of this police group, *Los Hierros*," Garcia said. "Do you believe the reports, and if so, do you think this sort of grassroots movement can be successful?"

Lorena cut her eyes to Max Arias, her secretary and senior advisor, who was standing by the director. He hastily stepped into the interview space, forcing the cameras to stop rolling. "I'm sorry," he said to Garcia and thrust a paper at him. "Perhaps you lost your copy of the interview questions."

"I thought the First Lady wanted to touch on current events," Garcia replied. He smiled at Lorena again, and if she hadn't been so annoyed with his departure from the script she might have wondered what he looked like without the suit.

"Stay with what was agreed upon," Max said and went back to stand next to the director.

The cameras started rolling again.

"Tell us a little bit about your typical day," Elsa Caso gushed.

"Fernando wakes me up every morning with a cup of coffee that he makes himself," Lorena said. She placed a hand on her bosom. "It is a symbol of our love."

"Oooh." Elsa clasped her hands in delight.

The rest of the interview went as planned, with Lorena weaving heartfelt concern for the Mexican peoples' welfare with sage political pronouncements prepared in advance by Max and his team. Elsa Caso unwittingly helped, supplying reactions and comments that painted the Betancourts' relationship as a fairy tale of enduring love. But Garcia held Lorena's gaze several times as if to remind her that he wasn't quite satisfied.

When the questions were all answered the *HOLA!* photographer took some still photos of her. Lorena spent a few moments adjusting her diamonds in the mirror over the Spanish sideboard and posed with one hand alongside the silver tea service. She changed clothes and jewelry twice, ending up in a strapless black evening gown with a sapphire and diamond choker, standing next to her husband's official portrait and gazing up at Fernando's stupid face as if inspired.

Max led out Elsa Caso and the film crew, the bouncy blonde woman evidently very pleased with Lorena's hard-hitting comments on relationships, balanced meals, and dressing for a woman's body type. Garcia waited stony-faced for his colleague as the *HOLA!* photographer snapped a last picture of Lorena ostensibly pouring her husband a drink at the end of a long work day solving the country's problems.

"Thank you, señora." The photographer bobbed his head at her and began to disassemble his equipment.

Lorena poured a second shot of tequila and carried both over to the big picture window. Garcia was sitting on a damask sofa. He stood and she held out a glass. "Maybe you'd like a drink, too?"

As he took the glass Lorena moved it so that his fingertips slid over hers. A corner of his mouth quirked up.

"To what are we drinking?" he asked.

"The success of your interview." She looked at him over the rim of her glass before sipping the strong liquor.

"I think you'll like the article when it comes out next week." He took a mouthful of tequila and tipped his head back. His Adam's apple moved as he swallowed. "But you should have let me ask my questions."

"They sounded boring," Lorena said.

"You didn't hear the exciting ones." He touched his glass to hers. The gesture could have been a toast or an invitation.

"Such as?" Lorena asked. She liked the way he stood up to her, flirting, using his sensuality to get what he wanted.

"Such as how does Lorena plan to finance her campaign?" he asked.

Many of the scripted questions had been phrased that way in

order to emphasize her name. She looked down, smiled and licked the rim of the narrow tequila glass. "The people will give Lorena the money."

Garcia raised his eyebrows. "Will the people give enough money for a viable campaign if the party tilts toward Romero?"

"The campaign has already started," Lorena said. Out of the corner of her eye she saw Max lead the *HOLA!* photographer out of the room, leaving her and Garcia alone. She stepped closer, the taffeta of her evening gown swishing.

Garcia didn't back away. "Romero will be tough to beat for the nomination," he said. "He's been a prosecutor, a professor, and a judge. Internationally known. Mediated with the terrorists in Colombia and the strikers in Argentina. Books have been translated into 20 languages. A stainless reputation."

"The people are with me," Lorena said dismissively. "I am their sister."

"Lorena's your sister." Garcia swallowed the rest of his tequila. "That sounds like a campaign slogan."

Lorena cocked her head. "I like it. It'll bring in the women's vote."

"If you use it will I get a royalty?"

Lorena finished her tequila and swished a step closer again. "Maybe we can discuss an exclusive," she said. "I want your magazine to write a series of articles, following my campaign from now until the election."

"That would be up to my editor," he said.

Lorena shrugged. "I'm not offering this exclusive to just any magazine. Or to just any writer."

"I see."

"Do you know the Hotel Arias?" she asked.

"In the Centro Histórico?"

Lorena slowly drew the empty tequila glass out of Garcia's hand and was rewarded with a stroke of his thumb across her palm. "I go there for lunch sometimes," she said coolly. "Max's father owns it."

"I hear it's very discreet," Garcia said.

Max stepped into the room. Garcia gave a nod. "Thank you for the interview, señora," he said and followed Max out.

Lorena put the empty glasses on the sideboard and took off the heavily jeweled choker. Max returned and handed her a card. There was the *HOLA!* logo at the top and the name Victor Garza. She smiled. So his name was Garza, not Garcia. Not that it mattered.

She pressed the card back into Max's hand. "Friday lunch at the hotel. Two o'clock."

"I'll make the arrangements," Max said.

Lorena gathered up the train of her dress. She watched as Max checked his agenda book then pulled out a cell phone. Max was in his mid-forties, trim, loyal, and discreetly gay. The perfect secretary and political advisor, Lorena mused as she went to change. Smart, well connected, and susceptible to pressure.

♦

Chapter 5

"Your hair isn't that horrible," Rosa said critically.

"Umm." Luz didn't look up. She had the Arts section from the *Reforma* newspaper spread out next to her dinner plate and was engrossed in a review of the October exhibits at the Tamayo Museum.

"I can't believe you came back last night looking like that." Rosa leaned over the table, grabbed the sides of Luz's hair and yanked it away from her face. "There. If you wore it back you'd almost look like la señora."

"Rosa," Luz yelped in protest. The other maid was pulling her hair so tight Luz felt her eyelids stretch. She batted Rosa's hands away.

"Come out with me and Manuel Wednesday night." Rosa sat back down. "Wear your hair back and we'll go to this rave place in Colonia Roma."

"You don't have Wednesday night off," Luz said. She smoothed her hair and pronged a forkful of *taquitos,* the stuffed and rolled tortillas that Marisol the cook had fried for the rest of the household staff before leaving for the day.

"You won't sneak out on my night off so I'll sneak out on yours."

Luz laughed and shook her head. Both maids wore a short-sleeved gray uniform dress with white collar and cuffs and apron but the similarity ended there. Rosa Perez Solana was barely 21, with a short, wiry perm and a petite frame. She was funny and irrepressible and reckless with men and an incurable gossip, finding the lives of her employers and movie stars equally fascinating. She'd worked for the Vegas for two years and Luz was continually surprised Rosa had lasted this long without getting pregnant or fired.

"You need to meet somebody," Rosa said with the authority of someone who had a boyfriend and regular sex.

"I don't like rave clubs." Luz was hardly going to waste the money she'd saved not getting a perm on a useless night out. Plus, she knew what kind of man she'd meet in a rave club. He'd be ten years younger, work in a *mercado* sorting fruit and vegetables, and grope her clumsily the first chance he got.

"Don't be such a--." Rosa was cut off when the swinging door to the breakfast room smacked open.

Francesca flounced into the kitchen. Tall and thin, with a shiny curtain of light brown hair, the middle Vega child was already a beauty at 14. She wore tight Prada jeans and a silk halter top. A school notebook was tucked under one arm. She looked around the kitchen, at the shiny stainless steel cupboards, counters, and appliances, then went to the desk where Señora Vega checked the household spending accounts, wrote out menus, and paid the staff.

Luz and Rosa pretended not to watch as Francesca rifled through the desk drawers and looked through the chauffeur's appointment book. They both knew she was looking for stray cash. Obviously not finding what she wanted, Francesca came over to the table where the two maids were sitting.

"Luz." The girl slammed down the notebook. "The cover needs to be decorated by tomorrow or I get a failing grade. Don't do anything stupid. You know what I mean. And the French homework is inside. Bring it upstairs when you're done." She got a *Coca* from the refrigerator and walked out.

"I would love to decorate your notebook and do your French assignment, Francesca," Luz said softly to the swinging door. "Right after I finish Victoria's homework."

Rosa snorted. Luz picked up the notebook and ran her thumb over the smooth paper cover. Most teachers required a decorated notebook as part of a student's grade for class preparation and Luz decorated a dozen notebooks and folders for the children every year.

The door opened again but no one walked through. The murmur of feminine voices came through from the breakfast room as the door swung lazily. Luz hurriedly tore the museum review out of the newspaper, stuffed it into her dress pocket and tossed the newspaper onto the recycling pile. Rosa caught her eye. They soundlessly counted to three together before hearing Francesca scream "*I hate you!*"

Señora Vega's voice came through. "You didn't tell me about the party. We're going to Valle de Bravo next weekend."

"I'm not going to Valle de Bravo. It's *boring*," Francesca shouted back from behind the door and the battle was on.

Luz and Rosa made mock sad faces at each other across the kitchen table as the mother and daughter shrilled at each other on the other side of the door, Francesca rebelling against the boredom of the Vega's weekend house in Valle de Bravo, her lack of new clothes, and her scant 3000 pesos per week allowance. The argument ended when Señora Vega said they could go to the Liverpool department store in Polanco on Saturday.

The swinging door opened and Luz and Rosa screwed on their stupid faces, the masks of servility and feigned incomprehension that every domestic in Mexico City wore at some time or another. Señora Vega stalked into the room, her high heels clicking on the *terrazzo* floor. Both maids stood up.

"Rosa." Señora Vega went over to the wall where keys to all the households' doors, windows and cars hung neatly below labels. She let the maids wait while she selected the keys to the big sedan, then pivoted on one stiletto and gestured at the younger maid. "Tomorrow you'll help me clean out all the closets. Luz, you'll go with Victoria to her swim lesson at the school. And you'll do some arrangements for the front room, too, for my luncheon on Wednesday."

"*Si,* señora," Luz murmured. A few years ago Señora Vega had sent Luz to the big *florista* school near the equestrian center in Chapultepec Park. Luz had passed all three levels and her arrangements always earned la señora lavish compliments.

Selena Obregon Javier de Vega was both the most demanding and most interesting employer Luz had ever had. First and foremost she was a true *castellano*. For the most part, Mexico's elite upper class was made up of *criollos*, people of pure Spanish blood born in Mexico. *Castellanos* were the elite of the elite, Mexicans whose Spanish heritage could be traced to Castile, region of kings and *conquistadores*. Señora Vega burnished her lofty place in Mexican society by claiming to have gone to college in Lisbon and affecting a Portuguese accent, which Luz knew to be fake because it disappeared when she was stressed or angry. It made all her "z's" turn into "sh" and she customarily referred to Luz as "Loosh."

"Señor Vega is working late and I have a parent-teacher conference." Señora Vega slid a bottle of water into her purse and checked her reflection in the steel surface of the big refrigerator. She was a decorative woman in her early forties, tall and fine boned and razor-thin from hours of spinning classes and tennis lessons at the club, and she gleamed from mornings at the spa being massaged and creamed and having her hair siliconed into a shiny spill of flat silk. She wore it in a ponytail, the near mandatory hairstyle for upper class women. Tonight she was wearing a tweed pantsuit and a silver rope necklace. There was a large leather Furla bag over her shoulder, a gold tag proclaiming its Italian pedigree.

"Will you need anything else tonight, señora?" Rosa asked.

Señora Vega narrowed her eyes at the remains of the two maids' dinner. Luz knew she was making sure they'd been eating off plates from the servants' cupboard and not using the family dishes.

"Alejandro's friends are still in the children's game room," Senora Vega said, with a manicured gesture at the door to the breakfast room. "Hector will take them home in the Suburban. Make sure the room is cleaned up before you go upstairs."

She click-clicked out the door to the garage, the Furla bag swinging. Rosa and Luz sat back down. A minute later, the bank of security cameras mounted on the kitchen wall above the steel work counter showed the gate opening and the car backing out. Raul, the ancient gardener, shambled across the camera's view and shut the gate. The security cameras were a necessity in Mexico City for a wealthy family like the Vegas. Señor Vega owned a publishing company and the Vega house was a veritable fortress on Fray Payo de Rivera, a narrow street of exclusive homes barricaded by 20-foot high stucco walls and elaborate iron gates.

"Parent-teacher conference," Rosa smirked. "Sure. And he's working late."

"*Segunda frente*," Luz murmured and ate the last bite of the now cold *taquitos* on her plate. The entire household knew the euphemism for Señor Vega being with his mistress, his *segunda frente* or second front, as the saying went.

"You were looking at *Reforma.*" Rosa carried their dirty plates to the sink. "Did you see the picture?"

"What picture?" Luz got out 9-year-old Victoria's school books and the little homework planner labeled *Mis Tareas.* It was only history and English tonight.

Rosa wiped her hands on her apron and fished the newspaper out of the recycling bin, clicking her tongue and shuffling the pages until she found what she was looking for.

"There," she said triumphantly and spread the paper on the table.

It was the *La Gente* section, the society pages that featured photographs of Mexico's elite at various balls and charity events. Luz followed Rosa's finger to a color photograph of a dinner dance to raise funds for the Colegio Americano. Francesca was seated at a table, wearing a clingy black strapless thing. Her hair and makeup made her look at least ten years older.

Standing behind Francesca and next to Señor Vega was a voluptuous young woman in her early twenties wearing a dramatic red gown with a full skirt and plunging neckline. Her cleavage was bursting out of the front of the dress.

"That's her," Rosa said. "She's a teacher at the school."

Luz looked up. "How do you know?"

Rosa tapped the newspaper. "I found a letter in the trash with her name on it."

"Doesn't prove anything," Luz said doubtfully.

"That dress probably got him hard as a rock," Rosa observed.

"*Rosa,*" Luz exclaimed, torn between laughter and embarrassment. "*Dios mio*! The things you say."

Rosa washed their dishes, as well as those of Raul who had eaten earlier. Luz finished the children's homework. The Colegio

Americano taught two concurrent curriculums; one in Spanish from Mexico's Secretariat de Educatión Publico and one in English from the *norteamericano* state of Texas. Both curriculums assumed a full six hour school day but at the Colegio Americano each was taught in just three hours in order to squeeze in both. Anything the teachers didn't cover during the compressed classes was assigned as homework.

Luz got out her colored pencils and drew a couple dancing the *flamenco* on Francesca's notebook, the man in a short embroidered jacket like a *mariachi traje*, the woman in a red dress with a wide, flaring skirt. The faces of both *flamenco* dancers were turned away. The woman's hands clapped over her head, further obscuring her features.

Rosa came over to the table with two empty trays and peered at the drawing. "Again, no faces."

"Doesn't matter." Luz shrugged. "I'm not ever going to be a real artist."

◆

Hector was sitting in the hall in his dark suit and tie, waiting to take Alejandro's friends home, and he nodded impassively as Luz and Rosa passed by with their trays. As a chauffeur, Hector was at the top of the social scale of domestic servitude, ranking even higher than Marisol the cook, and he never let the others forget it. Like Marisol, he didn't live under the Vega's roof but had a wife and children in a home clear on the other side of the city, near the airport.

The game room was a mess. Alejandro, the oldest Vega child, sprawled on the big sectional sofa with his three friends. He was a lanky teen with his mother's honey-colored hair and the beginnings of a scraggly beard. Luz and Rosa unobtrusively loaded their trays with dirty dishes, careful not to block the television or otherwise intrude upon the boys' cognizance.

It was the part of being a maid Luz loathed; that feeling of having to make herself invisible. When Alejandro's friends had arrived she'd led them to the game room and waited to take their jackets as they'd ignored her and said "How're they hanging, buddy," in English, showing off their Colegio Americano slang. They lapsed back into Spanish as they went through some weird teen-aged handslapping ritual.

The boys were watching the television show about the tall, funny doctor who lived with his father and gave people advice over the radio. The Vega's satellite service showed it in English. The doctor and his brother were arguing, his father's dog was digging up the carpet, and the dark-haired girl was saying something besides, and when the punchline came Luz caught it and laughed out loud.

She immediately clapped a hand over her mouth, surprised by her own indiscretion.

"Get out, Luz," Alejandro said in the voice of a teenager used to giving orders to servants.

"Unless she wants to stay and pretend to be a *taquito*," one of his friends said with a throaty laugh.

"She's got a body in there somewhere," jeered Alejandro. "Anybody got 50 pesos?"

Luz clamped on her stupid face as she and Rosa hauled away the trays of dirty dishes.

♦

It was close to midnight before Luz and Rosa went upstairs to the maids' attic bedroom, simply furnished with two twin beds and a wall of built-in closets. Luz changed into her nightgown, smoothed the art review she'd torn out of the newspaper, and reached under her bed for her collection of old school notebooks. For years she'd kept every interesting article she found, creating a tattered encyclopedia of painters and museums and people who created the beautiful things she never would. She glued the article into the current notebook and reread it, savoring every word. A Nadia Porov exhibit was at the Tamayo until the end of October. Luz had seen a Porov exhibit once before and it had been strange and breathtaking.

"Let me guess," Rosa said as she came out of the bathroom. "Museum stuff. *Jesu*, but you can be dull."

"The Tamayo is never dull," Luz said absently. She found

last year's notebook and flipped through the pages until she found the review describing the previous Porov exhibit.

Rosa climbed into her bed. "So why did you cut your hair?"

Luz sighed, put the notebooks away, and got under the covers. "My sister Lupe is pregnant and I need to save money."

Rosa made a face. "Is she going to get married?"

"She hasn't even told the father yet."

"Who is he?"

"She won't say."

The two twin beds were separated by a bedside table. A small lamp cast a soft glow over the mismatched blankets. Rosa turned on her side to face Luz. "A mystery father," she marveled.

"It's just so odd." Luz propped her head on her elbow. Late night was the only time to talk without fear of being overheard or interrupted by any of the Vegas. "Lupe never goes *anyplace*. She doesn't even work. I don't know how she did it."

"He has a car," Rosa said firmly.

"*Dios mio,*" Luz groaned. Rosa was always doing it in her boyfriends' cars. Of course, Luz had done it in a few cars herself, because single people never lived alone. Everyone lived with their families unless they were *muchacha plantas* like Luz and Rosa who lived with their employers. "It doesn't matter if he has a car or not. Lupe *never* goes out without the girls."

"Never?" Rosa, who escaped from her parents and the Vega house every chance she could, had a hard time with that.

"Church. She goes to church by herself and that's it."

"Oooh, a priest," Rosa breathed and sat up. "I saw a movie like that once. The priest was young and handsome and --."

"No, *no*," Luz protested. "Father Santiago is at least 100."

"Is he the only one?"

Luz blinked and her heart turned over in her chest. "No," she whispered. "Some seminarians stayed with Father Santiago a couple of months ago."

"Bet one of them was cute," Rosa chortled.

"That's why Lupe hasn't told him." Luz flopped on her back, suddenly needing air in her lungs. No wonder Carmelita hadn't known. "He would have been there in August but now he's locked in a seminary someplace."

"They don't wear anything under their cassocks," Rosa said knowingly.

Luz stared at the ceiling, her thoughts swirling. That was it. Lupe hadn't told this young seminarian that she was pregnant because she had no access to him. When she did, of course he'd offer to marry her. He'd leave the seminary and come to live with the family. He'd be some delicate young man, without any survival skills, a man who'd wanted to devote his life to prayer and charity and he wouldn't be fit to do anything else.

He'd be yet another mouth for Luz to feed.

◆

Chapter 6

It was just a nameless spot in Los Olivos, the little town that long ago had been enclosed by Mexico City's westward sprawl, with a serving counter at the back and Formica-topped tables and plastic chairs spilling out onto the sidewalk. The place opened early, serving breakfast to local workingmen; rolls and *huevos* and cups of the sludgy corn-based *atole* drink.

There wasn't a menu, just a chalkboard with options. Eddo and the other two men ordered coffee and *chilaquiles*, a hash made from leftover tortillas. The girl who'd slung down their plates had a greasy perm and a sullen expression. At least the salsa looked fresh. Eddo hoped there wasn't more salmonella in it than his system could handle.

They ate fast at one of the sidewalk tables in front of the serving counter, just three more casual laborers hoping to find work that day. Eddo wore the typical *barrio* workingman's outfit of faded baggy jeans, work boots, dark tee shirt and cotton overshirt. A dirty ball cap concealed his short hair and light eyes. Across the table, his closest friend Tomás Valderama Castro sported similarly worn and grubby clothes.

Tomás pushed aside his half-empty plate and gestured at Miguel Pintero Rojas, a young man with a smooth round face and metal-rimmed glasses who'd eaten his food with a mixture of trepidation and excitement at being in such a low class neighborhood. But Miguel needed to learn how to handle himself in places like Los Olivos and it was one of the reasons they were there.

Miguel pulled a tabloid newspaper from a backpack and handed it to Eddo. The front page featured a lurid photo of a body that had been literally shot to bloody pieces in a drug cartel firefight. "Page five," Miguel murmured.

Eddo fished out his reading glasses. Page five had a sheet of printer paper taped to it, showing a list of five userids, each comprised of 10 random letters and numbers. Under the list appeared to be directions how to use the userids to access a website.

"This was on a flash drive the Army picked up in the El Toro raid outside Nuevo Laredo." Tomás was two years younger than Eddo, with a muscular, stocky build, similarly short hair, and dark eyes that few knew how to read. The clothes he wore were a far cry from the suits of a Highway Patrol lieutenant

"The Army raid three weeks ago?" Eddo asked. His seat faced the sidewalk, with his back to the restaurant wall so he could watch who came by, but he closed the newspaper anyway to prevent someone seeing inside.

"Yes," Tomás said. The two friends exchanged an unhappy look. The Mexican army was battling the cartels and in many places it was open warfare, destroying any hope the police might have had of interrogating suspects or using informants. Of course the army had been called in because the local police were often in the pocket of one cartel or another and now everyone was wondering the same thing about the army. "The place was empty but some electronics got left behind and came to Miguel to look through."

An ancient red delivery truck lurched past, its tailpipe dragging and sparking along the broken pavement, and turned into the repair garage across the street. The place advertised brake work and oil changes and cheap retreaded tires.

"There were two files on the flash drive," Miguel said. He was just a few years out of college and pulling down a fat salary as the Judicial Police's webmaster. The kid knew things about computers that would have taken Eddo two lifetimes to learn. "One file with directions for accessing and uploading information to a website and another file with a list of userids authorized to access it. I can get to the log-in page it describes but without a password for any of the userids the directions are useless."

Eddo opened the newspaper again. The process for logging into the website was complicated and obviously designed to protect unauthorized access.

"The login process points the user to a real website that hosts business content." Miguel pulled his cheap white plastic chair closer to the table and pointed to the URL printed on the page. "Businesses buy private server space and put in data they only want their employees to see. When the company adds content, they get a certain number of characters to post a description. The directions explain how to post something using a specific attachment. Every time one of the userids wants to post something they're supposed to use the same article about how much it costs a country to host the World Cup."

"So they're using the postings description to pass information," Tomás surmised.

"You said it's a business site," Eddo said. "Who owns it?"

"The page that the userids access is just dangling," Miguel replied. "It's using the website's capabilities but isn't linked to any of the company registrations inside the site. A real pro set it up."

Two little schoolgirls walked by, their plaid uniform skirts swinging and their red bookbags bumping on the sidewalk. The metal door of the *abarrotes* shop next door to the restaurant rolled up with a clatter as the girls passed, revealing its stock of snacks and sodas and *Amigo* cell phone cards. Los Olivos was coming to life.

The salsa and the *chilaquiles* started to fight it out in Eddo's stomach. He leaned forward. "So basically what you're saying is that that the El Toro cartel is technically savvy enough to hack in a back door and use this content sharing site as if it was Twitter or something. Or at least that's what these directions from the flash drive would indicate."

Miguel nodded, clearly pleased that he'd been able to show off his computer skills to the two older men.

Eddo studied the paper again. "Is there a history? I don't recall seeing this kind of cartel activity before."

"Nothing this sophisticated," Tomás said. "But it was probably just a matter of time."

That the cartel was using modern communications technology to organize drug route activity wasn't a big surprise, nor was it germane to Eddo's job at the ministry, but it was the sort of good information they all shared whenever they found it. Eddo focused on the list of userids, each a combination of ten characters.

1612colcol
Hh23051955
BppBB16003
CH5299xyz9
44Gg449M11

The second userid contained a string of numbers that plucked at the back of Eddo's memory. May 23, 1955. "Fuck," he breathed.

"What?" Tomás said.

"Nothing," Eddo said, not wanting to say more in front of Miguel. He folded the newspaper again. "Anything we need to do with this? Suggestions?"

A paint crew, all wearing spattered white overalls, trooped up to the counter and noisily ordered cups of *atole* to go.

"Look, I could try to create another userid and get into the page," Miguel said when the painters left, a nervous thrill in his voice. "Post something and see what happens."

"No," Tomás said. "Whoever is on the other end would know they were hacked and shut it down."

"Maybe not," Miguel protested. "Maybe we could figure out where they are and raid them."

"A little early for that," Tomás said. "How about you try to figure out one of the passwords?"

"I'm not in this just to be stuck in front of a computer all the time," Miguel protested.

"You've done a great job, Miguel," Eddo said. "But I agree with Tomás. Let's just watch this for awhile. Try to crack the passwords."

His voice was low but the authority was unmistakable. "Okay, *jefe*," Miguel said, obviously mollified by the praise. He stood up. "I'd better go. Got to change and get to the office."

"You know how to get out of the neighborhood?" Tomás asked.

"Yeah," Miguel said. "Thanks for breakfast, *jefe*." He

grabbed his backpack and left, looking for all the world like a typical *barrio macho* looking for a day's work in Los Olivos instead of an honors graduate in systems engineering with an office job in a Colonia Cuauhtémoc high-rise.

"Smart kid." Eddo watched Miguel blend into the crowd near a bus stop. "But impatient."

"He'll learn," Tomás said. He tapped the folded newspaper on the tabletop. "What didn't you want him to know?"

"One of the userids," Eddo said. He opened the newspaper again and showed Tomás. "It's Hugo de la Madrid Acosta's birthday."

Tomas's eyes opened wide as Eddo refolded the paper. "Are you sure?"

"Big party in the office last May."

"Well." Tomás took a sip of cold coffee, obviously nonplussed. "Hugo involved with some weird cartel communications plan. Supports your investigation, doesn't it?"

"Still circumstantial." Eddo jammed the newspaper into his own backpack. "Would anyone really be so obvious as to use their own birthday?"

"Got to be something easy because you can't write it down." Tomás caught Eddo's eye with a meaningful stare. "Or you're too fucking arrogant to think anybody would ever catch you."

"*Madre de Dios.*" Eddo knew in his gut that Tomás was right. Hugo had lived at the top of Mexico's power pyramid for a very long time. It would be easy for him to think he was untouchable, invulnerable. Or maybe the cartel represented the ultimate thrill; a game full of excitement and risk, something to alleviate the boredom of being wealthy and successful and predictable.

Tomás shoved aside his coffee cup. "I'll ask Vasco if he can find out which Mexican companies use the website to post content. Maybe somebody using the site officially set up the piggybacking arrangement."

Vasco Madeira Suiza was a senior official in the Attorney General's office, the third member of their triumvirate.

"Wait." Eddo leaned forward, wanting to make sure Tomás

realized how serious this thing was going to get. "El Toro's got a long arm."

Tomás threw him an annoyed look. "What am I? Suddenly stupid?"

"This is my job. My investigation." Eddo paused, trying to find the right words. "If Hugo's in with the cartel and they come after me, I don't want anybody else to go down, too. You shouldn't be involved. Or Vasco. Any of the others. That way you and Vasco can keep things going even if I'm gone."

"Shut up." Tomás glowered at him. "You know why we're all involved. Vasco will say the same thing."

Eddo shook his head. "This could get bad. You know the cartels are going after family members of the cops and military up north. If this is Hugo and he's really in with El Toro . . ." He let the notion hang in the air, unspoken.

Tomás shrugged, the heavy shoulders moving easily. "We've handled worse."

Hugo de la Madrid and the El Toro cartel. *He'll learn of this investigation and when he does, you're a dead man. A dead man.*

"I'm not so sure," Eddo said.

♦

Chapter 7

On Tuesday morning, Luz arranged flowers while Rosa hauled clothes out of closets and bagged up everything that Señora Vega decided to throw out. The closet rampage had progressed to Francesca's room when Hector took Luz to the Colegio Americano for Victoria's swimming lesson. Luz met the little girl at the school's aquatic facility, got her suited up, then carried Victoria's towel and backpack to the bleachers.

The little girl scampered over to her class. The swimming teacher was Coach Carlos, a muscular young man who taught the children by walking along the edge of the pool in tight warm-up pants and no shirt, flexing his biceps. Most of the mothers sitting in the bleachers during swim lessons couldn't keep their eyes off him. There were far more maids than mother in the bleachers, however, all staring at the Coach Carlos show. Luz usually looked, too, although he was cocky and arrogant and way out of her league.

Coach Carlos said something to Victoria. He lifted her into the water, the muscles in his back rippling as he bent. *He probably has lots of parent-teacher conferences*, Luz thought. She pulled her eyes away and opened Victoria's backpack. English homework again.

When the lesson was over Victoria ran back to Luz to be dried off. They went into the locker room and Luz dressed Victoria in pajamas and robe for the ride home and an early bedtime.

They were walking toward the front gate of the school, where Hector waited with the Suburban, when Luz heard the click of high heels on pavement. A hand tapped her on the shoulder.

It was Señora Portillo, with her son whining next to her and the Portillo's chauffeur walking behind with the boy's backpack and swim bag. Señora Vega and Señora Portillo were friends, part of a circle of beautiful coffee-drinking women who met regularly at the upscale Café O on Monte Libano in Lomas Virreyes.

"Luz de Maria, are you free to work for me the Saturday after next?" Señora Portillo asked. "I need some extra hands for Enrique's birthday party and Selena said you can sometimes be helpful."

"Saturday after next?" Luz verified.

"Yes."

Luz was off again that weekend. If she worked for Señora Portillo on Saturday it meant she could not go home. But it also meant another 200 pesos and that was a real windfall so Luz said yes.

"Alberto can pick you up." Señora Portillo indicated the chauffeur. She extended a piece of paper to Luz with the date, time, and address on it. Her attention immediately refocused on a high-heeled mother strolling by who was obviously a friend.

The chauffeur nodded at Luz as his employer chattered to her friend. He was a blunt-faced tank of a man poured into a sharkskin suit. Almost certainly a former boxer. "I am Alberto Gonzalez Ruiz," he said.

He spoke formally, but his diction was sloppy. Luz had the sudden silly thought that he probably had gotten hit in the head a lot during his boxing career.

She gave him a weak half-smile.

"I shall be pleased to see you that day," he said meaningfully. Señora Portillo ended her other conversation and Gonzalez Ruiz followed her out of the school gate.

Luz watched him go, her mouth dry. Chauffeurs made lots of money. Lots. Hector made enough money to support a family and have his own house. Gonzalez Ruiz probably made as much as Hector, maybe even more.

"I'm not going to that party," Victoria said.

"What?" Luz said and fumbled the piece of paper into the pocket of her uniform.

"I hate Enrique," Victoria said, skipping a little in her pink chenille robe and slippers, her damp curls quivering as she shook her head. "He always says shitty things."

"Don't say 'shitty,'" Luz said automatically. As she settled Victoria into the back seat of the Suburban Luz pushed her thoughts beyond Gonzalez Ruiz and wondered what she would do with the rest of that weekend. She couldn't remember ever having a Friday and a Sunday off in the city with nothing to do.

◆

"Look at your ass in those jeans, Luz. You look *hot.*"

"*Dios mio*, Rosa, I can't believe she wants to throw these away."

Luz stood on her toes in front of the mirror in the maids' bedroom and smoothed her hands down the seams of the Dolce and Gabbana jeans. She'd never worn anything so expensive. They fit like a dream. She wore a white silk blouse with gold buttons, too, courtesy of la señora's closet cleaning, but it was badly stained.

"Here. Try this." Rosa rummaged in a trash bag as she sat on the floor by her bed, surrounded by bags of castoff clothing. She handed up a hot pink cardigan with matching velvet buttons and a label that said both "Chanel" and "cashmere."

"Where would I wear something like this?" Luz laughed. Pink was an impossibly impractical color. *La sopa* would leave the sweater peppered with soot.

"Don't be such a stick, Luz," Rosa said. "Just put it on."

The sweater was soft and beautiful and made Luz's face glow. She held her hair back with one hand and a stranger in designer clothes looked back at her in the mirror. "*Dios mio,*" she said.

"Nice," Rosa agreed. Señora Vega had consigned the bags to the trash but the younger maid had quietly hauled them up the back stairway after the Vega family had retired for the night.

"We can't keep this stuff," Luz said. "If she found out we'd even opened the bags she'd fire both of us."

"We're throwing tons away." Rosa gestured at the bags. "Nobody will miss a few things."

Luz shook her head. "I don't know . . ."

"Ricardo the streetsweeper is going to collect the trash, open the bags and sell everything," Rosa pointed out. "He's going to make a fortune. And he didn't have to do any of the work."

"I know." Luz bit her lip and looked in the mirror again at the slim woman in the dark jeans and bright sweater. She'd never worn anything so beautifully made, with such exquisite fabrics. "But la señora--."

"Has Señora Vega ever said not to take things out of the trash?"

"Well, no," Luz said, wavering. "Not exactly."

The handbag pushed her over the edge. It was a big Prada tote with tan leather on the sides and matching handles long enough to go over the shoulder. The front and back were some sort of multi-colored abstract patterned fabric with beads and sequins randomly scattered throughout the design. It was colorful and elegant and big enough to carry her sketchpad. In her mind's eye Luz saw herself carrying it into the Tamayo Museum, an important artist with her chin held high and things to discuss with the museum director.

In the end, she kept the jeans, pink sweater, stained blouse and the tote, plus a black cardigan, matching tee, and a Hermés scarf with swirling shades of pink and tangerine. Rosa kept a few tops and two of the purses. There was some old makeup, too; Luz took a charcoal gray eye shadow, pale pink nail polish, and a rosy lipstick Rosa said was boring. Rosa liked bright eye colors like violet and blue, and fuchsia and burgundy for her nails and lips.

They bagged up the remaining clothes, most of which were too small, and brought them back down to the kitchen. Trash went out first thing every day for Ricardo to pick up. Nothing was left out overnight when the wild dogs from nearby Chapultepec Park roamed the streets.

Luz and Rosa ended up on the floor in their nightgowns, yawning and painting their toenails.

"Would you go out with the Portillo's chauffeur?' Luz asked as she admired the pale pink polish against her skin.

Rosa looked up from her toes. "The really big guy? Wears those shiny suits?"

"Yes." Luz started on a second coat.

"I'm not sure I could imagine doing it with him," Rosa said meditatively. "He probably weighs a ton."

Luz jerked her head up. "I just asked about going out with him, not about sex."

"Who goes out with somebody and doesn't think about sex with them?" Rosa countered with a grin. She considered her toes with their burgundy polish. "He'd be the kind who gets all sweaty. And make grunting noises. Or fart."

Luz laughed but it took an effort. She walked on her heels to the bathroom and made a dye bath with coffee grounds to salvage the stained white blouse. The silk took the dye beautifully and darkened to a caramel color, completely covering the stain. After she rinsed it in cold water a dozen times it didn't even smell like coffee anymore.

Later in the dark, Luz thought about Gonzalez Ruiz, panting and heavy, pressing down on top of her. He seemed to be a simple man, who'd definitely looked at her with interest as if he was looking for a wife. Employers liked husband-and-wife teams, especially if they were both well trained. And if she worked for the Portillos she'd only have to clean up after one whining child instead of three.

There would be money for the new baby, and Lupe's priest, and college for Juan Pablo and Santa Catalina for the girls and coffee with milk whenever they wanted. Really, Gonzalez Ruiz was the answer to her prayers.

Luz cried silently until she fell asleep.

♦

Chapter 8

Max Arias slid onto a stool in front of the dimly lit and elegantly appointed bar in the Hotel Arias. His cousin Alvaro was the bartender, a slim and serious man who'd worked at the hotel his entire adult life. Max put his ever-present planner and cell phone on the bar and slipped off his suit jacket.

Alvaro held up a bottle of ruby port, Max's favorite. "Are you off duty?"

"For a while," Max replied and gestured for Alvaro to pour.

There was no one else in the bar at this hour of the afternoon, although it would fill with young professionals in the evening. Max had eaten lunch with his father in the hotel dining room, keeping a discreet eye on Lorena and her latest conquest at a corner table. The afternoon would go the usual way; Max was sure, meaning he had about two hours to himself.

"She's upstairs?" Alvaro asked. He set a cloth coaster and a glass of port in front of Max.

Max nodded and drank. The port was rich and smooth.

"They're never going to elect a whore, you know," Alvaro said. He took out a cloth and mopped the gleaming mahogany surface of the bar.

Max grinned and set down the glass. "All politicians are whores."

Alvaro shook his head, unsuccessfully suppressing a smile. "Another package was delivered for you while you were eating," he said. "I put it in your father's office."

"We're the unannounced campaign headquarters, you know." Max raised his glass in a toast to Alvaro.

His cousin cocked his head in the direction of the front stairs. "Maybe we'd better start charging her rent."

Max gathered up his items and glass and went into his

father's office around the corner from the bar. It was a large and comfortably untidy place, with the same heavy draperies and dark mahogany furniture as the rest of the small luxury hotel. There was a thickly padded envelope on the desk. He closed the office door, sat in the big desk chair and tore open the envelope. Inside was a sheaf of money orders, all for substantial but different amounts.

Humming to himself, Max fired up his father's computer. He navigated to the hosting site, tapped in the userid **1612colcol** and his password. He was automatically redirected to the right page. There was a new posting from **CH5299xyz9** using the agreed-upon code to indicate another shipment and another from **BppBB16003** indicating the shipment was received and forwarded. Using the **1612colcol** userid, Max created a posting with the right attachment and announced that the shipment had been finalized.

He logged off the website, used the computer's control panel to delete temporary files, and then shut down. Still humming, he went to the heavy wooden bookshelf full of antique books and selected a large old-fashioned corporate accounting ledger. It was one of a set, all identically bound in tan leather and faintly discolored with time and use. The others held three generations worth of hotel accounting, before everything went to computers, but this one had never been used until now. He copied the new posting into the ledger. Next to the entry he wrote out what it had actually meant, noting the amount and the date in the proper columns.

The column of deposits ran to eight pages. There were nearly the same amount of withdrawals, also neatly recorded.

Six months ago, Max's father and uncle had helped Max set up the whole scheme, the two brothers blending their knowledge of the hotel industry with their experience as influential businessmen in Mexico. Max's father was the manager and owner of the Hotel Arias while his brother, Max's uncle, owned a major hotel supply service. Max had also been able to draw on the talents of Lazaro Zuno, the software engineer with whom he'd had a discreet relationship for the past five years. So far the entire scheme had worked exactly as planned.

Max put the ledger back on its self, again hiding it in plain sight. He gathered his phone and planner, went back into the bar and had another glass of port, chatting quietly with Alvaro until Lorena texted him to say that she was ready to go back to Los Pinos. Max walked into the lobby, cell phone to his ear as he called the chauffeur and the First Lady's security detail to bring the car around. Twenty minutes passed before Lorena made her appearance, looking a little less put together than when they'd arrived several hours earlier.

Sitting next to her in the car Max nearly gagged on the smell of semen.

Lorena smiled in the slightly feline manner she always had afterwards. "A very nice lunch," she said and closed her eyes.

Max turned his head to look out the car window.

The woman had turned him into a pimp. Right under her husband's nose, too.

The car was turning into the circle in front of the entrance to Los Pinos before Max remembered he hadn't changed the password for **1612colcol.** He was still using the master password he'd been given along with the userid. The directions, too complicated to remember, were on a flash drive in his office.

"Tell me my schedule for tomorrow," Lorena said.

Max's planner felt oddly heavy as he opened it to tomorrow's page and started reading off the appointments to her.

◆

Chapter 9

Eddo was up to eight miles a day on the treadmill.

He pounded out the miles Friday morning, mentally readying himself for the monthly meeting of the ministry's senior executives that afternoon. Eddo had not seen Hugo since before the lunch with Bernal Paz.

At 3:00 Eddo took his seat in the ministry's big conference room. The space was a paean to Mexican history, with an enormous framed antique Mexican flag stretched across one wall and vintage photographs of Mexican government landmarks on the other side of the room. The dark wood conference table could seat 40 and was half filled with the Ministry of Public Security's top executives.

The monthly event was equal parts status check and social gathering. A late lunch was always served; this time it was pumpkin flower soup followed by elegant plates of *puerco en naranja* and a tart salad of shredded *nopales* and celeriac. Monte Xanic merlot from Hugo's favorite local winery accompanied the meal. Waiters took away the plates and set out a buffet of coffee and assorted *postres*, then discreetly left.

Hugo carried his coffee to his seat at the head of the table and the meeting officially came to order. It always started with a few words from Hugo; his views of how the ministry was doing and any information he felt his senior officials needed to know.

Eddo made a few notes as Hugo talked but otherwise deliberately kept his hands idle on the tabletop. Hands were always a giveaway. He laughed at Hugo's jokes--not too much-- and nodded at key comments. When Hugo was done those around the table each had their turn, updating the group about developments in their area of responsibility since the last time they'd met. At these meetings Eddo never mentioned investigations that were ongoing and therefore confidential, so today he just spoke briefly about the convictions of three Ministry of Agriculture officials who had been in the business of defrauding the government. Eddo wound up by mentioning that he'd been asked to speak at the Young Attorney Association's annual conference at the Hotel Franco in Polanco in a few weeks. He made a joke about not being able to get out of it, prompting guffaws from the group. His avoidance of the spotlight was almost legendary and assumed to be shyness.

The meeting ended in the early evening. As everyone got to their feet, Hugo motioned to Eddo and Luis Yanez Luna, head of the Financial Regulations Unit, the office that investigated financial crimes such as counterfeiting and bank fraud. "Stay, gentlemen, if you would be so kind."

Hugo was not a physically imposing man, but he had an intelligent face with regular features and a trim moustache. He had salt-and-pepper hair, a compact build, and a penchant for the same type of sleekly tailored Italian suits favored by Bernal Paz. He had been born into a tremendously wealthy family in Monterrey and had built his own media empire by buying up television and radio stations across Mexico and then branching out into news feeds for cellular phone service. His fortune had paved the way for a political career but not as an elected official. It was well known that his wife, Graciela, had absolutely refused to let him run for president in the last election, paving the way for Betancourt to be selected as the PAN's compromise candidate. Hugo had already announced he would not be a candidate in the next election, either.

"Well, my young friends," Hugo said. He'd shown the rest of the group out and now came back to the conference table where Eddo and Luis were standing. "I just wanted to pass on my appreciation to both of you for how well your offices worked together on this agriculture thing. I'd like to see more of this type of cooperation and this kind of result."

"There was good teamwork at every level," Luis said. A few years older than Eddo, he was an accountant and attorney. He'd never done field work but didn't seem mired in bureaucracy, either.

"It went smoothly," Eddo agreed.

"Excellent." Hugo leaned his hip against the table and loosened his tie, the picture of relaxation and goodwill. "Eduardo, who was your top investigator?"

"Conchita Félix Pacheco."

"Conchita?" Hugo appeared surprised that it was a woman.

"A Harvard Law School graduate who also happens to be president of the Young Attorney Association." Eddo smiled ruefully.

Hugo gave a short, seemingly genuine laugh. "Then I say 'well done' to her for both the investigation and getting you to the podium."

"I'll pass on your congratulations."

"Plan something for next month that I can attend," Hugo went on. "I'd like to give her a plaque and rally the troops. How about from your side, Luis?"

As Luis discussed the contribution from Financial, Eddo couldn't help admiring Hugo's gesture. The man was tough and demanding but he set high standards, paid attention to his people, and acknowledged excellence. It was why Eddo had gone to work for the man in the first place, why they'd been able to clean up the ministry after years of stagnation.

"Good, good," Hugo said as Luis wound up. "Let's keep the collaboration going." He turned to Luis. "Can you excuse us now, Luis? I want to talk to Eduardo alone."

Luis shook hands with the other two men and left. Hugo walked over to the dessert buffet. He perused the remaining sweets, his back to the room. Eddo slowly put his portfolio into his briefcase, his mind racing.

"I hear you're working long hours," Hugo said.

"No more than you," Eddo replied.

"Very good." Hugo laughed and turned around with a fruit tart on a plate. "Look, Eduardo, I really wanted to talk to you about Arturo Romero. I know you're very close."

Eddo nodded. Bernal Paz had talked and Hugo was going to say he knew about the warrant Romero had signed.

"Arturo is a good man," Hugo continued. "But politics is an erratic business."

"So I hear." Would it be a warning or an outright threat? Would Hugo try to explain or negotiate? Maybe the threat would be directed at Arturo as a way to force Eddo to stop the investigation.

"How close is he to getting the party nomination, do you think?" Hugo asked.

"I don't think I'm the right person to ask," Eddo said.

"Surely you have some sense of his backing. Rumor has it he likes you for Attorney General." Hugo chuckled. "There's a job with a lot of speeches."

"It's a long road to the nomination." Eddo didn't know where the conversation was headed, not sure if he was on solid ground or shifting sand.

"Romero can come across a bit dull," Hugo said. He bit into the tart, chewed, swallowed. "Too intellectual. Above the common folk, so to speak. He has to have other weak spots, too." It was almost a question.

Eddo shrugged.

Hugo finished the tart. "How much do you think his campaign for the nomination will cost?"

"I'm hardly a campaign strategist." Eddo kept his voice light.

Hugo tossed his empty plate onto the buffet and came back to where Eddo was standing. "When was the last time you had a good fuck, Eduardo?"

Eddo raised his eyebrows.

Hugo thumped Eddo on the shoulder. "For a young man, you're too serious." He made a jovial gesture of dismissal. "Get out and find yourself some women. Fuck their brains out and you won't care about that speech."

♦

Chapter 10

Raul shambled into the kitchen early Friday evening as Luz sat at the table pasting articles in her notebook and she realized he was expecting *la cena*. She rushed to set out warm *tortillas*, brew a fresh pot of coffee, and serve him a heaping portion of the *paella* Marisol had left. When the old gardener was settled she retreated to the other side of the table and resumed her work.

Rosa had left that morning for her weekend off and the Vegas had gone to Valle de Bravo immediately after school. Luz cherished the quiet. No worry that la señora was going to find fault with something, no need to sneak around corners to avoid Alejandro's groping hands or Francesca's temper. There was only Raul to feed and a few chores that Marisol had assigned. Luz planned to do the chores Saturday morning and spend the rest of the weekend reading the books in Señor Vega's study.

The recycling bin yielded some newspapers and a new copy of *HOLA!* There was nothing in the glossy magazine worth keeping for her notebooks but there was an interview with Lorena Lopez de Betancourt. The questions were all opportunities for Lorena to sound like a combination of the Virgin of Guadalupe and the country's fairy godmother and as she read it Luz laughed out loud.

"What's that?"

Raul was staring at her. He pointed at the magazine with a folded *tortilla*.

"An old *revista* from the trash," Luz said.

"You get ideas." Raul pushed half the *tortilla* into his mouth. "No good."

"Why is that?" Luz asked, surprised that he was actually talking to her. Raul was very old and kept to himself. Once a year Hector drove Raul to the huge plant market in Xochimilco but otherwise Raul hardly ever left the Vega property.

"You read too much," Raul said and shoved his empty plate away. "Like my son."

A son? Luz had never heard that Raul had been married or had children. "You have a son, Raul?"

The old man stared at her blankly. Luz swiftly removed his plate and replaced it with a slice of *pastel de tres leches* and a cup of coffee. He dumped sugar into the cup and slurped the coffee noisily. Luz slid into her chair with some coffee for herself and watched him expectantly.

After a few bites of the cake Raul seemed to realize that she was waiting. "He read about the United States and wanted to go. He tried to cross the desert but the Virgin abandoned him because what he was doing was wrong. He got lost and died in the sun."

"I'm so sorry, Raul," Luz said.

"His mother had a *retablo* made for the Virgin to have pity on his soul."

"I'm sure his soul rests in peace."

"When his mother died I had the *retablo* buried with her." Raul continued to eat.

They sat in silence for a few minutes, Luz's heart twisting in sadness. *Retablos* were primitive paintings of a scene of something that happened in a person's life for which they were giving thanks to the Virgin. But not this time. The son had died trying to get to *El Norte* and the mother had probably died of a broken heart.

Raul pushed the empty dessert plate across the table to Luz and got up. He walked over to the door, apparently having forgotten he'd said anything significant.

"I'm sorry for your loss, Raul," Luz called after him. "I'll light a candle for them."

Raul walked out, closing the door behind him.

Luz swallowed past the lump in her throat. Everyone knew someone who'd tried to cross the border into *El Norte*. Many *ilegales* made it and sent back good money to their families, but many were robbed and raped by *coyote* guides, left to die in the desert, or hunted down by *La Migra* immigration police and deposited back on the Mexican side of the border.

She got herself a cup of coffee, opened the next magazine from the recycling pile, and was soon engrossed in an *El Economista* article about people who were still rebuilding New York City after the terrible terrorist attack. There was a picture of a smiling woman named Dee Rodriguez who'd opened a flower shop called New Life Blooms. It was a wonderful article, all about courageous people and real change. The article continued and as Luz flipped the page a little card slid out of the magazine.

Instructions and a telephone number were printed in navy blue ink, Spanish on one side and English on the other. There was a tiny eagle in the upper left hand corner. The top read *Información sobre Visas.*

There was more than just the *ilegale* way to go to the United States where every job paid as much as being a chauffeur in Mexico. Go to the American Embassy on Reforma near the famous *El Angel* monument and *pay* for a visa.

The card stared up at her, full of crisp lettering and infinite promise.

Almost without thinking, Luz brought the card upstairs and got out her cell phone.

She got a recording. New visa appointments on weekday mornings cost 850 pesos. The applicant had to deposit the payment into the embassy's account at Banamex Bank and bring the bank deposit receipt to the appointment, with the account number printed on it by the bank, along with passport, birth certificate, and educational documentation.

Luz disconnected the call and sat back. The cost of a visa was triple what they spent all month for food in Soledad de Doblado. It was almost as much as her cell phone had cost and it taken a year to save for that. But Luz didn't have a year.

Go to New York. The thought made Luz dizzy. She could take her floral certificates and work for smiling Dee Rodriguez whose name was like an omen. She would finally see the wonderful Guggenheim with its undulating architecture and all the other museums she'd only ever read about. Maybe she could study art and learn to draw faces. She wouldn't have to marry

Gonzalez Ruiz.

Her hands shook as Luz pulled out her notebooks. In the pocket of the oldest one was a large envelope with her floral certificates, the letter from Santa Catalina that said how many years of school she'd finished, her birth certificate, and the passport she'd gotten two years ago when the Vegas had planned a trip to Spain but left her behind at the last minute.

♦

Monday morning before Marisol came Luz asked Señora Vega for an advance on her salary.

"An advance?" La señora's eyes narrowed with impatience. She was heading off to the club for a spinning class. She wore matching yoga pants and warm-up jacket, several gold chains, and a low-cut tank top that showed her sports bra. Her silky hair was pulled into the usual ponytail. "I don't give advances. You know that."

"I'm sorry, señora." Luz put on her stupid face and stared at the floor, appalled at the risk she was taking. "I've never asked before."

"You know the rules." Señora Vega made a dismissive gesture.

"My mother has to pay a school fee," Luz said, not moving.

Señora Vega drummed her fingers on the edge of the big desk. Looked at her watch.

"Please," Luz whispered, hating that she had to beg.

"Just this once," Señora Vega said archly. "I won't tolerate this sort of behavior again." She wrote out a statement that said Luz had accepted 850 pesos as an advance against her salary due Friday 29 October. Luz signed it. Senora Vega counted out the bills from her wallet.

"Thank you, señora. May I go send it?"

Señora Vega flapped a hand at her, unhooked her keys and left.

Rosa was busy cleaning Alejandro's bathroom. Luz ran up to the attic and called the visa number on her cell phone. When the recording ended she pressed the button to speak to a real person. She made an appointment for Friday morning, the day before the Portillo's party. Then she walked 20 minutes to the huge Banamex bank at the intersection of the big boulevards of Reforma and Prado Sur. She filled out a deposit slip and took a number. The tote board directing number-holders to a specific teller kept the lines of people moving. When the teller handed her the receipt with the embassy bank account number printed on it, Luz's knees nearly buckled with the enormity of what she'd done.

♦

Chapter 11

"Señor Cortez?"

Eddo looked up from the report on his desk. The junior secretary, Paola, was standing in the partially open door to his office, clutching a manila envelope to her chest as if for protection. He pulled off his reading glasses. "Yes?"

"A package for you, señor," she said hesitantly.

"Thank you, Paola. Leave it in the usual place, please." Eddo indicated the credenza along the wall adjacent to his desk.

Paola walked to the credenza and laid the envelope in the inbox. "It's marked urgent, señor," she said. "From Señor Cortez in Puebla."

Eddo got up, came around the side of the desk, and took the envelope out of the inbox. "Thank you, Paola."

The secretary disappeared out the door like a rabbit down a hole and Eddo carried the thickly padded envelope back to his desk. He cut it open with a scissors and pulled out a letter and a square cardboard envelope marked *Urgencia*.

The letter was from his uncle Bernardo explaining that the cardboard envelope had been sent to Marca Cortez from the Banco de Vieja Puebla and that he'd thought it best to send the package on to Eddo in Mexico City.

"*Madre de Dios*," Eddo swore under his breath. "Two weeks exactly."

The envelope contained an unmarked CD. There was no note, no message from Bernal Paz.

Eddo put the CD into the drive of his computer and pulled up a list of files. There were over 1000.

"*Madre de Dios*," he said again. He hit a button on his phone, told the senior secretary to only put through emergency calls or those from the minister, then double-clicked to open the first file.

It took him a few minutes to realize what he had. Each file was the record of either a deposit or a withdrawal into various banks accounts attributed to members of Hugo's family. There were several joint accounts for Hugo and his wife Graciela, and a joint account for Hugo and his son Reynoldo. The amounts in those accounts were substantial and relatively stable; there wasn't much activity. The accounts were in large, national banks.

But as Eddo kept clicking open files he saw other accounts in the name of either Hugo de la Madrid Acosta or Reynoldo de la Madrid. The accounts were in a bank called Banco Limitado.

Eddo got out a yellow legal pad and a pencil and started four columns: *Reynoldo deposits*, *Reynoldo withdrawals*, *Hugo deposits* and *Hugo withdrawals*. Toggling between files and the paper, he copied down the date, amount, and bank account number from each file on the CD and put the information under the correct column.

By the time he finished, the sky was dimming into twilight outside the big window behind his desk. Eddo took off his reading glasses and rubbed his eyes, wanting the pattern on the legal sheets to be wrong.

Several times a week deposits were being made into four different accounts held in Reynoldo's name. Each deposit was sizeable but not large enough to cause alarm. No two deposits were the same amount. It always varied; a thousand pesos here, a few hundred pesos there. The deposits appeared to be cash or money order, although some were wire transfers from a business called Montopa in Panama. Withdrawals were made only a little less frequently than the deposits. The withdrawals were never the same amount as any of the deposits and they were all for different amounts but by and large the same amount that was coming in was also going out.

The money withdrawn from Reynoldo's accounts was appearing within a few days in Hugo's accounts, the amounts modified by a few hundred pesos each time. About 80 percent of what came into Hugo's accounts was withdrawn within a week.

Eddo wrenched himself away from the desk and started to

pace the length of the office. Hugo was obviously trying to disguise the movement of the money by using multiple accounts and tinkering with the amounts. It was a classic money laundering scheme known as layering.

"Cartel money, Hugo?" Eddo muttered angrily. Layering was usually the middle step in the laundering process. "Where's it going next?"

The office was a big space but tonight Eddo felt closed in and suffocating under the weight of what he didn't know. He stood in front of the big window and looked down on the other buildings in the Colonia Cuauhtémoc business district. The Office of Special Investigations occupied the entire twelfth floor and the view was his only decoration. He'd never ordered any artwork or brought in any personal items. The place was as sterile and impersonal as it had been the day he'd walked in as the chief pitbull of the newly created anti-corruption office.

A long black car, followed by a black SUV, left the underground garage of the building across the street.

Eddo threw himself back into his desk chair. He unlocked the cabinet behind his desk, revealing a safe. He worked the combination and took out the list of userids and directions given to him that day in Los Olivos.

Miguel had uncovered a timestamp on the directions. They'd been created two weeks before the first deposit into Banco Limitado.

Eddo rubbed his eyes and thought about next steps. Getting an informant inside the El Toro cartel or Hugo's bodyguard cadre was next to impossible. That left the money trail; investigating Banco Limitado and tracing the Montopa company in Panama. It was a long shot but maybe Hugo's hard drive could be scanned for evidence of communicating with the cartel as **Hh23051955**.

Eddo dialed the private number to Los Pinos, identified himself, and despite the late hour got Betancourt's executive assistant, Ernesto Silvio. The Betancourts were in Guadalajara for the weekend, Silvio reminded him. They were dedicating the extension to the airport there.

Lorena's first salvo against the mayor of Guadalajara,

Eddo thought. "When will the president be back?"

"I can get you in for breakfast on Monday," Silvio said. "It's the holiday and his morning schedule is pretty open. Seven o'clock?"

"That'll work," Eddo said. The two men knew each other well enough to preclude any questions why the head of the Office of Special Investigations needed to see the president so quickly. After a few thin jokes about working too late the two men hung up.

Eddo had just grabbed a bottle of water and a protein bar from the stash in his desk drawer when the door handle turned. "Yes?" Eddo barked, heart suddenly pounding.

It was the cleaning supervisor; the night shift cleaners were already making their rounds. "Oye, señor." The man ducked his head sheepishly. "We'll come back later."

It took Eddo well past midnight to finish. The report, along with the deposit and withdrawal charts, went into a blue folder labeled "PEMEX" that was a permanent fixture in his briefcase. All bags were inspected going into and out of the building; the guards always saw the dogeared folder and never questioned the contents.

Eddo used a flash drive to run a program to erase his computer's cache and digital evidence of the bank records; hopefully it worked as well as Miguel claimed. He dropped the flash drive and the CD into his office safe, spun the dial and locked the camouflaging cabinet. The last thing he did was smear a bit of clay across the edge of the keyhole. Any attempt to open the cabinet would leave a mark in the clay.

♦

Chapter 12

The week passed with agonizing slowness. On Thursday Hector took Luz to the school to help out in Victoria's classroom. It was the class's combined Halloween and *Dia de los Muertos* party and the children screamed and shouted, fueled by too many chocolate skulls and candy *muerto* skeleton figurines. Victoria ate so much chocolate Luz was afraid she'd throw up during the swim lesson but she didn't.

♦

Luz got to the American Embassy at 8:15 am Friday morning, feeling like a pretender in the Dolce and Gabbana jeans and the elegant black sweater from the trash bags. The entrance to the visa pavilion was easy to find; the crowd swirled from Reforma onto a side street that ran alongside the embassy building. On the other side of the street Luz could see the Sheraton Hotel, several shops, and a small restaurant. The sidewalks on that side were crowded with relatives and street hustlers.

Luz shook her head at a man trying to sell her a folder as she went to the end of the line. Someone jostled her as she stood there, but she held her ground, her palms damp with nerves. She kept her arm clamped over the Prada tote, sure that someone would try to pickpocket her. No one in line talked to anyone else unless they had come with them but the people on the street sometimes darted in and out of the line, trying to get someone's attention. Luz was jostled again and her nervousness ratcheted up.

At about 8:45 am the line started to move. Luz found herself in a bare reception area where a clerk exchanged her bank receipt for a form on a clipboard. She was also handed a number like she'd gotten in the Banamex bank.

Luz passed from the reception space into the main room. The visa pavilion was huge, clean, and efficient. There were more than a dozen booths along the far wall, like tellers in a bank, except that there wasn't any glass and the tellers were sitting down. There were chairs in front of each teller. Dividers separated each booth so that the person being interviewed had a modicum of privacy. A big digital counter was mounted over each teller booth to direct number-holders. The center of the room was full of hard plastic chairs bolted to the floor like in the bus station. They were all placed at right angles to the far wall so that the counters could be seen from any seat.

Excited and scared at the same time, Luz looked at the number in her hand. 314. She fumbled her way to a seat and took out her pen. The room was quiet except for whispered questions and the scratching of pen against paper.

Luz filled out the form giving the address in Soledad de Doblado and her cell phone number. She put down "New Life Blooms, New York City" when asked to give her address in the United States. She wrote "Dee Rodriguez" as the point of contact.

Her number came faster than Luz thought it would. Her knees practically knocked as she walked up to the booth. She sat down in the chair and slid her clipboard and the copies of her documents to the young blonde *norteamericano* woman on the other side of the desk.

"Hello," Luz said tremulously in English. "How are you today?"

"*Buenos dias*," the woman replied automatically in Spanish. "Why do you want to go to the United States?"

"To work," Luz said in surprise. *Why did anyone want to go to El Norte?*

The woman sighed and skimmed Luz's form. "Is this where you'll be working?"

"Yes," Luz said. "New Life Blooms. It's a flower store. In Manhattan. I'm a *florista*." She pointed to the copies of the floral school certificates.

"You have a promissory letter?"

"I'm sorry?"

"A letter from, uh, let's see, Dee Rodriguez attesting to the fact that you have been offered employment in the United States with her company."

"No, I don't have a letter."

"Are you working at present?"

"Yes."

"In Soledad de Doblado?" The woman stumbled a bit over the unfamiliar name.

"No. Here in Mexico City."

"As a florist?"

"No."

"How long have you worked for your present employer?"

"Six years."

"Do you have a letter from your present employer regarding your intention to return to Mexico and resume your employment following your travel to the United States?"

"No."

"How long do you plan to work at New Life Blooms?"

"I don't know." Luz held onto the Prada tote with both hands to keep from shaking. The session was not going at all how she'd imagined it.

The woman wrote something down on Luz's form and rifled through the document copies. "Thank you for your application. You'll be notified by certified letter to your address of record as to the determination of your application. Have a good day." She rattled it off as if she had said it hundreds of times before.

Luz looked at the woman blankly. It was *over*? "I'm fluent in English," she blurted.

"I'll note that on your form," the young woman said crisply. "You should have your certified letter in four to six weeks." She shuffled papers, clearly suggesting that Luz should leave.

"Will the letter tell me when to come back to get the visa?" Luz asked. Surely there was more to getting the visa than this. They should take her picture, give her a receipt, something.

"The letter will notify you as to the status of your visa

application."

"Status?" Luz blinked in confusion. "But I've already paid 850 pesos for the visa."

The woman looked at her impassively, neither unhelpful nor sympathetic, like Hector. "The payment was for the appointment."

Payment was for the appointment. The words echoed as if Luz's head was suddenly hollow. The next interviewee was standing there, waiting for the chair to be free. Luz gathered up the Prada tote and moved away. A man in a uniform directed her to the exit.

◆

Luz found herself walking through the Basilica neighborhood, where virtually every shop was full of religious curios. She ignored the street vendors hawking rosaries and holy pictures like the one in the living room in Soledad de Doblado, and went through the giant gates of the enormous Virgin of Guadalupe religious complex.

The Basilica of the Virgin of Guadalupe was built at the base of Tepeyac hill where Mary had appeared to Juan Diego, whom the late *El Papa* Juan Pablo II had finally made a saint. Mary had appeared to Juan Diego as an *indio*, with cherubs at Her feet, and had left Her image on Juan Diego's garment, a shapeless poncho called a *tilma*.

As Luz crossed the huge Basilica plaza the diorama mounted on an enormous H-shaped pedestal started its show. Every half hour or so the diorama opened and a puppet theatre took place, with a recorded narrator telling the story of Juan Diego seeing the Virgin and trying to convince people, including a stiff-necked Spanish bishop, of what he'd seen. Luz went past the two old churches that each in their day had held the precious *tilma* but were now badly damaged by earthquakes, and went into the new Basilica, an architectural mix of church, theater, and spaceship.

Mass was always going on there, an endless loop of prerecorded consecration that took 20 minutes or so to play each time. There was no one on the altar until the priest came out to serve communion. Luz slipped into a pew that let her see the simple *tilma* in its glass case behind the altar and listened to the tinny recording start the Prayer of the Faithful. She tried to make her mind listen to the prayers, to find comfort in the familiar words.

But the place was noisy and full of movement. Visitors cruised around, bringing flowers to the communion rail, gawking at the *tilma,* or staring upwards at the rafters that looked like lace stretched across the ceiling. Some people actually stayed on their knees the entire time they were inside the Basilica, mouthing prayers as they kneeled their way to the communion rail to gaze upon the *tilma* and murmur their devotion to the Virgin.

Luz stumbled out and found the path that wound up the hill behind the Basilica to the actual site of Mary's visitation. She got most of the way up to the tiny *capilla* at the very top before she ran out of adrenaline and oxygen and sat down on a bench. Only a few other people were braving the hill in Friday's *sopa* and it was quiet. Luz sat there clutching the Prada tote, refusing to cry, trying to convince herself that she still had a chance at a visa, that she hadn't just wasted 850 pesos. As long as the *norteamericanos* didn't actually call Dee Rodriguez in New York she'd be fine. She tried to pray, to ask the Virgin to intercede, but all she could think of was how thoughtless and impulsive she'd been. When the tears came it was hard to gulp them away in the thin air.

Before she started back down the hill, she got out her cell phone and called Señora Velasquez who ran the *abarrotes* snack shop across from the Alba house. When Luz didn't come home, Maria or Juan Pablo would check for a message and pay Señora Velasquez 10 pesos for it. Few people in the *barrio* had telephones. Señora Velasquez probably made as much with her message service as she did selling soda and gum.

♦

Chapter 13

"My grandmother," Tomás panted. "Could have played better than you today."

Eddo pulled two bottles of water out of the carton he always kept in the back of his SUV and tossed one to Tomás. "Nobody's better than *abuela* Hortensia."

The back hatch of Eddo's SUV was open, affording the two men some shade from La Marquesa's Saturday afternoon heat. Both were streaked with sweat and grime from the dry dust of the soccer field.

Tomás drank down half a bottle in one swallow then wiped his mouth with a muscular forearm. "We got a new problem?" he asked.

Eddo pulled off his sweaty shirt, poured water into his hand, and rubbed his face. "Later."

There were still too many players there. More than a dozen cars were parked in the dirt next to the soccer field. The other players were all police and as dirty and sweaty as their captains. They traded water and sports drinks and good-natured ribbing about the game, which Tomás's team had won easily.

"Hey, *jefe,* next week we'll teach them, eh?" Diego, one of the best players, saluted Eddo with a wet towel. Eddo shook hands, clapped a few players on the back, forced a laugh about trashing the other team next week. Players shouted farewells and cars left the lot.

Finally Eddo and Tomás were the only ones left from the marathon game. "Bernal Paz came through with the bank records," Eddo said

"It's not good," Tomás surmised.

"Hugo's laundering money like an amateur," Eddo said. "Using accounts in his name and his son's. Money comes into the son's accounts, transits Hugo's and mostly disappears."

"Big money?"

"A couple of hundred million pesos so far." A few new cars drove into the lot. A group that looked like an extended family got out and started kicking a ball around by the far goal. "All in small chunks. Started a couple of weeks after the land sale in Anahuac and after the directions for how to use those userids."

"*Por Dios*," Tomás swore. "And nothing from his bank wondering what the fuck is going on?"

Eddo shook his head. "Probably isn't a real bank."

"Vasco can check."

"I'm meeting with Betancourt first thing Monday morning," Eddo said, watching the father and sons and cousins. He slumped against the rear seat of the SUV and let his feet dangle over the taillights. Played like shit. Missed two shots on goal he could have made when he was five.

"Monday?" Tomás wiped his face with the tail of his tee shirt. "You can tell us how it went at Ana's charity event that night."

Eddo stared at this friend, his brain sputtering. Finally it caught. Tomás's wife Ana was an architect and her firm had designed the new wing of a children's hospital. Eddo had promised weeks ago to attend the opening on behalf of Marca Cortez and make a company donation to the hospital. "Sure."

One of the children on the field missed a kick and the ball rolled toward them. Tomás hopped off the SUV's bumper and kicked it back, his cleat making a dull *thwap* as the ball connected. The child grinned with delight and ran after it. Tomás nodded in satisfaction.

"Come back to the house and have dinner with me and Ana," he said. "We'll hash out this thing. Figure a way to come at it that you haven't thought of yet."

♦

Chapter 14

Luz wore her usual uniform of gray dress, ankle socks, and black loafers but Gonzalez Ruiz still looked at her admiringly as she got into the front passenger seat of the Portillo's minivan. She nodded back, uncertain what to say. He drove with one thick hand on the wheel, the other on his fleshy knee, the cloth of his suit pants stretched tight. He wasn't much of a talker, however, and it was a silent drive to the Portillo's enormous house on Bosques de Almendros, a winding street in the Bosques de las Lomas neighborhood southwest of Lomas Virreyes.

The van slid into the driveway and Gonzalez Ruiz indicated that she should walk to the right. Luz went around the side of the house and found the back patio.

She paused before knocking on the kitchen door. On the far left of the expansive back lawn, a theatrical troupe was setting up a stage complete with big speakers, microphones, and footlights. On the other side of the yard several men in khaki pants and blue shirts reading FUN-A-MUNDO were using a motor to inflate a rocket ship that the kids would jump on. It was taller than the house with a cavernous entrance made to look like a loading dock. Opposite the back door of the house, more workmen were putting up food stalls for *quesadillas,* cotton candy, corkscrew potatoes on a stick, and other messy things that Luz would be wiping off children all afternoon.

Señora Portillo seemed pleased to see her on time and left Luz in the kitchen with Dolores, the Portillo's cook, and Nina, their maid. Dolores wore a white double-breasted chef's smock. Nina wore the standard uniform dress except that in the Portillo household it was navy blue instead of gray.

The Portillos' house was full of art and color, with high-quality canvases hanging on nearly every wall. Luz would have liked to study the paintings but she had come to work. Caterers were preparing a big patio-level game room for the adults, setting up six round tables, each seating ten. Luz and Nina set the tables with sterling silver flatware, three different wineglasses for each place, and napkins folded into fans. Then they got the children's tables ready.

The party started at noon. There were over 40 children, all wound up by too much sugar, too many *Cocas*, and too much sensory input. The inflatable jumping thing was a big success, until one child got sick in it and play was suspended while Luz and Nina cleaned up. The theatrical troupe was noisy, the speakers blaring music and campy pre-recorded dialogue. The actors ran around on the stage in Star Wars costumes until Luz hoped *El Ataque de los Clones* would happen *right now*. A gymnastics group spread mats on the grass and the kids tumbled and cartwheeled, with the inevitable spills and crying. There were several *piñatas* suspended by a rope controlled by Gonzalez Ruiz. The children sang screechily as they took turns hitting the papier maché figures. The candy that spilled out wound them up even more.

The adults stayed inside for the most part, eating the elegantly prepared buffet and discussing upper class issues. Much of the chatter was about the vacation house the Portillos had recently bought in San Miguel de Allende. A four hour drive northwest of Mexico City, San Miguel de Allende was famous for producing some of Mexico's finest paintings, metalwork, and handicrafts. Serious collectors went to San Miguel to buy the sort of artwork hanging on the Portillos' walls.

By 10:00 pm most of the guests had gone home. Luz and Nina helped the caterers pack up. Señora Portillo gave Luz 200 pesos in small bills, as if paying her was painful, and told her that Gonzalez Ruiz would take her home.

Luz followed the chauffeur to the Portillo's van and got into the front passenger seat. Backseats, like certain dishes, were always reserved for the employer.

It had been her second exhausting day in a row. Luz was glad for the silence. The van finally came to a stop opposite the Vega's house. Gonzalez Ruiz killed the lights.

"Thank you," Luz said. She pressed the unlock button and heard the click. Her hand was on the door handle when Gonzalez Ruiz pressed the master lock on his side. Suddenly there was no resistance as Luz tried the door handle.

He grabbed her left forearm.

Surprised, Luz pulled back hard but Gonzalez Ruiz was like a bull. He dragged her over the seat divider and kissed her, trying to force her mouth open with gummy lips. His free hand groped at her chest.

Luz twisted herself like a crazy person to get away but she simply wasn't strong enough. He wouldn't let go so she smacked him as hard as she could with her right hand, the crack of her palm against his cheek and ear surprisingly loud. She hit him, once, twice, *three* times before he finally let go.

"*Pendejo!*" Luz shouted. She slammed her hand on the unlock button and leaped out of the van.

Once upstairs, Luz locked the bathroom door, climbed into the shower, and scrubbed hard as if she could scour away the disaster of the past two days. Tomorrow would be better. She'd put on that impractical pink sweater and go to the museums, which were free on Sundays. First the Tamayo, then the Museum of Contemporary Art. Afterwards she'd walk into Chapultepec Park and eat at one of the taco stands that sold five tacos for 30 pesos. She could at least afford that.

And for a whole day she wouldn't think about the visa or Gonzalez Ruiz or Lupe's baby or anything else that would remind her what a shambles her life had become.

◆

Chapter 15

Eddo closed his apartment door and dropped his sportsbag and cleats on the doormat. The maid would take care of them the next time she came.

He slumped into the big chair across from the television and closed his eyes. Tomás and Ana were great company, the closest friends he had, but it had been a huge mistake to go over to their house.

As always, Ana was lovely and happy and glad to see him. He'd showered and changed in their guest room, then he and Tomás turned on the television and watched the Toluca *fútbol* machine grind yet another hapless victim into the dust. After a delicious dinner Ana steered him around the house, pointing out all the improvements since the last time he'd been there. The old Spanish-style house in the historic San Angel district was full of warmth and character and they'd done a lot to make it a real home. The stucco walls were softened with deep tones and bright artwork, and they'd added modern fixtures and appliances. There were numerous pictures of Tomás and Ana and their respective families, along with colorful pillows and throws. A thousand details said that this was a place where two people loved and made love and were building a life together. They'd been married a year and the glow was still obvious. Eddo could see it in the way Tomás lit up when Ana walked into the room, or the way Ana unconsciously slipped her hand into her husband's as they sat together on the sofa.

Eddo had said something lame about the charity event Monday night and left.

He turned on the television, the screen a ghostly glow in the dark room. He flicked through the channels and turned it off again.

His life had come down to sitting alone in the dark with a head full of secrets and suspicions. More of Bernal Paz's words came back unexpectedly. *In all that time you've been concealed. Lurking in the shadows.*

The only thing the old man had been wrong about was Eddo's father. Bolivar Cortez had been a crusader in his own way, and Eddo had watched him struggle against a never-ending web of bureaucratic and police corruption as Marca Cortez grew, fueled by his father's desire to improve the lives of workers in Puebla. But both parents had died before seeing what their son had accomplished. Sometimes he missed them like hell.

Eddo heaved himself out of the armchair and opened kitchen cupboards until he found where he'd stashed all the tequila he'd gotten last Christmas from ministry colleagues and subordinates who didn't know what else to get a cold sonuvabitch like him. He pulled out an unopened bottle of top grade tequila, found a water glass, and half filled it with the strong yellowish spirit. The stuff seared his throat and brought tears to his eyes. When it didn't come back up he finished the glass and poured some more.

He went back to the chair, shoving aside some newspapers in order to set the tequila bottle on the coffee table. He took another gulp and surveyed the dark room, mentally comparing it to Ana and Tomás's home.

"You live like a fucking monk," he announced to the bare walls. Between his ministry salary and his inheritance from Marca Cortez he could afford a palace, but an apartment in a building with good security and reliable plumbing was all he really needed. The place had two bedrooms, each with its own bathroom. He'd turned the smaller one into a gym. The dining room functioned as an office. He had good electronics and a lot of books but that was about it.

No color, no artwork. No connection to someone else.

The tequila took hold, warming him, letting the sadness inside expand. *A dead man.* Don César was right.

Eddo had confronted a lot of crime and evil during his career, but the investigation into Hugo de la Madrid Acosta was something else altogether. Something that was becoming a personal hurt. Eddo's own judgment and instincts had been so very wrong. He'd trusted Hugo, respected him, held him up as a model, the sort of man who could help make change happen. It was almost impossible to believe that Hugo had sold his soul for drug money and had sullied his son's name in the process. And for what? Hugo was already a rich man with all the power he needed. It didn't make sense.

As Eddo drank he wondered what the president's reaction would be at breakfast on Monday. Betancourt and de la Madrid Acosta were professionally, if not personally, close. The president would not appreciate hearing that a trusted advisor was almost certainly connected to a cartel, using some Internet back door to send messages, and trying to launder money through numerous bank accounts. And what would be the president's reaction when he realized that Arturo Romero had known first and signed the warrant? Anger? Revenge? *Fuck*.

Eddo got to his feet and staggered down the hall to his bedroom. The white apartment walls undulated like the billowing sails of a ship but he got to the dresser and took out his gun. It was the same Glock automatic issued to him by Highway Patrol as its youngest lieutenant and no one had ever asked for it back. Every year Tomás made sure he was issued a new carry permit.

Back in the living room Eddo shoved in the magazine, racked back the slide, and chambered a round. He played a warped and solitary drinking game, switching the glass and the gun between hands as his dexterity eroded. Finally he dropped the gun onto the coffee table.

He hadn't been this drunk since his freshman year of college in New Hampshire when he'd seen snow for the first time. The dorm had celebrated by introducing him to peppermint schnapps and Eduardo had morphed into Eddo. That had been a lifetime ago, when he'd known he would do hard things but they were still comfortably far away.

The neck of the tequila bottle clanged against the rim of the glass as he poured out the last of the liquor. He raised the glass and saluted the loaded gun. "To loneliness, old friend," he said, hearing the words through cotton wool. The title of a long forgotten book came back to him. "To the fucking loneliness of the long distance runner."

◆

Eddo woke sprawled in the chair, fist still wrapped around the glass. His head felt like granite. Making it to the kitchen was a major achievement. He managed to down water and aspirin, trashed the tequila bottle, unloaded the gun and put it away, stripped to his shorts and forced himself onto the treadmill.

He gasped through the worst of the pain. By the third mile his body fell into its normal rhythm and he could think clearly, the self pity gone. He had to get out of the apartment. It didn't matter what he did as long as it wasn't work. He needed to be with people, see real life, get a dose of the true Mexico that kept him fighting so hard.

A hot shower, clean clothes, a big coffee and breakfast roll at the Starbucks in Polanco and Eddo was human again. The sky was a surprising deep blue. His spirits lifted as he drove east on Reforma, past the Anthropology Museum. People on the wide sidewalks waited for the museums to open. He found a parking space on Avenida Mahatma Gandhi, in the dust that served as an urban parking lot, and aimlessly followed a group through a small wooded area toward the Tamayo Museum. He emerged onto a plaza and the huge glass museum burst into view.

Eddo stood still, taking it in, surprised at this massive structure he'd never seen despite having lived in Mexico City for so many years, always passing the giant curved sign on Reforma that announced the exhibits but never paying it any attention. The building was three stories high and he could see right through to the interior. The sun glinted off the glass façade.

But the place wouldn't open for 15 more minutes. Eddo was debating whether to wait or wander towards Chapultepec Park when he noticed a woman sitting alone on a plaza bench.

She was wearing a bright pink sweater, dark jeans, and a brightly colored scarf. Glossy black ponytail. There was a sketchpad balanced on her knees and she was drawing diligently, glancing back and forth between the sketchpad and the museum building. Her eyes were big and intelligent and her lips pressed together as she concentrated.

Before Eddo knew it the words were out of his mouth.

♦

Chapter 16

"May I see what you're doing?"

Luz froze.

Strangers *never* spoke to each other on the street in Mexico City unless they were thief and victim.

Heart thumping, Luz raised her head and looked around.

The man who had spoken was standing about ten feet away, close enough to speak to her, not so close as to be threatening. His hands were by his sides, not in his pockets, to show he wasn't hiding anything. There was no one else around, no potential accomplice, and there was plenty of room to run around him if she had to. She automatically checked that the Prada tote was still safely tucked between her feet. But he didn't look like a thief.

He was tall; probably a head taller than she, and everything about him said upper class. He was quietly but expensively dressed in crisp khaki pants and a white ribbed pullover shirt, the trademark weekend outfit worn by wealthy people who had someone like Luz to wash *la sopa* out of light colored clothes. He wore a well-cut brown leather blazer over the white shirt, a pair of snub-toed casual shoes, and *norteamericano* Ray-Ban sunglasses.

The only thing about him that wasn't standard upper class was his hair. It was only about a centimeter long, the sort of cropped military haircut that no one wore. Men of all classes wore their hair much longer and slicked back with gel.

"May I?" he asked. He gestured at the sketchpad. His voice was deep and strong, his diction clear and well-educated.

He took a few steps closer and pulled off the sunglasses, and Luz realized that he was the most handsome man she'd ever seen. His face was perfect, with a high forehead, excellent cheekbones, and a wide jaw tapering to a firm chin. His skin was darkened by the sun--if that was possible in Mexico City--and the effect against the white shirt was striking. But his eyes were more than striking, they were startling. They weren't black-brown like *mestizo* or *indio* eyes, not even pale brown like Señora Vega's. No, his eyes were hazel, a warm greenish gray that practically shouted out his elite position in Mexican society. He was probably pure *castellano*.

Luz slowly turned the sketchpad around. She'd drawn the building, making the glass soar into the sky, elongating and curving it slightly like an El Greco structure. But the sun was glinting off the glass façade and the shading was all wrong.

"It's very good," he said. He stepped to one side, a small athletic motion, glanced at the Tamayo, then back at the drawing. He raised his eyebrows in admiration. Luz couldn't help noticing they were perfect feathery lines above those remarkable hazel eyes.

An athlete, she guessed. He looked like pictures of European *fútbol* players, with clear smooth skin drawn tight over the hard edge of his jaw. The cords of his neck were well defined. The slouchy belt suggested narrow hips and a flat stomach. Maybe in his early or mid thirties, though, too old to be a professional player.

"Is this for the museum?"

"I'm sorry?" Luz realized she'd been staring and dropped her eyes.

"For the museum." He gestured at the Tamayo with the sunglasses. His hands were well kept, but not soft. "Are you doing some promotional work?"

"Who, me?" *Estupida.*

"Yes." He fiddled with the sunglasses. "The picture. It looks like something for the museum."

"No, señor," Luz said. "I'm just drawing. The Tamayo is one of my favorite places." She turned the sketchpad back around and looked at what she'd done so far.

"It's excellent."

"Thank you," Luz said. She looked up again and by some insane coincidence met his hazel eyes and forgot to put her stupid face on. For a moment they stared at each other. Luz caught herself before she smiled at him like some fool who didn't know her place.

"But I'm having a lot of trouble with the light today." Luz busied herself with her pencil case. "It's too bright."

"What do you mean?" he asked, taking a step closer.

Luz smelled leather and soap and citrus.

"Well, see this?" she heard herself say. Suddenly her finger was showing him where she'd drawn the reflection of the sun on the windows. "See how it's darker here, near the roofline? I'm not used to drawing light, there's usually too much smog. So I have to do it over and of course that sort of ruins the paper if I have to erase."

There were rules to keep the different social classes from getting too familiar with each other. Everyone knew them and Luz was breaking them all by chattering away like this. She shut her mouth and found her good gum eraser, the one with the brush on the end.

"Do you usually do things over until you get them right?" he asked.

"I usually get them right the first time," Luz said unthinkingly. She pushed up the sleeves of the pink sweater so she wouldn't get erasures on the beautiful cashmere and started to carefully rub off the pencil marks.

"Ah," he said.

Luz looked up, suddenly realizing how arrogant her words must have sounded. "I'm sorry, señor. That was a rude thing to say."

"Not at all," he said. "I can respect that. You're probably very good at what you do."

"Hardly." Luz continued to gently rub at the errant pencil lines. "I'm just stubborn."

"Do you mind if I watch?"

Luz swallowed hard. "Not at all, señor."

She brushed away the erasures and selected a soft lead pencil. She redrew the shading, her eyes moving between the Tamayo building across the plaza and the paper on her lap. She was acutely aware of the man watching her, glorious in his leather jacket and hazel eyes, sunglasses dangling from his hand.

Luz switched to a harder lead to fill in the three story stairway behind the glass facade, then chose yet a different one to soften the roofline with some fluffy clouds. As the drawing emerged in sharper detail, the humor was evident. The line of the building curved as if it was preening while the clouds leaned curiously, trying to see behind the glass.

"You're *fantastic*," the man standing next to her said.

Luz glanced up and electricity drilled right through her.

He was smiling a wide genuine smile that lit his face and made the hazel eyes sparkle. His teeth were perfectly straight and white. He could have been a toothpaste ad, the kind with "Cleanliness is Healthy" on the bottom.

"What are you going to call it?" he asked.

"My sketches aren't good enough to name," Luz murmured.

"I don't believe you."

"See for yourself." Luz held out the sketchpad.

"Do you mind?" He indicated the bench next to her and Luz nodded. He sat down--not too close, not too far away--and clipped the sunglasses to the neckline of his shirt. She handed him the pad; it was half-filled with about 15 sketches.

He studied the pictures. "These are very good." He flipped to a detailed sketch of Santa Clara, all sepia tones and sad gravestones. "There's a lot of *soul* in these pictures."

"Thank you," Luz said faintly. There was a humming sound in her ears and she was dangerously and inexplicably happy that this beautiful stranger liked what she'd done.

"But the funny ones are the best." He turned back to the picture of the Tamayo. "This one is important. You have to name it."

"Really?"

"Definitely." He handed back the sketchpad.

Luz selected a red pencil. She drew a tiny tomato sitting on top of one of the stairs about halfway up the flight. It was the only spot of color in the otherwise black-and-white drawing. She gave it a green stem and it became a perfect miniature vegetable, poking fun at the grandeur of the preening museum. She started to grin as she wrote "Tomato Tamayo" at the bottom.

Luz turned the sketchpad so he could see it.

"Tomato Tamayo?" He gave "tomato" the English pronunciation; he had understood the rhythm of the words right away. "Excellent. Very clever. But you didn't sign it."

"It's just a sketch." Luz folded her hands primly in her lap, very conscious that he was solid and confident and knit together with a sort of taut energy. The humming sound was still in her ears. She fought a crazy urge to reach up and feel the muscle over his jaw and the smoothness of his shave. She put the red pencil back in the case instead.

"You should sign everything you do," he said seriously.

"All right." She found a pen and wrote "Luz de Maria" in black ink across the bottom corner. "There."

He cocked his head. "Your name is Luz de Maria? Is that right?"

"Yes."

"Luz de Maria. That's lovely."

"Thank you," Luz said. The humming mixed with the scent of leather and soap and citrus to make her lightheaded.

"I'm sorry for not introducing myself sooner. I'm Eduardo. Eduardo Cortez Castillo."

Of course his name is Eduardo Cortez Castillo, Luz thought wearily, crashing back to earth. There were no two more Spanish surnames in all of Mexico. He could probably trace his bloodline directly to Hernán himself.

He looked at her expectantly.

"I'm Luz de Maria Alba Mora," Luz said, feeling all over again that she had no business talking to him.

He offered his hand and she shook it. His grip was firm and dry. He didn't try to hold her hand any longer than was appropriate or do anything else but give it a friendly shake.

"It's been a pleasure meeting you this morning, Luz de Maria Alba Mora. Thank you for letting me see an artist at work."

"You're welcome," Luz said. The humming was gone and she felt vaguely dishonest and foolish. Dishonest for letting him think she was a real artist, foolish for feeling so let down.

Some people walked by, heading for the museum, and Luz

glanced at her watch. He saw her looking at the time and stood up.

"I guess the museum is open now?"

"Yes." Luz felt cold. She pulled down the sleeves of the pink sweater.

He took a step backwards and looked at the museum. The huge doors were open. "Thank you for your time," he said.

"Enjoy the exhibits, Señor Cortez."

He nodded at her, almost a bow. A formal, old-fashioned gesture. He walked a few steps toward the museum then turned back to her. "Are there any exhibits you'd recommend?"

"Oh. Well." Luz tried to look nonchalant and not supremely happy he hadn't just walked away. "I have the review of October's artists if you'd like to see it."

"There's a review?" he asked.

"I read it every month." Luz dove into the Prada tote for her notebooks and found the current Tamayo review. "Let's see. There's an exhibit of 'vast multi-dimensional multi-medium works reflecting the solitude and insanity of the polar winter.' It's by an artist from Finland whose 'works were expressed directly onto his personal structures.'"

"Ah."

Luz looked up. "I think that's a nice way of saying big murals with odd things jutting out of them, done on a barn door. And that he used lots of white."

Eduardo Cortez Castillo laughed, the wide smile lighting up his face. "Thank you for the translation. I think. What does what does 'multi-medium' mean?"

"Like this." Luz picked up her pencil case and rattled the pencils inside. "The pencil and the paper are *my* mediums of creativity. It just means what the artist uses to create. This artist just used many different things to create a single piece of artwork."

"I get it. So this ought to be pretty good?"

"Yes."

"Anything else?"

"Well, there is a new exhibit from Nadia Porov. She's Russian, very clever." Luz read the review to him. "'Nadia

Porov proves once again that she can enthrall and stimulate the viewer with her exceptional choice of materials, elevating the mundane and juxtaposing the ordinary with the necessary to achieve the sublime.'"

He gave her a questioning look, seemingly on the brink of laughter.

Luz fought a great wave of silliness. "Nadia Porov is really quite good. I saw one of her exhibits two years ago. Took up the entire wing." Luz gestured at the left side of the Tamayo. "It was *amazing*. She'd made this enormous ship, all out of . . . of . . ." Luz trailed off as she remembered.

"Yes?"

"It's not important."

"But now I need to know," he said, as if she was making a joke.

"Toilet paper," Luz replied, her face scarlet to be sure.

He threw his head back and roared unabashedly.

"Are you laughing at me?" Luz started to giggle.

"Yes," he said breathlessly. "How many rolls?"

"Seven thousand four hundred and two." It had been a memorable exhibit.

He dropped onto the bench and his shoulders shook with laughter. The silliness rolled over Luz and she found herself nearly hysterical. Several people in the plaza looked at them, helpless with mirth on the bench.

"Ah, *Madre de Dios*, I needed that." Eduardo Cortez Castillo took a deep breath and shook his head. "I haven't laughed that hard in a long time."

His eyes sparkled at her. The museum and the woods and the people in the plaza all faded away. The sun shone brightly and Luz felt happiness bubble up inside her.

They kept smiling at each other, something connecting, the electric current humming again, until Luz remembered who she was. She closed the notebook and picked up the pencil case just so her hands would have something to do.

"Right. Of course," he said and stood. "I guess I'd better go see some art before the crowds get too bad. My apologies again for intruding on your time."

"Not at all." Luz didn't meet his eyes. "It was very nice meeting you, Señor Cortez."

"*Egualmente*, señorita." He bowed again, that beautiful formal gesture, then turned and went toward the museum. Luz watched him go. He had a powerful, athletic stride; one foot precisely in front of the other. The back of the leather blazer swung gently from side to side as he walked away.

Luz leaned against the back of the bench and closed her eyes. She needed to head to the zoo or *el lago* and come back later. If she went into the Tamayo now she'd see him again and do something stupid.

As she bent over and put everything back into the Prada tote, she suddenly found herself looking at the crisp hems of a pair of khaki pants.

"I don't suppose you would consent to take some time off from your work to play tour guide?" Eduardo Cortez Castillo asked.

Luz craned her neck.

"I hate listening to those recordings, you know," he went on. "The kind you carry around that tell you what you're seeing."

"They don't have them at the Tamayo," Luz said faintly.

"Ah, well." The perfect eyebrows went up and down in mock consternation. "Right." The sunglasses tapped across his thumb. "So. The problem is worse than I thought."

"A predicament, señor," Luz said. Her bones left and she sagged against the bench.

"You would be doing the art world a great service."

"How's that?"

"Educating the ignorant."

The sun was still shining. He stood there and smiled at her. Luz drank in the close-cropped hair, expensive clothes, hazel eyes. She simply had to walk away.

"I would be honored to be your guide, Señor Cortez," a voice like hers said. Luz stood up and put the Prada tote on her shoulder, straightened the Chanel sweater, and flipped her ponytail loose from where it had gotten caught up in the Hermés scarf.

"My friends call me Eddo." He held out his hand and Luz shook it for the second time that morning. Maybe it was her imagination or just wishful thinking but the handshake lasted a little longer this time.

"Eddo, then," Luz's voice said.

"And do your friends call you Luz de Maria or just Luz?"

"Luz is fine."

He made a courtly little gesture for her to proceed and together they walked across the plaza and into the Tamayo.

◆

The first thing they saw was the "polar night" exhibit, composed of huge murals of rough pine, white and complicated. According to the museum description the artist had painted the murals after his wife died of exposure during a harsh winter.

"He must have loved her a lot," Luz sighed when she finished reading about the artist and his dead wife. And then cringed inside because she'd said *love* to a man she hardly knew.

"These are his scars from loving her so much," the man she hardly knew said. Luz blinked in surprise.

They wandered to an exhibit of short video presentations by a Danish filmmaker. Nine flat screens were arranged in a pattern against three black walls. They flashed on as Luz and Eddo stood in the dim room. Each showed a different view of the same train in fast motion, complete with blaring soundtracks. The effect was immediately shocking and disorienting. As they stumbled out of the room Eddo said "Tell me how that was art," and Luz honestly replied "I can't, I'm too dizzy," which made him laugh. He put out a hand to steady her and the clatter of the trains gave way to the humming in her head.

Next was a curving wall of seascapes by a Chilean painter, long horizontal canvases of rocks and angry seas. Luz pointed out the *impasto* technique, making Eddo step close to the canvas to see the individual daubs then back away so that the whole picture emerged.

They walked through several more rooms of sculpture, paintings, and an exhibit of gigantic silk banners decorated with

Japanese characters. According to the description, the banners contained important modern poetry railing against the electronic world.

Eddo turned to Luz. "I guess it's too much to expect that you read Japanese."

"I used to," Luz replied, her tongue running away with her. "But then my cell phone destroyed my artistic soul."

Eddo gave an unexpected guffaw. "Let's go, Kagemusha." He ushered her toward the Porov exhibit.

The exhibit hall was full of enormous puffy white sculptures. They were twice as big as life size. The centerpiece was a fire truck, complete with ladder and hoses and tires as tall as Luz. It was surrounded by faceless firefighters holding hoses. The odd white material, combined with an eerie lighting and discordant background music, gave the space an other-worldly quality.

"What's this medium called?" Eddo asked, running his hand over the truck wheel.

Luz stepped closer, realized what Porov had used, and her face flushed. "Napkins," she murmured.

"What?" Eddo said, bending his head down to hers. "Did you say napkins?"

He smelled *wonderful*. "Yes," Luz whispered.

"Dinner napkins? Paper?"

"Not that kind."

"Cotton?" Eddo was still touching the fire truck. Luz wished the guard would tell him to stop but of course no one did.

"Sanitary." Luz could barely get the word out. "Feminine hygiene products."

Eddo snatched his hand away as if he'd been burned.

Luz swallowed laughter. "'Exceptional choice of material,'" she quoted softly.

"Are we done here?" Eddo's mouth twitched.

"Yes, I think so."

Once outside they both burst out laughing.

"*Dios mio.*" Luz found a tissue to wipe her streaming eyes. "Nadia Porov is just . . . so . . ."

"A con artist," Eddo supplied.

"No, that's why the Tamayo is so wonderful. People with imagination, such *nerve*."

"Nothing as good as your drawings," he scoffed.

"No." Luz shook her head. The ponytail swung. "I just have these little sketches and some paintings at home. No nerve."

While they'd been in the Tamayo the plaza had filled with people. The crowd was mostly *mestizo;* noisy knots of people with baby carriages and children eating cotton candy from the vendors in front of the nearby Anthropology Museum.

"I'd like to pay you back for being such a great guide," Eddo said. "Let's go over to Jardin del Arte. You must know it. I want to show you that your pictures are better than anything else out there."

"Yes, I know it," Luz said, surprised at his suggestion. Jardin del Arte was a huge outdoor art market, where every Sunday hundreds of artists brought their paintings to sell. It was also the cheapest place to get paints, drawing supplies, frames, and blank canvases.

"My car's parked just on the other side of the trees." He gestured to indicate the dirt lot on the edge of Avenida Mahatma Gandhi.

Luz swallowed. Going into the museum was one thing, getting into a car and letting him take her someplace was another. A lot of women had died getting into cars with strangers in Mexico City. But this charade she was playing was even more dangerous. Obviously he assumed she was someone other than a *muchacha* on her day off.

He mistook her hesitation for something else. "Were you supposed to be meeting someone?"

"No," Luz said automatically and mentally kicked herself. He'd given her an opportunity to walk away and she'd missed it.

"Is your car here?"

"No, I walked," Luz said.

"You walked? From where?"

"Lomas Virreyes," Luz said, watching for his reaction, waiting for him to finally catch on.

"Good for you." He checked out her rubber-soled work loafers with seeming admiration. "So on to Jardin del Arte?"

"I don't think so." Luz took a step back, trying to put some distance between temptation and the smart thing to do. "But thank you for asking."

"Look," he said. "I don't want you to think I'm some sort of lunatic who goes trolling for pretty women at the museum. There are a lot of *locos* in this city but I'm not usually one of them." He pulled out a slim leather wallet and thrust it at her. "Here."

"I don't want your wallet," Luz exclaimed, more surprised than if he'd pulled out a gun or cocaine or a monster. No one flashed a wallet in Mexico City unless they wanted to lose it immediately and die at the same time.

"Take it," he said and tipped the corner toward her. "If I do anything in the car you don't like, toss it out the window. My license is in there. I guarantee I'll stop the car to go get it."

Luz laughed shakily and pressed a hand to her temple. Everyone knew that getting or renewing a driver's license was a bureaucratic horror, requiring multiple visits to *delegación* offices and a couple of bribes as well. Replacing a lost one would be an endless nightmare.

"You must be a terrible risk taker," she said.

"More of a creative problem solver."

Luz took the wallet and opened it. The license was encased in a plastic display pocket. "Eduardo Martín Bernardo Cortez Castillo," she read aloud. There was an address on Avenida Constituyentes and an impossibly handsome grainy ID picture.

"That's me," he said. "Although I'll have to ask you to forget the Bernardo. Named after my uncle."

"Was he *loco*, too?" Luz snapped the wallet shut and tried to hand it back. "I'm not taking your wallet."

"Yes, you are. I want you to know you'll be all right with me." He put his hands in his pockets.

She couldn't keep standing there holding the wallet in middle of the crowded plaza so Luz put it in the Prada tote, trying not to think how reckless she was being. Eddo crooked his elbow, another of his charming courtly gestures, and she slipped her arm through his. A little thrill rippled down her spine as they walked through the woods to Avenida Mahatma Gandhi.

♦

Eddo Cortez Castillo drove a late model Japanese SUV. It was smaller than the Vega's Suburban but nicer inside, all charcoal leather and smelling like coffee from an empty Starbucks cup. Luz tucked the Prada tote under her feet so that no one looking inside the car could see it, and put on her seat belt. Eddo nodded his approval. He put the car in gear and bounced over the curb onto the street.

"So do you usually sketch on Sunday mornings?"

"When I can," Luz replied but it occurred to her that she'd have to keep the conversation away from herself and what she did. "So. What brought you this morning?"

"That's a good question." His eyes flickered as he checked his mirrors and turned onto Reforma. He drove skillfully, even better than Hector. "Art meant a great deal to my father. Said it gave him perspective."

Luz noted the past tense. "Did he pass away recently?"

"Almost 15 years ago. Lost both my parents in a car accident."

"I'm so sorry," Luz said. "Were you very close?" The car swung around *El Angel*, turned by the Sheraton and headed east on Lerma. They passed the United States embassy and her stomach fluttered.

"We . . . we shared a lot."

"I know how you feel." Luz thought about the timing. "My father died about the same time. Hit by a bus."

"*Madre de Dios*. I'm sorry." The car stopped at a light. Eddo looked at her, warmth and sadness in his hazel eyes. The fact that they had both lost parents formed a small bond.

A dirty street urchin scrambled onto the hood and the spell was broken. The child grinned and squirted soapy water from a plastic bottle onto the windshield. Eddo nodded at the child and Luz had the impression that he'd checked first to see if there were accomplices--men often robbed motorists as a window washer distracted them--but she hadn't actually seen Eddo look around. Nonetheless she knew that he'd decided the situation was safe, as if the *castellano* man had the instincts of a street fighter.

The child industriously cleaned off the windshield. Eddo tipped him 10 pesos. Luz was astonished; the going rate for a windshield cleaning was no more than 2 pesos.

Eddo caught her expression as the light changed and the car moved forward. "He's got a quota to make. If he doesn't bring enough to his handler, he doesn't get any food."

"I've heard that," Luz said as if she'd never had nightmares of her brother cleaning windshields.

"So do you take after your father?" Eddo asked as the car moved through traffic. "Was he artistic, too?"

"In his own way, I think he was. I used to draw a lot of pictures for him--." Luz caught herself. The pictures had been designs for things he could make in the forge such as candlesticks and lamp bases. If Eddo asked what her father had done for a living it would lead to a question about what Luz did for a living. "The museum," she said hastily, trying for a neutral topic. "In the museum. What did you call me? 'Kagemusha?'"

"Sorry." Eddo grinned. "It was just those big Japanese banners. They reminded me of the scene with the armies all lined up, the big banners rippling in the wind, all this great samurai armor and horses."

Luz stared at him. She had absolutely no idea what he was talking about. The social gulf between them suddenly widened into a dark, sucking chasm. "It's a movie?" she groped.

"Yes. *Kagemusha.* A great movie by Kurosawa. Although a pretty obscure reference, I admit."

"A movie." A safe subject, even if it made her feel stupid. "What was it about, apart from banners?"

"Great plot." He took one hand off the wheel to gesture. "Medieval Japan. Kagemusha is this peasant who impersonates a dead warlord. The impersonation is necessary to prevent the warlord's enemies from defeating the clan."

Luz's heart stopped and her back went rigid as he said *peasant* and *impersonates.* Of course. He was mocking her, telling her that he knew who she really was. He'd seen through her coffee-dyed blouse and scuffed work shoes and flat coarse hair. She dropped her eye to the door handle. But the car was still moving and all she could do was say "Really?"

"Most beautifully shot movie I've ever seen," Eddo continued. "Cast of thousands in medieval Japanese armor and of course those rippling banners. The military scenes were--." He stopped. "I'm probably boring you."

"No, not at all." Luz's jaw was so tight she could hardly speak. "What happened in the end?"

"Kagemusha does pretty well for awhile but eventually he's revealed as an imposter," Eddo said. "Gets run off. The clan is wiped out. Didn't matter if it was the real warlord or the imposter, without him the army just fell apart. I guess the lesson is that appearance is everything."

He knew. If he'd come out and said he knew who she was she could have dealt with it, but *no*, he'd chosen this cruel, humiliating, upper class way to do it.

"At least I think that's what the movie was about." He gave a rueful chuckle. "Saw it years ago in Paris in Japanese with French subtitles. I kept thinking that if I just knew what *jusqu'à* meant I'd know what was going on."

"It means 'until,'" Luz managed.

"*Now* she tells me," he joked and deftly dropped the car into a parking space on the edge of the Jardin del Arte.

Luz undid her seat belt, her hands shaking and her heart pounding. Everything was blurry.

"Are you all right?" Eddo took the key out of the ignition and looked at her. "Do you have allergies?"

Before she could answer, he reached over the armrest, pulled two bottles of water from a shrink-wrapped carton on the backseat floor, and held out one to her. "This city is the worst place in the world for people with allergies."

His face was full of concern, no deceit or hidden message there at all.

"Yes," Luz said. "Do you mind waiting?"

"Take your time."

Luz found a tissue, blew her nose, and drank some water. He opened her door, like she was a queen, and they waded into the sea of paintings that was the Jardin del Arte.

♦

They strolled slowly, occasionally being bumped into each other by the crowd. Jardin del Arte was big, about three city blocks long and one deep. They pointed out their likes and dislikes and Eddo listened as Luz explained the different techniques--"you mean 'medium,' right?"--acrylic, watercolor, pastels, oils.

There were hundreds of canvases for sale. There were brightly colored rural Mexican scenes with the inevitable donkey, the inevitable old houses, and the inevitable dark-haired girls holding terra cotta jugs. There were rows of seascapes, mostly monochromatic monstrosities like the one in the Vega's living room, and lots of odd modernistic things that neither of them liked. But here and there they found a few gems; a tiny painting of an apple that looked amazingly real, a series of white flowers against dark backgrounds, a filmy watercolor of the Xochimilco canals.

"Watercolors are hard to use here, though," Luz said regretfully. "You can't hang a watercolor on a stucco wall. It's not substantial enough. You have to hang oil or acrylic on stucco."

"I have no idea what you're talking about," Eddo said.

Luz tried to explain about texture and decorating with art but he laughed and said, "You should stop while you're ahead. I know what 'medium' means," and Luz said, "Well now, Kagemusha."

Finally there was nothing new to see. They drifted back to the car, talking about the few pieces they'd liked and the many pieces they hadn't.

"You know," Eddo said, putting the keys into the ignition. "I've never learned so much or had a better teacher."

"Thank you," Luz said. She tucked the Prada tote under the seat like she'd done before.

"May I at least buy you some dinner? In gratitude for no longer being so ignorant?"

"I've imposed too much on your time already," Luz said. She'd been planning to ask him to drop her off at the museum.

She couldn't keep up the charade forever.

"But I'm the one asking." He started the car. "There's an excellent Argentine place at the Centro Commercial de Santa Fe."

The suggestion was unexpected and unnerving. Santa Fe was a huge mall at least 40 minutes from where they were, west on Reforma back past the museums, until the big street turned into the eight lane highway that ran through the new western suburbs. A bastion of the upper class, the Santa Fe mall was ostentatiously guarded by an army of private security in bulletproof vests. It had all the very best stores; branches of Palacio de Hierro and Liverpool, and specialty European stores like Massimo Dutti and Prada. Cinemas, restaurants, a betting club, and an enormous children's play village rounded out the mall's attractions. Luz had been there before, in her uniform, carrying Señora Vega's purchases.

"That sounds fine," she breathed.

♦

El Rincon de Santa Fe was the most elegant restaurant Luz had ever been in. Touches of wrought iron separated the big place into sections. The walls were covered in big sepia murals of *gauchos* riding through the *pampas*, punctuated with antique photographs and leather saddles and bridles. Dark bottles of red wine snaked along a high shelf above the bar. Guitar music invited patrons to linger.

The waiter led them to a skirted table near the center of the room. Eddo took the seat facing the door to the mall. Luz could see the big bar over his shoulder.

She looked around surreptitiously at the other diners. Was anyone staring at her? Did she look out of place? She caught Eddo's eye and started guiltily.

"I think the bathrooms are through the archway by the bar," he whispered conspiratorially.

"Thank you," Luz whispered back.

She found the ladies room, used the facilities, and then put on some of la señora's lipstick, appalled to find that her hand was shaking worse than when she had the visa interview. There were a few other women in there, upper class women dressed in ponytails and tight designer pants and pretty tops. They took no notice of Luz.

There was a menu lying on her place at the table when she came back. Eddo stood up as she approached and sat when she did. He'd taken off his jacket. The white short-sleeved shirt hugged his chest, revealing a heavily muscled but lean physique. Luz had an impure thought about what he would look like without the shirt.

"What would you like to drink?" he asked.

"What are you having?" She'd just do whatever he did.

"I think I'll have a beer."

Luz hesitated. Señora Vega never drank beer.

"How about a sangria?"

"Yes, thank you."

The waiter came by and took their drink orders. They opened their menus and Luz nearly passed out. The prices were *staggering*.

"What do you think, the mixed grill?" Eddo asked.

Luz thought she might have a stroke. The mixed grill for two was 1200 pesos.

"That's fine," she said.

"And a salad?" he asked.

But there was no salad fork, just a dinner fork and hadn't Señora Vega drummed into her head the rules about the proper utensil for the proper food? If she ate her salad with the dinner fork would it be a dead giveaway? Would everyone notice? The fork and the prices and the day-long charade were all too much. "There's no salad fork," Luz said, mortified as soon as the words came out of her mouth.

"Oh," Eddo said.

The waiter brought drinks, appetizer plates, a cold salad of *bayos blancos,* and small condiment dishes of *chimichurra* and *salsa roja.* Eddo murmured to him and the waiter immediately fetched two extra forks. He took their order for salad and the mixed grill, collected the menus, and disappeared.

The sangria was tall and cool, the limeade and chilled red

wine separated like oil and water in the glass. Luz swirled the two colors together with the straw and sipped. The sweet alcohol hit her empty stomach, warmth radiated out, and she relaxed a fraction.

Eddo drank his beer directly from the bottle, like every other man she'd ever been with, and that helped, too.

"So," he said. "*Tomato Tamayo*. Your English must be pretty good."

"I'm practicing to go to New York. To see the Guggenheim and the Metropolitan Museum of Art." It was the most personal thing she'd said to him so far and immediately felt like a mistake. She covered by serving him a plate of bean salad with artistic dollops of the garnishes.

"Excellent. Thank you."

"You're welcome." Luz put some of the beans and garnishes on a plate for herself.

"So you need to practice your English." Eddo put the cloth napkin on his lap and Luz followed suit. "Maybe I can help." He switched to English. "How are you this evening, Miss Alba?"

"I am well, thank you," Luz replied carefully in the same language. She racked her brain to find something to impress him. "How're they hanging, sir?"

He'd been in the middle of drinking from the beer bottle, holding it lightly, and his eyes widened over the neck as he choked. He nearly dropped the bottle and grabbed his napkin, laughing and sputtering beer. Luz froze, fork halfway to her mouth, as she tried to think what she'd done wrong. *How are they hanging, how're they hanging*, but maybe it was *how are them hanging*.

"Luz, do you actually know what that means?" He was back to Spanish, hazel eyes twinkling with fun.

"A greeting. Something you say to friends." Luz laid her fork in her plate, unable to eat a bite, knowing the blunder was somehow huge.

"Male friends only," Eddo said softly, leaning over the table, his face still twitching with suppressed laughter. "It refers to a man's *cojones*. Literally. How are *they* hanging."

"*Oh.*" Luz clapped her hands to her face, utterly

embarrassed. She'd said something *vulgar* to him. *Again.* First *toilet paper*, and then *napkins*, and now this, the worst of all.

"Where on earth did you hear that?" Eddo leaned back and forked some beans.

"Kids. From the school," Luz fudged, blinking back tears. "I'm sorry. *So* sorry. I feel like such a fool."

"Well, don't. Just another part of a very memorable day."

The electric smile warmed her as he chuckled again and Luz started to laugh, too. The conversation moved on, to what they'd seen at Jardin del Arte and what they knew about other art bazaars in the city. Luz ate her beans and the delicious *chimichurra* relish. The sangria went down quickly, and Eddo ordered them both another round. She was well into the second drink when the main course came.

The waiter laid out dinner plates and a salad big enough for four. An enormous charcoal brazier was centered on the table. Several different cuts of veal and beef sizzled on it, smelling like heaven.

Eddo served this time, putting more meat and salad on her plate than Luz could possibly eat. They talked and ate and every time the conversation veered toward the personal Luz steered it away. She didn't ask what he did for a living, despite her growing curiosity, afraid that he'd do the same, so the conversation stayed light.

But somewhere between her second and third sangria, Luz realized he truly had no idea who she was because he asked her what type of books she liked to read.

"*Masters of the Light Within*," she replied, smearing the dark green *chimichurra* over a bite of mouth-watering beef, exactly as he was doing.

"*Masters of the Light Within*," he repeated. "This is revenge for *Kagemusha*, right? Aliens?"

"Close. Painters."

"Ah. Of course. Lots of snappy dialogue? Gripping plot?" His table manners were impeccable. She could have watched him eat all night.

"More like a textbook," Luz said. It was her favorite from Señor Vega's study. "Profiles of famous painters."

"The only famous painter I know is Frida Kahlo."

"Yes, she's in it. But she's hardly my favorite."

"She's not?" Eddo put down his knife and fork. "I thought she was a Mexican icon."

"Her paintings do define a certain Mexican style." Luz had never had a conversation with someone who used words like *icon*. She felt like a part of her that had been asleep was waking up and spreading its wings. "But so many of her paintings are terribly depressing. Frida Kahlo was too absorbed with death for me."

"No, that's not you at all."

"No, no, it's not." It was unnerving the way he had said that, as if somehow he knew her very well.

"So if Frida Kahlo isn't your favorite, who is?" Eddo pronged some beef.

"El Greco," Luz replied.

"El Greco? I haven't a clue. Tell me."

So she told him about El Greco, the man from the island of Crete who captivated Spain in the late 1500's with his powerful images of Christ and the saints. El Greco's most famous pictures were crowded with people, and Luz always felt he'd known what it was to live in Mexico. She got carried away as she told Eddo how his wife's madness was the great tragedy of the painter's life. People said El Greco was mad, too, or maybe he just had bad eyesight, because all his paintings had a strange vertical elongation to them, but Luz felt it was because the paintings were stretching toward heaven. Her artist's hands demonstrated the vertical force of El Greco's works and the feeling she always had of reaching toward God when she saw pictures of *The Baptism of Christ* or *Burial of the Count of Orgaz*.

"If I'd had a teacher like you," Eddo said. "I would have paid attention in school."

Their eyes met and Luz felt the heat rise in her cheeks. "So what are you reading?" She picked up her fork and started to eat again.

"*El Cantar de Mio Cid*."

"Really?" Luz was both surprised and impressed. *El Cantar de Mio Cid* was like *Don Quixote;* everyone knew the story but no one actually *read* it. But unlike *Don Quixote*, which was a book, *El Cantar de Mio Cid* was a difficult three-part poem written in medieval Spanish. "Why?"

Eddo told her how he'd found a copy of the poem after reading a contemporary biography of the Spanish general, whose real name was Rodrigo Diaz de Vivar and who'd lived nearly 1000 years ago. He was called El Cid Campeador, a title that reflected the esteem in which he was held by both the Moors and the Spanish. *El cid* was derived from the Moorish *al-sidi*, meaning sir or lord, while *campeador* meant champion in Spanish.

Eddo's voice pulled her into the story. El Cid had already made a name for himself fighting the Moors for King Ferdinand I of Castile when Ferdinand died and the lands he'd ruled were divided among his five children. They immediately started fighting each other. Sancho, the son who'd inherited Castile, named El Cid commander of his armies. When Sancho was assassinated his brother Alfonso was the chief suspect. El Cid made Alfonso publicly proclaim his innocence. Angered, Alfonso forced El Cid into exile without his daughters and beloved wife Jimena. On his warhorse Babieca and brandishing his sword Tizona, El Cid became a mercenary. Eventually he was recognized by Alfonso, reunited with his family, and conquered Valencia where he and Jimena ruled in Alfonso's name until El Cid died in 1099.

"He sounds like an incredible leader," Luz said over her sangria glass, feeling like she'd just seen a great movie. "Someone who inspired others. Otherwise how could he have survived and won all those battles?"

"He was ahead of his time, really," Eddo said, picking up his fork again. "He used to study military history and ask his men for suggestions. They fought for him because he listened to them."

His beautiful jaw flexed as he swallowed and Luz realized she wasn't the only one in the restaurant engrossed in Eddo Cortez Castillo's discourse on Spanish history.

Two women were sitting at a nearby table, piles of Liverpool bags at their feet. They were both staring at Eddo as if he was the grand prize at La Feria, the big amusement park, and they were waiting for their turn at the games. But he was completely oblivious to their blatant interest. Luz wondered if he ever looked in a mirror.

"El Greco and El Cid weren't contemporaries," Eddo said. "But I think they lived in a world of passion and righteousness that has passed our generation by. Honor and loyalty meant something then."

"A world of passion and righteousness," Luz repeated slowly. It was amazing to think she was sitting here with a man like this, talking about art and history and abstract concepts of life and living. "Maybe hard sometimes, but a place where life was lived to the fullest."

"Yes," Eddo said. "They did what was right, not what was easy. Life probably felt very precious. Now we take so much for granted."

The conversation moved on again, to movies about El Cid, and Mexican movies and *norteamericano* movies, and life in Mexico City. As the charcoal in the brazier crumbled into white ash, they started talking about the upcoming presidential elections and the candidates that were jockeying into position for their respective party nominations.

"I'd like to hear the perspective of a woman on something," Eddo said. He sliced the end off the last piece of beef, a tender *lomo*, and dropped it on her plate. "Lorena Lopez de Betancourt says every woman in the country is her sister and will vote for her. It was in Friday's *Reforma*."

"'My *sister?*'" Luz exclaimed. "She actually said that?"

"Sure." Eddo drank some beer. "Lorena's going for something simple that people who can't read will hear and repeat: 'Lorena's your sister.'"

"Lorena's going for the uneducated vote?"

"Well, there's plenty of it, unfortunately," Eddo said wryly. "We only require six years of primary school. Probably 25 percent of adults are functionally illiterate."

"Illiterate doesn't have to mean gullible," Luz said.

"Maybe the next election will prove you right," Eddo said. "We've got a real multi-party system now. The PAN attracts intellectuals and strong Catholics. PRD is way out on the left. The PRI means union affiliations and the revolution."

"How about a new revolution," Luz hazarded. "An education revolution."

"You're an idealist?"

"That would be better for Lorena than running a campaign built around that sister thing. PAN could be the party that brings real education to Mexico."

"You vote PAN?" Eddo asked. "Did you vote for Betancourt?"

"Yes, but the PAN could be more than it is," Luz said.

Eddo seemed amused. "It needs an identity?"

"Yes. Like how the PRI is the party of the revolution."

"Which did so much for all the folks who still can't read."

"There you go." Luz waved a finger at him. "Revolution should mean looking forward, not being dragged down by the past. PAN could mobilize an education revolution with a symbol that energizes people. Even if they can't read now they'll join because they know their lives will change when they can. That's better than catchy words because Lorena wants to keep living in Los Pinos."

The waiter brought Eddo a fourth beer and Luz a fourth sangria. She stirred and smiled as the colors swirled together. Eddo's mind was quick and agile and she was keeping up.

"The only problem with your ideas, Kagemusha, is that they're too dangerous," Eddo said. "This country's entire social system is predicated on the majority of the people being tolerant. Educated people find things out and aren't quite so tolerant after that."

"That's a terrible thing to say," Luz said, the straw frozen in her hand, momentarily taken aback.

Eddo picked up his beer bottle. "So we let illegal immigration be the pressure valve."

"But that's where the jobs are," Luz said.

Eddo took a long pull from his beer bottle. "The *ilegales,* and the *coyotes* who get them out, are a kind of system. They siphon off the smart ones who might get restless and cause trouble because they're sick of being cheated all the time. The remittances they send back from *El Norte* are a quarter of this country's income. Drug money is another quarter. Think of it. Half of our national income comes from negative activity that drains our human resources but which we don't control or regulate."

Luz blinked at him, struck by the intellect behind his words. "So how do we change that? Make the country . . . healthy."

"Reform is hard." He seemed about to say something else, but stopped.

"But if nothing changes," Luz said, thinking about the dwindling opportunities for Juan Pablo. There would be even less for Martina and Sophia. "What will happen?"

Eddo shrugged. "The leftovers will remember Lorena's catchphrases. That's all she wants them to do."

He was saying such hard things. Luz leaned forward. "Do you mean to tell me Lorena is happy to cry for the pain of the people if it means they'll stay uneducated enough to vote for her?"

"'Cry for the pain of the people?'" Eddo leaned forward, too. "What are you talking about?"

"That interview in *HOLA!*," Luz said. "There was this one question. 'What makes Lorena laugh and what makes Lorena cry?' She was in all these pictures, dripping with diamonds, and she answered the question with 'Every day I cry for the pain of the people.'" Luz stabbed a bite of beef as Eddo's mouth started to twitch. "Please, I could cry myself. All she has to do is sell one bracelet and she could feed the people for a year."

"So you probably won't vote for her," Eddo chuckled.

"I'm voting for El Cid." Luz grinned. "What would he do?"

"Hmmm. Maybe gather everyone round for a brainstorming session."

"Study his history to get some perspective," Luz offered.

"Sharpen Tizona."

"Give Babieca a carrot and cinch the saddle a little tighter."

They smiled at each other, both savoring the humor and the imagery and the sense that they were the only two people in the world who knew what they were talking about. The waiter came and replaced the brazier with a candle in a clear glass holder.

"So," Eddo said. His smile faded into seriousness. "I guess I know what makes Luz de Maria cry. Now I'd like to know what makes Luz de Maria laugh."

"Well." Luz's heart raced, fueled by too much sangria and the look on his face. "Nadia Porov exhibits, of course. Old episodes of *El Chavo del 8*. Cantinflas movies. My nieces."

"Nieces? How many?"

"Two. My sister's girls."

"So you have a sister. Older or younger?"

"Younger. I'm the oldest."

"Any brothers?"

"One. Juan Pablo's much younger." *Enough about me.* "What about you?"

The waiter finished clearing the table, leaving their half-finished drinks.

"I was the baby brother," Eddo said. "One sister, much older."

"Let me guess. A naughty little brother." Luz had an image of him at five or six, getting away with murder because his parents were wrapped around his finger.

"Spoiled rotten," Eddo said. "I made up stuff about her to scare away her boyfriends. Trooped my friends through her parties, even shot her in the head with an arrow. My archery phase. She had to go to the hospital."

"How old were you?"

"I was seven and she was 16."

"Has she forgiven you yet?"

"I think so." He laughed. "She lives in Atlanta now. Married a *gringo*. I have a niece, too."

"That's nice," Luz said and put down her sangria glass.

The line of Eddo's shoulders shifted. His face tensed and Luz realized that their hands were inadvertently touching. The humming filled her ears again. This time Luz knew he heard it, too.

Eddo reached out with a forefinger and slid it between her first and second fingers. Another finger followed until he had laced their hands together.

"What's your favorite flower? A gentleman should always

know what his lady likes best."

"Violets," Luz said on a breath.

"I'll have to look for those."

"So what are your favorite things?"

"Hmm." He gently rocked their clasped hands. "Favorite day: Sunday. Favorite museum: Tamayo. Favorite restaurant: El Rincon. Favorite--."

The waiter appeared. Luz pulled her hands back into her lap.

"Do you want coffee? Or dessert?" Eddo asked.

"No, thank you." Coffee was probably 1000 pesos a cup here.

"Maybe later?" Eddo asked and Luz said yes, maybe later, and gave back his wallet.

The waiter laid the little tray with the bill on the table. It was outrageous, over *3000* pesos. Eddo paid in cash. Luz couldn't believe she'd been walking around with that much money.

"Thank you for a wonderful dinner," Luz said.

"It was my pleasure."

He helped her on with her sweater and got his jacket. They walked out of the elegant restaurant, past the two thoroughly ignored women.

◆

Chapter 17

Some idiot had left Liverpool shopping bags in the aisle of the restaurant and Eddo put out a protective hand to make sure Luz didn't trip. He was acutely aware of her next to him as they strolled into the mall. The top of her head came up to his mouth and he found himself staring at her hair and her cheekbone and the sweet curve of her neck.

Eddo guided her toward the sound of live music, looking for any excuse to prolong the evening. A jazz band was playing on a stage on the ground floor. An enormous coffered skylight high above reflected the energy of the music and the crowds. The second and third floors of the mall were fronted by mezzanines that circled like great glass and chrome ribbons. People stood along the railings and watched the band. Eddo found a place for them along the second floor railing.

"Pretty good, aren't they?" Eddo asked after they'd listened for a while.

"Yes." Luz beamed at him then turned back to the scene below.

Everything about her was damn attractive, from her sense of humor to her bright clothes to the athletic way her body looked and moved. And she had a talent and a creativity that amazed him. But the thing he liked best was her sense of serenity. There was nothing shrill or noisy or needy about Luz; her company was more relaxing than that of any woman he'd ever met. He'd said nothing about his government job or being part of the Marca Cortez business empire. And she hadn't asked about things like that, as if she was only interested in him, not power or position or money.

Eddo stole another look at her, happier than he'd been in a very long time. He certainly hadn't laughed this much in years.

Several times during the day she'd said something funny or a little risqué. Her eyes had widened in this priceless *I shouldn't have said that* expression and he'd found himself laughing again.

As Luz watched the band, her mouth curved into a smile and her body swayed a little to the music. If Eddo was any judge of people, she was completely unaware of how sexy she was.

"You should draw this," he said.

"All right." Her mouth was a little too big for her face and her smile was dazzling.

He found a bench and Luz sat and pulled out her sketchpad. As Eddo watched, she drew swiftly; first the dramatic setting with the skylight and the mezzanines, then the band.

People clustered around to watch her and Eddo stepped behind the bench so he could survey the crowd better. Luz stopped drawing, instinctively pulling in her elbows, and Eddo knew what she was thinking. Crowds in Mexico were often unruly and rarely safe. He reached out and stroked the back of her neck, letting her know he was watching out and that she was fine.

Luz looked up and caught his eye, then finished the drawing. The crowd applauded and she blushed and closed the sketchpad.

The crowd dispersed. Eddo sat down next to her and opened the sketchpad again. He could almost hear the music coming from the drawing. "This is terrific. But there are no faces?"

"I know." Luz sighed. "I can draw everything except faces. They always come out blank. Like there's no brain inside."

"Sign it," he reminded her.

Luz wrote her name then tore the drawing out of the sketchpad, along with the *Tomato Tamayo* drawing and handed both to him. "Here," she said. "It's not much but thank you for everything today."

The gesture took Eddo by surprise. He couldn't remember the last time he'd gotten such a personal gift. "Thank you," he managed and took her hand.

They walked outside and crossed the parking lot, the signs for Liverpool and Palacio de Hierro huge against the building. The night sky was its usual milky white.

"You almost never see stars here," Luz said, breaking their silence. "I'll bet there's nowhere else in the world like it."

"Well, Los Angeles can get like this from time to time," Eddo said.

They got in the car. Eddo laid the two drawings on the back seat and cleared his throat.

"I was wondering," he said, as nervous as if it was his first time. "If you'd like that coffee now. At my place."

She didn't immediately reply and Eddo found himself holding his breath.

"Coffee," Luz said finally. "Yes, I would."

♦

Eddo looked around the living room in dismay as they walked into his apartment. "Sorry about this," he said and kicked the soccer cleats to one side. "I have help on Tuesdays and Fridays and the rest of the time I'm hopeless."

Luz looked around the living room and he followed her gaze as it took in the rustic pine coffee table, the flat-screen television, and green suede sofa and chairs. The blank walls.

"Have you lived here long?" she asked.

"Couple of years. A little bare?"

"A little."

"You see why I needed an art education," he said.

Luz smiled but she was nervous, he could tell. She put her bag by the front door and twisted her fingers together.

"Please make yourself comfortable," Eddo said and mentally kicked himself. *Fuck,* he sounded like he was inviting her into his office for a business meeting. "I'll get that coffee going."

In the kitchen, Eddo filled the coffeemaker carafe with water from the *garrafon* dispenser, dumped ground coffee into the filter and turned on the machine. Luz came over to the granite-topped counter. As he placed two colorful *talavera* cups on a lacquer tray she rearranged the apples in the basket on the counter into a red pyramid.

"Sugar?" Eddo asked. "Milk?"

"No sugar, thank you. Just milk."

"Milk. Great. I've got milk." In another minute he'd be babbling like a teenager. Eddo gave himself a mental shake, poured milk into each mug and tossed two spoons on the tray. He nodded toward the living room. "Shall we sit in there?"

Luz went over to the sofa and took off the pink sweater. The definition in her upper body showed through the thin material of her tan blouse. Eddo swallowed back a surge of pure lust, poured coffee into the mugs and carried the tray into the living room.

"Here we go." Eddo set the tray on the coffee table, sat on the edge of one of the armchairs and handed her a mug.

"Thank you," Luz said.

Eddo picked up the other mug. The *talavera* was full of a viscous liquid that smelled burnt. He half expected the bowl of the spoon to dissolve when he stirred it. The coffee tasted as bad as it looked. "*Madre de Dios*, this is terrible," he said.

"No, it's fine," Luz said.

"How you lie, Kagemusha." Eddo brought both mugs into the kitchen and dumped their contents into the sink. She had him so wound up he couldn't even make decent coffee. "I'll make a new pot."

Luz followed him into the kitchen. "Let me do it," she said. She rinsed the coffee carafe under the faucet, dried it thoroughly with a paper towel, and then started to fill it with water.

Eddo looked at the back of her neck, at the softness of her skin, and couldn't wait any longer. He stepped behind her and kissed her right where he'd touched her in the mall. "Luz."

She stopped the water, slowly put down the glass carafe and turned to face him. "Yes," she said softly, as if he'd asked her a question.

He smiled and kissed her, easy and unrushed. Her mouth was warm. He felt her hands travel up his arms, her touch feather light.

They kissed for a long time in the little kitchen, the heat growing. They pressed together, both of them touching, exploring, gently at first and then with urgency. Eddo pulled her hair loose and untied her scarf.

It went on until Luz made a sound and Eddo realized he'd

trapped her between his body and the edge of the countertop. He was hard against her jeans.

Eddo stepped back. "You all right?" he asked.

She didn't reply, just grabbed the sides of his shirt. Eddo sucked in his breath and the shirt came untucked. Luz pulled it over his head.

Her hands splayed across his bare chest, her touch flooding his senses. Eddo fumbled at the buttons on her blouse, his fingers thick and clumsy.

There was a tug at his waist and a pressure against his groin that was sweet agony. "Your belt," Luz whispered.

"I'll get it," he said, still focused on those little gold buttons and he couldn't get them unfastened and there was no time so he simply pulled apart the two panels of silk.

The *plings* of metal bouncing on granite brought Eddo to his senses. He was on an unfamiliar emotional precipice with this woman and acting like a caveman. He swallowed hard, reminding himself to keep his head together.

Luz looked at the blouse on the floor. To Eddo's surprise she shyly raised her arms. Almost of their own volition his hands reached around and unfastened her bra.

◆

Chapter 18

When Eddo stripped back the white matelassé coverlet to reveal white linen sheets Luz opened her legs for him to do what every other man she'd ever been with did right away. But Eddo came down beside her and said "No rush, no rush," even though she could see that his body was more than ready for her.

They kissed again and again, their hands slipping over each other, the tension growing, until Luz thought he must want to do it *now* and she tried to position herself for him. Again he didn't let her but instead arched her over him so that their bodies crossed.

"I want to know what you like," Eddo murmured. He gently slid his fingers into her and Luz gasped.

It went on and on, Luz stretched across him, his to play on, and he tightened her like a guitar string. She couldn't make a sound, couldn't do anything except feel the tension build and her blood pound. He touched her and kissed her and stroked her until the dam broke and the force of the climax curled her up. Only then did he stop stroking and instead pressed his palm between her legs, pushing so that she could feel her muscles pulse against his hand. Every time he moved his hand another pulse would shake her and she wouldn't be able to catch her breath. When the last one died out Luz forced her eyes open and saw him watching her, his eyes dark with intensity.

"Okay?" he asked.

"Yes." Luz finally could speak again. "It just . . . wasn't what I was expecting." She'd climaxed before during intercourse, but it was never something her partner had deliberately made happen.

"I wanted you to be ready."

Luz looked at him. He was gorgeous, lithe, *erect*. "I'm

ready."

Eddo found a condom in the bedside table drawer and slid into her easily, heat radiating out from his body and warming hers. He stayed far above her, taking his weight on outstretched arms and Luz had a near-perfect view of his near-perfect body. She caught his rhythm easily, watching how his abdominal muscles flexed in a pattern as all his taut energy thrummed in and out of her. He looked at her, but didn't make a noise, didn't smile, didn't stop the rhythm until he seemed to thicken inside her. His eyes closed involuntarily and he stopped moving. All the muscles in his neck and chest tensed, the veins and cords bulging in sharp relief. Then the tenseness faded.

Luz waited for there to be more, but there wasn't.

Eddo opened his eyes and settled onto his elbows and kissed her. Luz put her arms around his neck and relaxed her legs, feeling uncertain without knowing why. He started to slide away.

"Don't go," Luz said, not wanting it to be over, wondering if she'd done something wrong.

"It'll make a mess," he said regretfully and slid all the way out, making sure the condom stayed where it was supposed to be. He went into the adjoining bathroom and there was the sound of running water.

Luz sat up. The heat was gone. She felt self-conscious all of a sudden, naked and in this man's bed.

Eddo reappeared in the bathroom door, minus the condom. "Let me show you why I bought this place."

An immense oval tub set into a marble platform was filling rapidly. Eddo pressed a button and the water churned into white bubbles.

He helped her in and Luz practically had to swim over to one end. The water frothed around them. Eddo tickled her hip with his toes and she saw that his feet were battered. Several toes had been broken, the heels were calloused, and some nails were missing.

"*Fútbol* feet," Luz said.

"Since I was old enough to walk." Eddo smiled. "When I was little I wanted to grow up and play for Cruz Azul. Now I want to grow up and play for Toluca."

"I'll cheer the loudest of anybody for you," Luz said.

"So what are you doing way over there?" He held out his arms and Luz pushed herself through the bubbles until she was on his end of the tub. He pulled her back against his chest and wrapped his arms around her. The uncertainty faded.

"It's 1:00 am," Luz said. There was a small clock on the rim of the tub.

"It's too late to take you home." He kissed her neck and slid his hands over her wet breasts.

"I was just wondering how long since we met." Luz closed her eyes.

"We met, what? About 10:00 am? Fifteen hours ago."

Fifteen hours. A lifetime ago. Luz shifted to kiss him and as she moved she realized he was hard again. She reached under the bubbles and grasped him gently, feeling how he was made and where it all connected.

"Lift up," she said softly. She ran her hands along his sides, making him kneel. The bubbles played around his thighs. This time she was going to do to him what he'd done to her.

"The water," he said as if he could read her mind.

"No matter," Luz said and slid to her knees, too, like a prayer. She bent and closed her mouth over him, the bubbles playing around her chin. She'd never done such a thing before but somehow she knew what to do.

"Luz," she heard him say. He turned off the bubbler and the room got very quiet. Luz kept her mouth on him and stroked him at the same time, her right hand squeezing up and down, her left hand touching everything else.

She went on and on, immersed in the sensations of how he tasted and reacted to her touch. He started to tremble. She thought she heard him say "stop" but she wasn't sure and looked up. He was braced, arms outstretched and holding onto the rim of the tub on either side, head down, staring at her, his face contorted with tension, his breathing hoarse. She slid her left hand between his legs and up the other side while stroking with her right, the skin under her hand hot and silky and taut. As she bent to him again he made a sound, something between a groan and a sob, and white syrup fountained out of him. As her hand kept up the rhythm his body jerked helplessly and he cried out her name.

She kept stroking until he reached down and grabbed her hand and made her stop. "*Madre de Dios*," he rasped.

They settled back into the water, Eddo pulling Luz against his chest again. She couldn't see his face and didn't know if he was pleased or angry. Neither turned the bubbler back on. The room was moist and silent.

"Why did you do that?" he asked after a long time.

Luz bit her lip. She knew it was not something good Catholic girls did. "You don't lose control very often, do you?" she asked in return.

"What do you mean?"

"Even before . . . you wanted me to feel wonderful," Luz said. "And I did. But then you held back. I got the feeling you don't ever really let go." She paused but he said nothing. His arms around her rose and fell with her breathing. She went on. "I wanted you to know that you could with me. That it would be all right . . . to just let go. So you could have what you'd given me."

"*Madre de Dios*," Eddo said.

He turned her around and they moved gently against each other, needing reassurance, knowing each other in a way they hadn't an hour ago. Luz stroked his shoulders, loving the way his body now seemed completely relaxed. Eddo moved his hands into her hair, brushing it away from her face. But then he pulled back and grinned like a fool.

"*Madre de Dios*, Luz, it's all over your hair."

Luz reached up and felt her hair, sticky and already getting crispy in a couple of places. She started to redden and caught his eye. He looked absurdly proud. She laughed and so did he.

"I'll have to wash it out," Luz said. There was only soap on the tub rim. "Do you have any shampoo?"

"Let me check." He leaned halfway out of the tub. As Luz admired the sight of wet loins, he opened the cabinet under the sink and took out a dusty box of Klorane herbal shampoo. It was the kind Señora Vega bought for 140 pesos at the pharmacy.

"You use this?" Luz asked.

"It was a gift," Eddo said, sinking back into the tub. He took a bottle out of the box.

"Oh," said Luz. Of course. It was a woman's product, a gift from a girlfriend. He had a girlfriend. She suddenly couldn't look at him. "Never mind. She didn't mean for you to give it away."

"It's not what you think," Eddo said, taking Luz's chin in his hand and making her look up. "I was with some journalist but it ended last spring. I've got nothing to hide on that score."

"Okay." His eyes were too honest to doubt.

"I'll tell you something, Luz." Eddo smiled. "After a year she didn't know me half as well as you know me after *one day*."

He lathered her hair as Luz sat blissfully in the middle of the giant tub with her arms around her knees. The touch of his wet hands on her head was achingly intimate. He kissed her as he rinsed her hair and told her she looked like *la sirena*--a mermaid.

"There," he said. "Squeaky clean." He helped her out of the tub and enveloped her in a big bath sheet.

"What about you?" Luz pulled the towel around him as well, wrapping him in her body heat. His response was immediate.

It was so much more this time, the sharpest, sweetest thing Luz had ever known. Eddo stretched over her, skin-to-skin, no distance between them at all and Luz forgot where she ended and he began. There was rapture as he pulsed deep inside her. But then he stopped moving and said, "I just need to look at you." With their heads close together his eyes searched her face and Luz slid her hand over the line of his jaw. She arched against him and he started thrusting again.

When he said hoarsely, "It's coming, Luz. Like a freight train," she lifted her legs and locked her ankles behind his shoulder blades. He rocked even deeper inside her, the angle had changed, and as they stroked together, the rhythm got quicker and his shoulders grew rigid under her hands. Luz stopped breathing as the tightness broke and the climax roared through her body, making the muscles deep inside her clench around him. She was shaking as his rhythm grew jerky and uncontrolled.

As his body juddered between her legs he cried out. Luz held onto him as hard as she could, never wanting the moment to stop, letting him let go as long as he could.

♦

They made jokes afterwards, lying on the bed and touching each other possessively, until Luz's stomach growled and Eddo insisted on finding her something to eat. He rolled off the bed and tacked unsteadily down the hall. Luz found her pink panties and put them on. It seemed like the right thing to do. She didn't really know the protocol--she'd never spent the night in a man's house before.

Eddo came back with a plate of cut up apples. "This is how Adam and Eve got started."

"That's right." Luz burrowed into his pillows and crunched a wedge. "But they had to leave Eden. I liked your story about Rodrigo and Jimena better. They ended up in Valencia."

"Of course, I doubt Jimena ever looked this good." Eddo ran a finger over the silky pink fabric of her panties. "She probably wore big linen bloomers."

Luz laughed. "And I heard Rodrigo needed a haircut."

Eddo stretched up to kiss her and they smiled as they kissed because they both tasted like apples. He stayed there against the pillows, suddenly quiet and intense.

"What?" Luz could tell his mood had shifted; he wasn't joking or being funny anymore.

"In *El Cid*, people are always saying to him, 'You were knighted in a fortunate time.'"

"A fortunate time," Luz echoed. "Is this a fortunate time, Eduardo Cortez Castillo?"

"I didn't think so until today," he said slowly. "It's not fortunate to be in a place where there isn't ever any stillness. But you're the sort of person who carries stillness with her, Luz."

"Thank you," she said, surprised at the poetry in his words.

"I've been waiting a long time to feel this way with anyone."

"Me, too," Luz murmured.

They finished the apples in silence, bare feet touching.

Eddo slid off the bed, went into the bathroom, and emerged with a new toothbrush still in the wrapper. "For you, Jimena."

When Luz came out of the bathroom Eddo was clad in boxers and had put a CD into the small stereo on the dresser. His keys and cell phone and wallet were on a little tray next to it. "How about some Miguel Bosé?" he asked. "It's good music to help you fall asleep."

It was cool enough to need the matelassé coverlet. The white night sky glowed behind the shades and Luz could just make out Eddo's face as they laced their fingers together. Miguel Bosé sang softly.

"Luz, do you believe in fate?" Eddo asked.

"Sometimes."

"This is one of those times." His fingers tightened around hers.

Luz closed her eyes and nestled a fraction closer.

◆

Chapter 19

The title of the article in the *norteamericano* newspaper was "Betancourt's Embarrassment" and Lorena breathed fire as she read it. She was referred to as a "political pet poodle" in a long commentary full of snide comments about her "barely competent" speech in Guadalajara and the "inane" interview in *HOLA!*. The article predicted that she wouldn't be able to hold her own against Romero for the party nomination, much less win anything but a rigged election if by some miracle she did manage to be the party's candidate. Her background was examined and torn apart; the legacy of wealth from her grandfather's mining business, meeting Fernando when she was a graduate student and he was a professor, and his divorce and remarriage to her. The article belittled her degree in literature, harping on how she should have studied foreign relations or law or economics. It went on at length about the fact she'd never held a paying job. There was hardly any mention of her charitable work or how she'd supported Fernando's career.

She threw the newspaper to the floor. One of Max's flunkies prepared a morning brief for her every day so she could see what the press was saying and plan her next campaign event. Not everything was favorable; of course, a seasoned politician like herself had to expect that. But this was too much. Fernando would have to do something. Sue the newspaper. Arrest that *yanqui* reporter for libel or treason or threats to a foreign government.

Lorena finished dressing, putting on a beaded brocade suit for the day's visit to a children's center, then charged down to Fernando's office. She ignored a warning look from gatekeeper Ernesto Silvio in the antechamber and threw open the ornately carved door. "Fernando, you must--," she started but stopped short when she realized there was someone else in the office with her husband.

An extremely attractive man, with the short hair and stiff bearing of a military officer, was sitting with Fernando at the round table on the far side of the room. They'd obviously been breakfasting together, but there were also papers next to their plates. The attractive man swept all the papers into a blue folder before both men stood up to acknowledge her.

"I didn't know you had company," Lorena said. She smiled warmly at the attractive man and waited to be introduced.

"Lorena," Fernando said. "This is business. I'll be with you shortly."

"I don't mind." Lorena came over to the table and took a roll from the basket. Up close the man was absolutely delicious. He had on a perfectly draping suit and expensive cologne.

"Lorena." Fernando adjusted his metal spectacles. His tie was loose, his suit jacket was off and he looked surprisingly rumpled for so early in the morning. There was a glisten of sweat on his forehead below the receding hairline. "We will discuss whatever it is later."

"It will only take a minute, Fernando," Lorena purred. "I need you to do something right now. I'm sure your guest won't mind."

She stood close enough to bump the attractive man's arm, still expecting to be introduced. The man's mouth flickered with the faintest of smiles but otherwise he had no reaction. It wasn't the usual way men responded to her and Lorena was intrigued. She kept her gaze on him and let her tongue touch her upper lip. The attractive man's expression didn't change.

To Lorena's surprise, Fernando plucked the roll out of her hand, grabbed her elbow and propelled her across the room. "We'll speak later, my dear." His voice was strained.

"Where are your manners, Fernando?" Lorena hissed. She tried to drag her feet but it was impossible in those heels. "You haven't even introduced me to your guest."

"We'll speak later," Fernando repeated and deposited Lorena outside his office. The door shut abruptly behind her.

Ernesto Silvio and the secretaries had their heads down but

she knew they were secretly laughing at her. Lorena had never been so humiliated in her life. And there was still the newspaper problem to deal with. She stalked over to Silvio's desk and glared at him, her best *you ignorant shit* look. "Who's that with the president?" she snapped.

Silvio was an energetic man in his early forties and Fernando depended on him for virtually everything. Sometimes she wondered if Fernando even knew how to pee by himself.

The man met her eyes with a bland expression. "Have a nice morning, señora," he said.

♦

Chapter 20

Luz woke up alone in the bed.

The apartment was quiet, no sounds of a man in the bathroom or the kitchen. Luz edged into the hallway and called Eddo but there was no answer. She poked her head into the living room and checked the dining room, and called some more but there was nothing.

She walked back into the bedroom, not sure what to do, and saw the digital numbers of the little steel travel clock on the bedside table. It was 10:00 am.

She was supposed to have been at work in the Vega's kitchen *four hours ago.*

Panic hit hard as Luz looked around for her clothes. They were folded on the dresser top, right next to the stereo and the neat stack of CD's and a 200 peso bill in the little tray where Eddo's wallet had been.

The room shimmered around her.

He'd left her 200 pesos and disappeared.

He'd left her 200 pesos because he'd thought she was a prostitute.

A prostitute. The kind that pulls off men's shirts and does unspeakable things in tubs.

A whore.

A *puta.*

Putting on her jeans took forever. The blouse was worthless; there was no way to keep it closed. She found her shoes and socks, lurched into the living room, and stuffed the ruined blouse into the Prada tote.

Luz ran out the front door, wearing the sweater buttoned over her bra. She slammed the door hard and a draft churned angrily through the apartment.

Some paper near the coffee maker swirled off the kitchen counter and fluttered to the floor.

◆

Chapter 21

Lorena seethed all morning, barely hearing the preschool brats sing as she toured the place and avoided dirty hands. When Fernando sat down for *la cena* she gave him a furious lecture, letting him know that she expected Ernesto Silvio to be let go immediately. And for that *norteamericano* newspaper reporter to be expelled from the country and sales of the newspaper banned in Mexico.

Through it all, Fernando said nothing, just mechanically spooned soup into his mouth like a robot. When Lorena ran down, he gave a sigh and wiped his lips with his napkin. The servant came in and removed the soup plates.

"Well?" Lorena demanded. "Did you even hear me?"

The servant came in with the main course, served each of them, and went out.

Fernando prodded at the chicken on his plate with his fork, rearranging it like he always did with his food and everything else. "My dear, you'll learn in politics that all sorts of people have very disturbing agendas," he said when the chicken was no longer touching the rice. "Sometimes it's easy to ascertain the agenda, other times not so simple. You have to probe. Get to the bottom of what is going on before taking action yourself. Never be hasty."

Lorena banged down her glass of white wine, swearing under her breath as it slopped over the bowl and onto the tablecloth. "Ernesto is insufferable," she said.

"Ernesto is excellent," Fernando said. An offending grain of rice was pushed to the proper side. "He has neither his own agenda nor political passions."

Lorena rolled her eyes. "He doesn't like me and he doesn't want me to become president after you."

Fernando stopped fussing with his plate. "Lorena," he said testily. "If you can prove without a shadow of a doubt that wrongdoing is underway, then let me know. But I'm not listening to any more conspiracy theories without adequate proof today."

Lorena's blinked. "Conspiracy theories, Fernando?"

Fernando sliced his chicken into uniform pieces. "Political *tonteria*," he said. "It's probably all just nonsense."

♦

Lorena saw the attractive man again that very night at the Lomas Altas Children's Hospital benefit. He was positively gorgeous in a well cut tuxedo and shiny shoes.

Of course, she was gorgeous herself with her hair swept up and secured with a diamond clip. Her gown was a strapless amethyst silk with a small train. Max escorted her in and introduced her to various hospital patrons and made sure the right photographs were taken.

The event was held in the hospital cafeteria, with a band and champagne and waiters serving canapés. A small stage had been set up and the hospital director made a speech and then Lorena was asked to step up and say a few words. Of course Max had prepared for this. Her statement embraced those who worked so hard for all the wonderful children of Mexico.

Some boring people talked next and she realized the attractive man was one of them. According to the program he was Eduardo Cortez Castillo, legal advisor to the Marca Cortez company. He pledged a surprisingly large sum to the hospital on behalf of the company, and called for a round of applause for the architectural firm that had designed the wing, noting the way they had created innovative space for physical therapy, family consulting rooms, and other things Lorena supposed were important.

After the speeches and the tours and the rest of the formalities, Lorena circulated, making the sort of small talk expected of the First Lady. At the same time she discreetly assessed who at the benefit would support her candidacy and kept an eye out for Cortez. Really, how had this company minion managed to have a private breakfast with the president of Mexico?

Lorena eventually found Cortez. He was in a corner stuck like glue to a couple he appeared to know well. The woman was one of the architects he had recognized in his speech. The man next to her looked thick and menacing despite his tuxedo.

They were obviously having a private conversation and Lorena couldn't get close enough to overhear them. But whatever they were talking about, Cortez was happy about it. In fact the little threesome looked positively animated. The woman hugged him, he shook hands with the man and left without speaking to anyone else.

In the limousine going back to Los Pinos, Lorena asked Max about Eduardo Cortez Castillo and Marca Cortez.

"*Talavera*," Max said. "It's the largest *talavera* maker in the country. Exports everywhere."

Lorena almost laughed. She really shouldn't take Fernando for granted the way she did; he still could surprise her now and then.

The papers on the breakfast table were probably some special design for her campaign.

Dear Fernando. He was giving her dishes.

◆

Chapter 22

Luz didn't get fired, but only because she starting sobbing hysterically in the middle of Señora Vega's angry tirade.

She got back to the Vega's house well after 11:00 am. The traffic on Constituyentes was terrible and she couldn't find a *colectivo* minibus to take her through Chapultepec Park. There should have been buses near the Pantéon Dolores, the huge cemetery, but the street corner was thronged with people, all going in and out of the cemetery or buying flowers at the crowded *florista* stalls on the adjacent street. So Luz ended up walking an hour through the huge park alone, terrified that she would encounter a pack of wild dogs or thieves looking for easy prey.

Raul met her as soon as she unlocked the gate. "La señora is waiting for you in the kitchen."

It was like walking a gauntlet. Señor Vega was reading in the living room. He looked up and frowned as Luz passed through the adjacent hallway. The Vega children were eating in the breakfast room and they stared as she went through the swinging door. Rosa and Marisol and even poor Inez who came to do the laundry were in the kitchen, all wearing their stupid faces. Señora Vega was sitting at the big desk, with an expression like thunder. Her mouth twisted in anger when she saw what Luz was wearing, and then she launched into a biting diatribe that lasted forever, until Luz's stupid face dissolved into tears of humiliation and bottomless sadness.

In the end, Luz lost her Wednesday afternoons for a month.

She was back in uniform and upstairs cleaning by noon. Hector took Victoria to a friend's house, Alejandro and Francesca started fighting in the game room, el señor migrated to his study, and la señora went upstairs to her bedroom.

When the gate buzzer sounded Luz ignored it. Rosa and Raul were both downstairs.

"Luz." Rosa appeared a minute later in the doorway of Francesca's bathroom where Luz was scouring the tub ring. "There's somebody at the gate for you."

Eddo. Luz sat back on her heels, her heart jumping. But the servants were not supposed to have callers. La señora would *kill* her.

"What's he look like?" she gulped.

"Tall. Slim. Hot." Rosa's eyes sparkled. "If you don't want him I'll take him."

"*Madre de Dios*," Luz breathed. She rushed past Rosa, flew down the stairs, and ran to the gate.

It was Juan Pablo.

"What are you doing here? What's wrong?" She gave him a quick hug and kiss. He was supposed to be home, in Soledad de Doblado. In school.

"Nothing's wrong," Juan Pablo said. He had on jeans and his navy blue sweatshirt with the big zippered kangaroo pocket in front and "Santa Catalina" in white letters across the back. "You didn't come home this weekend."

"I left a message," Luz said. "Didn't you check?"

"We got the message." Juan Pablo shifted his feet.

"Something's wrong," Luz insisted. "Is Mama all right? Lupe? The girls?"

"You didn't come home this weekend," he said again.

"I know I didn't come home this weekend," Luz said impatiently.

"You didn't come home, so you didn't bring home any money." Juan Pablo looked miserable.

"Mama took you out of school to collect my pay?"

"I came with Tío."

"*Tío?!*"

"Yeah. He knew somebody coming to the city so we hitched a ride."

"No." Luz had a sudden vision of Juan Pablo in the back of a truck with a bunch of Tío's drunken friends as they passed around a bottle of rotgut *mezcal*. She gulped with relief when she heard him say they were returning on the 4:00 pm bus.

"Where's Tío now?" she asked.

"At the newspaper stand down the street." Juan Pablo waved his hand toward the intersection with Virreyes. "I'm supposed to meet him there in a few minutes."

Luz left him at the gate while she got her pay and the 200 pesos she'd earned at the Portillos, so that all together it was only short 650 pesos. She made Juan Pablo put the money into the zippered pocket of the sweatshirt to avoid pickpockets.

"Did I get you in trouble, coming like this?" Juan Pablo looked at her closely.

I'm a mess. Luz knew that her eyes were red and swollen. Her hair was a tangled ponytail secured with a brown rubber band. Her hands had been shaky since morning.

"I'm fine," Luz lied. She grabbed his arms and gave him a squeeze. "I should yell at you for missing school."

"There wasn't any school." Juan Pablo kissed her swiftly. "Today's a holiday. *Dia de los Muertos.*"

The Day of the Dead.

"Of course," Luz said.

◆

Chapter 23

Hugo de la Madrid Acosta propped himself against the pillows, pulled the sheet to his waist, and poured himself a glass of champagne. His performance had been exceptional. He'd stayed hard for a long time, making her writhe and shout until he'd exploded into her like a stallion mounting a wild mare.

The Dom Perignon was cold and crisp. He drank two large swallows and watched the woman at the dressing table pin up her hair. Her glass of champagne was on the table in front of her and she occasionally sipped from it, her lips sensual as they pressed against the glass.

She was a diamond. Flawless. Glittering bright and white. A class of one, an elite woman, descended from Spanish royalty, educated and beautiful, deserving of the biggest stage in any country.

Graciela was still his wife and the mother of his child. But she was a round river pebble compared to this sparkling, faceted diamond.

Lorena pushed a last pin into the thick white hair she'd caught up in a twist at the back. She often did her hair afterwards, sitting naked in front of the vanity table in the room they always used. He liked when she did that, liked the knowledge that she was preening for him. She'd never had children and her belly was still flat and her breasts firm.

She put on her underwear, wisps of La Perla lace unlike anything that Graciela had ever worn, and stepped into a navy silk sheath dress. She came to the bed. "Zip me up."

Hugo slid his hand through the opening in the back and caressed her lace-covered breast. Lorena made a noise deep in her throat. She let him continue for a moment then twisted to signal he was done.

Hugo zipped up the dress. "Where are you off to?"

"Downstairs." Lorena let a hand trail across his chest before reaching for her champagne glass. "Max is going to show me the campaign website."

"The website or the data sharing site?"

She shrugged as she sipped. "The one with the pictures of me."

"The official website," Hugo verified.

"We're going to have a big kickoff party for it," Lorena said. "Can you come?"

"Can you come away with me on the boat?" Hugo countered. It had been months since he'd been on the small yacht he kept in Puerto Vallarta and they'd never gone there together.

"After the election," Lorena said. "Then we can do anything."

"I want to fuck you right in the middle of the ocean."

She poured them both more champagne. "*HOLA!* will do another interview," she said, obviously not interested in fantasy sex talk. "They'll cover the rallies, too."

"How many rallies?"

"Every major city." Lorena touched her glass to Hugo's in a victory toast. "We'll start in Oaxaca. A sharp stick in Romero's eye."

"What about Valdez Obrero?" The popular mayor of Guadalajara was sure to be the PRI candidate and tough to beat in the election.

"We'll save Guadalajara for after the nomination," she said.

"I want to talk to Max just to make sure everything's on track," Hugo said. Once the rallies started and they were counting down the weeks until the nomination conference, Arias would spend the money as fast as it came in. Hugo wanted to keep the snotty little shit from pocketing anything for himself and his boyfriend. "Send him to my office next week."

Her campaign was like a fire in his blood. The complexities of getting her on the roster at the nominating convention, developing her platform, catering to the PAN party backbone and convincing them that Lorena could win a general election was the ultimate business deal, the biggest one Hugo had ever taken on. But the political game was only half of it; setting up the funding had been a stroke of genius, coupled by fortune's smile. Hugo felt more alive than at any time when he was building up his company, buying other companies, being first to crack the monopolistic Mexican telecommunications market or even as he blew fresh air through the Ministry of Public Security. He was pulling it all off, with a partnership of huge risk and huge reward. But when Lorena won Los Pinos, his diamond would give him the power that was rightfully his.

"Max is being brilliant with the campaign funds," she said.

"Anyone can be brilliant with that much money."

Lorena caressed him through the sheet. "Are you having second thoughts about funding the campaign? Is Graciela being mean about the money?"

"Never mind about Graciela." Hugo leaned forward and kissed her, then spoke with his lips against hers. "Your slogan will be everywhere. Lorena's your sister."

"Romero can't compete with that." Lorena's tongue played with his before she pulled away. "He's hardly visible at all, just blah-blah-blah out of him about legal reform and being important at the United Nations. I don't know why he's so popular. You never see him doing anything fun."

"Don't worry." Hugo watched her ass sway as Lorena went back to the vanity table, relieved she hadn't pressed him about the money or his wife. "You'll be the first woman president. And the most beautiful."

She laughed knowingly at that, even as she studied herself in the mirror and began applying makeup. Hugo liked the way Lorena knew her value, how well polished she kept the diamond even after spending most of the afternoon acting like a whore, biting and sucking and screaming.

"Sure you need to rush off?" he asked, wondering if he could get hard again.

"Dinner with some of the PAN *deputados* tonight," Lorena sighed. "It will take me hours to get ready."

"So how is Fernando these days?" Hugo decided to be content with the afternoon's activity. He finished what was left in his glass then poured himself more champagne. "Working on his legacy of strong leadership for the Mexican people?"

Lorena half turned to him, mascara wand raised. "Fernando is buying me dishes."

Hugo chuckled and drained his glass. "Dishes?"

"Probably for the campaign." She fluttered her lashes in the mirror and applied a coat of mascara. "I think it's a specialty *talavera* pattern. A surprise."

"But why dishes?"

"Honestly, who knows what goes through Fernando's head besides numbers and economic theories." Lorena flapped her hand dismissively. "But he had someone from Marca Cortez in his office very early last week. Pretended that it was all very important."

Hugo set his glass on the bedside table. "Someone from Marca Cortez was in his office?"

"Yes." Lorena brushed powder across her cheekbones. "A man named Eduardo Cortez Castillo. He went to the same benefit I did that evening. That's how I found out his name. Fernando wouldn't even introduce us."

"Cortez was in Fernando's office?" Hugo practically shouted.

Lorena dropped her brush. "What is the matter with you?"

"Eduardo Cortez Castillo is the director of the Office of Special Investigations," Hugo frothed. "He's my top anti-corruption investigator."

Lorena frowned. "No, he works for Marca Cortez. Making *talavera*."

"He works for me. His family owns Marca Cortez." Hugo got out of bed and hauled on his pants. "Eduardo gives their money to charity now and then."

"My dishes," Lorena insisted. "Why else would he be in Fernando's office?"

"*Dios mio,* Lorena." Hugo hurriedly stuffed his shirt into the waistband of his pants. "What did I just say?"

She stood, clearly annoyed with his tone. "You mean, investigating something?"

"Reporting an investigation to the president."

"But you said he worked for you. Wouldn't he report to

you?"

Hugo couldn't believe he had to spell it out. "Not if I was the subject of the investigation."

"You mean you and me?" She gestured at the bed.

Hugo was speechless for a moment, livid at her selfishness, then Lorena put her arms around him and he calmed down. Of course that's what Lorena would think, she didn't know the truth. He took a breath, put his hands on her waist even as he wanted to grab his phone and call Luis to make sure the dogs were sniffing around Cortez. "I can find out, make sure it wasn't anything about you."

Lorena kissed the tip of his nose then moved away to find her shoes. "If this Cortez works for you, can't you get rid of him? If he's a troublemaker send him away on a trip or a conference. Make him go check your boat and drown."

Hugo started to laugh. At first it was a tinny chuckle tinged with hysteria, then it became genuine laughter that shook his body and made his eyes water.

Lorena put a hand on her hip, gorgeous in her upswept hair and form-fitting dress. "What is so funny?"

Hugo was laughing so hard he could barely speak.

"The last time we spoke." He stopped to wipe his eyes. "I told Eduardo to get fucked."

♦

The old man was senile, Hugo decided. They'd been sitting in the bar at the Hotel Arias for more than an hour. He'd listened to Bernal Paz's economic drivel and compared stories of raising boys until Hugo could bring up the fact that Bernal Paz had been seen having lunch with Cortez a couple of weeks ago. Bernal Paz didn't ask how Hugo knew about the lunch, which was good because Hugo's resources were none of the old fart's business.

"I have no intention of becoming involved in the affairs of your ministry, Hugo," Bernal Paz said.

"Eduardo didn't ask you for information?" Hugo asked.

Bernal Paz pursed his lips. "I was a friend of Eduardo's father," he said testily. "I have an obligation to the man's memory to ensure that his son treats the name of Cortez with respect."

Hugo nodded in sympathy. "You're worried about Eduardo, Don César?"

"He is a man who cares nothing for his heritage," Bernal Paz sniffed. "No offense to you and the ministry but Eduardo should be running Marca Cortez."

Hugo settled back in his thickly upholstered chair, resigned to giving Bernal Paz one last try. The bar in the Hotel Arias was excellent; darkly paneled and dimly lit and perfect for quiet conversations. "Eduardo runs a very efficient department," he offered. "He's very good at his job. Why he recently caught some contractors who'd managed to wangle millions of pesos out of the government. Knows where to get information and how to use it."

"I'm sure he does," Bernal Paz said.

Hugo nodded thoughtfully. "But I worry about that," he said. "So, if Eduardo had, say, overstepped his bounds, I'd need to know. For example, if he was asking you to use your connections to provide him with information he's not entitled to have."

Bernal Paz drained his glass of single malt scotch. He coughed a little with the glass still on his lips.

"That really would have been a misuse of his position," Hugo went on. "And he would have been disrespecting your position as well."

"Our families have been close for years." Bernal Paz spoke slowly and deliberately, as if he needed Hugo to understand something important. "Eduardo used to play with my son Octavio."

"Really?" Hugo mused. "How interesting."

"Marca Cortez has always banked with my family." Bernal Paz's voice wavered for a fraction of a second.

Hugo almost didn't catch it. "A considerable amount of business, I assume."

The old man adjusted his silk tie and stood slowly, unfolding like a metal coat hanger being straightened into a length of wire. "I really must be going, Hugo. It's been such a pleasure catching up."

Hugo stood and offered his hand. They shook as Bernal Paz's gaze fixed on something over Hugo's shoulder. When Bernal Paz tottered out a bodyguard who'd been sitting at a table by the door rose and followed him.

The waiter padded by on the thick carpet and picked up the empty glasses. Hugo ordered another drink and brooded. The old man was afraid of Cortez's leverage over the Bernal family, but that didn't necessarily have anything to do with Lorena's campaign.

As he waited for the damn waiter to get back Hugo looked at the other patrons. The younger types who had more money than brains clustered around the long mahogany bar. Those who came for the hotel's famous discretion were in the high-backed upholstered chairs. The slim, urbane man in the corner with a laptop was Max Arias's boyfriend.

Hugo was more than a little drunk by the time his bodyguards got him into the car and the chauffeur drove home. Graciela had waited up. She wore some sort of sweat suit made of a thick fabric. There were stripes on the pant legs that made her look like a painted ball.

"Go to bed," Hugo said sourly.

"You didn't call," she said. "Again. Reynoldo wanted to talk to you about that school trip. You told him you'd discuss it tonight."

"Don't make demands, Graciela," Hugo muttered. He pushed by her, went into his library, and closed the door. He went to the computer, belched heavily, and fumbled through the login routine, cursing as he messed up twice. He hit all the right keys in the right sequence the third time and there was the page. He hated the clever attachment routine but the messages wouldn't post otherwise. Each message could only be so long so he ended up posting two.

Hh23051955: Possible intruder. Removal assistance required.

Hh23051955: Use more 7s at Site 1 for secure shipments.

♦

Chapter 24

Luz's week dragged. The children went to school. Señora Vega went to the spa and Café O and had more parent-teacher conferences. Señor Vega drank heavily in his study, smoked *cubano* cigars, and ranted at meals about the upcoming elections, the high cost of pulp paper, and the mythical *Los Hierros*. Luz did her chores like a zombie, fended off Alejandro, didn't take off early on Wednesday, and wore her stupid face all the time to keep from crying.

Eddo invaded her thoughts when she was tired, but he was probably some type of criminal. If he wasn't, wouldn't he have told her what he did? She told herself that things had turned out for the best.

Really.

Really.

Sunday evening Rosa came back from her weekend with two big plastic bottles of *toronja* soda. She'd spent Friday at home in Cholula with her family but returned to Mexico City the next day to be with Manuel. She'd slept with him in his car Saturday night and spent Sunday watching him use a red rag to wave traffic into parking spaces in front of a church.

"Luz, can you believe how much he made? He said I was his good luck charm."

They were upstairs in their room. It was 10:00 pm and the house was quiet. Manuel had made 400 pesos and that was probably all he'd make for the entire week. Luz tried not to think of the 3000 peso dinner she'd had a week ago.

"Okay," Rosa went on. "Enough of the martyr thing. I'm beginning to think you're turning into Santa Lucia or something and I'm going to see your eyes on a plate any day." She handed Luz a bottle.

"Thanks." Luz put the *toronja* soda—a Fresca imitation--on the bedside table. She put on her nightgown and curled up on her bed.

"Don't thank me until you've tasted it." Rosa slipped into her own nightgown and made a *come on* motion.

Luz unscrewed the cap, took a healthy swallow, and nearly choked. "*Madre de Dios*," she gurgled, pulling the bottle away from her lips. The cheap soda was liberally laced with even cheaper tequila. It hit her stomach like a bomb and made her eyes water. A curdling heat spread throughout her body.

"Keep going," Rosa admonished.

Luz widened her eyes and took another big swig. Maybe some cheap tequila was just what she needed. By the time Luz was a third of the way through, she told Rosa about meeting Eduardo Martín Bernardo Cortez Castillo at the Tamayo and going with him to Jardin del Arte.

"He gave you his wallet?" Rosa was shocked. "How much was in it?"

"I don't know," Luz said. Her voice sounded higher than usual. "I didn't look. But he paid 3000 pesos for dinner. *Effectivo*." *Cash.*

"You are a liar," Rosa breathed. "There's no dinner in the world costs that much."

"Santa Fe," Luz said proudly. "Argentina. El Rincon de Santa Fe." The "s" in *santa* came out sounding like "sh" and that sounded like Señora Vega. *Loosh.* Luz giggled and drank some more *toronja*-and-tequila. The concoction tasted like fizzy motor oil but it was smoothing out the edgy weepy feeling she'd had all week.

"You ate at a restaurant?" Rosa was clearly impressed with Luz's great adventure. "A real restaurant, not the food court?"

Luz started looking at the situation from Rosa's point of view. Which was a lot nicer than her own. She told Rosa all about El Rincon, how Eddo had thought she was looking for the bathrooms, and the salad fork crisis, which prompted Rosa to do a fairly good imitation of Señora Vega ("Loosh, how many times do I have to tell you, the salad fork on the outer left"). Fueled by the tequila, Luz described Eddo's apartment, his terrible coffee, and how good he'd looked naked. Rosa was agog and Luz got increasingly glib.

They discussed Eddo's physique at length, until Rosa said he was too handsome to believe and that Luz had to be making it up.

Luz was beyond embarrassment and real coherent thought by the time she was two-thirds of the way through her bottle and she giggled uncontrollably as she told Rosa about being in the bathtub with Eddo.

Rosa's jaw dropped. "You blew him in the bathtub?!"

"Yes, I did," Luz said to both Rosas sitting across from her. "And he liked it, I swear to the Virgin."

"Of course he did," Rosa said thickly. "Manuel wants me to do it to him. How was it?"

"*Muy sabroso*," Luz said and it seemed to be the most delightfully wicked thing she'd ever said, calling Eddo *tasty*.

"You're my hero, Luz." Rosa took another deep swallow and coughed a little.

"And then we did it again in the bed."

"He was a three-timer?" Rosa suddenly seemed to be having a little trouble following the story.

Luz laboriously counted on her fingers. "Yep. Three."

"Manuel can only do it once a night." Rosa started giggling.

Luz started laughing, too. "But in the morning he thought I was a *puta*."

"You were *good*," Rosa roared.

"I was *great*." Luz tried to put her bottle down and she missed the bedside table and the bottle fell on the floor but it didn't matter because it was empty. The bottle skidded a little and that was hysterically funny. Then Rosa rolled the neck of her bottle between her lips suggestively and that was *hilarious*.

As the room spun in circles, Luz laughed helplessly until her sides ached. Rosa threw up her tequila in the bathroom, still giggling over the toilet bowl.

◆

Chapter 25

Now and then, when it wasn't occupied, they met at the safe house to make sure their keys all still worked and the place hadn't been tampered with. It was a small brown stucco house south of the main business area, near the big medical center and the Lazaro Cardenas subway stop, where the neighbors were just short of poor and no one asked questions. A front company separated from Marca Cortez by seven degrees of complicated but legal paperwork owned the place and paid the water and electricity bills. The house had been used more than a few times, most recently for a homicide detective from Acapulco who'd been targeted by his union for refusing to participate in a pyramid bribe scheme; he'd been relocated to a private security firm in Toluca.

A tall concrete wall topped by rolled barbed wire enclosed the property, similar to other houses on the street. Eddo clicked a remote and the solid iron gate rolled out of the way. Motion controlled lights blinked on. He drove into the small courtyard, noting the two cars already parked there, and hit the remote again. The gate slid back into place.

As he walked into the house he called out his name, announcing himself so nobody shot him. He was rewarded with noise from the dining room and headed that way, admiring the place as he went. A few months ago Ana had spruced it up and the result was a pleasant combination of soft terracotta tones and Spanish colonial-style furniture.

Vasco and Tomás were seated at the dining room table, jackets and ties off, with a pile of still hot *empanadas* on a take-out tray in front of them. "I bring the gods beer," Eddo said and set down the six-pack he'd brought.

"Pork. Chicken. Mushroom." Vasco pointed out the various

types of *empanadas* and indicated an empty plate.

"All fried," Eddo muttered as he took off his own suit jacket and loosened his tie. "Are we eating anything green?"

"Here you go." Tomás opened a beer and set it in front of Eddo. "Hops."

The three men clinked their beer bottles together and tackled the *empanadas*. Eddo ate slowly and felt himself unwind a little in the company of his friends. *Madre de Dios* but he needed it badly.

"Got something on the funky website." Vasco reached for his briefcase on the end of the table and pulled out a sheaf of papers. "Canadian company owns it. Took some convincing but they gave us a list of clients."

Eddo wiped his hands on a napkin, found his reading glasses and leafed through the papers. "Over 200." He passed the papers to Tomás.

"The only Mexican entity using the hosting site is Lorena's election campaign." Vasco said.

Tomás snorted. "Who knew she'd be that organized?"

"No Mexican banks or investment companies," Vasco said.

"Anything from Panama?" Eddo said.

"No." Vasco took back the papers from Tomás, replaced them in his briefcase and took out a folder that he pushed across the table to Eddo. "But I ran down Montopa, that Panamanian company that wired some of the money into Hugo's accounts. Construction."

"Good research job, Vasco." Eddo opened the folder to find a commercial database profile of the company. Montopa was privately owned and profitable, with fewer than 100 employees. The company's corporate address, major bank, insurance company, and top three executives were listed. The folder also held a reprint of an article from the Panamanian newspaper *La Prensa* on refurbishing the old part of Panama City known as Casco Viejo. Montopa was one of the firms buying up historic buildings and turning them into boutique hotels and upscale restaurants. Eddo read part of the article out loud and looked at the two men across the table. "What are the odds the company is legit?"

"Construction on old buildings." Tomás picked up the newspaper clipping. "Bet Montopa has a lot of problems. Delays. Cost overruns. Payoffs."

"Dozens of opportunities to launder money," Vasco agreed. He took the last chicken *empanada*. "But just to play devil's advocate, maybe Hugo's media company is a legitimate investor?"

Eddo swallowed his beer before answering. "But if his company was legitimately involved with Montopa, why put money into accounts in his son's name?"

"How about the other way around?" Vasco threw out. "Make the accounts look legit by connecting them to a proper investment?"

"Montopa's a cartel front," Tomás insisted.

"More devil's advocate," Eddo said. "What are the chances there's a connection to Lorena?"

"Because Lorena's campaign site uses the same business website as those userids?" Tomás asked.

"There's nothing." Vasco shook his head. "You're grasping."

"How about those userids and Lorena's page?"

"That was one of the first things I checked," Vasco said. "I gave the site administrators the userids from the postings directions without saying where they came from. No matches with any of the companies using the website, including Lorena's campaign."

"Miguel hasn't gotten any further." Tomás drank the last of his beer and unsuccessfully suppressed a burp. "Hasn't been able to figure out any passwords and actually see what's going on."

Eddo leafed through the list of companies using the postings website. Most were well-known international companies. No connection to either Hugo or the El Toro cartel. "You think the postings page is a dead end?" he asked.

"Probably," Tomás said. "Unless Miguel figures out a password."

The takeout tray of *empanadas* was empty. Vasco pushed the tray and their dirty plates to the far end of the table and produced three Cohiba cigars from a leather case. Tomás found an ashtray and lighter in the sideboard and set them in the middle of the table. Eddo took a cigar, appreciating the rich woody scent of the tobacco. He'd eaten three *empanadas* and downed two beers; the most food he'd eaten at one time since El Rincon de Santa Fe on Sunday.

"Lorena's got a surprisingly big campaign machine gearing up," Vasco said idly as he puffed on his cigar to get it drawing. "A lot of userids posting to her page."

"Probably all trying to raise money," Eddo said. He slid the colorful Cohiba label off his cigar. "Somebody named Arias called the Marca Cortez offices."

"Probably Max Arias, her top flunky." Tomás lit his cigar and waved it at Eddo. "I swear you can be such a dumb shit sometimes. Lorena was smacking her lips over you the other night at the hospital benefit. He was probably calling to invite you to make a contribution at one of her so-called lunches at the Hotel Arias. His family owns it."

"Everybody knows that's her favorite sex spot," Vasco added.

"Fuck that," Eddo exclaimed, nearly coming out of his chair.

"What would Luz de Maria say, eh?" Tomás grinned even as he puffed on his cigar.

"Luz thinks Lorena's an idiot." The words slipped out before Eddo even thought about it. He felt a flush creep up his neck and busied himself with the cigar.

"Luz de Maria?" Vasco asked, light brown eyes glowing behind funky designer tortoise shell glasses. In his late thirties, he was a good-looking guy and the closest thing to a playboy Eddo had ever met. He was currently dating his way through the women in the Danish embassy. "Do I know her?"

Eddo stuck the cigar in his mouth and flicked the lighter furiously, trying to get a flame.

"Nope," Tomás answered for him. "But the way he told it, she's smart, she's hot, and this is more than serious."

"No kidding?" Vasco had been tipping his chair on its rear legs and now he let it down with a thump, happy surprise plastered all over his face. "Our boy's finally in deep?"

"Over his head. She's a high school art teacher."

"Is he going to tell her?"

"Said he would."

"That is more than serious."

Eddo couldn't light the damn cigar but his face was sure on fire. He'd been incredibly stupid, mouthing off to Tomás and Ana at the hospital benefit like some love-sick moron. Now if he never saw that bitch Luz de Maria again it would be too soon.

"So when do I meet her?" Vasco asked, smirking around his cigar. "See the woman who's making you blush like an altar boy in a--."

"Hey," Eddo said sharply, torn between abject humiliation and the need to start throwing punches. This was the problem with having friends who were lawyers and cops. Fucking interrogators. "A major investigation here and you're both thinking with your dicks."

Tomás and Vasco exchanged broad grins.

"I'm going up to Anahuac in a couple of days," Eddo went on. "Betancourt listened to everything I had to say but the only thing he was willing to authorize was an investigation of the bank with Hugo's funny accounts by the Financial Regulations Unit. I'll meet the unit's guy there."

"Wait and minute, wait a minute," Tomás broke in, the grin gone from his face. "Why the hell do you need to go up to Anahuac?"

Eddo shrugged. "Betancourt isn't going to do anything until there's a solid link between Hugo's accounts and the El Toro cartel. The way the money's moving between accounts so fast and with amounts changing all the time somebody there has got to be moving it for Hugo."

"What about the userid?" Vasco asked.

"Betancourt didn't buy it," Eddo said. He had just started explaining the userid scheme to Betancourt when Lorena came in. The interruption made Betancourt regroup, decide he wasn't going to deal with the issue, and hand Eddo a bunch of classic stalling routines. "It wasn't enough. Said he needed hard proof. Independent verification."

"Fuck Betancourt," Tomas spat. "Too many people are

getting involved. Arturo Romero, Bernal Paz, whoever in the central bank traced the accounts."

"The three of us." Vasco took up the count. "Miguel knows about the website but not about the link to Hugo."

"Anybody from your office?" Tomás asked.

Vasco shook his head.

"And now Luis Yanez Luna and his boys in Financial." Tomas smacked the table with the flat of his hand. "Are we really going to trust them?"

"Look." Eddo gestured with his still unlit cigar. "Luis tends to think he's smarter than he is but he's come through on a couple of things. If he can do as well with Banco Limitado maybe I can wrap this up before Hugo catches on and goes to Betancourt with some bullshit story the president is just gullible enough to believe."

Vasco nodded. "Trace the money trail and Betancourt won't be able to ignore the evidence."

"You don't have to go to Anahuac," Tomás insisted stubbornly.

Eddo finally managed to light his cigar, then focused on Tomás. His friend had his elbows on the table, shoulders hunched and tense, eyes pinched and dark. "What's really the problem?" Eddo asked.

"We lost two plainclothes Highway Patrol up there yesterday," Tomás said after a beat. "They'd been called in to investigate a body in a truck by the side of the road. Last we heard of them, they'd found a guy with his head in his lap. Literally."

Eddo leaned forward. "You mean two Highway Patrol guys are missing?"

"Found the car but no bodies." Tomás nodded unhappily. "No ransom calls, either. Either they were targeted and the body was a decoy or they were dealing and something went sour."

"Shit," Eddo said. He slumped back, the cigar forgotten. "Any of ours?"

"No."

"Look." Vasco shifted uneasily in his chair. "I think I'm with Tomás on this one. If Hugo found out you were in Anahuac asking questions it would be easy to make you disappear up there."

"The story is I'm visiting my sister in Atlanta."

"You got some other papers to use?"

"Yes." Eddo had a passport, identity card, and credit cards in another name. A man could buy just about anything at the Lagunilla market these days.

"Take your gun," Tomás said glumly. "Keep it with you."

♦

Chapter 26

It had been a month since Luz had been home. The adjustment from the Vega's sterile atmosphere to the clutter and color of the Alba house was harder than usual. But Luz smiled and hugged the girls as they climbed all over their Tía Luz, bubbling with news. Martina had a new teacher and Sophia would play Mary in the Christmas *posada* at the church this year.

It was only six weeks until Christmas, Luz realized, staving off the thought that she would have to tell Maria about the visa application this weekend. Soon she'd be getting her *aguinaldo*, the traditional Christmas bonus of an extra week's salary. Other people who served the Vega household, like the water *garrafon* delivery man and Ricardo the streetsweeper, would get *dispensas*, boxes of basic household staples like oil, rice, and beans. Pre-packaged holiday *dispensas* would appear in the grocery stores soon. Hector would be dispatched to buy a dozen and Luz and Rosa would hand them out.

Luz stepped behind the ironing board and made Maria sit down. Her mother was red-faced and a little breathless but said that it was just because she'd been so busy that morning. Lupe looked thicker and a little tired but insisted she was feeling fine. She came to the kitchen table with her sewing and the girls did their homework and everyone talked about the *posada*.

Tío and Juan Pablo joined them for *la cena*. Lupe had made *arroz a la tumbada*. But after a round of compliments about the seafood dish, the dinner chat subsided into a tense stillness. Luz tried to catch Juan Pablo's eye but he just shook his head at her. Even the girls were quiet, as if they had run out of things to say about Christmas.

"Your pay was short last time." Tío pointed his fork at Luz, breaking the silence.

"My pay doesn't concern you, Tío," Luz said in surprise. His trip to Mexico City to make Juan Pablo collect her pay notwithstanding, her salary was none of Tío's business and never had been. She would account for the missing 650 pesos to Maria, not to Tío.

Tío made a spitting sound. Luz ignored him.

"Why was your pay short?" Lupe asked quietly.

Luz put down her fork. Her sister was at the other end of the table, sitting across from Juan Pablo. Maria sat at the head. The girls shared the foot of the table near Luz and Tío. Everyone always sat in the same place, except when Tío didn't show up, and then Martina sat at his place facing Luz.

"This isn't the time to talk about this, Lupe," Luz said quietly. "Mama and I will talk about it later."

"Luz, please," Lupe said, sounding almost tearful.

Luz blinked at her sister. Lupe's bottom lip was trembling. "Okay," Luz said, drawing it out. A tiny white lie could put this awkward conversation to rest and Maria could be told the truth later. Luz took a deep breath as if embarrassed. "I . . . uh . . . broke a dish."

"Six hundred fifty pesos for a dish?" Tío shouted. Everyone jumped. Someone's spoon clattered to the floor.

Luz shrugged. "It was *talavera.*"

Tío's hand hit Luz's cheekbone with a stinging *smack.* Her head snapped back, her eyes watered, the room sparkled with vertigo and she tasted blood.

Through a curtain of dizziness, Luz watched Juan Pablo rise up and throw a wide looping punch across the table. He put his weight behind it, his chair spurting out behind him, his feet nearly coming off the floor. Fist connected with jaw and Tío spilled to the floor.

"Don't you touch my sister!" Juan Pablo yelled furiously.

"She's a stupid girl," Tío roared, scrambling to his feet. "Breaking dishes when her family needs the money."

"So you can drink it?" Juan Pablo was barely in control.

"Lupe is *pregnant*," Tío shouted.

"If you're so worried, why don't *you* get a job?"

Tío threw a counterpunch across the table but Juan Pablo

was younger and faster and sober. He jerked back to avoid the blow, then lunged forward, and suddenly they were snarling and grappling like two wild dogs, hands locked in each other's shirts. The table between them rocked wildly as they wrestled over the dishes and the *tortillas* and the clay *cazuela* full of rice and seafood, ready to kill each other in the small cramped kitchen with everyone else sitting like shocked statues. Plastic glasses spun crazily and tipped over, flatware clattered to the floor, and Luz's plate slid onto her lap.

It ended when the girls started screaming. Tío and Juan Pablo let go of each other and Tío stalked out the back door, slamming it so hard the door didn't catch but swung to and fro until Luz got up and closed it. Maria took Martina and Sophia upstairs. Lupe followed.

Juan Pablo ran some cold water on a kitchen towel. He held half of it to Luz and she put it against her cheek. Juan Pablo wrapped the other end around his fist.

"Thanks," Luz said shakily. She reached for his free hand. "But I don't want you fighting. You both have to live here."

"He's a *borracho* who drinks like a fish," Juan Pablo growled.

Maria came downstairs alone and started to make tea.

"I didn't break any *talavera*," Luz said.

She talked quietly as they sat at the table again, telling Maria and Juan Pablo that she'd applied for a visa, how much it had cost, and where she would go in the United States if the visa was granted. Be on the lookout for a notice from the postal service, she said, because it would be the certified letter from the embassy.

"No," Juan Pablo said.

"No what?" Luz turned to look at him.

"No, you're not doing this."

"Juan Pablo, look--."

"*No. NO.*" He cut her off. "You are not leaving and going someplace so far away." He jumped up and Luz was surprised to see tears running down his cheeks. He'd just been ready to kill Tío and now he was crying because she'd applied for a visa. He was still between a boy and a man.

"Listen, sunshine," she started.

"*No, Luz.*" Juan Pablo's voice was loud and angry. "You keep saying 'we'll manage, we'll manage.' But this isn't managing, this is *leaving*." He ran up the stairs and slammed his bedroom door.

"He'll get over it." Maria sighed. "You did the right thing. If you get the visa you'll go."

Luz sat in her chair like a lump, unable to move. It seemed as if too many things had happened in the last month and she was a different person and everyone at home was different, too. Her brain was too tired to maintain its defenses, and she had a sudden memory of being in Eddo Cortez Castillo's bed, feeling beautiful, her fingers entwined with his. It was as if she wanted time to stop and just let her be in that wonderful moment for the rest of her life.

Her heart felt like lead as she watched her mother wash the dishes.

♦

The little church was full of people when Luz walked in Saturday morning. Father Santiago was supervising a First Communion rehearsal.

I'll never buy a Communion candle for a child of my own, Luz thought, and almost left. But Carmelita was there with her oldest daughter, Bianca, and so Luz stayed.

They chatted for a few minutes in the vestibule about the First Communion until Bianca went off to join her friends and Carmelita gently touched Luz's cheek. Tío's hand had left a faint bruise. "Everything okay?"

Luz shrugged. "Tío and I had a disagreement. Nothing important."

Carmelita frowned. Luz hugged her and caught Father Santiago's eye. He nodded and Luz walked into the sacristy behind the altar.

It was a simple, homely room, with a cabinet for candles and altar cloths, a closet for Father Santiago's mostly threadbare vestments, and a table where he counted the Sunday collection, wrote his sermons, conducted marriage counseling, and kept the books for the bishop's office to review every six months. A yellowed poster of the late *El Papa* Juan Pablo II blessing the crowds during a visit to Mexico City curled away from the age-stained wall, next to a faceless Madonna that Luz had painted years ago.

The noise in the church died away and Father Santiago came in. He was wearing corduroy pants, a threadbare sweater, and his usual patient smile. "I'm so glad you came." He filled two glasses of water from the dispenser, handed one to Luz and gestured for her to sit down at the table.

"I have sort of a family problem, Father." Luz sipped some water, feeling uncharacteristically nervous in front of the old priest.

"Ah," said Father Santiago

"Lupe's pregnant, Father."

"Ah," said Father Santiago.

"She won't say who the father is."

"Ah," the priest said again.

"I . . . uh . . . thought it might be one of the seminarians who was here in the summer." Luz felt herself blush.

"No." Father Santiago gave his head a slight shake. "The father of Lupe's baby is not a seminarian."

"Father, you--." Luz didn't finish. The priest's eyes were knowing and sad. Lupe had evidently told Father Santiago but he would not violate the sanctity of the confessional.

"You are concerned for your sister?" he asked.

"I'm concerned that if she won't say who it is, how is he going to provide for this baby?" Luz heard the irritation in her voice.

"Lupe and the father are responsible for what happened and for their child."

"No," Luz said. "It'll be me. It's always me."

"This isn't like you, Luz de Maria." Father Santiago frowned slightly. "Is something else the matter?"

Luz realized she'd drawn a heart in the condensation on her glass. "I'd like to make my confession now, Father."

Father Santiago made the sign of the cross with her.

"Bless me Father for I have sinned." Luz murmured the familiar start to the sacrament of Penance. "It has been three months since my last confession. In that time I lied to my employer to get an advance on my salary. I lied to my family about what I did with the money when really I applied for a visa to the United States."

"Ah," said Father Santiago.

"I told Mama and Juan Pablo about it last night," Luz said miserably. "Juan Pablo's so mad he won't speak to me."

"Do you have a job in the United States?" asked Father Santiago.

"No."

They sat silently for a minute.

"There's more, Father," Luz said, wishing she had some of Rosa's tequila-and-*toronja* handy. "I met someone and I slept with him even when I knew it was a sin. But he . . . he's special. He has a car and a nice apartment in Mexico City. It was . . . he . . ." Feelings she'd tried to ignore for weeks bubbled to the surface. "He's smart. Cares how I feel. Listens when I talk. About art. Politics. Anything I say."

"How old are you, Luz de Maria?"

Luz frowned at the unexpected question. "Twenty-nine."

"Hmmm." Father Santiago sighed and smiled. "I honestly have a hard time telling you it's a sin to be 29, unmarried, and sleeping with the man you love."

"Love?" Luz echoed in surprise. "Who said anything about love? He thought I was a prostitute."

"Is this what you are trying to tell me, Luz de Maria?" Father Santiago sat up straight in his chair. "That you sold yourself to make money for a visa? Or Lupe's baby?"

"No. *No.* It had nothing to do with anything." Luz shook her head. "We had a wonderful time. But then he left 200 pesos on the dresser and disappeared."

"Because he thought you were a prostitute?"

"Yes. But I didn't take the money."

"Is there any other reason he would have done that?"

"No." Luz got up and went to the window, too agitated to stay seated. "I knew he didn't know that I was a *muchacha.* I didn't realize he thought I was a prostitute."

"You didn't tell him about yourself?"

"Not about being a *muchacha*, of course."

"Who did you tell him you were?"

"I didn't really say anything. He was . . . is . . ." There was nothing more to say. She was sorry, sorry, *sorry* and wanted absolution. Maybe then she could get the image of Eddo Cortez Castillo out of her head. "Father, what is my penance?"

"Your penance for what, Luz de Maria?"

"Father," Luz said impatiently, returning to her chair. "I have confessed to the sin of sleeping with a man to whom I was not married. What is my penance?"

"Let us consider." Father Santiago folded his hands. "If he hadn't left the money and didn't, as you claim, think you were a prostitute, would you still be sleeping with him?"

Luz looked at the heart on the misty glass. "Yes."

"Luz de Maria," Father Santiago said. "You cannot expect absolution for a sin for which you do not feel remorse."

"Of course I'm sorry for what happened."

"You feel remorse because he misunderstood who you were pretending to be. Isn't that true?"

"Well, yes," Luz said uncertainly.

"So if that misunderstanding didn't exist you would still sleep with him."

Luz stared at the old priest. He was right; she couldn't very well claim to be sorry for the sin of having slept with Eddo if she still wanted to be committing the sin. But that meant Father Santiago was not going to give her absolution.

"It's not a sin to love someone, Luz de Maria," the priest said gently. "You deserve to love someone and have him love you. But the real sin here is that of false pretense. Maybe if you'd been more honest about yourself none of this would have happened."

"I couldn't have told him," Luz said. "Someone like him would *never* be with a *muchacha*."

"Did you give him a choice?"

"It wasn't like that," Luz faltered.

"But you believe he wanted to be with you?"

"Yes, but only because he didn't know I was a *muchacha*."

"And being thought of as a prostitute is somehow better?"

"No, I *hate* that's what happened." Luz's head began to pound.

"Luz de Maria, you are not being fair to this man," Father Santiago said sternly. "He ought to know who he was truly with, rather than thinking he was with a prostitute. Because by letting him believe that, you led him into sin, too."

What she'd done was sounding worse and worse. Luz found a tissue in her jeans pocket and waited to hear how many rosaries she was going to have to pray for her penance.

"You must talk to this man and explain who you are." Father Santiago reached out and patted her arm. "As your penance you must make your peace with him."

"*What?*"

"You need to be honest with him, tell him who you really are and make sure he understands his mistake."

"This is my *penance?*" Luz blinked at the old priest, serene in his apparent insanity. "Father, *wait.* I can't go back and talk to him!"

"Do you know where he lives? Could you see him your next weekend off?"

"Yes, yes, of course," Luz babbled. "My next weekend off is in two weeks. But Father, *no.* I'll say a thousand Hail Mary's, Father, a thousand Our Fathers, as many prayers as you like. But I *can't* go back there. I can't face him. *Please.* What would I say?"

Father Santiago gazed at her mildly. "God will guide your words, Luz de Maria. Let us pray the Act of Contrition together."

◆

Chapter 27

Anahuac was about two hours southwest of Nuevo Laredo, a congregation point for *ilegales* who wanted to cross into *El Norte* and the *coyotes* who guided them. The drug routes into the United States followed the *ilegale* routes and vice versa. The rival cartels and the street gangs that served them fought over the routes and anything along the way, ranging through the once sleepy town in open warfare.

On the ragged eastern side of town, Eddo met the Financial agent in a boarding house popular with migrants. Javier Sotos Bild had been told that Banco Limitado was suspected of cartel activity and that Eddo was an Army officer working cartel issues.

Sotos Bild was young and aggressive and made it clear that he regarded Eddo as an old crank from Mexico City. The night they'd met Eddo sat stoically while Sotos Bild lectured him on the proper way to conduct a financial investigation, never realizing how close he was to having his nose broken.

They cased the area around the bank for several days, just another two *machos* looking for day jobs or a cheap way to get across the border. Banco Limitado was on the top floor of a narrow 2-story building. It overlooked a strip of stores on a main street in the combat zone where everything reeked of urine. The first level of the building was occupied by a tailor shop, a fruit and vegetable stall, and a small hardware store that was no bigger than a closet, with rope and chains and plastic mats spilling onto the sidewalk. There was a doorway between the tailor shop and the hardware store with a number and an intercom plate screwed into the concrete wall. When the door opened they could see a steep stairway leading to the second floor.

There were more businesses along the street but then the commercial section gave way to a trash-strewn vacant lot on one side and a cement block shantytown on the other. During the day the area was busy. Battered cars lurched down the street as pedestrians hustled across in the dry heat, bent on getting their errands done before something bad happened. The area closed at dusk, when whichever gang that currently owned this part of town came out to play. Eddo spent each night in the boardinghouse with the Glock in his hand, listening to the sporadic gunfire and assessing its distance.

An alley, nothing more than a narrow strip separating cement buildings, ran parallel to the main street. Sotos Bild was furious when he realized that Eddo meant for them to pose as itinerant garbage-pickers but he went through the motions as they gradually crossed the vacant lot and accessed the alley. There was a rickety iron staircase on the outside of the Banco Limitado building leading to a second floor door crisscrossed with security bars. A truck was parked at the base of the iron staircase with a couple of guys, almost certainly cartel *sicario* foot soldiers, smoking and playing cards on the tailgate. As Eddo got familiar with the street's routines he realized that various trucks came and went in the alley but there was always one parked in it, guarding the stairway.

Only one person appeared to work at Banco Limitado. A painfully thin woman in her mid-forties arrived each day around 10:00 am, used a key to unlock the door between the shops, and left in the late afternoon.

A few other people occasionally went into Banco Limitado after announcing themselves via the intercom and waiting for the door to buzz open. They were all men, dressed in jeans and boots like the *coyotes* roaming the bars or the card players in the alley. A few carried backpacks which looked lighter when they left and Eddo marked them as cartel couriers.

The best vantage point for Eddo and Sotos Bild was a pool hall half a block down on the opposite side of the street, a dark cavernous place where there was a knife fight every few hours. There were four pool tables in back, where the air was so smoky it was hard to see. In front, tables spilled out onto the sidewalk by a low wall decorated with torn posters advertising a parade in honor of Santa Muerte. The patron saint of death's black skeleton face leered from the faded paper.

Anyone sitting outside the pool hall had to deal with beggars and kids selling everything from pencils to their sisters. In contrast to the rest of the street, the place never seemed to close. Eddo suspected that the owner paid protection money to all the gangs.

The night of the third day Eddo hid a tiny microphone in a crack in the concrete by the Banco Limitado doorway while Sotos Bild drank a beer outside the pool hall with the receiver and a digital recorder in a backpack. The next day they captured several brief conversations between the woman inside the building and men at the door; in each instance they gave her the same password after which she buzzed open the door.

They talked through their next step that night. Bild was out of patience with Eddo's slow and methodical casing and Eddo wasn't sure how much longer their migrant cover would hold. They'd had to continually avoid fights and brush off the *coyotes* and Eddo couldn't hear one more scared teen boast how he was going to outwit *La Migra*.

The plan was simple. Sotos Bild would try to open a bank account at Banco Limitado with the money and false identity that had been provided for just that purpose. He'd get an account and set up wire transfers to another bank, which Financial could hack. With the information Financial got from the operation, they could potentially trace the bank's other transactions. Although Sotos Bild did not know it, Financial's chief would then personally work with Eddo to trace where the funds from Hugo's accounts went next.

"Do it just like we rehearsed," Eddo warned late the following afternoon. They were slouched on a street corner, both in jeans and cotton shirts and backpacks. The woman appeared to be alone in the bank. A group of couriers had just left; they'd almost certainly been the last of the day. The truck in the courtyard had changed about an hour ago when a new crop of card players had taken up their vigil at the base of the iron stairs. "I'll be waiting for you at the pool hall in an hour," he reminded

Sotos Bild and nodded toward the shantytown. "The grocery is the emergency meet. Use your radio if there's any problem."

"I know," Sotos Bild muttered. He was shorter than Eddo, with light brown hair and a square jaw that bespoke a German ancestry. "Here we go, *abuelo*."

Eddo watched the kid cross the street by the tailor shop. Sotos Bild was an insufferable asshole but he was smart with numbers and he had balls, too. He was armed with a cell phone with a push-to-talk radio feature and a small automatic he'd probably never fired before. Eddo was betting the kid was glib enough not to need either.

Eddo's Glock was a reassuring pressure against his side in its shoulder holster under his cotton shirt as he ambled down the street. Out of the corner of his eye he saw Sotos Bild speak into the intercom. The door swung outward and Sotos Bild disappeared inside.

Eddo loitered at the hardware store. He bought a lottery ticket, then drifted back and skirted the alley. The truck was still there, with four men looking bored and slapping cards down on a makeshift table in the truck bed. Another urinated against the wall of the adjacent building.

Parched in the dusty heat and listening hard to the street noises for anything out of the ordinary, Eddo made the block and went into the pool hall. He bought a beer at the bar and carried it outside to one of the small plastic tables with a view of the Banco Limitado door. The drink was lukewarm but helped to wash down some of the grit in his throat. Eddo wondered if he'd ever feel clean again.

"Eh, *amigo*." A boy of nine or ten sidled up to him and showed him a couple of bootleg CDs. The covers showed masked men with long guns holding a scantily clad woman. "*Narcocorridos*," the boy said. "The latest. Ten each CD."

Eddo shook his head. *Narcocorridos* were banned songs extolling the drug cartels and their opulent lifestyle, mostly recorded by amateurs but sometimes by well-known musicians.

"They're cheap, *amigo*," the boy said but stopped his sales pitch when a hand gripped his shoulder.

"Move along." The speaker was a short wiry man, made

leathery by sun and hard work. He wore jeans, a plaid shirt, expensive tooled boots, and a dirty New York Yankees baseball cap. His expression was wary and confident at the same time.

The boy slipped inside the pool hall and the wiry man sat on the edge of the other plastic chair at Eddo's table. He had a *Coca* and raised it to Eddo in kind of a salute before taking a swallow.

Eddo said nothing, his brain churning. He and Sotos Bild had definitely seen this man go inside the bank two days ago.

"You looking for work, *amigo*?" The wiry man wiped his mouth with the back of his hand.

"You hiring?" Eddo replied.

The man grinned as if Eddo had said something funny. "Nobody here has work." He slid his eyes away, then back again. "But other places, yes."

"How much?" Eddo asked.

"Depends." The man scanned the street. "Do you have a family?"

It was a strange question for a *coyote* or cartel courier to ask. "Today I'm alone," Eddo parried.

"But you have children?" the man persisted. "How old?"

Eddo watched the activity around them as well; it was if they were both talking to the street rather than to each other. "You starting a school?"

The man grinned even more broadly this time. "Sure."

Eddo felt the blood thump in his ears. If this asshole was selling kids into prostitution he was going to pull his head off. "Where?"

"On the way to--." The man broke off as a big blue truck lumbered past, the bed full of swarthy men. He stood up. "Go tomorrow to the house behind the church of Santa Agneta," he said. "Bring your children."

He walked off swiftly, disappearing into the shantytown and Eddo watched as the shops all started to close, even as the sun continued to glint off car fenders and bake the sparse grass. A woman with a bale of secondhand clothes scurried past, panting as she went. The rolling door of the hardware store clanged shut. Precious inventory was left on the sidewalk; chains, rope, a stack of blue plastic buckets. A watermelon rolled into the street, the fruit vendor in a rush to pull everything inside and close the shop.

Pedestrians melted away. The street was suddenly deserted and noiseless.

The big blue truck came down the street again and the eerie silence was broken as the men in the back whooped and shouted and fired into the sky.

Eddo threw himself out of his chair and onto the ground, rolling toward the bulwark of the wall behind him. Men boiled out of the pool hall in a noisy tangled mass of confusion and anger. The street erupted into violence, the chaos doubled by the long afternoon shadows.

A different truck screeched around the corner and Eddo saw it was the one most recently on guard in back of the Banco Limitado building. It skidded to a halt in front of the pool hall and a man who'd been standing in the truck bed screamed and pitched out of the vehicle backwards into the trash on the side of the street, his neck spouting blood. The gunshots were no longer sporadic but a pitched battle for control of the street. Another truck skidded around the corner. Several men started beating on the doorway between the tailor shop and the hardware store with rocks and a metal baseball bat.

An unmistakable sound pinged off the wall behind Eddo. He scrambled to his feet, snatched up his surprisingly intact beer bottle, and sprinted for the shantytown, aiming for a street that ended in the alley behind the bank. He heard another shot and footsteps behind him and ran as if he was playing Toluca for the title, dodging, weaving, his feet barely touching the broken pavement, the backpack on his shoulder nearly horizontal behind him.

He darted into a gap between two crumbling cement walls, waited a beat for his pursuer to catch up then stepped out, ramming the moving man under the chin with an elbow. At the same time Eddo brought the bottle down hard on top of the man's head. The man gave a low gurgle from his mangled windpipe and collapsed onto broken glass.

Eddo hauled out the Glock, wheeled around and ran for the alley. There was only one person on guard, a skinny youth with a long gun held inexpertly; and Eddo was on top of him before the kid could react. The barrel of the Glock cracked against bone and the kid was suddenly unconscious in the dirt, his head streaked with blood. Eddo grabbed the long gun and took the winding iron stairs two at a time. He slowed halfway; the iron was only loosely fastened to the concrete wall and the whole thing swayed as he went higher.

The door was locked but cheap. Eddo blasted out the lock and shoved the door inward, using it as a shield against the boom of buckshot as he rammed into the room. Eddo fired around the edge of the door and an older man with a shotgun slumped to the floor.

Eddo stepped out from behind the door and managed to shove it closed. He found himself in an office that had been touched by a tornado; two desks were intact but at odd angles while broken lamps and chairs and electronic equipment littered the floor. The thin woman they'd seen going in and out stared at him mutely, her face contorted with fear.

"I'm not going to hurt you," Eddo said rapidly. "Who else is here?"

The woman didn't move or speak.

Sotos Bild was a bloody figure on the floor behind a desk, cell phone in one hand, gun in the other. Eddo felt for a pulse that wasn't there. An older man in a denim shirt was also dead, sprawled on the opposite side of the room, a gun still clenched in his hand. The man Eddo had shot was still alive but unconscious. Raucous sounds of looting filtered up from the floor below.

"They came. All of a sudden," the woman said. "They broke down the door while that man was here and . . . and . . ."

A door on the far side of the room was barricaded with a filing cabinet. "Why didn't you leave?" Eddo jerked his chin at the battered doorway he'd just come through.

"I don't have the key," the woman whimpered.

A thunderous crash from the other side of the barricaded door announced a renewed assault on the bank. Eddo kept the Glock in his right and rifled through Sotos Bild's pockets with his left, scooping up everything and dumping it in the younger man's backpack, leaving only a false identity card. Eddo would find the body at the morgue later; make sure Sotos Bild was laid to rest properly.

He stood up and grabbed the woman by the arm. "Get your files and let's go."

She seemed frozen and he gave her a shake. "Banking files," he barked. There was a laptop on the floor and he snatched it up, yanking cables out of a router as the banging on the door grew more intense. The file cabinet fell over with a crash, spilling out folders.

The woman jerked into life. She grabbed the folders off the floor. Eddo grabbed the rifle and eased open the door to the iron staircase. He peered into the alley. By some miracle the rival gangs hadn't taken the fight to the back of the building. The guard was still unconscious where Eddo had left him. Eddo half shoved, half dragged the woman down the stairs and into the maze of streets in the shantytown.

◆

Her name was Sonia Velardo and she had been a senior teller at a Banamex branch office until her son Ramon got involved with a gang and began using cocaine. When she stole money from the bank to support his habit she got fired. About six months ago her son's friends needed someone with her skills. Since then she'd worked at the office above the hardware store moving money between accounts and filling out money orders. She didn't seem to know that she was dealing with accounts held by the Minister of Public Security or that she was working for the El Toro cartel; she'd never met any of them, never gone to any meetings. When Eddo asked her if the office was called Banco Limitado she said yes, but that the name was like a joke and no one said it very often.

For three hours Eddo and Sonia traveled, walking and changing buses and finally taking a taxi to the small resort hotel south of Anahuac where he'd left the SUV and had a room booked in a different name. He was sure they weren't followed. Once in the room Eddo called Tomás. Sonia sat on the small sofa, obviously unsure whether to regard him as savior or kidnapper. She made no attempt to get away from him but Eddo kept the Glock visible just in case.

"What's your name?" she asked, her voice shaking a little, as he hung up the phone.

Eddo was ready for the question. "Reynoldo," he said.

Sonia blinked and her eyes slid to his backpack, which now held the laptop and folders taken out of the Banco Limitado.

"What would you like to eat?" Eddo asked.

She looked at him blankly. He ordered for both of them from room service.

He turned on the television while they waited for the food to come. A Nuevo Laredo station showed local news, all horoscopes and fluff.

The food came on two trays. The waiter put them on a table in front of the sofa. Eddo let Sonia sit there and pulled out the desk chair to sit across from her. He was ravenous but after three bites he was ready to throw up.

Eddo put down his fork. "Sonia, tell me again what you did in the bank."

She shrugged around a forkful of rice. "I made sure all the transactions looked just like a real bank."

"How many accounts?"

"In the whole bank?"

"Yes."

"Sixteen." Sonia ate in small bites as if she had a hard time chewing. "Including yours."

The central bank data had shown four accounts each in Hugo's name and that of his son Reynoldo. The other eight accounts might be connected to Hugo or to another El Toro affiliated operation; something for Vasco to deal with. "And you handled them all?"

"Yes."

"How did the money get into the accounts?"

"Money orders. Or wire transfers." Her eyes slid to her plate.

"Who sent the money orders?"

"You did."

Eddo didn't say anything for a few minutes. Sonia finished

her food. She was so thin that the veins on her hands and forearms were like blue cords.

"You moved the money between the accounts in the bank." Eddo made it a statement but Sonia nodded as if he'd asked a question. "And then moved it out of the bank. Always within four or five days."

Sonia swallowed hard, the veins in her neck pulsing.

"Where did the money go, Sonia?" Eddo asked.

"Just money orders," she said.

"To whom?"

"I don't remember," she whispered.

"Always the same place?" Eddo demanded.

"No." Sonia wrung her hands, bony fingers pressing down on those fragile veins. "Different. I don't remember."

"How did you know where to send the money each time?"

"They told me," she faltered and her eyes darted to the backpack again.

"You wrote it all down, didn't you?" Eddo reasoned slowly. "It would have been a lot of places, seeing as all the accounts got emptied at least once a week."

"No."

She started to sob, frightened now as well as confused. Maybe once she had been attractive, but now she was wraithlike and broken. She covered her face with her hands and rocked as she sat on the sofa. "I have to go back. My son . . . my son needs me."

Eddo put the trays in the hall. Sonia looked at him hopefully as he came back through the doorway then cried again as he double-locked the door behind him.

"Tell me what happened today, Sonia," he said.

She nodded, now trying to please him, obviously worried that she'd done things with Reynoldo de la Madrid's money without his permission. "The man who came in said he could shut down the office unless we gave him money."

"We?"

"Rico was there."

"Rico?" Eddo frowned. When Sotos Bild went in they'd been sure she was alone.

"The tailor. He . . . he helped me with the bank. And Ramon."

"Ramon? Your son lives in the bank?"

"In a room . . . over the tailor shop."

"And Rico stayed with him? Got cocaine for him?"

"Yes." Her voice was barely a whisper.

Eddo digested this information. Ramon was probably little more than a hostage, kept close by and filled with cocaine so that Sonia would continue to use her banking skills for the cartel. "So finish telling me about what happened today."

Sonia swallowed convulsively a few times. Eddo got some tissues out of the bathroom and thrust them at her, feeling the stress beginning to break him down.

"People came . . . with the usual papers." She swallowed again. "Then in the afternoon a man came up who wasn't anyone who'd come before."

Sotos Bild. "And what did he do?"

"He knew the password and I thought he was like the others." Sonia wiped her eyes. "Bringing papers or money. He was nice at first. Made some jokes. I had fun talking to him." She looked wistful and Eddo had a glimpse inside a life that had fallen into an abyss; subservient to cocaine, locked in a one room office, frightened by the cartel henchmen who passed through and probably used her when they had nothing better. "But then he said that the *federales* knew about the bank," she went on. "He said if we gave him money he would make sure the *federales* looked somewhere else and left the bank alone. But we had to pay him right now."

Eddo went cold. "You're sure that's what he said?"

"Yes." She cried again, but softly, as if she was too drained to make more of an effort. "He had a phone in his hand the whole time. I think it was on and someone was listening. When Rico said no, the man said that the bank would change hands. That's the way he said it. Change hands. But I don't think the people who came were his friends like he thought they were."

"Go on." Eddo didn't want to believe what he knew she was going to tell him. Rage battled with relief that Sotos Bild had never known his true name or identity. *Or had he?*

"We heard fighting in the street and someone said the password but Rico wouldn't let them in." Sonia talked in between soft sobs. "But they broke down the door and a man with a gun came in. Rico managed to barricade the door again but the man shot him and the man with the phone, too. Then you came in and shot him."

Eddo rummaged through Sotos Bild's backpack, coming up with his wallet, bottles of water, a spare shirt, and two cell phones. One was the phone Eddo had taken out of the dead man's hand, the other was the phone with the radio feature he'd seen Sotos Bild use during the week. The call log of the first phone showed three calls to a cell number Eddo didn't recognize. He hit redial and called the number again. It wasn't in service. On impulse, Eddo rifled through the wallet, finding a few pesos, a piece of paper with the mystery cell number on it, and a spare SIM card that could be inserted into either cell phone to change the number.

"Fuck," Eddo swore.

Cross and double cross. All that untraceable money had been too much to resist. But once Sotos Bild had shown the rival gang the bank, he'd become a liability.

Eddo sucked in air and paced the hotel room. Sonia stopped crying and was motionless. For the first time Eddo noticed that her hair was streaked with gray. Her feet in their flat brown sandals were dirty from all the walking they'd done. She wore a print blouse and navy skirt and both were old and cheap. Everything the cartel had paid her had probably gone up her son's nose.

Or her own. Sonia's eyes were ringed with shadow and her skin was translucent. She was probably as much an addict as her son.

She looked up at him. "I have to go back now."

"If Ramon's friends still control things they'll wonder where you've been and how you got out alive," Eddo said. "They won't trust you any more and they kill people they don't trust. If the other gang is in charge they'll make you tell them everything you know about Banco Limitado and then they'll kill you for having been part of it. Either way you can't go back."

Sonia's bony shoulders slumped in despair.

It was past midnight. Eddo got up, his body sore inside and out, and put a hand on her shoulder. "Get some sleep and we'll decide what to do in the morning. You take the bed."

Sonia crawled into the bed fully clothed and they turned off all the lights except for the one in the bathroom. Eddo sat in the chair, his feet on the sofa and the Glock in his hand.

He woke Sonia a little after 5:30 am. She looked like hell as she went into the bathroom. Eddo heard her vomit.

Sonia walked out of the bathroom and gave him a thin smile. "Thank you for not . . ." She indicated the bed.

"Let's get you some help, Sonia," Eddo said.

♦

Chapter 28

44Gg449M11: 7s at Site 1, multiple arrangements.

44Gg449M11: Site 2 interrupted, shipment delays.

Gustavo Gomez Mazzo considered if there was anything else to say about the firefight at Banco Limitado and decided against it. The bank had been caught in the crossfire of a gang rivalry in Anahuac, which meant either that some upstart didn't realize he was in El Toro territory or didn't believe the stories of what happened to people who didn't respect El Toro. But it was a situation that Chino would deal with as soon as he got back to Mexico. It wasn't too serious; Gomez Mazzo had lost a few replaceable *sicarios* and the accountant had disappeared. Her body might turn up, likely raped to death, and maybe it wouldn't. A new location for Banco Limitado would be up and running in a week or so. He logged off the website, handed the laptop to Chino and got himself a rum cooler. "Your turn."

Chino wasn't so good with computers and it took him almost five minutes to laboriously type in the required information, find the attachment and set up a posting. Gomez Mazzo read over his shoulder, unconsciously bracing himself against the gentle swell of the deck.

CH5299xyz9: Intruder team @ Site 3 in 5 days.

"Good workers?" Gomez Mazzo asked.

"Best." Chino's reply was characteristically brief, delivered in his flat, whispery voice.

"Just have them make it fast," Gomez Mazzo said. "El Toro doesn't like going into the city."

Chino logged off the site and closed the laptop with almost visible relief. He nodded at Gomez Mazzo and left the main cabin.

Gomez Mazzo leaned back in his chair and put up his feet.

He could hear the happy sounds of his grandchildren in the lounge on the upper deck. Some cartoon marathon with the Saudi children from the yacht three slips down. The breeze carried a slight salt tang and kept the day from being too hot. Later they'd swim in the pool and then go ashore for dinner.

He'd come a long way from the brickyard in Culiacan and wasn't done yet. He'd been just 16, with two children and 12 years hauling bricks behind him, when he went north and joined a rip crew stalking the cartel mules who crossed the border with packs of drugs on their backs. He was so scared he pissed his pants that first night, but he'd impressed the leader of the rip crew when they found a group walking north and ambushed them. He was a big, powerful teen, able to kill a man with his bare hands. It was hard work but in one night he made more than a month's salary from the brickyard. A week later he killed two men with a knife, gutting them with arms made strong hefting sand and stone. When the leader of the rip crew was killed by a gang working for the Colombian cartel that owned the *plaza*, or smuggling route, Gomez Mazzo struck a deal with the man most likely to become the new leader. Gomez Mazzo would let him keep his penis and he'd let Gomez Mazzo take over the crew. The deal lasted two days and then Gomez Mazzo killed him. Those were the best years, he sometimes thought, the years when he was stronger than anyone else and learning the taste of freedom and power.

The rip crew grew. Eventually Gomez Mazzo pushed out the Colombians. His organization became known in northeast Mexico for its ruthlessness, mobility, and financial acuity. The specter of the brickworks in Culiacan pushed him hard and Gomez Mazzo moved around restlessly, never staying in one place too long, buying a succession of local officials to ensure his freedom of movement. He became an obsessive money manager. Those within his own organization who tried to cheat were dealt with swiftly. He prized loyalty.

He earned the name El Toro after he hung a rival's body from an Osborne Brandy black bull-shaped billboard, a message to the dead man's adherents carved into his chest. By the time he was 35, Gomez Mazzo controlled all the drug routes in northeast

Mexico and was pushing west, into Zetas territory, buying gangs and freelance *sicarios* and killing with impunity to consolidate his territory. The legend of El Toro was large.

Chino, the son of a Chinese whore and an unknown Mexican father, had started on a rip crew, too. He'd grown up on the streets of Nuevo Laredo and knew the eastern border area better than anyone Gomez Mazzo had ever met. Chino wasn't sure how old he was, but Gomez Mazzo guessed he was about 27 or 28, strong and wiry from years of living on the edge of survival.

Chino ran things on the ground, moving between Anahuac, Nuevo Laredo, and wherever Gomez Mazzo happened to be. The thin man with the papery voice and slanted eyes wasn't the dealmaker, but the enforcer and the transportation chief. Gomez Mazzo was still in charge but trusted Chino to move the stuff and avoid the free-lance rip crews, to hire gangs to consolidate territory, to get rid of witnesses and the temporary cocaine factories and the rivals who were stupid enough to try and challenge El Toro. To make sure the local officials knew who they worked for.

If **Hh23051955** had a problem, Chino would take care of it.

The deck moved, just enough to remind Gomez Mazzo where he was. It was a comforting feeling, knowing that he could order the anchor to be raised and head out whenever he wanted. No one else told him where to go, when to get up, what load to shift. There were no brickworks on the water.

He reached into the cabinet next to his chair and got another rum cooler. He unscrewed the cap and mentally toasted **Hh23051955**. A man had to move fast to catch fortune in both hands whenever it came flying by, Gomez Mazzo had always believed, and he'd done just that when they'd met at that yacht show. Gomez Mazzo had known who Hugo de la Madrid Acosta was, of course. They were well into the negotiations and a third bottle of brandy when Hugo finally realized that Gomez Mazzo was the notorious El Toro. Realization had spread over the man's face, yet he didn't blink. Hugo was all about money and the power. And the woman.

There were bound to be a few bumps along the way. Hugo's

nattering about who they were recruiting to mule across the border, the occasional person who had to be eliminated--these were all to be expected. But if his partners didn't lose their nerve, in a year the new president of Mexico would have the army take care of the Zetas and then go back to barracks.

Leaving El Toro in control of the entire northern half of Mexico.

♦

Chapter 29

"The key is this Hermanos Hospitality company," Vasco said. For the past hour he'd taken notes from the files taken out of Banco Limitado. "Sonia kept busy moving all the account money around, using at least 12 accounts. But according to her code, eventually there'd be a money order made out to Hermanos Hospitality."

"She said there were 16 accounts," Eddo said, slumped in his chair at the dining room table. At some point his coffee had gone cold.

"Eight we knew about from the central bank records," Vasco confirmed. "Sonia used another four to park money from time to time before moving it on. The other four are registered to different names and don't seem to be as active. More deposits than withdrawals and not much money. Give me a couple of days on those."

"I bet we're going to see connections between the userids, the fake bank shit, and this company," Tomás said.

Eddo nodded, although he was too wrecked to read all the stuff Miguel had printed out. Sonia's laptop had yielded a treasure trove; one of the five userids, along with the password, had been stored on her browser. When Miguel logged in with Sonia's userid, **BppBB16003,** he'd been able to access the page and print out all the postings from all five userids. The same password worked for two of the other userids, **CH5299xyz9** and **1612colcol**.

"That Panamanian company Montopa hasn't shown up so far," Vasco said. "My guess is they made a mistake early on, letting Montopa touch Hugo's accounts."

"So what are you saying?" Eddo asked. "Montopa is the beginning of the money trail and Hugo and Reynoldo's accounts are at the end?"

"The accounts are two steps removed, I'd say." Vasco stood up and tore a sheet off his pad. "Hermanos Hospitality is the end of the line and the postings are the dialogue along the way." He left Eddo and Tomás sitting at the dining room table and went into the living room. The sound of Miguel's fingers tapping a keyboard slowed. Vasco's voice was heard indistinctly and then the tapping resumed, faster than before. Diego said something and Vasco replied.

Eddo studied the printout, too tired to focus very well. The page showed about 40 postings in reverse date order, each showing the userid of the sender. The latest posting was only a few hours old. Several of them referred to activity taking place at Site 1 or Site 2. More recently, a Site 3 was mentioned. There was only one reference to a Site 4, which appeared to be a place all the userids had met. "What are these different sites they're talking about?"

Tomás shrugged.

Eddo took off his reading glasses and pinched the bridge of his nose. He'd made the trip back from Anahuac in 18 hours, stopping only to piss and get gas and leave Sonia in a rehabilitation center in San Luis Potosi. Vasco and Tomás had met him at the safe house with Miguel. Diego was there, too, a tough young Highway Patrol cop who was one of the regular Saturday soccer players. Diego didn't know shit about computers or money laundering but he was loyal as hell.

"You call Luz de Maria yet?" Tomás asked.

"No," Eddo said. Eventually he had to tell his friend that he wasn't seeing Luz, that he'd been wrong about her, but tonight wasn't the night.

"Look." Tomás reached across the table and shook Eddo's shoulder. "That Sonia woman is going to be all right."

"I didn't save any kids." Eddo pushed away his cup of cold coffee.

"What?"

"Ran into a *coyote*." Eddo wondered tiredly what would have happened if he'd gone to the house behind the church of Santa Agneta. "Asked if I had kids and told me to meet him with them the next day."

Tomás's face darkened. "Selling kids?"

"Probably." Eddo caught the edge in Tomás's voice and wished he'd kept his mouth shut. Kids were a sore subject with Tomás; Ana wanted to start a family but Tomás was reluctant. Too many risks involved in police work.

Tomás got up and collected the takeout trash from the table. He took it into the kitchen and reappeared empty-handed just as Vasco, Miguel, and Diego burst into the dining room.

"Miguel found an address for Hermanos Hospitality," Vasco said excitedly

Eddo sat up "So?"

"Same address as Hotel Arias," Vasco said. "Lorena's sex palace in the Centro Histórico."

"Fuck," Tomás said.

Eddo rubbed his eyes, willing his brain to make the connection hovering just on the edge of his understanding. "Could the hotel be one of the sites they're talking about?"

"Hard to know." Miguel slid into the chair next to Vasco, the young man puffed with importance at his latest find. Diego lounged against the edge of the table.

"So a connection between Hugo and the Arias family," Eddo said slowly. "And El Toro."

"And Panama," Vasco said.

"Montopa," Eddo said. "Ideas for next steps?"

"I say we start at the end of the trail and work backwards," Tomás said. "A good look at Hermanos Hospitality and the Hotel Arias."

Eddo nodded. He watched as the other four men planned surveillance on the Hotel Arias, the two younger ones visibly excited at the prospect. Eddo felt a certain uneasiness that Miguel and Diego were learning about the tie to Hugo, but he was too tired to think of an alternate plan.

He got up and made his way upstairs to one of the bedrooms. Anahuac had been bad, but at least he'd found something useful. The flash drive found in the Army raid had shown five userids. If Sonia was **BppBB16003** and Hugo was **Hh23051955**, only three userids were still unidentified. When

Eddo wasn't so tired he'd read all the postings and sort out the information in his mind but already the references to various sites stood out. If they could figure out where the sites actually were maybe they could catch Hugo in the act. Betancourt could hardly keep stalling then.

Ana had put an old pine spool bed in the biggest bedroom and Eddo fell onto it, not bothering to take off his clothes. He stared up at the ceiling, drained but sleepless, and his mind tumbled back to that night with Luz. Her body in his bed, her skin warm against his own. As if it had been yesterday, he remembered the curve of her cheekbone, the taste of the nape of her neck, the way her hair spilled over the pillow like lush, heavy linen.

It hurt all over again, but at least the hurt told him he still had something inside. He wasn't a dead man just yet.

◆

Eddo spent the next morning in the office, reviewing the status of cases with Conchita Félix Pacheco. She was a tiny thing in a designer suit and sleek ponytail, full of ambition and fire. On a personal level she was exhausting, but on a professional level she was the best investigative attorney he had.

They wrapped up before lunch and Conchita gathered the folders from the credenza. "You haven't forgotten about the Young Attorneys Association?" she asked.

"Friday at three, right?"

She nodded, pleased that he'd remembered, and left.

Eddo worked for a few more hours, going over the figures in a fraud case, then closed down his computer and headed out.

Luis Yanez Luna worked out at a gym in one of the big hotels near the *glorieta* Christóbal Colón, the roundabout anchored by the huge statue of Columbus. The hotel parking garage was equipped with security cameras, so Eddo parked a few blocks away and walked through the lobby with his gym bag, flashing a room card at the uniformed hotel doorman as he passed.

The room card got him into the executive locker room by

the spa and gym. There was no one else there, just as he expected, except for the attendant, an older man who handed out towels and kept the spacious locker room clean.

"I'm a guest of Señor Yanez Luna," Eddo said, slipping the man 200 pesos. "We'd like privacy.

It took the old man a few beats to get the message. Eddo smiled and widened his eyes and the attendant left the locker room.

Luis reserved the entire gym twice a week at this time, working out alone as his bodyguard waited outside. Eddo grinned to himself as he wondered if the small fortune Luis was paying for the private gym time included discretion as well. If not, Vasco would probably be the first to hear the new rumor about the head of Financial.

Eddo changed from his suit into workout gear and stowed his clothes in a locker.

The gym was modern and over-decorated. Two walls were tiled to resemble ocean waves and the other two walls were mirrored, so that patrons could watch themselves get seasick as they worked out. The machines were the latest in chrome, with placards by each one giving directions how to use it.

A small room off the main gym was for serious weightlifters, with a bench, free weights, and a heavy bar with interchangeable weight plates. Eddo went in there and turned on the light. More tiled waves encircled the room. If he stood in the near corner he could see the glass doors leading into the spa and gym area as well as the locker room door.

After a few minutes he saw Luis and his bodyguard get off the elevator. Luis went into the locker room. The bodyguard, a beefy type in a dark suit, stationed himself outside the glass door leading to the gym. In about five minutes Federal cops were going to appear and start asking the bodyguard about his carry permit.

Luis, wearing a sleeveless black tee shirt and basketball shorts, came out of the locker room and stretched. Eddo pressed himself into the far wall. Luis realized that there was a light on in the weight room and approached.

Eddo stepped away from the wall. "Hello, Luis."

"Eddo?" Luis blinked. "When did you get back? Why didn't you call?"

Eddo moved fast, pinning Luis's right arm behind him with one hand and closing the weight room door with the other. A shove with his shoulder and Luis's face slammed into the tiled wall. Eddo's cross trainer kicked apart the other man's feet. Feet spread and dick against a wall made most men feel vulnerable.

"What the fuck?" Luis's voice was tight.

"Your man in Anahuac," Eddo said softly, his face close to Luis's. "Turned out to be rotten and I'm wondering how far up it goes."

"What are you talking about?" Luis grimaced from the pain of his arm twisted behind him.

"Sotos Bild. The man you hand picked nearly got me killed."

"What?"

"Your man sold out the investigation," Eddo snarled, remembering the violence that had poured over the street in Anahuac. "He knew just who to call. Funny part was, once he'd delivered the bank they didn't need him. He's in the already overcrowded morgue up there."

"He's dead?"

Eddo jabbed a knee into Luis's ass, shoving the man's crotch hard against the tiled wall and ignoring the resulting sob of pain. "You said he was taking orders straight from you. Nobody else was supposed to be involved."

"Eddo," Luis breathed into the wall. "I swear. I didn't set you up. We're friends. Sotos Bild was my best man up there."

"When things went down in the street, somebody came after me." Eddo yanked Luis forward then smashed him back against the wall. "Was that the plan? Take me out so this investigation could disappear?"

"I swear." Luis wasn't nearly as strong. His attempt to pull away made another landing against the wall that much more painful.

"Who are you working for?" Eddo demanded. "The Zetas? El Chapo? Get Sotos Bild to deliver the bank and you'd split the commission? Or El Toro? Make it looked like the bank closed so we'd drop the investigation? How much were they going to pay you?"

"Nothing," Luis gasped. "I told the kid the cover story and the instructions just like we agreed. Did he get the codes?"

"No codes but you weren't really expecting any, were you?" Eddo knew Luis hadn't been this roughly handled since grade school. He gave the man's twisted arm an upward shove as his knee kept up the pressure. "You gave Sotos Bild my name? My true name?"

"No, no." The wall tiles were wet from the spit dribbling from Luis's mouth and the tears of pain rolling down his cheeks. "Come on, let me go."

Eddo hauled Luis away from the wall and threw him down on the weight bench.

Luis held his arm, his expression a mixture of pain and fear. "Sotos was a good kid," he said huskily. One side of his face bore the imprint of tiny squares and his hair was disheveled. "He was plugged into a lot of stuff going on up there. Knew who the players were. If he tried to cut a deal it was his doing. Not mine."

"And he's not here to say otherwise."

"He had his orders from me and it was exactly what you and I had agreed on." Luis wiped his mouth.

"You think I'm just going to believe that?"

"I'll give you his files," Luis said. "Everything he was working on."

Eddo stood between the door and the weight bench, stomach tight and muscles taut. He'd only told Luis that Banco Limitado was a cartel bank and had omitted the link to Hugo, but couldn't be sure that Betancourt hadn't said anything. Either way, it was hard to know if Luis was clean or not.

Luis dropped his head and rubbed his eyes.

"I'm going to finish this investigation," Eddo finally said, his voice low. "You're going to give me everything you've got and then Financial's out. I may step on your toes, I may foul up something else you're working on. Nobody's going to give a shit. Get in my way and I'll put you down, whether you were pulling Sotos Bild's strings or not."

"I swear, Eddo," Luis started again but then he saw Eddo's

face and stopped. They stared at each other until Luis blinked. He looked away and attempted a half smile. "It just fucking never ends, does it?"

Eddo went into the main gym, fired up a treadmill, and started running fast. Luis shuffled into the locker room, stayed a few minutes, and then came out wearing street clothes. He pushed through the glass doors. The two cops with the bodyguard smiled and nodded and moved off. Luis and the bodyguard got into the elevator.

The reserved time period was over and people drifted into the gym. Eddo dressed and left. He passed Diego in the lobby sipping a cup of coffee and reading a copy of *El Universal*. They didn't acknowledge each other. Eddo knew that within the hour a name would check out of an executive level room and the key he'd used would no longer work.

The next morning there was a package waiting for him in the office. Notes from Sotos Bild's current investigations.

Most of it was shit.

At noon, after he'd paced a dozen miles, he called Conchita into his office and asked her to open a classified investigation into Luis Yanez Luna. No one else would know about the investigation, she would have no assistant to help her, and any leak would be highly dangerous. He told her what happened in Anahuac and gave her Vasco's contact information. He also gave her Sotos Bild's phones, the extra SIM card and everything Miguel had found out about it, as well as information about the four extra Banco Limitado accounts. He had a hunch, he said.

For her own protection, he didn't give Conchita anything connected to Hugo. The CD from the central bank and the list of userids stayed in his office safe, hidden inside the cabinet with the clay smeared across the keyhole.

◆

Chapter 30

Señora Vega was deep in the throes of Christmas and New Year party planning and sharp-tongued with stress. Francesca pouted about needing new clothes for the family's January trip to France. Alejandro managed to squeeze Luz's breast one morning as she handed him his lunch. Luz was glad to escape onto the bus for the four hour trek to Soledad de Doblado on Friday even if it was the dreaded penance weekend.

Maria was ironing in the kitchen. Luz kissed her mother and put down her backpack, ready to take over when Maria pointed wordlessly at a yellow postal notice on the table.

It was a long walk to the post office and Luz was scared every step of the way. After waiting in line for almost half an hour she presented the notice and her identification card to the man behind the counter. He handed her a white envelope with an eagle and an address printed on the upper left hand corner.

When she got back to the house, Juan Pablo and the girls were home from school and Lupe was back from the craft afternoon at Santa Clara. They were all sitting around the table looking like ghosts. Lupe put down her crochet hook. Maria unplugged the iron. Juan Pablo folded his arms and stared doggedly at the wall.

Luz opened the envelope and drew out a single sheet of paper. It was very stiff and very clean. She read that she had not been granted a visa but that she was free to apply again after six weeks from the date of the letter. No reason for the denial of the visa was given.

Luz looked at her mother and shook her head. She pushed the letter to the center of the table and left the house.

She walked blindly through the *barrio*. As the sun went down, Luz found herself near the church. The gate was open and she walked around the gravel path to the cemetery.

Luz brushed some dried leaves off her father's grave. *I've made a mess of things, Papa,* she thought. *And I'm trapped in it.* She squatted by the tombstone until her legs got stiff and then she slumped onto the nearby bench, feeling empty and sad.

She'd wasted her family's money, still had no way to pay for the new baby and college for Juan Pablo, and her penance loomed like a death sentence. On Sunday she'd take the morning bus back to Mexico City and be at Eddo's apartment by early afternoon.

"Hi."

It was Juan Pablo. He had on his big school sweatshirt. His hands were jammed into the kangaroo pocket.

"Are you talking to me now?" Luz asked.

"I was an idiot." Juan Pablo settled onto the bench next to her. "I'm sorry."

Luz didn't reply.

He nudged her arm with his elbow. "So I guess you're going to stick around some?"

"I guess." Luz pulled the sleeves of her sweatshirt over her fingers. Some crickets chirped, but soon it would be too cold for them.

"I'm sorry you didn't get it," Juan Pablo said, slouching so that their shoulders were level.

"No, you're not."

"I'm *trying* to be."

"You know why I wanted to go?" Luz jerked toward him. "If I went to New York City I could be something more than a *muchacha.* Work someplace where I'm not invisible. Go to art school, be a real painter. You can do that there. But here, once you're a *muchacha,* that's all you ever are. It's *what* you are forever and you can never want more."

"Luz--."

"Sometimes I hate being a *muchacha* so much I think I might smash every dish in that *maldita* house." Luz's sadness spilled over. "Do you know what I'm most afraid of? That time will stop as I'm scrubbing a toilet and I'll be stuck in that same moment for the rest of my life. On my knees scrubbing--."

"Here's the deal," Juan Pablo cut in loudly. "I finish Santa Catalina and you stop talking about college. Or I quit Santa Catalina and you stop talking about college. Your choice."

Luz made a hiccupping noise.

"We're not going to talk about college any more," Juan Pablo said. "When I graduate I'm getting a job. You can quit. It'll be my turn."

"No," Luz begged. "I want you to become *licenciado*."

"Stop it, Luz," Juan Pablo said. "We're done talking about this."

"*No*. You're so smart--."

"Stop it." Juan Pablo's voice was harsh and flat. "We both know it's not going to happen. Getting me through Santa Catalina was a miracle and I'm grateful. But that's enough."

"*Dios mio*." Luz realized his jaw was set. "You're hard as nails, aren't you?"

"We'll manage, Luz," Juan Pablo said.

◆

Chapter 31

His talk at the Young Attorneys Association meeting at the Hotel Franco in Polanco had gone well. Despite being a Friday, there was a full house. Conchita had introduced him, referring to notable investigations that were now public knowledge, and everyone asked questions. Eddo had loosened his tie and put Hugo and the scenes from Anahuac out of his mind. He'd even gotten the crowd laughing a couple of times.

He stopped at the gift shop in the hotel lobby and bought a big bouquet of roses and some cigars to take to San Angel. Dinner tonight with Tomás and Ana. An opportunity to make up for being such bad company the last time he was there.

Tonight they'd decide what to do about the surveillance on the Hotel Arias. After a week they had discovered exactly nothing. The problem was twofold. They didn't know what they were looking for and they only had the manpower to cover the hotel in the evenings; everybody had a day job. Whatever new plan they came up with they would share with the guys tomorrow during *fútbol* at La Marquesa.

Rush hour traffic was starting and the milky sky was darkening as he drove out of the hotel parking garage. A dark sedan came out of the garage right after him without stopping. Eddo felt a sting of adrenaline along his spine. He drove a purposely erratic route through the fancy suburb's streets. The sedan stayed with him.

A small truck replaced the sedan. After a few turns Eddo knew they were both tailing him, taking turns riding his bumper, obviously not caring if he knew they were there or not. There were three or four men in the sedan and two in the small truck.

Eddo's cell phone was plugged into the charger. He speed dialed a number and turned on the loudspeaker feature.

"Time's up," he said as soon as Tomás answered. "Got a tail and they know I know."

"Where are you?"

"Polanco. Marina Nacional. Two vehicles."

"I'm already in San Angel," Tomás said. "Can you get on the Periferico? Head this way?"

"Hold on," Eddo said. He swung the car into the right lane, crossed over the interchange with Calzado Melchor Ocampo and stayed to the right. He kept going until the road forked and he was on Avenida Parque Via. The two cars were still in his rearview. "Still with me."

"I'll call in Diego and some others," Tomás said. "Get on the Periferico and get off at Barranca del Muerto. We'll be there by the time you are."

"Okay," Eddo said. "Barranca del Muerto."

He disconnected, driving west through the choppy traffic, and took his gun out of the divider between the seats and slid it under his right thigh. Maybe this was just a warning, but he didn't think so. Either Luis was dirty or Bernal Paz had talked.

A left turn off Reforma across from the Loma Linda restaurant brought him into the posh Lomas Virreyes neighborhood. He'd avoided the area in the past month--not that he usually had much reason to drive through it--half thinking he'd pull up next to some car and Luz would turn and look at him and they'd pretend not to recognize each other. He shook that thought out of his head, turned onto Virreyes and worked his way through the streets leading to the Fuente de Petroleos monument surrounded by rosebushes. The SUV juddered over the old railroad tracks, past the street vendors packing up their wagons. A minute later Eddo swung onto the southbound Periferico highway. The traffic was thick and fast, no backups at all.

His cell phone rang and he hit the talk button.

"Where are you now?" Tomás asked.

"Periferico. Just passed Papalote." The huge yellow children's museum was a well-known landmark.

"Friends still with you?"

"Yep. Kept on me all through Lomas Virreyes." Eddo kept

scanning his mirrors. The big sedan was still behind him, letting two or three cars stay between him and them. The truck was weaving in and out of the three lanes and would be right up his ass in another minute or two. Former *transitos*, Eddo decided.

"We're six. Spread out on both sides of the Barranca del Muerto exit and on Revolución. Come off and work your way east."

Eddo gave Tomás the make, model, and *placa* numbers for both vehicles but didn't disconnect as he concentrated on the aggressive traffic and the bad road surface. He kept the SUV in the middle lane as much as possible; both the right and left lanes of the highway were peppered with recessed gratings that could take out a tire.

He was just about a kilometer from the Barranca del Muerto exit when they made their move. The sedan suddenly accelerated, jinking around the cars in the left lane, almost hitting the concrete barriers on the shoulder of the road, and swung up beside Eddo, pushing him to the right.

Eddo jammed his foot on the accelerator and saw the sign for the Barranca de Muerto exit. The sedan kept pace with him. Eddo saw the front seat passenger window slide down and the ugly muzzle of a sawed-off shotgun appeared.

"Not going to make it," Eddo said out loud and hit the brake.

The SUV's tires locked and there was a screeching squeal as the vehicle fishtailed and slowed, but didn't spin. The sedan shot by and Eddo cranked his wheel to the left and bulled the SUV back into the middle lane, away from the dangerous concrete barriers and recessed gratings.

But the sedan was waiting for him ahead, almost stopped in the middle of the highway as the heavy traffic buzzed by on the left and Eddo had no choice but to swing to the right again.

The boom of the shotgun was followed by the blast of his left rear tire being blown to hell and then the harsh metallic clatter of the vehicle rolling over a recessed grating. The SUV flew up, the right side tires clawing high up the concrete barrier and then Eddo was tumbling sideways, the vehicle airborne. The roof of the SUV hit the highway with a sickening sense of gathering motion and the teeth-jarring grind of metal against tarmac. Eddo managed to keep his hand on the Glock as the SUV rolled side over side over side across all the lanes of traffic and slammed into the concrete barrier on the left side of the highway.

A delivery van smacked into the rear corner of the SUV, swinging it around so that it lay on the passenger's door with the nose pointing down the highway like a crippled horse waiting to be put out of its misery. The noise of the fast-moving highway traffic coming to a screeching halt was deafening.

Dazed from the disorienting tumble and dangling from the seat belt shoulder harness, Eddo managed to cut the ignition. He tried to unfasten the seat belt when there was a shot and the shoulder harness ripped apart where it was attached to the frame, dropping him abruptly into the passenger side of the vehicle. He heard bones grate and pain flashed through his body.

Another shot pounded into the roof of the SUV, then another and another. The windshield was a maze of glass that had crackled but not shattered but it was the only way out of the vehicle that didn't put him into the line of fire. Eddo leveraged himself and dove shoulder first through the crumbly glass mosaic, still gripping the Glock. He bounced over the mangled hood amidst a spray of glittering shards and dropped messily onto the debris-covered road.

All three lanes of traffic were stopped, cars slewed at crazy angles, people screaming and honking in the dirty half darkness. Eddo was dizzy and bloody as he got to his feet but stayed hunched behind the SUV's bulk, bits of tire and glass and plastic clinging to his suit pants and crunching under his shoes.

The sedan was waiting against the concrete barrier on the far right but the small truck was stopped in the middle lane near the SUV. Two men were using the vehicle's open doors as cover. Chips flew around Eddo as a round nicked the barrier behind him and then something slammed into the left side of his head and pressed him against the cold concrete. But he didn't fall and he didn't feel the pain any more. It seemed phenomenally heavy but he sighted the Glock and fired again and again, staggering with the recoil that would have been less with two hands but he couldn't raise his left arm. The door windows of the truck shattered and the men stopped shooting.

Eddo walked toward the center lane, aiming now at the sedan, waiting for a shotgun blast to cut him in half. But the vehicle took off. Eddo fired at the windows, squeezing off the rounds as fast as he could, but the side of the car scraped against the right side concrete barrier and then it was gone.

Eddo lowered the gun, dully aware of the sounds of engines and people screaming, of the stink of blood and burned plastic. He walked over to the small truck. Glass was everywhere, twinkling in the gray light.

The two men were dead, both shot in the head. He looked at their bodies and then for some reason felt he should put the Glock into his shoulder holster. To his surprise he wasn't wearing it. There was blood on his white shirt and on his tie. His knees buckled and Eddo dropped to a kneeling position.

His left side felt very odd, as if it was melting in a blue flame. The pavement seemed very deep, as deep as the ocean, as he pitched face first into it. Something trickled through his hair. Now it hurt to draw a breath and so he stopped trying and just watched a dark puddle seep out from under his cheek. He smiled because it looked like her hair in the water the night he kissed the mermaid.

◆

Chapter 32

Hugo's secretary had done a fine job putting together the ministry's Christmas party, although all she'd really had to do was book the hotel ballroom for Sunday evening and agree to all the event planner's suggestions. Waiters circulated with trays of *ceviche* in martini glasses and mini corn tortillas heaped with caviar. Champagne flutes lined up like wings on either side of an ice sculpture that towered over a vast skirted table.

Hugo was feeling particularly jovial as he greeted his guests. Over the past few weeks he'd orchestrated solutions to problems that would have caused a lesser man to fold. As a result Lorena was creeping up in the polls, now trailing Arturo Romero by only 12 points. Romero was helping by staying in Oaxaca and being a starchy intellectual whose public appearances revolved around foreign affairs or legal reform; hardly issues to excite the average Mexican voter.

Lorena was across the room, fabulous in a white satin gown, acting like the presidential candidate that she was. Fernando was there as well, entertained by Hugo's senior staff. It was clear that Fernando still suspected nothing.

Key PAN politicos circled around, sniffing the wind, as did senior officials from other ministries. Everyone was wondering about Lorena and Romero going head-to-head for the PAN nomination but no one was talking about it.

Hugo had just helped himself to another delicacy from a passing waiter, his wife Graciela smiling nervously at his elbow, when Luis Yanez Luna edged through the crowd and came up beside him.

"Luis," Hugo beamed. "I don't believe you've met my wife."

He introduced Graciela to Luis. They exchanged

pleasantries and then she had the good sense to excuse herself, saying she had to mingle.

"Excellent evening," Luis said. "I'm glad you didn't cancel."

"Cancel?"

"Cortez Castillo's attempted carjacking."

"Yes." Hugo nodded gravely. "The random violence in this city is out of control."

"I read about it in yesterday's newspaper," Luis said. "Horrific crime."

"Shot in the head." Hugo eased past a group of women in evening dresses.

Luis followed until they were relatively alone on the edge of the party. "How bad is it?"

"He's in a coma. Hooked up to a million monitors, bandaged up to his eyeballs."

"Did you see him?"

"Yes." Hugo didn't have to feign a shudder. Cortez had been unrecognizable. "Yesterday in the hospital. Neurologist says his brain swelled and recovery is unlikely. Marca Cortez issued a press release. Family moved him to a private clinic in Puebla this morning. If he survives he'll be a vegetable."

"Good," Luis muttered. "Fucking scary bastard."

"Won't be roughing you up again any time soon."

"I held my own," Luis said.

Hugo made as if to bring his knee up to groin height and Luis flinched. Hugo chuckled and raised his glass. "To Eduardo and his family."

"To friends with the right skill set."

Hugo snorted. "To a direct approach."

It was a slam against the botched job in Anahuac and Luis glowered for a moment, then touched his glass to Hugo's. They drank. Hugo waved to a passing waiter who refilled their glasses. A few partygoers drifted over and they made polite conversation for awhile. When the others moved on Hugo maneuvered so that Luis ended up in a corner by a big palm and Hugo's back was to the rest of the party. "I'll go to Cortez's office tomorrow," Hugo said. "Express my sympathies to the staff. There's some woman there nobody knows. She can be the acting head of the department for awhile."

Luis bobbed his head. "I'll let her know that Financial is at her disposal."

"Find out if he passed anything to her."

"I doubt it." Luis drank more champagne and eyed an attractive woman in a halter dress across the room. "Cortez was such a solitary bastard. Never did anything more interesting than play *fútbol* with his old police cronies."

"You'd better hope you're right," Hugo said. "Banco Limitado is back in operation and I want it to stay that way."

"I've got a stake in this, too," Luis reminded Hugo.

As if he needed reminding. Every peso that went to Luis to keep people like Cortez from finding out was another peso diverted away from Lorena's campaign.

"I'm still not convinced Bernal Paz didn't give Cortez something," Hugo said. "Keep looking. I don't like loose ends."

"Relax," Luis said. "I know what I'm doing."

"You know how to sleep with Cortez's secretary to find out his lunch schedule," Hugo said.

◆

Chapter 33

Luz stood in front of Eddo's apartment door, trying not to hyperventilate. All the wrong words ran through her head.

Señor Cortez. I see you have company. Is she a prostitute? Because I'm not.

Hello, Eduardo Martín Bernardo Cortez Castillo. I hope you realize I didn't take your maldita *200 pesos.*

Eddo. It's me. I love you.

It was four weeks since they'd met. What if she rang the bell and he didn't recognize her? She'd pulled her hair back, put on makeup, and was wearing the Dolce and Gabbana jeans, a simple white tee shirt, and the black sweater she'd worn to the visa interview. The Prada tote was tucked under her arm.

She looked around nervously. Eddo's apartment was on the lobby floor. A uniformed guard in an enclosure by the courtyard gate had buzzed her into the building. The big marble and glass lobby was empty except for a nicely dressed man who was probably waiting for someone. He paid no attention to Luz.

She took a breath and pressed the bell.

The door was opened by powerful, thickset man of medium height. He wore pressed khaki pants, a pale blue button-down oxford shirt, expensive shoes, and a gun slung under his arm as if he was in a *norteamericano* police movie.

"Uh," Luz said.

"Fuck," he said. "Are you Luz de Maria?" He pulled her into the apartment. Someone came in right behind her. The door shut with a sharp click.

Luz found herself surrounded by five men, all staring at her like schoolboys who'd found a dead cat. One was the man from the lobby. All were armed. None were Eddo.

"I'm sorry," Luz faltered. "I must have rung the wrong

bell."

"Can I see your identification?" asked the man who'd opened the door.

She was hemmed in. Luz handed over her wallet.

"Knew it," the man said smugly. "You're as pretty as he said you were." He handed back her wallet and said to the others, "*la novia.*" The girlfriend.

As the men nodded and smiled at her, Luz realized she was in the right apartment after all. There was the green suede sofa and chairs, the iron kitchen barstools, and even the familiar basket of fruit on the bar. But the place was littered with packing boxes and rolls of bubble wrap, as if Eddo was moving.

"Hey, Luz de Maria ought to see some ID, too," the man said. He flipped open a worn leather wallet so Luz could see a shiny Highway Patrol badge and a police credential with a photo identifying him as Lieutenant Tomás Valderama Castro. "Just so you know you're among friends."

Each of the men in the apartment came forward and showed her some sort of police credential, grinning and nodding at her like she was someone important who made them a little nervous. They were all cops; two others from Highway Patrol, one from the Judicial Police, and one from the Diplomatic Protection police. Valderama Castro was the most senior and very obviously in charge.

As Luz looked at the badges, the situation suddenly made sense. Eddo was a *drogista*. That's why he hadn't told her what he did. Now he'd been arrested and the police were confiscating his things. Luz didn't know why they would think she was his girlfriend but if they did she could be in big trouble.

Luz pulled on her stupid face and sidled toward the door. "Yes, well, thank you for showing me."

"Did you have a date tonight?" Valderama Castro asked, stepping in her way. "Eddo didn't tell me."

"Not a problem," Luz murmured, trying to keep sidling.

"*Cristo,*" Valderama Castro swore. "You don't know about the accident."

"Accident," Luz repeated. Maybe that's what they were calling it now when *drogistas* got caught.

"On Friday," Valderama Castro said. "Car's a total loss."

"A real accident?" Luz asked in spite of herself.

"It was a near thing," Valderama Castro said. "Concussion and a cracked collarbone--."

"And a--," one of the others started to say but Valderama Castro jerked his head for him to shut up as Luz staggered a little. Valderama Castro caught her by the elbow and steered her to the sofa. She sank gratefully onto the soft green suede. She loved that sofa.

Valderama Castro sat next to her. "Car rolled across all three lanes of southbound traffic on the Periferico. Eddo went headfirst out the windshield."

"He went out the windshield?" Luz gasped. *"On the Periferico?"*

"It was a *monster,*" one of the younger men said excitedly from behind the kitchen bar. Luz looked at him as he went on. "Man, *el jefe* is tough! The car rolled across the highway and then a truck smashed into it, too. So they're shooting, see, and *el jefe*, he's trapped in the car and he can't get the seat belt off because he's like stuck and they shoot the seat belt apart. *Oye,* how lucky was that?! So *el jefe* goes out the windshield and over the hood and he's kept his gun the whole time and he starts shooting back and takes out two of them, *Cristo*, just by the exit." He grinned at Luz, proud as hell of *el jefe*. "We was there and then Tomás is calling and, *Cristo*, we drove down the wrong side because traffic was stopped and there he was, lying right in the middle of the road with two dead guys, like the devil's own *pistolero.*"

"*What?*" Luz shrilled.

"Shut up, Diego!" Valderama Castro barked at the same time. He shook his head at Luz. "They made it look like a carjacking attempt. But it was de la Madrid Acosta. You have a right to know."

"The Minister of Public Security?" Why did the young cop call Eddo *el jefe*? Was Eddo some kind of cartel chief? Luz could hardly breathe, let alone think.

"Look, Luz." Valderama Castro flicked his eyes around the room and the other men melted away. He turned back to her.

"When the government wanted an anticorruption pitbull, de la Madrid Acosta got just what he asked for."

"Anticorruption pitbull?" Luz echoed faintly.

"Yeah, well, no doubt Eddo described his job in the ministry to you a little differently. Federal attorney? Prosecutor? Director of the ministry's Office of Special Investigations? Right?"

Luz nodded vaguely. Of course Eddo had said those things.

"You know that big PEMEX thing was Eddo."

"*Oh.*" PEMEX was the state-owned petroleum company. Two years ago the government had recovered 300 million pesos and jailed senior PEMEX officials for embezzlement. It had been one of the Betancourt government's few major successes.

"But de la Madrid Acosta apparently never thought that Eddo would find *his* dirty laundry."

"*Dios mio,*" Luz moaned softly, catching on immediately.

"Yeah," Valderama Castro said. "Looks like a little deal with the El Toro cartel."

He paused, waiting for Luz to say something but she couldn't. Her mind was reeling.

"But *Los Hierros* is going to put an end to this, Luz de Maria," Valderama Castro said firmly. "We're not going to lose *el jefe.*"

Luz dropped her jaw.

"Hey, Tomás." Another young cop leaned over the kitchen bar with a bottle in his hand. "Do we have time to toast *el jefe's* lady? We found some Cuervo Especial."

"Thanks, Miguel. I think she could use it." Valderama Castro pulled Luz to her feet. "Are you all right?"

"No. Yes." Luz was overwhelmed, hit by too much unexpected information in too short a time. Eddo was a federal attorney and *el jefe* of *Los Hierros*. And she'd slept with him. "Thank you for trusting me," she managed.

"He said he was going to tell you."

Luz blinked and opened her mouth to ask how he knew that, when a metallic screeching sound made them both flinch.

"Give us a hand, Tomás." Two of the cops tried to pull the big stainless steel refrigerator away from the wall. Others packed dishes and glasses into boxes.

Luz sat on one of the stools in front of the bar as the cop named Miguel poured the expensive tequila into tall shot glasses. With Valderama Castro's help the refrigerator gradually slid forward. The lieutenant unplugged it, picked up two grimy pieces of paper from the floor that had been caught underneath and handed them to Luz. "This must have been for you," he said.

Luz matched the pieces together along the tear line.

> *Dear Luz –*
>
> *I have an unavoidable early morning meeting. Make yourself some decent coffee, and when you want to go home take a sitio taxi from the stand around the corner. Taxi fare is on the dresser.*
>
> *Leave your number before you go. My cell is 55 5406 6200, the house is 5257 1490.*
>
> *Can I take you to dinner on Wednesday? And to the store of your choice. I owe you a blouse--a debt I'm happy to pay.*
>
> *Eddo*

♦

Tomás ushered Luz into an old house in a part of Mexico City she'd rarely visited. Two of the young men from Eddo's apartment, Miguel and Diego, came with them.

The entrance was warmly decorated in shades of terracotta and brown, with heavy wood trim, antique Spanish furniture, and a muted tapestry on the wall. A handsome man in glasses a few years older than Luz closed the door behind them.

"Luz de Maria, this is Vasco," Tomás said and put down the suitcase they'd brought with them.

Vasco shook her hand and smiled. "A pleasure, despite the circumstances," he said.

"So how's he doing?" Tomás asked.

"All right, I guess." Vasco nodded at a flight of stairs carpeted with a patterned runner. "Still hasn't eaten much. Won't take what the doctor gave him for the pain, either."

Luz followed Tomás up the stairs, torn between fear at the

strange situation and elation that she would see Eddo again. A door at the top was halfway open. They walked into a large bedroom decorated in the same comfortable style as the hallway downstairs.

Eddo was stretched out on top of the bed. He had on gray sweatpants. His upper body was bare but a thick bandage wound around his left shoulder and the upper part of his chest. A sling kept his left arm close to his side. Purple bruises seeped out from under the white gauze of the bandages and spread across his pectoral muscle.

The left side of his face was swollen and discolored from hairline to cheekbone. Much of his hair on that side had been shaved off and a row of butterfly bandages closed a gash that extended at least three inches around the side of his head. A cold pack like the kind a coach had once given Juan Pablo was on the bed, along with a copy of *Reforma* and a remote control. Opposite the bed, a television was broadcasting a *fútbol* game with the sound off.

"Hey, Eddo," Tomás called softly. "Somebody here to see you."

Eddo slowly rolled his head in the direction of Tomás's voice. His eyes opened in a puffy squint.

"How's it going?" Tomás asked.

"The food's like shit and the nurses are ugly," Eddo said. His voice was hoarse.

"This ought to cheer you up. Look who I've brought."

Luz stepped out from behind Tomás, her heart hammering.

Eddo's mouth fell open.

"She packed your stuff," Tomás said, resting the suitcase against an old dresser.

"How'd she get here?" Eddo's expression changed from shock to tension.

"Came by your place while we were packing," Tomás said slowly, watching both Eddo and Luz. "We talked."

"Give us a minute," Eddo said.

"I'll be downstairs with the guys." Tomás shot Luz a glance she couldn't fathom, then walked out and shut the door.

Luz was left alone near the foot of the bed. The

awkwardness was palpable.

"If I'd known you were coming," Eddo said tightly. "I would have dressed for the occasion." He plucked at the sling with his right hand and Luz realized how much he must hate being like this. Dependent. Not in control.

"I packed some of your things." Luz made a tiny motion toward the suitcase. She'd found the Hermés scarf and the tiny gold buttons from her blouse in his sock drawer. "Clothes. Your toothbrush. The clock. *El Cid.*"

She trailed off.

He blinked at her.

The room got deathly quiet.

"You're married," Eddo said.

"What?"

"You're married," he repeated, struggling into a sitting position against the pillows. "Your husband was away or you had an argument with him and amused yourself with me for a day."

"*No,*" Luz exclaimed.

"No?" Eddo bit off the word, the pain in his eyes terrible to see. "I thought there was something there, Luz, and then you just *disappeared.* You didn't leave your number. You didn't call. No explanation. Nothing. *Of course you're married.*"

"You left 200 pesos on the dresser," Luz blurted. "I thought you left me money because you thought I was a *puta.*"

"*Are you joking?*" Eddo's face went gray with pain as he started to swing his legs off the bed. Luz moved to his side and eased him back against the pillows. He grabbed her wrist. "Why would you say that? I swear to the Holy Mother I never thought that."

"I just saw the money and that's what I thought," Luz said wretchedly.

"I left you taxi fare."

"I didn't see your note until today," Luz said. She took a deep breath and let it out in a rush of words. "Two hundred pesos is a whole day's salary to me. I'm a *muchacha.* A *muchacha planta.*"

"A *planta?*" Eddo let go of her wrist.

"Yes." She'd done the penance and it felt awful.

"Why?"

"Why what?"

"*Why such a fucking bullshit story*," Eddo shouted, making her jump. "If you never wanted to see me again, all you had to do was *keep staying away*. Why bother to come here with some *maldita* bullshit story about being a *muchacha*? Do you really think I'm so stupid?"

"No, no." Luz felt herself falling apart as she sank onto the edge of the bed, totally unprepared for his disbelief. "It's true. I work for the Vega family in Lomas Virreyes."

"You're an art teacher," Eddo insisted.

"No, I'm a *muchacha*. I shouldn't have even *talked* to someone like you. I'm so sorry. I knew better."

"What the hell . . ." Eddo's right hand moved restlessly across his bandaged chest and then he pointed at her. "You know English. French. Taught me about art. We talked politics."

"I talked to you like I talk to no one else." Luz wanted to die. "But I'm just a *muchacha*."

"I don't believe it," Eddo said roughly.

"That doesn't change anything," Luz said, suddenly angry at what she had lost and was losing all over again in some strange house. "My father was dead and there was no money and I was the oldest. I left school and cried for a year but it's what girls like me do to feed our families."

There was silence.

"How old were you?" Eddo asked at length.

"Sixteen."

Eddo looked away, as if he'd finally understood. Silence filled the room again. Luz watched the television, too drained to move.

"Why did you go over to the apartment?" Eddo asked. "Why now?"

Luz shrugged, unable to meet his eyes. "Father Santiago said for my penance I had to tell you who I really was."

"You went to confession?"

"Well, I'd slept with you, you know," Luz said uncomfortably.

"*Madre de Dios*," Eddo said. He started to laugh but a spasm of pain contorted his face. "Shit. I can't even laugh."

Luz picked up the cold pack, glad for the distraction. "What hurts the most?"

"My head. It feels like it's in a vise."

"Lie still," Luz clucked at him. She gently pressed the cold pack against the butterfly bandages on the left side of his head.

Eddo closed his eyes.

"Why didn't you tell me you were an attorney?" Luz asked.

"Didn't I?"

"It doesn't matter." Luz adjusted the cold pack and inspected the butterfly bandages. "You must have a head like concrete. Tomás told me you jumped through the windshield."

"What else did Tomás tell you?"

"*Los Hierros*," Luz said. "I'm very proud of you, for what it's worth."

"I was going to tell you."

Luz moved the cold pack again. "I'll keep the secret."

"Thank you," Eddo said, eyes still closed. He exhaled. "I'm sorry I left that morning the way I did. I had a breakfast meeting at Los Pinos. I should have woken you up, got your number. Made sure I knew where things stood between us."

"It doesn't matter," Luz said. "You go to Los Pinos and I scrub toilets."

Eddo was still as Luz held the cold pack. "Do you regret being with me?" he asked. "Is that really why you went to confession?"

"I committed the sin of falsehood." Luz's throat was tight. "I pretended to be someone else."

"I don't think so," Eddo said. "Aren't you the person who drew me pictures and showed me lunatic Russian artists? Trashed Lorena and ate apples in my bed?"

"Yes."

"Then you're the same woman." The hazel eyes opened and bored into her. "The day we shared was the best day of my life."

Even bruised and broken he was a taut and powerful presence. Luz was drawn to him so strongly she couldn't stand it.

Eddo reached up and pulled at her hand. Luz dropped the cold pack. He laced his fingers with hers and pressed their hands to his chest. "I've got an investigation I can't let go," Eddo said. "It'll probably get worse before it gets better but one way or another I'm going to nail Hugo and be done. Say you'll celebrate with me when it's over."

"It's bad, isn't it?" Luz rubbed the bandages on his chest with her fingertips.

"Another few weeks to run things down and then we'll put it all on the president's desk. Force him to do something."

"President Betancourt?" It was almost too much for Luz to absorb.

"Yes. Say you'll wait, Luz. It won't be forever."

The look on his face said he truly didn't care who she was because he knew the real Luz and wanted to be with her. He would fight and he would win and she'd be there for him when he did. *Rodrigo and Jimena.* There was a low, familiar humming in Luz's head.

"Tell me you'll take what the doctor gave you and I will," Luz said.

"I'll take it."

They smiled at each other and Luz's heart danced in her chest.

She shook out a pill from the little bottle on the bedside table. Eddo swallowed it with some water, then made room for Luz beside him on the bed. She pressed her cheek against his unhurt shoulder and tucked her arm around his waist. Despite the sling, his body was achingly familiar.

"I thought about you a lot," he murmured. "Took me a long time to realize you weren't coming back."

"I'm sorry," Luz said against his skin.

"Me, too. I never should have left without waking you up."

Luz closed her eyes. For a few wonderful minutes the room felt like heaven.

"Until this is over, you don't know me, haven't seen me, nothing," Eddo said, breaking their silence. "You've never been to this house. Anything you know about Eduardo Cortez Castillo is just what you read in the paper."

"Oh." Luz really got it then; the danger and the risk of what he was doing.

The door creaked open. Both were instantly alert. But it was only Tomás and Miguel.

"Probably should be getting Luz de Maria out of here, Eddo," Tomás said apologetically.

"I know," Eddo said. "Luz, give Tomás your cell phone."

Blushing, Luz sat up and found her phone. The lieutenant keyed in his number, adding it to the phone's short list of contacts. He showed her how she could speed dial him just by pressing the number 4. Luz wrote her cell number and the Vega's address on a pad on the bedside table.

"Luz," Eddo said. "Keep your phone with you all the time. If anything worries you, call Tomás immediately."

"Okay." Luz bent and kissed his unbruised cheek, wanting to do something for him but there wasn't anything to do. She picked up the Prada tote and Tomás opened the door for her.

"*Mi corazón*," Eddo called. "Promise me something."

Luz turned around in the doorway. "What?"

"Take your pictures to Jardin del Arte some Sunday. They're better than anything there."

"All right." Luz nodded, surprised. "I'll tell you how I made out."

"Luz. I meant what I said. The best day."

It was as if an invisible thread connected them, shining and tuning with emotion. It would stretch as far as it needed to, and when he was ready, Eddo would wind it all the way back to her.

"I know," Luz said. "It was the best day ever."

♦

It was a dirty dry *la sopa* night. The city had never seemed so grimy, the buildings so drab, the people so sullen. Luz gave Tomás the Vega's address then sat quietly in the car, her thoughts trying to catch up to her emotions. In the back, Diego and Miguel were silent, as if her bodyguards.

"You okay?" Tomás asked after 15 minutes of silence.

"He should be in the hospital," Luz said.

"He is," Tomás replied evenly. "Just like it said in the newspaper."

"He . . . oh." Luz realized what he was saying.

"He'll come through this, Luz." Tomás talked as he drove, telling her about how he and Eddo had joined Highway Patrol at the same time. They were the only two college boys, and naturally gravitated toward each other, often having to prove with their fists that they were tough enough for the job. Together with Vasco they'd organized *Los Hierros*, but Eddo was the driving force. *Los Hierros* only existed because of Eddo's personality and Marca Cortez money. They would keep it secret as long as they could.

"Marca Cortez?" Luz asked.

"*Talavera,*" Tomás said. "The Cortez family owns Marca Cortez, half of Puebla, and the land the new Volkswagen factory is on. Eddo is still the family's legal advisor and sits on the board of directors. Don't know how he finds the time. It helps that he never sleeps."

Eddo is rich. Richer than the Vegas, even richer than the Portillos. "Puebla," Luz said. "The city or the state?"

"Both."

Phenomenally rich.

The car pulled up next to the Vega's gate. "Nice place," Tomás said.

Luz unfastened her seat belt then turned to him. "Did he say I was an art teacher?"

"Yes. Said you took him to a museum. That must have been something."

"I'm not a teacher," Luz said. "I'm a *muchacha.*"

Tomás raised his eyebrows. "You making a joke?"

"No."

"You don't look like a *muchacha.*"

"We had a mix-up but he knows now." Luz swallowed hard. "Is that going to be a problem for you?"

The muscular man stared over the steering wheel, his face immobile. A street light illuminated the other side of Fray Payo de Rivera, causing the concertina wire topping the neighbor's wall to look like spun candy.

"I only care that you're not a bitch to him," Tomás said finally. "He's my best friend and he's going through a rough time."

"Thank you." Luz impulsively kissed him on the cheek. "For taking care of him."

Tomas's expression didn't change but Luz knew he was blushing. "Call if you need anything," he said gruffly. "Number 4 on your phone."

Luz said goodbye to Diego and Miguel, who both acted as if they hadn't heard the exchange, then went inside. She was in bed listening to Rosa snore before Luz recalled that Eddo had called her *mi corazón.*

My heart.

♦

Chapter 34

On Wednesday Luz had her first free afternoon since being grounded by Señora Vega. She hustled down Fray Payo de Rivera to the intersection with Virreyes, crossed the wide boulevard divided by a grassy median, and then walked up Monte Athos to the fancy shopping area on the northern end of that street. She spent 68 pesos from her emergency fund at the Batiz art store on two small canvases and some oil paints.

Luz was heading back, passing La Sumesa, the gourmet grocery store, when her cell phone rang. She fumbled it out of her backpack. The display read *Valderama*.

"What happened?" she gasped in lieu of a greeting.

"Luz de Maria?" There were traffic sounds in the background.

"Yes. What happened?"

"Nothing. He's fine. Up and walking around. Irritating people."

Luz sagged against the side of the La Sumesa store, right beside the bulletin board with notices advertising English lessons and jobs for chauffeurs with excellent references. "That's good," she gulped.

"I'm heading toward your neighborhood. I want to talk to you."

They agreed to meet at the cafe around the corner from the art store. Luz window shopped for 15 minutes, not daring to go into any of the upscale shops in just her old jeans, sneakers, and a sweatshirt. Tomás showed up just when he'd said he would, dressed in a beautiful double-breasted gray suit and red silk paisley tie.

"Luz de Maria," he said politely, keeping whatever thoughts he had about her appearance under wraps. He ushered her into the café and they sat down at a small table. The waitress gave Luz a hard stare and Luz automatically pulled on her stupid face. Tomás said "Coffee?" to Luz. She nodded and he ordered two. The waitress stalked off.

"You keeping your cell phone with you all the time?" Tomás asked, fiddling with the empty ashtray.

"Yes."

They sat in silence until the waitress delivered the coffee and went back behind the counter.

"Eddo had some stuff in his office at the ministry that we need to get out." Tomás poured three sugar packets into his cup and stirred. His voice was low.

"What sort of stuff?" Luz asked, matching his tone.

"Some of the evidence about what de la Madrid Acosta has been up to."

"Oh."

"I had an idea that you could help us out."

"Go on," Luz said cautiously.

"We've been watching the building since the accident, trying to get someone inside but they've never been able to get near Eddo's office. The one person with access can't afford to get burned."

Luz nodded her understanding.

"At night the building is empty," Tomás went on. "Except for a cleaning crew that comes in at 11:00 pm. Two male supervisors. Everyone else is female."

The coffee in Luz's mouth suddenly turned to bile.

"You could pretend to be one of the cleaning crew," Tomás said, watching her face. "Get into the building. Get the stuff out of his office."

Luz didn't say anything, her thoughts swinging between humiliation and the desire to help.

"Time is not on our side, Luz de Maria. We have to do it before the weekend. There aren't any cleaners then and the office will probably be searched. The evidence will be gone."

Luz pressed her hands between her knees. Friday morning Rosa would leave for Cholula or Manuel's car. Marisol left weekdays after *la comida*. There were no parties planned at the

Vega house for the coming weekend.

"I could do it Friday night," she said.

◆

Chapter 35

Max walked through the bar of the Hotel Arias. The place was full, the dark paneling and heavy draperies obscured by wealthy young people in suits and ties or elegant dresses, having a drink at the famed Hotel Arias after work and before a late dinner or theater date. Jazz played just loud enough to soften the edges of the conversations and the clink of glasses. There was no one there Max knew; Lazaro was working late and would meet him in a few hours.

There were two other bartenders behind the mahogany counter with Alvaro, helping to deal with the Friday evening crowd. Max squeezed between an Armani suit and a Chanel purse and picked up his glass of ruby port. He nodded thanks to Alvaro, eased his way out of the crush and went into his father's office.

The heavy door blocked out the chatter and music from the bar. He didn't turn on the light, just dropped his planner and cell phone on the desk and took his drink to the window. There was a filigreed iron security grid on the other side of the glass but he could see the manicured garden and the low wall that separated the hotel property from the street. The security guard was there, along with the parking valets in their green vests and black pants.

Max wanted out of all of it. Lorena wasn't a candidate; she was a money-sucking machine, buying baubles, flyers, radio air time and full color ads in fashion magazines with money she thought was coming from Hugo's media empire. Romero wasn't doing any of that but was still ahead in the polls. The only thing Lorena's campaign could do to even the odds was pay the party faithful before the nominating convention.

Max held his breath every time Lorena met someone new and wanted a lunch date. She was becoming less and less discreet and at some point either Hugo or the president were going to find out. Max would be blamed, he knew it, and Hugo would throw him to the wolves on the other side of the postings page.

But it was Max's role in getting rid of Eduardo Cortez Castillo, who apparently was more than a *talavera* salesman, that had him waking up in a cold sweat. Four men had shown up at the hotel the day that **CH5299xyz9** had said they would. They'd been crude cartel thugs from Chihuahua and walked into the bar like they owned it, which had nearly given Alvaro a stroke. Max had shown them a picture of Cortez and a few notes from Hugo on the man's schedule. When they took their worn cowboy boots and greasy shirts out of the hotel Max had logged in as **1612colcol** to say that the team could not return.

The men from Chihuahua had been successful and Cortez Castillo was now a vegetable. Lorena and Hugo had celebrated in the bar with a champagne lunch and then a romp in their favorite room.

Max finished the port. He should have brought the bottle. On the other side of the window, a big SUV pulled up to the valet stand and one of the valets ran around to the driver's side. Max envied those valets the simplicity of their lives.

He pulled himself away from the window and turned on his father's computer. The screen glowed blue across the keyboard.

The door opened, throwing a wedge of light into the room. A man in a suit walked in, shut the door behind him, and stood with his back pressed against it.

"This is a private office," Max snapped.

"You're Max Arias, aren't you?" the man asked.

Max took his hands off the keyboard. "If you're looking for the manager he's in the restaurant right now."

The man stepped away from the door. Max couldn't see his face in the dim room. "You're running a company called Hermanos Hospitality out of this hotel," the man said. The voice was younger than Max's and touched with nervousness.

Max's tie was too tight as the blood rushed to his head. "Never heard of it," he managed.

"Money is being sent to Hermanos Hospitality from

accounts in a bank associated with the El Toro cartel," the man continued. "The accounts are in the name of the Minister of Public Security Hugo de la Madrid Acosta and his son."

Max couldn't have reacted even if he'd wanted.

The man put a sheet of paper on the desk. It was a printout of micropostings including some by **1612colcol**. "A man named Eduardo Cortez Castillo has figured out the whole thing. Money comes out of some operation the El Toro cartel has near Anahuac, filters through a front company in Panama, moves around the minister's bank accounts, and is finally sent by money order to Hermanos Hospitality."

"I don't know what you're talking about," Max said without breathing.

The man made a gesture taking in the office and the hotel beyond. "Maybe Cortez will ask Lazaro Zuno what he knows. He's the software engineer who set up that page where all the attachments are the same."

The blood left Max's head as fast as it had come.

The man went on. "Took a long time, making all the connections. Zuno is a systems consultant. Does some work for the Canadian conglomerate that owns the site. Sits in this hotel bar at least three nights a week waiting for you. But you're busy with Lorena's campaign. Which is the only Mexican entity on the postings site. You see how things connect?"

"Cortez is in a coma," Max said.

"Eduardo Cortez Castillo isn't in a private hospital in Puebla. That was all a fake. Unless somebody stops him he's going to blow your whole operation wide open."

"Who are you?" Max asked when he was sure he wasn't going to pass out.

"Call me Juan."

"Presumably there's something you want?"

"Cortez is always in charge." The man leaned over the desk and for the first time Max had a clear view of his face. The eyes behind the glasses were glazed with anger and self-loathing. "Everybody loves him. They'll go to the ends of the earth for him. But I do all the work. *I* do it."

"You want his job." Max said.

"You could say that." The man grinned, flashing white teeth. He was definitely younger than Max, and hungry to make his mark.

Something inside Max relaxed. He'd been in service to politicians for nearly 20 years and had met this kind before. Ambitious, with information to sell to the highest bidder.

They never lasted.

◆

Chapter 36

The tall building faced Reforma. The service door was at the rear of the building, in an alley parallel to the big boulevard. A straggly line of cleaning women, dressed in old clothes just like Luz, waited to get in for the 11:00 pm shift. Luz put on her stupid face, both to blend in and to keep from betraying her nervousness.

Luz wore jeans and a sweatshirt and held her old backpack. She had Eddo's keys and had memorized the safe combination. Tomás and two others were positioned around the office building and she knew the plan: in quick, out quick. The rendezvous point was a newsstand a block away.

As Luz followed the line down the stairs, the plan was immediately in trouble. Uniformed security personnel inspected the bags of anyone entering or exiting.

She did what the other women did and walked through an archway by the guards' table. A beeping started and the guard barked at her to empty her pockets. Luz showed the keys, saying they were her house keys. Her backpack was given a cursory check and shoved back across the table. Luz followed the group into the service elevator. A few of the people seemed to know each other and muttered greetings. Luz pressed the button for the twelfth floor.

Workers got off at other floors. No one got off with Luz. The elevator doors swished behind her and she was left in a darkened hallway with a gray linoleum floor. The only light peeped from around a partially opened door.

"Hey, nobody's going to pay you to pose for pictures." The door smacked open all the way and a man walked out. "Usual girl is sick. You the sub?"

Luz nodded, her knees shaking.

"Put your stuff in here," the man barked, gesturing to where he'd just come from. It was a janitorial closet about the size of a bathroom. Cleaning supplies were piled against brooms and a large upright vacuum cleaner. An upholstered office chair was pulled up in front of a rickety folding table with a small television on it.

Luz put her backpack on the floor. The man pointed to a bucket containing trash bags, rags, and bottles of bleach and furniture polish. She picked it up. The man locked the closet door, crossed the hall, and unlocked a door. He relocked it after they'd passed through and Luz found herself standing in a wide carpeted hallway.

"Ashtrays first, then dust, water the plants, empty trash cans. When you're done come back for the vacuum cleaner." The man strode down the hall, unlocking doors with a passkey dangling from a long thin chain attached to his belt. He was short and round, with breath like sour beer. He wore brown pants and a grease-stained gray shirt. Luz wondered what he did while the cleaning people worked.

"Break at 2:00 am," he went on. "No vacuuming, no break. Done by 5:00 am."

Luz transferred the bucket to her other hand as she followed him down the hall. She counted 14 doors before they reached the reception area with damask sofas and brass tables that Tomás had described. The door opposite the reception area had a plaque reading "Director, Eduardo Cortez Castillo."

They moved on. The hallway on the other side of the reception area had 16 offices.

"Start here and work your way back," the man said after unlocking the last door. He turned and walked back the way they'd come. When he disappeared around the corner Luz put down the bucket and padded noiselessly after him on the thick carpet. She didn't see him again but she heard the unmistakable sound of the service door being unlocked and opened, then closed and relocked. Luz ran into Eddo's office.

It was the domain of a powerful man. An enormous L-shaped desk faced the door to the hall. There was a credenza against the wall; 12 feet of gleaming dark wood. Upholstered wing chairs in front of the desk were for important visitors. A big conference table and chairs took up a quarter of the room and books lined the far wall.

The cabinet was behind the desk just as Tomás had said it would be. Luz knelt, sheltered by the desk, and unlocked it. Inside was a two drawer combination safe. Luz spun the dial, remembering the instructions, and the drawer slid open.

Heart thumping, Luz found the paper with the list and the CD in a glassine envelope.

She hurriedly searched Eddo's desk. The deep drawers on the left side contained an assortment of food and bottled water, including a dozen chocolate protein bars, the kind that Señora Velasquez sometimes sold in the *abarrotes* shop for the staggering price of 30 pesos each. The drawers on the right under the computer held expensive dress shirts still folded and wrapped in paper from the dry cleaners. Finally in the center drawer she found a scissors.

She cut the printing from the paper into slips, folded each one into a little square and slipped them into her sneakers. Then she stuffed the CD into her panties.

Luz shut the safe, relocked the cabinet, ran to the service door and banged on it.

"What do you want?" The manager's voice was slurred.

"I'm not feeling well," Luz called through the door.

"If you puke you clean it up," he shouted back.

Luz's mind raced, trying to think of another way out that didn't involve abandoning her backpack and her precious cell phone. But she could think of nothing.

She picked up the bucket of cleaning supplies and went into the first office.

◆

By the time she had done all the offices on the first half of the hallway and was back to Eddo's, Luz was shaky with fatigue and hunger and residual adrenaline.

She sat on the floor behind the desk again, as if it was her private hiding place, and took a chocolate protein bar and a bottle of water from the desk drawer. The bar was thick and moist and crunchy with nuts, almost like a dense chocolate *pastel*. It was so good she ate another, thinking that she'd have to pay Eddo at least 60 pesos but she didn't care.

After a few minutes she had the strength to head back to work. And stopped dead.

The two sketches she'd given Eddo in October were framed and hanging to the immediate right of the door, directly opposite the desk so he could see them when he was sitting. The framing was beautiful--wide white mats and narrow black frames carved to look like rope. Displayed like that, her unimportant sketches looked professional and expensive. Like *real* art.

As she looked at the pictures, the back of her neck prickled just *there* and she whirled around, sure that he had touched her, but of course he hadn't; there was no one else there.

The feeling was at once both steadying and unsettling, as if he'd shaken the thread connecting them and she'd felt the reverberation.

◆

Luz surrendered her backpack to the security guard in the basement and he gave it a cursory check. She took it back wordlessly, climbed the stairs to the exit and left the building with the other workers. Saturday was just dawning, the gray-white sky giving way to a soft blue that might last until mid-morning. A car pulled up next to her and she saw to her relief that it was Tomás.

"Where have you been?" he practically shouted as she fell into the passenger seat.

"I had to clean the entire floor." The car pulled away from the curb and Luz closed her eyes. "They lock the workers in. Don't let them out until the shift is over. I cleaned 30 offices. And bathrooms."

"Ah, fuck."

Luz groaned in reply and unzipped her jeans.

"Hey, *hey*, wait a minute," Tomás said. Luz felt the car swerve.

If she hadn't been so tired she would have laughed but instead she pulled down her panties and took out the *maldita* CD. She had dozens of tiny cuts all over her abdomen from the corners of the envelope. Tomás drove without speaking as she emptied her shoes.

By 6:00 am Luz was in the Vega's kitchen waiting for Ricardo to ring for the trash.

The rest of Saturday was like a nightmare. She fell asleep at the kitchen table at noon and woke with a start when Francesca came in for a *Coca*. Luz started drinking coffee after that, so she'd be awake when la señora came to punish her, but her brain stayed hazy while her heart raced and she felt so agitated she wanted to scream.

When Alejandro cornered her in the hallway and started in on her she had no patience to deal with him adroitly. Without thinking about the consequences she grabbed the front of his pants and squeezed until his eyes watered.

"*Keep away from me*," Luz hissed. She shoved him aside and went back into the kitchen. She fell into bed at 10:00 pm after taking off her panties, shaking from nerves and too much caffeine, the paper cuts stinging.

♦

Chapter 37

"You're sure about this, Eduardo?" Arturo Romero asked.

"Let's get it done before I go," Eddo answered.

"'Regarding current income from and holdings in Marca Cortez,'" Arturo read from the paper in front of him. "'Upon your demise, a quarter of said assets to your niece. A quarter to the Marca Cortez Medical Fund, a quarter to Lomas Altas Children's Hospital, and the final quarter to Luz de Maria Alba Mora of Lomas Virreyes, Mexico City.'"

"Where do I sign?"

"Here. And here. And again here." Arturo arranged the papers on the table so that Eddo could sign the will.

The room was silent except for the scratching of Eddo's pen. Arturo signed as the witness.

They were in Arturo's study in the big house in Oaxaca. The French doors to the patio were open, a breeze gently moving the long white draperies gathered to one side. Cotton slipcovers on the upholstered furniture were a cooling contrast to the dark wood of the library table and the brown leather armchairs. An eclectic mix of landscape paintings, family pictures, and memorabilia from Arturo's distinguished career decorated the walls.

From where Eddo sat he could see the mountains rising greenish brown beyond the far wall enclosing the Romero compound. Some of the peaks were perfectly pointed; everyone knew there were unexcavated pyramids out there but no one had enough money or energy to tackle them. The ancient city at nearby Monte Alban was enough for most people.

It was the second time he'd come to this house to heal. The first had been when his parents had died. That time his soul had been broken, this time it was his body. His cracked collarbone had knit well, but it was still sore. The scars were red and angry, but they would fade in time, and he'd let his hair grow to conceal the one on the side of his head. He'd started exercising as soon as he could and his strength had come back quickly.

"Does Pilar know?" Arturo asked.

"About the will or that I'm going to Panama?" Eddo asked.

Arturo slid the will into a file jacket then settled back in his chair, still long and lean despite being in his early sixties. His hair was silvery gray and his features were sharp and aristocratic but never cold or aloof. "Both."

Eddo stood and walked to the French doors. Several hundred meters away, an armed security guard walked the perimeter of the razor-wire topped wall. Peace and a tight-knit family were inside. Outside were the pressures and dangers of being a judge, a presidential candidate, and a crusader against the weak laws and official corruption that enabled the drug cartels.

"I told her I was changing the will," he said. "She was fine with it. After all, her share of Marca Cortez is just as big."

"But you didn't tell her--."

"I just told her I'd be traveling for awhile," Eddo said. "And, no, I didn't tell her about Luz, either."

"Why not?" Arturo poured two cups of coffee from the service on the library table.

"Vasco has put together all the evidence we have so far," Eddo said, not ready to talk about Luz. "He's briefing Fonseca." The Attorney General, Ignacio Fonseca Zelaya, was old and his role was largely that of a figurehead but he still carried considerable influence.

Arturo handed Eddo a cup of coffee. "Do whatever you have to do in Panama to complete the picture. Let Fonseca take it to the president."

The coffee cup in Eddo's hands was fine china, expensive but faded from everyday use, a symbol of the house and the life that Arturo and his wife Imelda had built together. In contrast, Eddo didn't even have an apartment anymore, much less a bone china teacup. He pushed aside a feeling of rootlessness. "Betancourt stonewalled before," he reminded Arturo.

"Fernando can be slow to decide." Arturo gave a nod. "But

faced with an overwhelming amount of evidence he won't have a choice."

Unless Betancourt is afraid of Hugo. They both walked back to the armchairs and Eddo took a deep breath but before he could speak there was a knock on the door and Imelda came in.

Arturo's wife matched him for height and elegance. Her most striking features were her large brown eyes, an extremely short hairstyle, and a cascade of smile lines that betrayed her age. Eddo knew she wasn't beautiful in the conventional sense but even movie stars paled in her presence.

Right now she was wearing baggy jeans, an old tee shirt, and reading glasses on a string around her neck. She kissed each man on the top of his head and plopped down in another armchair. "Ignore me," she said. "I just want to be around sane people for ten minutes."

Arturo topped up his own coffee cup and handed it to her. "Wedding plans?"

Imelda took the cup. "All I ask is that both Maria Elena and Duarte make it to the church in appropriate clothing. The rest of this is nuts."

Eddo smiled. Arturo and Imelda's daughter was getting married in a couple of months. Planning the wedding was more complicated than putting together the presidential campaign.

Imelda chatted about the wedding for a few minutes, making them laugh. The driver would be ready to take Eddo to the airport at 6:00 pm, she reminded them, and left.

"The campaign needs to move to Mexico City," Eddo said. "Lorena's loud and obnoxious but she's making you look remote. Ask Nestor." Eddo liked and respected Nestor Solis, Arturo's campaign manager. During his recuperation Nestor had encouraged him to outline a book on legal reform that would come out before the nominating convention.

"Nestor also tells me I'm not telegenic," Arturo said wryly. "He says we have to balance my dullness with the image of a young, dynamic Romero team."

He got up and went to his desk, rifled through papers, and came back to Eddo with a folder. "Nestor wants to build that team image around you. Here's his plan for getting you in front of the public."

As Eddo looked through the materials in the folder, Bernal Paz's words echoed in his head. *In all that time you've been concealed. Lurking in the shadows.* Well, not with this plan. Nestor had scripted an impressive campaign to introduce Eddo to the country with interviews, editorials, and speeches at law schools and police graduations. There were radio and television appearances, too.

Eddo closed the folder. "This is great, Arturo," he said. "But have you and Nestor thought about what might happen if I get enough evidence in Panama? If it gets known that someone connected to your campaign took Hugo down, you could lose a lot of party support."

"Not a consideration." Arturo leaned forward, eyes like flint. "We'll do what's right."

Eddo shook his head. "If it's a choice between me being part of the campaign and Lorena getting the nomination, I'm out."

"No," Arturo said. "There are only a handful of people who can keep this country from crumbling. You are the best man for Attorney General and I will stand by that."

Eddo nodded, nearly bereft of words in the face of Arturo's loyalty. "I'd better go pack."

The two men embraced.

"*Vaya con Dios*, Eduardo," Arturo said.

♦

Chapter 38

On the Monday after the feast day of Our Lady of Guadalupe, the air was so gritty it stung Luz's eyes. More grit would come in January and February, the height of the dry season. But it didn't matter as Luz floated down Virreyes to the big Bancomer Bank.

It had been a Soledad de Doblado weekend but she'd left Sunday on the early bus and gone straight to Jardin del Arte. As a result, along with her cell phone, there was now a Bancomer check in her pocket for 1850 pesos from the sale of two small paintings. Her money problems were solved.

A zigzag line of at least 30 customers waited patiently for the tellers, guided into place by velvet ropes and brass stanchions. They were mostly laborers in paint and plaster-daubed work clothes. Luz filled out a form to cash the check at a mahogany counter then went to the end of the line.

It moved very slowly and grew very long. Luz had ample time to look around. The bank was an elegant place of glass and darkly veined marble where people had hushed conversations. The business being transacted was too venerable for a normal tone of voice.

Luz was only about eight customers away from the teller windows when a man wearing a beautifully tailored dark suit walked into the bank. In the midst of the rough looking laborers, he stood out, tall and good looking.

He consulted his jeweled Rolex and eased into the line directly in front of Luz. No one he passed reacted at all. The security guards on either side of the line appeared not to notice.

Luz stared at the finely stitched wool in front of her. Maybe it was the boldness of knowing Eddo or the check that said she was a real artist or the fear that Marisol would punish her for taking such a long time, but she tapped him on the shoulder.

"Excuse me," she said. "The end of the line is back there."

The soft murmur of banking conversations abruptly ceased.

The man turned around. He was younger than Luz, maybe in his early twenties. He looked her up and down, taking in the gray uniform, old sweater, short socks, scuffed shoes, high cheekbones, and flat hair tucked behind her ears. Luz tried not to wilt.

"What the fuck?" he said and sniffed as if she smelled bad. Then he walked ahead of the next three people in line. They all stepped to the side to let him pass.

Shaking with impotent rage and humiliation, Luz could do nothing except clamp on her stupid face. The stares of the people in line felt like razor cuts.

She finally got to a teller window and slid the form, the check, and her identity card under the glass barrier.

The woman on the other side of the glass tapped an unseen keyboard and shook her head. "This check is not valid." The teller handed back Luz's identity card.

"What?"

"The signature on file doesn't match the one on the check," the teller said smugly. She inserted the check into a tiny machine and there was a whirring sound. The check was swallowed then spit out. The woman slid it back under the glass barrier. "Next."

Red ink across the back proclaimed that the check had been invalidated.

1850 pesos gone. No.

Luz was shouldered aside by the next customer, a man in plasterer's overalls. He looked at her darkly, with a barely concealed *serves you right* expression.

"Wait." Luz pushed her way back to the teller. "How am I going to cash this now?"

"Come back in 15 minutes," the woman said dismissively and turned to the man in overalls.

Come back in 15 minutes. The universal Mexican response meaning *get out of my face, go away.* It wasn't a literal expression. Nothing was going to be different in 15 minutes and everybody knew it.

Luz reeled out of the bank, blinking back tears.

There was no telephone number on the check and the address was a street in Cuernavaca. She could hardly take a bus there and wander around.

Luz furiously tore the check into pieces and dropped them on the sidewalk. Her artwork wasn't the solution to anything. She wasn't a real artist, wasn't anything but a stupid, stupid *muchacha*.

As Luz headed back to the Vega house, a big dark sedan with a long white scratch on the passenger side door passed her. She thought she recognized the person in the front passenger seat, but no, it was just another insane fantasy, like being a real artist or a woman in love with an attorney.

The day dragged, the lost money never far from her thoughts. She was already in bed when Rosa waltzed into their room at 11:00 pm and snapped a 100-peso bill at Luz.

"Alejandro just gave this to me for doing it with him in his bedroom."

"*What*?" Luz sat bolt upright.

Rosa giggled and did a little shoulder shimmy. "He doesn't know *anything*. I had to show him where to stick it in. He popped off like a wet firecracker and then cried." She went into the bathroom.

Luz scrambled out of the bed and went to the bathroom door. "Rosa, did he use a condom?"

"Nah." Rosa came out of the bathroom in her nightgown and stuffed her clothes in the laundry basket. "He's too young for anything to happen."

"Oh, Rosa." Luz wanted to shake her. "What about Manuel?"

"He said it was all right as long as I split the money with him."

♦

Chapter 39

Tuesday morning was busy. Not only were the *dispensa* boxes piling up, but the Vegas were hosting a cocktail party for el señor's senior managers that evening. Luz and Rosa did their morning chores, handed out *dispensas*, aligned fine china and old silver on the buffet, and arranged the mountains of poinsettias that Raul and Hector brought in.

After *la comida* Marisol sent Luz to La Sumesa. Luz put on her heavy sweater and grabbed her cell phone, sticking it into her pocket with Marisol's list and 250 pesos from Señora Vega.

Rosa got off early on Tuesdays and the two maids left the house together, chatting of Christmas presents, sure that Señora Vega would give them their *aguinaldo* bonus on Friday.

"I might get him an Alejandro Sanz CD," Rosa said, bubbling with anticipation. She was on her way to see Manuel and give him his 50 pesos.

Luz slowed. The scratched sedan she'd seen Sunday was parked on the side of the street.

"Are you paying attention?" Rosa said impatiently. "Alejandro Sanz."

"I like Miguel Bosé." Luz stared at the car as they passed. The driver was studying a map book. A passenger was reading a newspaper.

A car with waiting men in it was not unusual. They were probably a chauffeur and a bodyguard. Maybe la señora was visiting friends or their important personage had business in the nearby United Nations building.

"Do you want to go to the rave place tomorrow?"

"What?" Luz pulled her attention back to Rosa. "Not that again, Rosa."

They were almost to the corner of Fray Payo de Rivera and

Virreyes when Luz heard a car engine rumble behind them. She knew without looking it was the big scratched sedan. Luz loitered on the street corner, drawing out her good-bye to Rosa. Hopefully the sedan would pass them, make the turn onto Virreyes, and go away. Rosa eventually turned right on Virreyes toward the intersection with Prado Sur. Luz went straight, crossing the oncoming lanes of Virreyes and stepping onto the median by the Monte Xanic wines sign. The sedan turned right, passed Rosa, and sped off.

Luz told herself it was a coincidence as she walked up Monte Athos. Christmas was in the air and the south end of the street was lively. The florist was taking delivery of huge red amaryllis plants. The veterinarian's office door was open. The receptionist's three-legged miniature collie wore a plaid bow.

Luz crossed the big boulevard called Explanada, and after two more blocks reached the big shopping area with the café, the Batiz art store, and La Sumesa. Traffic was slow there. Street vendors were out in force and shoppers dodged around cars to get from one side of the street to the other. Luz was just about to walk into La Sumesa, past the toothless crone selling chestnuts and the smarmy guy selling fake Fendi purses, when she saw the scratched sedan in the line of cars cruising north on Monte Athos toward the intersection with Reforma.

Luz turned around and pressed "4" on her cell phone.

"*Bueno?*"

"Tomás? It's Luz de Maria."

"What's the matter?"

"There's a car I've seen a few times," she gulped. "I think it's following me."

He made her describe the car then told her to do the shopping and go straight back to the Vega's house. She should call him when she was back. Meanwhile, he'd get the boys rousted and they'd start looking for the sedan. Nobody would bother her.

It only took Luz a few minutes to buy the things on Marisol's list: Bloody Mary mix, seltzer water, tonic water, lemons, limes, a can of shrimp, boxes of crackers, and some fancy olives. She carefully pocketed the receipt and the 25 pesos change.

She started briskly down Monte Athos, not even stopping to ogle the Batiz window display. To her relief the dark sedan was nowhere in sight. She'd be safely back at the Vegas in 15 minutes.

After a block she was breathless from the gritty air. The plastic bag with the glass bottles was heavy and cut into her hand. She slid her wrist through the loop to take some of the strain.

◆

Luz had just put her foot on the median, thinking irrelevantly that the grass looked brown and dusty here because Explanada wasn't maintained by a corporate sponsor the way Virreyes was, when she heard a car accelerate as it traveled west on the big boulevard.

The scratched sedan bounced over the curb, chewing grass and spitting pebbles. Before Luz could understand what was happening, the back door on the driver's side opened. Iron hands snatched her up by the waist and hauled her backwards.

The plastic grocery bag looped around her wrist came, too. Luz dropped the others and flailed at the side of the car, trying to get a handhold that would prevent her from being dragged inside. But the car swallowed her up, bag and all.

♦

Chapter 40

The man who'd said to call him Juan had delivered on his word and those louts from Chihuahua had picked up Cortez's girlfriend. Max didn't want to know what would happen to either the woman or Cortez. He'd do this last thing because he couldn't afford to leave any loose ends. But then he was done.

He put the old ledger into his briefcase and left a note on his father's desk. As he left the office he turned off the lights. He joked with Alvaro as he passed through the bar, just like always. Max's father was in the kitchen and Max nearly wavered, but he straightened his spine and left the hotel without saying goodbye. If he saw his father Max knew he'd spill everything and no one, no one, could know.

Juan was waiting at the appointed place and time, eager to be going. He'd been equally eager to talk, once he had assurances that he'd be taken seriously and that rewards would come his way. He'd given them interesting information but he'd also said a lot of nonsense about this fictional *Los Hierros* bunch. How there were cells all over but nobody knew more than a dozen members, like they were the French Resistance or something. Max agreed with Hugo that Juan was making that part up, trying to seem more important than he was. Juan was an attention hound and Max wanted him gone.

So Max could go, too.

Juan hopped into the passenger seat of Max's car, shoving aside Max's planner. "Introductions, you said," Juan said as Max pulled away from the curb.

"People who can help you in your career," Max replied.

"They understand that *Los Hierros* is serious business?" Juan adjusted his glasses.

"Absolutely." Max headed north, towards the anonymous

housing blocks of the Satellite City neighborhood. "They know you're a serious player."

"Good."

They traveled in silence, following the heavily trafficked main artery and bailing out into a typical Satellite development. Max pulled up in front of a house and two men came out. Both were dressed casually, in contrast to Max and Juan's suits. One of the men pulled open Juan's door. Juan shot a look at Max, who nodded back encouragingly. "Go ahead," Max said. "I'm right behind you. Just need to call Lorena. Check on the campaign."

He made it sound like a confidence only he and Juan shared. Juan got out of the car. Max pulled out his cell phone as soon as Juan disappeared inside the gate with the two *sicarios*.

Lazaro answered on the first ring. Everything was packed and ready to go.

Max made it to Lazaro's apartment in 20 minutes. The two men held each other for a moment, nerves jangling and hearts racing.

"I've got the ledger," Max said when they broke apart. "It's our protection if they come after us."

"I'll make the copies," Lazaro said.

"I transferred it all to the Canary Islands account." Max found himself breathless at his own audacity. "Cashed today's shipment."

Lazaro put out a hand to steady Max. "I closed down Hermanos Hospitality online. It's like the company never existed."

"But you left the postings page alone."

"Of course." Lazaro took Max's planner and started making copies of the pages. The printer-copier was the only thing left on a desk that was usually cluttered with two laptops, an extra hard drive, and various other computer paraphernalia. "We'll need to keep watching it."

"Of course," Max echoed.

The protection went into Max's carry-on bag, along with the fake passports and bundles of American dollars curled up in socks. Lazaro had the same amount in his bag and both carried money orders for cash as well as bonds and stock certificates.

The last thing wasn't hard at all. Max put the planner copies into an envelope and addressed them to Ernesto Silvio. The courier service came, collected the envelope, and left without incident.

The taxi ride to the airport was excruciating. The two of them leaving with suitcases was sure to arouse suspicion if Lazaro's apartment was being watched. Max expected the taxi to be attacked. But nothing untoward happened.

The airport was mobbed, as usual. They checked in for the first flight, which would take them to Madrid. Lazaro's knuckles were white as they went through Security. Max wondered how long his heart could pound before he had a stroke.

No one questioned the bulky socks in their carry-on bags. They found the gate and boarded with the other first class passengers. The flight attendant offered them newspapers, champagne, orange juice, movie cassettes, the dinner menu. Max took juice but didn't drink it. His father would be reading the note by now, finding out that his son was gone.

After an eternity the big jet rumbled down the runway and lifted into the air. Max didn't realize he was crying until Lazaro reached over and thumbed away the tears.

◆

Chapter 41

Luz was trapped in the middle of the back seat, her left arm twisted across her back by the man on her right. The man on her left worked a thin braided leather belt around her neck. Bile and panic rose in Luz's throat as her breathing was nearly cut off. They pressed her head down onto her knees. Luz was more frightened than she'd ever been in her entire life. They would rape her, kill her, or she would choke on her own vomit.

It was a long time before they let her sit up, dazed from the awkward position and her labored breathing. The man holding the noose snapped the loose end like a whip, opening a cut on Luz's chin. "Is this the right one?" he barked at the front seat. He was a broad Mexican with small eyes and pockmarked skin.

"Straight hair!" the driver roared. "He fucking said she had straight hair." He was loud and argumentative. Luz stared at him in the rearview mirror, memorizing the curl of his lip and the lift of his eyebrow as he shouted at the others and squinted at the road.

The man twisting Luz's arm was dark and sharp-featured like an *indio*. He pulled her toward him, making her cry out in pain, even as the noose tightened. She saw blood on the front of her uniform dress and thought stupidly that Señora Vega was going to be very angry when she saw it. Blood stains never came out.

"What the fuck is he doing with a maid?" The front seat passenger was sharp-featured like the man holding her arm, with lank hair slicked back from a low forehead.

"Maybe the uniform gets Cortez hard," the man holding her arm said.

The noose slackened. "You saw Eduardo Cortez a while ago."

Luz gulped air.

"Answer me, bitch." The man slapped her. "You were all prettied up. Fancy jeans and a flashy bag. That was you, wasn't it?"

"No," Luz said and he pulled the noose so tight her eyes rolled back and she felt herself start to slip away.

He grabbed her hair and tipped her head back and her vision cleared. "You know a cop named Valderama?"

Luz couldn't say anything if she'd wanted to. The lack of air and the sour body smells of the four men in the confined space gagged her. Blood ran down the inside of her throat, a salty, gummy taste. Her tongue swelled and her thoughts were a crazy jumble of fear.

"Cortez. Valderama. You know them?"

The car turned onto a highway. Luz saw a sign for La Marquesa. The park where Eddo and Tomás played *fútbol* and families had Sunday picnics. Where there were desolate places only wild dogs roamed.

"You saw Cortez, no?" the man went on. "Sometimes they call him Eddo. I hear you climbed right in his bed."

"No," Luz whispered.

"Do you clean his house?"

"No. I don't know him." He still had her by the hair, her head pinned against the back of the seat, her left arm trapped behind her.

"I don't believe you." He let go of her hair and nodded at the other man in the back seat.

With an unseen movement, someone dislocated Luz's left shoulder.

With the noose around her neck, Luz couldn't even scream. Hot tears of agony flowed down her face as pain pulsed through her body and she passed out.

◆

They slapped her awake, the pain white and consuming, the movement of the car excruciating. "Next time I'll let him break your neck," the man said and Luz knew he would. "Tell me about Cortez."

"I don't know," Luz choked.

"Where is he?" he roared at her and the other men were yelling now, yelling at him to hurry up, they didn't want her puking or pissing in the car, just find out where Cortez was and do it now.

"Where?" He started punching her face, each time sending a hammer of pain through her shoulder and down her back and into her stomach.

"House," Luz mouthed, hardly aware of what she was doing, blood and vomit in her mouth.

"Do you clean his house?"

"No."

"He's fucking her, then," one of them said. "More money than God and he's fucking a maid."

"He pay you?" The front seat passenger leaned over the seat and leered in Luz's face. "Cortez pay you to be his *mamacita*?"

"I didn't take the money," Luz gasped and they all roared.

"So where is he now?"

"I don't know."

"Don't you want him to fuck you again? Or maybe you want a big one, no?"

The man who'd dislocated her shoulder put his hand under Luz's dress and tried to pry her legs apart. She wanted to push him away but her right arm was weighed down by the grocery bag full of glass bottles still looped around her wrist. She could only scream soundlessly.

The cell phone in her pocket rang.

The man groping Luz found her cell phone. The noose slackened and Luz sucked air. He held the phone to Luz's ear.

"Luz, you didn't call me back. Where are you?" Through the haze of pain Luz recognized Tomás's voice.

"The old highway to La Marquesa," she croaked.

The noose cut into her throat again. Suddenly Luz's lungs were bursting, there was no air, and she passed out again.

◆

They hadn't slapped her awake this time. Luz's head pounded but the pain in her shoulder seemed less, as if her body had adjusted to the awfulness.

The car moved easily along the old highway, well past the worst congestion of the little towns between Mexico City and Toluca.

"He's in fucking Panama." The front seat passenger waved Luz's cell phone in a gesture of surprise.

Sitting limply between the two men, her eyes closed as if she was still unconscious, Luz realized she'd given them what they needed--a way to get at Eddo.

The big glass bottles full of Bloody Mary mix and seltzer water were still in the bag looped around her right wrist. Her attackers weren't paying her any attention, the two in the back seat slanted forward to communicate with those in the front. No one noticed as Luz laced the necks of the bottles between her fingers, praying she was strong enough to lift the bottles with one hand and that she wouldn't pass out from the pain if she did.

She was strong enough.

She didn't pass out.

Luz heaved the grocery bag with the bottles in it to her left, smashing the Bloody Mary mix into the man's face, shredding the plastic bag and raining tomato juice and bits of glass all over the backseat. The man grunted and went limp. The noose unraveled. Luz swung her arm in the opposite direction, over the front seat and into the face of the right seat passenger. The effervescent seltzer water exploded like a glass bomb, leaving her clutching the two jagged bottle tops like a desperate bar fighter. The remnants of the plastic bag flapped around her wrist, a shredded wet bracelet. The driver started shouting and the car slewed on the highway.

The foreign man on her right grabbed at her. Luz reflexively rammed her elbow into his face, yelling for him to let go of her. Something cracked loudly and he curled away from her.

"Stop the car! *Stop the car!*" Luz screamed. The dislocated shoulder vented white-hot pain into her head but Luz leaned forward, pressed the jagged glass in her hand into the driver's neck and twisted as hard as she could, yelling at him to stop, stop the car, let her out, that she'd kill them all. He scrabbled ineffectively at her hand with his own. Luz ground the glass into the driver's neck, needing to survive like a wild animal, wanting to see the life pour out of him. The brakes squealed and the car fishtailed, bucking all over the road as the driver's blood spurted over her arm.

"Get her out!" the driver sobbed. *"Get her out! OUT."*

The car swerved crazily and the front seat passenger came alive. He reached over the seats and flailed at Luz. She clapped the bloody handful of glass straight into his face, seeing a long shard disappear into his eye. He started to shake and shriek.

"Stop the car! Stop the car! STOP THE CAR!" The man to her right joined the bedlam, his nose caved in and streaming blood. He lunged at her, trying to wrestle her down. Luz pulled the bloody glass out of one man's face and shoved it against the other man's crotch. She put her weight into it. He shrieked like a dying thing and clawed open the car door.

The car was still moving as she half fell, was half thrown. The driver's sobs to get her out, to kill her, to shut her up, rang in her ears along with her own animal cries.

She hit the ground heavily, the glass in her hand flying back at the car. Luz retched as the bones in her dislocated shoulder grated together and then her head rapped into concrete. She was unconscious as sounds like *Cinco de Mayo* fireworks exploded around her. One hit her a massive body blow, folding her up with a wave of leaden pressure as the sedan careened away.

Blood blotted across the front of her dress, creating quite a big stain.

♦

Chapter 42

Tomás's face flickered into view.

"I'm dead," Luz mouthed.

The look on his normally hard face was one of pure relief. "You're in the hospital," he said. "You've had surgery but you're going to be fine."

Highway Patrol officers had found her lying by the side of the highway. A rib had shattered along the path of the bullet and it had taken surgeons nearly four hours to pick out the bone fragments. A large compression bandage encircled her torso and her right hand was swathed in gauze. Her left shoulder was back in the socket and she could use her arm but there was a burning ache. There was an IV line in her hand and an oxygen tube under her nose. As her vision focused, Luz realized that the young cop named Diego was also in the room.

"Where's Eddo?" she managed. Her throat was raw.

"He's safe," Tomás said. "Can you tell me what happened?"

Hardly able to speak above a whisper, Luz told Tomás and Diego everything. At a certain point the two men exchanged a meaningful look. Tomás turned back to Luz. "Can you tell me what they looked like?" he asked.

"I need paper," Luz said. Tomás sent Diego to find some.

A doctor and two nurses came into the room and the conversation stopped. The doctor checked Luz's various bandages, the nurses discreetly shielding her breast with a cloth as he looked at the stitches over her ribs. An angry red trench was held together by black stitches, making the whole thing look like the decayed teeth of a snarling animal. The entire side of her ribcage below her breast was black and blue.

The nurses left roses in a vase and an array of magazines and DVDs for when she was feeling up to some entertainment.

The hospital hairdresser would come tomorrow. She'd probably be able to have real food in a day or so. The doctor made sure the correct dose of antibiotic was in her IV and then they all left.

Despite her bandaged hand Luz drew the man who'd held the noose, capturing his thick jaw, flat nose, greasy hair, and pockmarked skin. Then she drew the odd man who'd dislocated her shoulder, remembering his hawk-like features and intense expression.

The front seat passenger was easy to draw with his low forehead and lank hair. The driver was fleshy, angry, trying to be in charge.

Tomás gathered up the drawings. "We'll find them, Luz."

"I didn't want to say I knew him." Luz's eyes felt heavy.

"Luz, just rest," Tomás said. "We're going to have somebody with you all the time. Anything you want, you say so. Don't worry about a thing."

"You need to call Señora Vega and tell her where I am," Luz whispered groggily.

"We sent somebody over there already, Luz. Just rest."

The next day she only half remembered drawing the pictures. But Diego was there, along with another cop named Benito, and they made sure she had everything she needed.

♦

Chapter 43

Eddo shut the door behind Tomás. Handshake turned into bear hug. His newly healed collarbone protested the pressure but *Madre de Dios*, it was good to see Tomás.

"You look like an old fucking rock star," Tomás said when they broke apart.

Eddo grinned. He'd let his hair and beard grow to give himself some camouflage and it was like hiding behind itchy foliage. "Second career."

"Good choice." Tomás looked around the expansive hotel room with its carved door and two big beds. "So. Panama City's not bad."

"As long as you like rain," Eddo said.

He'd been there a week, staying at the El Panama hotel in the heart of the commercial district. The Casco Viejo area was just a taxi ride away. There he'd found that Montopa looked fairly legitimate, with a small office and a secretary who knew nothing and could not make any appointments for him; all the company's management was traveling. A few workers roamed the buildings that Montopa was ostensibly restoring. Local tax records listed Montopa's bank as Credit Britannia Limited, a bank located in St. John's, the capital of the tiny Caribbean nation of Antigua and Barbuda.

Tomás sat on the bed closest to the door and took a folder out of his carryon bag. "You ready for this?"

"Yeah."

Tomás handed the folder to Eddo. "Luz's drawings of the men who attacked her."

Eddo spread them out on the other bed, feeling the anger and anxiety bubble up all over again. The four pencil sketches were each a portrait in evil. "She said she couldn't draw faces," he muttered.

Tomás said something but Eddo didn't reply as he remembered the call. How Tomás's voice had cracked as he'd told Eddo that the El Toro cartel had Luz. Eddo had agreed to a meeting, knowing he'd be trading himself for Luz. The next hours were agony until Tomás called again with the news that Luz had been found alive but injured.

But the meet was still on.

"Start at the beginning," Eddo said.

Tomás was halfway through the story when Eddo began pacing the room. Fifteen steps from one end to the other and he kept his arms folded so he wouldn't slam a fist into the stucco wall.

"I knew it had to be one of us," Tomás wound up unhappily. "From what she told me, her attackers knew who she was and where she lived. Diego and Miguel were both in the car when I took her back to Lomas Virreyes."

"Miguel," Eddo said flatly.

Tomas nodded. "Nobody's seen him since the day it happened. Cell phone's out of service. His mother is frantic."

"You think he connected with Hugo?"

"Like that kid in Anahuac," Tomás said. "Couldn't resist the money."

Eddo rubbed the side of his head where the scar tingled under the shrubbery. Sotos Bild, Yanez Luna, Miguel. The lure of cartel wealth was as much of an addiction as cocaine or meth.

"He would have told him we knew about the postings page," Tomás went on. "Banco Limitado."

"*Los Hierros.*" Eddo slumped down on the other bed. "This won't make tomorrow night any easier."

"Here's your leverage." Tomás got a CD case out of his carryon and tossed it to Eddo. "Central Bank records and everything else we've turned up. Vasco, Conchita, and Ana have backup copies."

"Conchita got the Central Bank CD out of my office?"

"No." Tomás wiped his palms on the cloth of his pants. "With her investigating Yanez Luna, Vasco and I decided we didn't want her to take any chances. Luz got it out."

Eddo was pretty sure he'd heard wrong. "What?"

"The week after your so-called accident we paid off the regular cleaner who does your floor and Luz substituted. She opened your safe and got the stuff out."

"And cleaned my fucking office?" Eddo sputtered, jumping to his feet. "When were you planning on telling me? Maybe that's how they got to her!"

"Yes, she cleaned your fucking office," Tomás shot back. "And no, they didn't trace her."

"You used her." Eddo had a hard time staying in control.

"We were out of time and we couldn't afford to burn Conchita."

"Luz was there, all by herself?"

"We had a team picketed around the building. I picked her up."

"*Madre de Dios.*" Eddo slammed a hand against the wall, suddenly hating hotels. He hadn't wanted Luz to be touched by this mess and she'd landed--badly hurt--in the middle of it.

Tomás found some miniature bottles of whiskey in the minibar, poured one into a water glass and held it out to him. "Look, Luz could have said no. But she didn't and handled everything like a pro. She's really something."

Eddo shotgunned the whiskey and took a couple of deep breaths. "You sure it was Miguel?"

"Yes."

"Fuck." Eddo turned away from Tomás and put his empty glass on the dresser, feeling like a clock ticking down the last seconds before the alarm went off. "Let's go do some recon."

When Tomás stood up Eddo swung around and punched the heavier man, frustration and anger weighting the blow. Tomás fell backwards onto the bed, unconscious.

"*Oye*," Eddo said in surprise. He never expected to knock out Tomás. But it had been like hitting a cement truck. His hand hurt like hell.

By the time Eddo came back with ice from the machine down the hall Tomás was coming around.

"What did you do that for?" he croaked.

"That was for asking Luz to get the CD," Eddo said calmly.

He wrapped a towel around some ice. "Here. Put this on your face."

Tomás sat up and fingered the welt rising under his eye. "Not bad for a has-been rock star."

♦

Chapter 44

The ocean rippled gray under the night sky. In the far distance they saw the lights of ships lined up to pass through the Panama Canal. The soft rain made Eddo feel soggy but no cooler.

Panama City's Amador Causeway ended in a parking lot that led to a pedestrian plaza lit by streetlamps and surrounded by water on three sides. A cluster of popular restaurants served people from the cruise ships docked nearby. Further from the parking lot, with the water lapping up to the railings, was a Duty Free store and a restaurant called Alfredo's Café. Across the wide open space was a private marina full of glittering white yachts with signs to keep out those who didn't belong. The marina was full.

People could be seen through the windows of Alfredo's Café. The sound of muted speech and laughter drifted along on the moist air from the covered outdoor seating areas of the restaurants beyond the parking lot. Eddo and Tomás strolled along the water's edge, the only people outside in the soft night rain. Eddo resisted an urge to look at his watch.

"Ana and I decided to . . . uh . . . do the family thing when I get back," Tomás said. His face was still puffy from yesterday's punch.

"About time," Eddo said, forcing a smile. *If you get back.*

A thin man in black, no bigger than a shadow, crossed the plaza from the distant parking lot. He stopped several yards from them, vaguely Asian in the uneven light. "Cortez?" His voice was a gravelly whisper.

"Yes," Eddo said.

"Follow me."

The thin man walked past them and they followed him to

the marina gate. He unlocked it and gestured for them to step down onto the floating pier. Eddo heard Tomás say "Fuck" as the pier heaved under their weight.

They continued walking down the pier, the boats on either side moving gently in the swell caused by their passing. At the end of the pier the thin man indicated a boat. He said something to someone on board and a light flashed on.

The boat was one of the smallest in the marina. Eddo grabbed the ladder at the stern and clambered up. Another man dressed all in black met him at the top and pulled him into a dark cabin. Tomás got similar treatment.

From inside the cabin, the boat's running lights glinted through the windows, making small, angular patterns on the walls. Engines revved and the boat began sliding out of the slip, throwing Eddo and Tomás against the built-in benches that lined the cabin. No one spoke as they were righted and roughly patted down. The lights of the Amador Causeway receded as the boat picked up speed, churning the gray ocean into dirty foam. They passed a few yachts anchored beyond the marina and kept going, apparently headed for open water.

Eddo's cell phone was pulled out of his pocket and handed to a guard who left the cabin. Through the window they watched him dump it over the side. Tomás swallowed a protest as his phone went overboard, too. The man in black found the CD.

"Señor Cortez can keep his CD."

The overhead lights came on in the cabin. The speaker, a heavyset man in his late forties with thick black hair and an impressive set of jowls, was seated alone on a swiveling upholstered chair bolted to the floor. He wore a plaid button-down shirt, khaki pants and a navy blue windbreaker. Except for a scar disfiguring one eyebrow, he could have been a banker, a doctor, the friendly father-in-law.

Gustavo Gomez Mazzo, otherwise known as El Toro.

Eddo took back the CD. "Nice boat," he said.

"It belongs to a friend." Gomez Mazzo gestured to a cushioned bench bolted to the wall. "Please. Sit down."

Eddo and Tomás came forward, bracing themselves against the pitch of the boat, and sat. The boat moved swiftly and the fishy tang of the Pacific night blew in. Apart from the patterned upholstery, the cabin was colorless and impersonal.

"Even the most zealous public servants enjoy a beverage now and then," Gomez Mazzo said. One of his bodyguards opened a cabinet door to reveal a well-stocked refrigerator. The bodyguard took out a rum cooler and handed it to his boss. Eddo counted six bodyguards, all wearing black and all armed. El Toro's version of Hitler's elite.

Gomez Mazzo raised the bottle and looked at Eddo and Tomás inquiringly.

Eddo shook his head. "This is a business meeting."

"This is your funeral." Gomez Mazzo grinned, baring his teeth.

Eddo tapped the CD against his palm. "This is a complete record of your arrangement with Hugo de la Madrid Acosta including every bank transaction he's made through Banco Limitado, its connection with Montopa, and the money laundering transactions. Shut down your operation with Hugo and you can keep it."

Gomez Mazzo took a long pull from his rum cooler before speaking. "There is no operation with Hugo de la Madrid Acosta."

"No one operates in the Anahuac corridor without your support," Eddo said. He felt himself sweating as the El Toro bodyguards lounged against the cabin walls, obviously accustomed to the movement of a boat.

Gomez Mazzo spread his hands apart, one still clasping the incongruous rum cooler. "I am a simple businessman here in Panama. Hugo is Mexico's very important Minister of Public Security."

"You sold him the land near Anahuac before or after you moved to Panama?" Eddo asked. Gomez Mazzo had large, scarred hands. Two nails were missing. The hands didn't go with the conservative clothes and the tidy boat.

"Very nice, Señor Cortez." Gomez Mazzo was amused. "What comes next?"

"Drugs into *El Norte* along the Anahuac route. Some of the money gets laundered by your company here in Panama and some goes into the quasi-legitimate Banco Limitado and out to a bogus company in Mexico City called Hermanos Hospitality." Eddo paused and then threw the dice. "From there it gets piped into Lorena Lopez de Betancourt's presidential campaign."

Gomez Mazzo grinned. "So our meeting tonight is not a waste of time."

"If she wins you'll own the presidency," Eddo said.

"I will own every drug route in and out of El Norte," Gomez Mazzo corrected him.

One of the bodyguards left the cabin. A few seconds later the engine quieted and the boat slowed. No one said anything as they heard the anchor run down. There was only darkness outside the cabin windows.

Another bodyguard collected the empty rum cooler bottle. Gomez Mazzo sighed, stretched out his legs and crossed his ankles. "The rumor is that Lorena is a hell of a fuck. Did you do it with her, too?"

"No," Eddo said.

"Now it comes back," Gomez Mazzo said, waving his scarred hand idly as if remembering. "You're the one with peculiar tastes. Of course not so peculiar as Hugo. He likes children. Is that why you two don't get along? You should just let him buy you off."

Eddo heard Tomás make a noise. His friend's face was green in the dim cabin lighting, either from seasickness or rage Eddo couldn't tell. The color contrasted with the red welt.

"Keep the CD," Eddo said. "Withdraw your support from Hugo's operations and he's out of business. Do what you want with Montopa."

The Asian, who'd been a silent shadow standing against the wall, got Gomez Mazzo another rum cooler. The cartel leader chugged some down, belched, then pointed the neck of the bottle at Eddo. "Lorena's money dries up and her campaign stops. That's not necessarily in El Toro's interest."

"She's not going to be president, either with or without your money."

"If you go public with this information you won't last a week."

"You'd have to send out better than last time."

Gomez Mazzo made an expansive gesture. "Maybe the ocean swallows you up tonight."

"If we don't come back tonight the CD is released to the media in Mexico, Panama and the United States tomorrow morning."

"Hugo has much of Mexico's media in his pocket," Gomez Mazzo countered. "The story may die, too."

Eddo held up the CD. "It will be front page on every major *norteamericano* newspaper and website."

"You'd destroy your own government," Gomez Mazzo said. "The *yanquis* would descend like locusts, screaming that *los mexicanos* can't run their own country."

"Once they finish screaming, the *yanquis* will find you," Eddo said.

"They're not very smart."

"They will be with this information."

Gomez Mazzo tapped the cooler bottle thoughtfully. "This is very creative."

"As a simple businessman, I thought you would appreciate that."

Gomez Mazzo laughed, a shouted bark that rang in the cabin. "El Toro likes this man!" he exclaimed to his bodyguards. He leaned forward. "A mutual blackmail, no? We have each other by the short hairs, eh?"

Eddo grinned and it felt like death.

"El Toro keeps the CD and Hugo's, ah, operation, as you say, goes away." Gomez Mazzo waved the rum cooler bottle in the air, his battered hand dwarfing it. "But you have a copy of the information and can take it to the media or the army or whoever you think will help if I don't keep my part of the bargain. But if you make it public, we leak that you made a deal with the El Toro cartel." He took a pull from the bottle, still smiling in triumph. "Romero's pretty boy the dirtiest of them all. You would not survive prison."

"That would appear to be the deal on the table," Eddo said evenly.

Gomez Mazzo gestured at another bodyguard who took out

a small laptop. Eddo handed over the CD. He could feel Tomás rigid next to him. Gomez Mazzo watched the screen intently. His jowly face hardened as he toggled through various files.

Eddo lost track of how long they sat in the cabin, the boat rocking gently as Gomez Mazzo combed through the data on the CD. Tomás was seasick for sure. His breathing was hoarse and his fingers dug into his thighs.

"We can come to an agreement, Señor Cortez," Gomez Mazzo said at length. "El Toro may have lost a president but won an Attorney General."

Eddo swallowed back a retort and took out copies of Luz's sketches and a picture of Miguel. "These men aren't part of the agreement," he said. "If I find them, I will kill them."

Gomez Mazzo looked at the Asian whose only reaction was a barely perceptible lift of one shoulder.

"These are not El Toro's men," Gomez Mazzo said.

"So you won't miss them."

A smile flickered at the corner of Gomez Mazzo's mouth. "She was a maid."

Eddo met the other man's eyes. "Nobody touches her."

"Some maids are very good with . . . starch."

"Just so we understand each other," Eddo said.

Gomez Mazzo stood and rapped on the ceiling. Almost immediately they heard the sound of the anchor chain going up and the engines starting. The boat pitched and gained speed. Gomez Mazzo and the Asian left the cabin, walking easily on the rocking deck.

Outside the windows, the dark horizon shifted as the boat turned. Tomás looked green and desperate.

Eddo hauled Tomás to his feet. The bodyguards tensed. "Look, he's going to puke," Eddo said. "Needs some air."

One of the bodyguards went ahead and led them out onto the deck. Tomás leaned over the rail and gulped salt air. To Eddo's relief, the Amador Causeway twinkled in the far distance. On the other side of the boat, almost hidden behind the bulk of the cabin, Eddo saw Gomez Mazzo talking to the Asian.

As they neared the marina, lights came on in one of the big yachts. Gomez Mazzo, as if he'd known all along that Eddo and

Tomás were on deck, turned and saluted. Eddo raised a hand in return. Gomez Mazzo went back into the cabin. Eddo needed a bath.

As the boat maneuvered into its slip, the thin Asian man handed Eddo a cheap cell phone. "From el señor," he said in his thready voice. He led them off the boat and locked the marina gate behind them. All the restaurants were closed. Eddo and Tomás were left alone in the dark at the end of the plaza.

Two hours later, as they sat in the airport, Eddo scrolled through the cell phone's applications. The only thing he found was a series of numbers and letters listed as an address.

"They're coordinates," Tomás said, peering over his shoulder. "GPS coordinates."

◆

Chapter 45

The hospital decorated for Christmas. Luz's bruises faded. The bandages came off her hand and the doctors and nurses all told her that she was making a wonderful recovery from the surgery. A police officer was always with her and today it was Diego, whom she liked very much.

In the afternoon Hector came. Luz introduced the two men and waited for Hector to say he'd brought Rosa.

"I am sorry for your misfortune." Hector was his usual impassive self in a dark suit and tie. He nodded at Luz then wheeled in a brand new black suitcase with a retractable handle. He slid it over to the wall near the window and took out two envelopes.

"Diego, could you go outside for a few minutes?" Luz asked softly.

Diego gave Hector a hard look and walked out.

"You have my *finiquito*, don't you?" Luz asked when the door closed.

The legally mandated *finiquito* severance payment was a *muchacha's* only safety net. It was the most specific thing in the vague contract between employer and domestic employee. If a domestic servant quit, there was no payment. But if the employer let the servant go, the employer paid a *finiquito* of one month's salary, plus an amount equal to twenty days of salary for each year worked.

"You have to sign this first." Hector handed her one of the envelopes.

It contained a document from an attorney stating that Luz accepted the amount of 15,300 pesos as *finiquito* associated with the termination of her employment with the Vega family. By accepting it Luz acknowledged that she was being terminated because of the theft of 250 pesos.

"I never took 250 pesos," Luz protested.

"You were given 250 pesos to buy food for la señora's party," Hector said. "You didn't bring the food and you haven't given back the money."

Luz looked at him in utter disbelief.

Hector shrugged impassively, as if to say he was only the messenger.

"This isn't even enough *finiquito*," Luz pointed out. "They owe me six years worth."

Hector looked around the room and made a small motion. His meaning was clear. The rest of her *finiquito* was paying for the hospital.

Anything you want, Tomás had said. Luz had eaten gourmet dinners, had her hair done, and watched movies without a thought as to who was paying for all this luxury. She'd been *el jefe's* lady for a while, cared for by the best in Eddo's world, but it had been just another charade.

"I didn't know," Luz said dully.

She signed the paper. Hector took it and gave her the other envelope. He nodded at her without expression and left.

♦

In the afternoon Luz convinced Diego to get them each a cappuccino from the shop in the lobby. The kind with chocolate on top. She'd be fine by herself for a minute or two.

When he left Luz got out of bed and dressed, wincing from the effort. She left a note on the dresser. There were no nurses at the desk as she wheeled the big suitcase down the hall and out the back entrance of the hospital, avoiding the lobby. She managed to walk around the big building to the *sitio* stand where a driver took her suitcase and put it in the trunk of his taxi.

The *sitio* took her to the bus station. Luz was in a pain-filled daze as the bus bounced along the highway. A cheap *libre* taxi took her home. Dragging the big suitcase across the concrete yard and up the steps took more strength than she had. She passed out as she walked into the living room.

◆

Chapter 46

Gomez Mazzo toggled through the files again, once more impressed with the information that Cortez had put together and the nerve the man had shown. Fortune had showed up and he had again grabbed it with both hands. Without Lorena as a distraction, Romero almost certainly would win the presidential election. Cortez would be the best asset El Toro ever had.

There just remained the problem of Hugo and what to do about Site 1. And certain other things that were no longer useful.

"Chino." Gomez Mazzo gestured to the cabinet.

Chino got up, selected a rum cooler, and opened it.

Gomez Mazzo took a long pull from the bottle. He belched with satisfaction then pointed at Chino. "When we get to shore call Pepe. He and the boys can take a holiday."

"How long?"

Gomez Mazzo smiled. "Find something else for them to do."

Chino looked at him quizzically.

Gomez Mazzo closed the laptop and drank more rum cooler. "Send the intruder team up there."

Understanding spread across Chino's face. "A test, eh?"

"They're useless now." Gomez Mazzo grinned at his own cleverness. "Except to show us what kind of guts Cortez really has."

Chino made a sound like a dry cough.

Gomez Mazzo handed Chino the empty cooler bottle. "Go tell the captain to come here. See if we can't pick up the speed a bit."

Chino left the cabin and Gomez Mazzo stared out the window. The sky was a brilliant blue and the sea was a sheet of glass.

The feeling of freedom and power was exhilarating. There was nothing in El Toro's way.

♦

Chapter 47

The army convoy sounded like a swarm of bees as the trucks drove over the unpaved road northwest of Anahuac. Tomás and Eddo were in the third truck, wearing the same camouflage uniforms and body armor as the soldiers. As they bounced in the ruts and the army sergeant driving the heavy vehicle swore, Eddo checked his phone. No service.

The vehicle's GPS unit showed that they were almost to the coordinates.

The radio crackled with instructions. Together with the soldiers in the truck bed, Eddo and Tomás pulled on the black fabric balaclavas that masked their faces and prevented them from being identified. Metal clicked as everyone did a weapons check.

The convoy passed a small village tucked into the sparse shadow of a rocky hill. There were a few houses, a sheltered well, a store, and an outdoor restaurant. The place seemed empty. No one came outside to wonder at so many trucks or to sell drinks to the soldiers. Doors swung open in the ripple of wind caused by the passing of the trucks.

"Look," Tomás said over the noise of the trucks. "Whole fucking place is empty."

They'd seen no sign of humanity as they'd traveled the narrow road between Anahuac and the GPS coordinates. A few stray dogs and a goat, but that was it. The trucks rumbled on for a few more minutes and then a gray smudge appeared in the distance.

"Think we found it," the driver called.

Some of the trucks moved off the road now, allowing the convoy to approach in a fan arrangement. The gray smudge composed itself into a long steel warehouse backing up to a rocky rise.

Eddo knew the soldiers were sweating in anticipation of an ambush. But it wasn't a good location for that; it was open and any potential threat could be seen from quite a distance. The place seemed deserted but his scalp prickled with anticipated danger.

The trucks slowed and stopped about a quarter of a mile in front of the warehouse. As the air stilled around the stopped trucks, the acrid smell of human feces was an immediate assault.

"*Madre de Dios*," Eddo said.

"Latrines," Tomás said and jerked a thumb toward a line of open pits.

Vultures circled overhead, lazy black harbingers of fear against the dry blue sky. The windowless warehouse made of corrugated steel glinted like molten metal, broken only by a black door with exposed tracks wide enough for a vehicle to go in and out. Tire patterns were ground into the dirt in front of it. Along one side of the building a few scrubby pines sheltered a collection of plastic tables and chairs, most toppled over in the dirt. Piles of trash bags were torn apart, likely by scavenging birds and desert animals. Debris was everywhere.

Someone was sitting in a plastic chair in front of the wide black door. The figure didn't move or acknowledge the convoy in any way. Vultures stalked between the chair and the trash.

The colonel gave the signal and everyone spilled out of the vehicles and took up assigned positions. Two small units moved ahead, circling around the hills on either side of the warehouse. Eddo's body armor was surprisingly light as he and Tomás grouped with the colonel and the group approached the warehouse.

A gasp snaked along the lines of men from those in front all the way to the back. There were exclamations until the colonel barked out an order for silence.

The figure in the chair held its head in its lap. The hands were arranged to hold it in place. The body was dressed in a suit that had once been gray and a shirt that was a solid sheet of dried blood. The sandy ground beneath the chair was stained dark brown.

Most of the face had been pecked apart. A pair of metal spectacles was half buried in the sandy dirt by one foot.

"Miguel," Eddo said.

"Played and lost," Tomás muttered.

Soldiers moved the body to one side, the birds fluttering away in angry protest. The wide metal door was padlocked and a soldier with huge metal cutters stepped forward to snap apart the lock.

It took three soldiers to roll open the door. The tracks squealed a metallic protest until the door clanged into the fully open position.

The colonel entered first, flanked by Eddo and Tomás. The stench and heat were almost unbearable.

Eddo was startled to see people blinking in the light suddenly pouring through the open doorway. Dozens and dozens of people. Many were children.

Everyone looked dazed and listless. No one said a word.

As they moved further inside the space Eddo tried to assess the numbers. At least 200 people were jammed into the space, along with meager belongings. Backpacks, blankets, dishes and plastic bottles were strewn about. Toys. A child started to cry.

"What the fuck," Tomás said, his voice muffled by the balaclava. "What are all these kids doing here?"

The colonel turned to a man sitting on a pallet with a young girl in his arms. "Why are these children here?"

"She's seven," the man replied.

There was movement at the back of the warehouse. A man holding a gun to the neck of a child approached. Even in the dim light the sharp features Luz had drawn were unmistakable.

"We got a lot of hostages here," the man said.

The man was quite a bit taller than the child. Eddo had a clear head shot.

He wondered if the army would back him up or cut and run.

♦

Chapter 48

Carmelita came, as did Father Santiago. Everyone was shocked by Luz's story of being robbed and shot while buying groceries in Mexico City. The holidays passed in a sad blur.

A few days after New Year's Luz went to the free clinic. The stitches itched terribly. Juan Pablo went with her and they waited three hours before Luz was seen. A young man picked inexpertly at the thread with a variety of scissors. When he was done the lips of the wound gaped and Luz was panting from the pain. He put some gauze and tape on it.

By 6 January, *el Dia de los Reyes*, she had a raging fever and the incision was infected. Luz took an antibiotic and watched as Martina and Sophia moved the three king figures next to the Holy Family to complete the *navidad* scene set up on the cabinet in front of the picture of the Virgin.

For Luz, the holiday was marked by despair. She had no way to get in touch with Eddo. Her cell phone was gone and she hadn't memorized Tomás's number. Her only hope was that Eddo would catch her attackers and find her cell phone. He'd key through the contact list, call Señora Velasquez, and leave a message.

To make matters worse, Luz had lost all the little treasures from her glorious day with Eddo. The castoff clothes hadn't been in the suitcase Hector brought to the hospital. She'd hidden Eddo's torn note, the Hermes scarf and the tiny gold buttons in the Prada tote and now they were all gone, as if he'd never existed.

The infection finally petered out at the end of January. Lupe helped her take off the last bandage and together they stared at the scar in the bathroom mirror.

The stitches had clearly come out too early. The result was a jagged, lumpy weal as thick as Luz's forefinger under her left breast. Much of the scar was sunken into the place where the rib had been, so that the surface was uneven. The skin around it was puckered and numb and Luz felt like a monster.

◆

Chapter 49

Lorena was furious. Max had simply disappeared and everyone who'd worked on his staff had resigned. Hugo tried to find out where Max had gone but so far had turned up nothing. In the meantime, her campaign was out of money. It was outrageous to think that she was just months away from defeating Romero for the party nomination and she didn't even have enough money for new shoes.

Romero's poll numbers went up five points just on the strength of her press statement canceling the first rally in Oaxaca. The political pundits hooted that she didn't have the nerve to face Romero on his own territory and when she chided them they accused her of being shrill and defensive. The slogan "Lorena's Your Sister" was still getting air time because Max had bought weeks worth of advertising in some places, but it didn't seem to be making any difference.

To make matters worse, her new assistant was a dolt and Ernesto Silvio had become a major annoyance. In fact, he'd been the one to hire Natividad, with Fernando's blessing. Natividad had an impressive resume but frankly, the woman hadn't any staff of her own, didn't know anyone important and had little success in booking interviews and events. The fool didn't seem to realize that Lorena was running for president.

Silvio appeared at her office door as she dictated a letter to the editor of a magazine, disputing a laudatory article about Arturo Romero. "Señora, the president would like to see you in his office," Silvio interrupted.

"I am particularly busy right now," Lorena said and swung her gaze to her secretary. "Natividad, is there time in my schedule to see the president today?"

"Natividad, la señora will let you know when she comes

back," Silvio said.

Natividad left the office, nodding at Silvio as she went. The bitch.

Lorena stood up. "I'll thank you not to--."

"Señora, the president is waiting."

Silvio followed her as Lorena stalked down to Fernando's office. Really, this business with Silvio trying to push her around was going to end. Silvio opened the door and Lorena charged in, only to stop short at the sight of Hugo and that ancient relic Ignacio Fonseca Zelaya. Next to Fonseca were two men Lorena didn't know: a younger man and a haughty looking aristocrat nearly as old as Fonseca.

"Lorena, dear." Fernando looked tense as he came around his desk and took her by the elbow. "You know Hugo and Ignacio, of course."

Lorena greeted Hugo as if they hadn't fucked the afternoon away two weeks ago, giddy with champagne. She extended her hand and made the usual pleasantries to Fonseca as well. The man looked like dried beef in a suit.

"This is Vasco Madeira Suiza from Ignacio's office," Fernando went on.

Madeira Suiza was attractive in a smug sort of way. Lorena decided, with Hugo in the room, not to give him any of her special looks.

"And senior governor of the Central Bank, Don César Bernal Paz." Fernando introduced the other man. He was a man who wore his position in society on his immaculately tailored sleeve, just like Lorena's own father.

Fernando had them all sit down, including Silvio whom he asked to be notetaker. There was an enormous seal of Mexico behind Fernando's desk, the eagle with the snake in its talons looking triumphant. Lorena shifted in her chair. She was going to have some wonderful portrait pictures taken next to that seal when she got to be president.

"We can make this a relatively quick meeting," Fernando said. "Ignacio has some news."

Fonseca cleared his throat. "Luis Yanez Luna, the head of the Financial Regulations Unit, was arrested this morning on charges of participating in an organized crime ring and laundering money through a fraudulent financial institution."

Lorena gave Fernando her annoyed but patient wife look. Why on earth had he made Silvio drag her here to listen to this? She didn't know Luis Yanez Luna.

"We felt that as his superior, Hugo," Fonseca continued in his quavery old man's voice. "You should be officially informed of this."

"Yes, yes of course," Hugo said. He sounded nonplussed. "Thank you for telling me. This is most distressing."

Madeira Suiza handed something to Hugo. "The financial institution was called Banco Limitado. All the funds have been confiscated."

"The Central Bank has been able to trace the movement of funds in and out of this bank," Fernando said. "This is why I've asked Don César to be here."

Bernal Paz looked as if he might have a stroke.

Lorena saw Hugo's face go blank and worry niggled at the back of her mind.

"How," Hugo began. He licked his lips. "Exactly how much was confiscated?"

"Over 800 million pesos," Madeira Suiza said. "From 16 different accounts."

Lorena darted another look at Hugo, the worry growing.

"My office is actively searching for Yanez Luna's accomplices," Fonseca said.

"Accomplices within the government," Fernando said, as if correcting Fonseca.

"I expect that you have sufficient evidence to indicate there were accomplices?" Hugo asked.

"Yes," said Madeira Suiza. He looked forcefully from Fonseca to Fernando as if he expected one of them to say something else.

Bernal Paz gripped the arms of his chair but did not speak.

Silvio cleared his throat.

"The Attorney General's office is mainly concerned with the impact on government operations." Fonseca made a small, vague gesture.

"The arrest of one man should not precipitate the breakdown of the social order," Fernando said primly. "We do not turn on each other like dogs. But of course a line must be drawn. Especially if it involves . . . indiscretions."

Lorena held her breath. She was in the audience, watching a sparsely-worded drama unfold on a stage. Surely the principal actors would not tear apart one of their own.

"I cannot believe anyone of stature was involved," Fonseca added. "Hopefully, my office can close the investigation . . . into government accomplices . . . very soon."

Hugo cleared his throat. "Fernando, I appreciate this information but I'd like to turn the conversation to a different issue."

Madeira Suiza slid to the edge of his chair, too intense to be handsome any more.

Bernal Paz might have been stuffed, his body was so rigid.

Fernando made a go-ahead gesture from behind his desk.

"Graciela has not been well," Hugo said. His face tightened in an expression of grief. "We're going to see some specialists. Overseas."

Fernando looked sympathetic. "I'm sure I speak for everyone in offering my best wishes."

"Thank you, Fernando," Hugo said. "But I'm afraid the situation has caused me to neglect my duties as minister." He looked down and grief turned to remorse. "I should have caught this situation with Luis before Ignacio's office was involved."

Fernando nodded. "What are you saying, Hugo?"

"I offer you my resignation, effective immediately," Hugo said. "I'll give you a formal letter this afternoon. Graciela and I will be traveling out of the country shortly."

Madeira Suiza jumped to his feet and was pulled back down by Fonseca.

"I accept your resignation," Fernando said. He came around the side of his desk. "Send the letter by courier."

The two men embraced. Hugo pulled away from Fernando and looked at Lorena. She didn't dare say a word.

Silvio opened the door and Hugo left. Fernando started to sit back down behind his desk as Madeira Suiza jumped up again.

"President Betancourt, you can't just let him--," Madeira Suiza started.

"Ignacio, César," Fernando interrupted. "Thank you. That will be all."

Silvio opened the door. "This way."

Madeira Suiza walked out, his face a mask. Fonseca, Bernal Paz, and Fernando exchanged a nod of mutual satisfaction before the two older men left.

Lorena stood to leave as well. Something here had happened that she didn't understand. She needed to get in touch with Hugo, find out exactly what all this meant.

"Lorena, please stay," Fernando said.

Silvio closed the door, leaving Lorena and Fernando alone.

"Well," Lorena said. "This was all very sudden, wasn't it?"

"It leaves me with an important position to fill," Fernando said. He took off his spectacles and rubbed his forehead.

Lorena regarded him with loathing. Just like always, it was Fernando first, before anything that was important to her.

"I would like you to consider taking over as Minister of Public Security," Fernando said. "For the remainder of my presidency."

"Me?" Lorena flounced into a chair in front of the presidential desk. "Fernando, seriously. You know that a sitting minister cannot also be a political candidate. The law is very specific."

"I'm asking you to put your country first, Lorena," Fernando said.

Lorena leaned forward to argue and her eye fell on some papers on her husband's desk. The handwriting was familiar. Max's handwriting. Max's handwriting on pages from a planner. Lorena read the words *Hugo lunch, Hotel Arias.*

♦

Chapter 50

Luz and the girls decorated the house with lacy *papel picado* streamers for Maria's fiftieth birthday. Father Santiago came, and Carmelita and the Rosales family, and several of Maria's friends whose lives also revolved around their children and the church.

Tío was working a few hours each week in an upholstery shop and brought his new employer to the party. Esteban Jimenez Cruz was compact and barrel-shaped, with dark brown eyes and straight black hair hanging over his collar. He was her age, Luz guessed, with the padded look of a man who had a few too many *tortillas* at every meal.

Luz and Lupe put out the food: *tamales, cuaresmeños jarochos, bayos refritos con salsa, ensalada de nopalitos*, fried fillets of *tilapia* fish, *arroz rojo*, and *tortillas*. Everyone helped themselves and sat wherever they could find a chair. Beer and *Cocas* were passed around for toasts to Maria.

Luz sat on the sofa next to Lupe with a plate of food and a bottle of beer, and unwrapped her *tamale*. The spicy pork and chiles formed a tangy red counterpoint to the white slab of *masa* corn paste nestled inside the folded and steamed corn husks. Without the meat and spices the *masa* would be filling but tasteless.

The party had pleased Maria immensely but she was flushed again, her face an unhealthy red as she drank copious amounts of *Coca*. Luz watched her mother with concern. Something had to be done about Maria's intermittent breathlessness and increasingly ruddy look. Maybe Maria had developed high blood pressure, like Señor Vega. There was a blood pressure machine next to the pharmacist's desk in the big grocery store. Luz resolved to take her mother there to check.

There was a birthday *pastel* and pastries. Lupe got up to help Sophia wash her hands. Esteban Jimenez Cruz appeared with his dessert plate.

"Do you mind, señorita?" he asked and sat.

"Not at all," Luz said.

"Your cooking is excellent," Esteban said. He leaned forward and forked up the cake on his plate. "I've never had such good *tamales*."

"How kind of you to say," Luz murmured. She watched him out of the corner of her eye. He wolfed down his cake in three large bites, like he wasn't sure there would be food tomorrow.

"This is excellent, too," Esteban said around his last mouthful.

"I didn't make it," Luz said. "I bought it at the *pasteleria*." People were standing around, still helping themselves to dessert and coffee and *Cocas*. She couldn't start cleaning up yet.

"Armando tells me you were a *muchacha* in Mexico City," Esteban said, trying to get her attention. He put his plate on the floor and wiped his mouth with the back of his hand. "But you had an accident there."

"Armando?"

"Yes, Armando." Esteban gestured at Tío.

"Oh. Yes." Luz had almost forgotten that Tío had a real name. For once Tío had showered and shaved and looked marginally presentable. Martina was sitting on his knee.

"I live with my family." Esteban paused. "The house is a good size."

"Yes," Luz said, because he seemed to expect her to say something. Single people always lived with their parents. Unless they were wealthy and lived in a nice apartment in Mexico City.

"My mother says our kitchen is large enough for another cook," he said.

Madre de Dios, Luz thought. She searched desperately for another topic as she unconsciously wrapped her left arm over her ribs and hugged the scar. "Do you enjoy your work?"

"It is a fine living," Esteban said.

Luz listened with a pasted-on smile as he talked about the shop he owned with his brother. They had three employees and reupholstered old pieces as well as making custom pieces for a *decoradora*. They had their own delivery van. The shop was going to branch out and start making curtains. As he talked she knew there was no artistry to what he did, although there might have been. For him it was all about stretching the fabric and stapling it into place. That and using the least amount of the customer's fabric so that there would be leftovers to sell. Or use himself.

Luz had a mental image of what the inside of his house looked like: a hodgepodge of mismatched upholstered pieces, the inevitable shrine to the Virgin, and a mother who would insist on telling Luz how to make *caldo de mariscos* for his hangovers.

"Are you interested in the presidential elections?" she asked abruptly, cutting off Esteban's description of the sewing machine they'd bought for their expansion into drapery.

"The elections?" Esteban smiled uncertainly. He wore a dark blue shirt and brown pants. He didn't have help who came in twice a week to care for white shirts and khaki pants.

"Yes, the presidential elections," Luz said.

"I am in the union," Esteban said proudly, as if that was all he needed to say.

And it was. Being a member of a union almost certainly meant that Esteban automatically voted for PRI candidates. He took a pack of Boots cigarettes out of his shirt pocket and offered it to her. Luz shook her head. He lit one for himself and put the pack away.

"What about Lorena Lopez de Betancourt?" Luz asked.

"Lorena?" Esteban held the cigarette in his right and tapped the ash into his cupped left hand as if it was an ashtray. "President Betancourt's wife, no?"

"That's right. Did you read her interview in *HOLA!*?" There was a long pause while Luz looked brightly at Esteban and started to feel mean.

"She is the president's wife?" he asked. Again.

"Yes," said Luz.

"You think she would like to be president?" Esteban took a long, thoughtful drag on his cigarette.

Every day I cry for the pain of the people. "Yes."

"Did she ask her husband?"

"I think he knows she wants to be president," Luz said.

"If she is president, who will make his dinner?" Esteban said, as if he had resolved an important issue. He finished his cigarette by putting it out against his thumbnail. The butt and his handful of ash went onto his dessert plate.

He smelled of onions and cigarettes and hair gel.

"Excuse me," Luz said abruptly. She got to her feet too quickly and the pain in her side flared. She swayed a little. Suddenly Juan Pablo was there. She shook him off and went upstairs.

◆

"Mama," Luz said. "I think you should have your blood pressure checked."

"I'm fine," Maria said from behind the ironing board.

"We'll walk to the big grocery store and have it checked at the pharmacy." Luz poured iodine into the water in the sink and added stalks of cilantro and some tomatoes. "After the shirts get picked up."

"You worry about nothing," Maria said. "I'm just tired today, that's all. The party kept me up too late last night."

After helping Luz clean up the detritus of Maria's birthday dinner, Lupe had gone to the Friday craft afternoon at Santa Clara. Juan Pablo and the girls were still at school.

"Tomorrow then," Luz insisted. She let the cilantro soak for a few minutes then shook it dry, wiped the tomatoes, and carried everything to the chopping board on the table to make *salsa fresca*.

"That Esteban was nice," Maria said.

Luz diced a tomato. "I guess."

"A good eater." Maria ran the iron over a shirt placket, her face ruddier than ever. "He ate four *tamales* and three *cuaresmeños*."

Luz bent her head over the chopping board and minced the cilantro stalks into damp green dots. Her mother had counted how many *tamales* and stuffed *chiles* the man had eaten. Like gluttony was an important quality. A more important quality than, say, intelligence.

"He would be a good provider for you, Luz de Maria."

"Mama, you can't be serious." Luz scraped the cilantro into a bowl and tried not to laugh.

Maria panted as she hung the shirt on a hanger, shrouded it in plastic, and stapled the coupon to the shroud. "Why not?"

"Mama, please." Luz minced another stalk with swift strokes of the knife. "Talking to him was like watching paint dry."

"He's a good son. He goes to church."

"He's thick and round," Luz groaned. "His hair is too long. He has the table manners of a goat. He doesn't read and he hasn't any opinion of his own and he doesn't care about my opinions, either. He's so dull it would kill me." She narrowly missed slicing off her finger and knew she was far too worked up.

Luz dropped the knife and clamped her arm around her ribs. It was like comparing *molé* and *masa*. *Molé* was sharp, tangy, and complicated. For special occasions. The sauce was hard to make, requiring many ingredients and hours of cooking and grinding and stewing and mixing. But the end result was a unique and wonderful experience, full of the flavor of fruit and cocoa and *pasilla* chiles.

Masa was just the opposite, bland and simple and requiring only *masa harina* flour and water. *Masa* dough was everywhere. Thin it for *tamales*, thicken it to make *tortillas* or fried *tlacoyos* or *gorditas*. It was plain and unremarkable. On every street corner and in every kitchen.

"There's someone else, isn't there," Maria said.

Luz bit her lip. She'd told no one about Eddo, not even Carmelita.

"So?" Maria rested the iron on its heel.

"He's an attorney, Mama." Luz resumed chopping as her face reddened with guilt. "He's very smart. Travels a lot. Loves *fútbol*. Very athletic. Like Juan Pablo." She swallowed. "His family makes *talavera* and owns a lot of land."

"*Criollo?*"

"He went to college in the United States and then studied law at UNAM." Luz tried to ignore her mother's tone. "I went to his office once. It was very nice."

"This is why you keep going to the *abarrotes* store?" Maria demanded. "For messages from a *criollo* man? Where is he?"

"I'm not sure."

"Almost 30 and you still don't know your place." The scorn in Maria's breathy voice was unmistakable. "*Estupida*. You don't know where he is because he lied to you."

Luz said nothing.

"That sort of man just uses women like you." Maria shook her finger at Luz. "You keep with your own kind."

"He was just nice . . . and I thought he might leave a message. That's all."

"That's foolishness," Maria scolded. "Think about Esteban. His mother and I think you two would be a good match. You could get married in June. After Lupe has the baby."

"I'm not going to marry Esteban," Luz sniffed. "Or anybody else. I've got a great big scar across my ribs and no man is ever going to see it."

"In 17 years of marriage your father never saw my ribs," Maria admonished and picked up the iron again.

Luz grinned in spite of herself.

There was a noise by the stove. Luz looked up just in time to see Maria turn the color of an eggplant and slump awkwardly in the tight space between the table and the ironing board. The iron fell out of her hand, clanging onto the tile floor with the crack of metal on cheap *saltillo*. The board tumbled, slamming into the rack of shirts. The plastic shrouds swayed around Luz's head as she screamed. Then the rack pitched forward, snapping apart as it hit the table and sending the plastic-covered shirts slithering over the floor next to Maria's body.

◆

Four days after saying Maria's funeral Mass, Father Santiago was murdered by a gang that broke into the church to steal the collection from the Sunday masses. His body was discovered Monday morning by the old man who tended the cemetery. A young priest named Father Patricio moved into the rectory and Luz hated him for not being Father Santiago.

♦

Chapter 51

"You don't have to do a thing," Hugo said. "Just tell Fernando you're thinking about the job."

"And that the campaign can't be turned off like a switch," Lorena said.

"Make sure Silvio doesn't sneak around behind you and pull the radio advertising or close down the websites."

The phone connection was clear and Hugo heard Lorena catch her breath. "He wouldn't dare."

"He's Fernando's man."

"I hate him."

For the first time since he'd known her she ready to give up and he was damned if she would. "Just give me some time to figure this out, Lorena," he said. "Keep stalling Fernando. Don't give him an answer."

"But he knows there's no money," she hissed. "And Max is gone. There's nobody to run the campaign."

It had been nearly two weeks since Hugo had resigned. Luis hadn't lasted long in prison; he'd been found stabbed to death in his cell. Meanwhile, Max's trail was still cold.

Hugo had sent a cryptic note to Gomez Mazzo about Site 2 "shipments" being confiscated but had not received a posting in reply. Even so, Hugo was optimistic that all he had to do was reconnect with Gomez Mazzo and make sure the operation at Site 1 was still running. A network like that, making that kind of money, didn't just evaporate overnight. Gomez Mazzo might still be bringing in the cash but he'd know it belonged to Hugo. They'd set up another fake bank, like before when Luis's man had messed things up in Anahuac and Gomez Mazzo had fixed it. Only this one would be fake enough to stay under the Central Bank's radar. Bernal Paz must have been shitting his pants that night over drinks at the Hotel Arias. The thought made Hugo smile grimly to himself.

"I can fix this, Lorena," he replied. "Right after I get back from Canada. Graciela will have a physical at some hospital in Vancouver, they'll tell us she's fine and we can all act relieved."

"You're leaving me here all alone?" Lorena shrilled. "With Fernando pushing and pushing me every day?"

"After Canada we're going back to Monterrey." Hugo felt her anger vibrate over the cell phone connection. Somewhere a microwave tower was emitting sparks.

"What about me?"

"I've got a business to run, Lorena," Hugo said. "We'll keep the campaign going from there."

"With what money?" Lorena raged. "I need the money now."

Hugo got off the sofa and went to the bar in the corner of the study, phone clamped between his shoulder and ear so he could pour himself a drink. "I'm working on it," he insisted. He'd use his own business to filter the money, he decided, siphon off what he could from the books and use several of the smaller subsidiaries the same way that Arias had used the Hermanos Hospitality shell company. He'd have to work out the arrangements and find some new accountants but it could be done.

"Am I important to you or not?" Lorena demanded.

"I promised to make you president," Hugo said, the drink halfway to his mouth. "And I have a plan. You just sit tight for a couple of weeks."

Los Pinos was still within his grasp.

♦

Chapter 52

"I should quit school, Luz," Juan Pablo said.

Luz handed him a cup of *manzanilla* tea and sat on the sofa next to him. It was Saturday. Lupe and the girls had watched *Sabado Gigante* and were now upstairs in bed. It was time for the news. Sticking to routine was how they had survived the weeks since Maria's death.

"I paid your tuition through to graduation." Luz stirred her tea. "It's not refundable."

Juan Pablo's jaw dropped. Luz smiled for the first time in forever.

It was so hard to be the only decision maker now. Carmelita had helped; taking Martina and Sophia for sleepovers with her girls, bringing over food, and talking quietly to Lupe who seemed incapable of doing anything these days. But Luz was head of the family now, solely responsible for the future of the Alba family. She moved into Maria's shabby bedroom and lay awake nights, wondering if she had the strength to keep going. The house felt more claustrophobic than ever, as if shrunken by sadness.

"You shouldn't have done that," Juan Pablo protested. "Nobody's working."

"We had a deal," Luz said. "You'll finish Santa Catalina first."

"Luz, that was before--."

"No," Luz cut him off. "I have an appointment on Monday with a placement agency. I'll get a day job in Veracruz so I can help Lupe with the baby at night."

"You got it all figured out, then," Juan Pablo said grudgingly.

"We'll manage, sunshine," Luz said with more confidence

than she felt. Taking a bus to and from Veracruz meant a 14 hour day.

Juan Pablo kissed her on the cheek then turned on the television. Luz watched him out of the corner of her eye. He had neither mother nor father, now, just her to keep him from ending up waving cars into parking spaces with a red rag.

They sipped their tea while the advertisements urged them to buy La Costeña beans and Jumex juice and brush their teeth with Colgate because Cleanliness is Healthy.

The main news story was about the increasing violence on the border with Texas, centering on Nuevo Laredo. The drug war between competing cartels was heated and bloody, with the battle lines blurred by cartel rivalries and police and military involvement. The camera panned across two bodies which had recently been uncovered in the desert south of the city. The dead men had both been shot in the head and buried, making identification difficult. The only clue was a Highway Patrol badge. The camera zoomed in on a sand-scoured badge and then swept across the dirty bodies. The heads were covered but one body wore light colored pants.

Luz dropped her cup.

This was why Eddo never called. Tomás had taken her pictures but they hadn't helped and somehow, out in the desert, both Eddo and Tomás had been killed.

In her mind's eye, Luz saw the gun jerk and Eddo's eyes glaze and his jaw slacken as his brains sprayed out of the side of his head. Those men had found him because of her. Everything Eddo had worked for was all gone; lost in a puddle of blood that had dried up and blown away across the desert.

"Are you okay?" Juan Pablo went to get a rag.

Luz walked over to the shrine. The Virgin looked as serene as if She hadn't abandoned Eddo in the desert like Raul's son.

Juan Pablo said something but a roaring sound drowned him out and Luz threw the votive candles across the room. The glass cups shattered against the concrete wall.

"You let this happen!" Luz screamed at the Virgin in Her dark green robe with the stars and the cherubs at Her feet. "You *let it!*"

She hurled away the ribbon and the rosaries. The beads made little rattling sounds as they hit the floor. Luz grabbed the heavy picture and hauled it out of the iron tabletop easel her father had forged long ago.

"*That's enough,*" she yelled, not knowing why or what she was saying. "*I've had enough!*" The pain in her side flared and burned. Luz gasped and the room swam but the Virgin no longer deserved any prayers.

Luz swung the heavy picture and belted the wooden cabinet and the concrete wall and the coffee table, staggering with the weight and the awkward movements. The frame shook and splintered in her hands.

"Enough!" *SLAM. SLAM.* She raised the picture over her head and smashed it against the wall, then blasted it into the edge of the cabinet again. Momentum carried her across the room, the picture scything everything around it. Chips of wood and bits of canvas flew around her head.

"Luz! *Luz!*" Juan Pablo shouted.

There was a roaring and it was deafening, louder even than Juan Pablo or Lupe's screams or the shrieks of the girls from the stairs. All of them were shouting and crying because Tía Luz, the calm one, the strong one, had suddenly gone mad.

"*Stop it*, Luz. *Stop it.*"

"Tía Luz! Tía Luz!!"

"*Enough! Enough!*" *SLAM. SLAM.* Splinters and shreds filled the air as the picture smashed into the sharp corner of the doorframe.

Luz swung the picture again but suddenly Juan Pablo's arms were around her from behind, bending her over and pinning her down.

"Luz, what's wrong? What's the matter?" Juan Pablo's arms were like iron. His voice sounded like a grown man's.

Her pain in her side was blinding.

"*Luz,*" Lupe cried from the stair landing. "*Please.*"

Luz dropped the smashed picture and hauled in air.

"Talk to me, Luz," Juan Pablo said insistently.

She wanted to tell him to let go, that she wasn't done, but she couldn't speak. The pain was rich and dark and hot and Eddo was dead.

Juan Pablo continued to hold her, her back against his chest, doubling her over so she wouldn't pass out. Eventually the pain subsided and Luz pushed him away.

"What's going on, Luz?" He hung onto her arm.

"Get it out," she panted. "Of the house."

Lupe crept down the stairs. "Luz, please tell me."

"I don't want to see this picture ever again," Luz shouted. The pain rose up and darkened her vision. She had to bend over again to find some air.

"The picture of the Virgin?" Lupe asked.

"You don't mean that," Juan Pablo said at the same time.

"Tía Luz, what's the matter?"

Sophia and Martina came down the stairs. Both of them were still crying. Martina picked up the rosary beads from the floor but Sophia just clung to Lupe's leg and sobbed.

Luz looked around the room. The picture of the Virgin was in ribbons. Pieces of the frame and bits of glass from the votive candles were scattered all over the living room.

"*Madre de Dios*," she murmured and slumped against Juan Pablo.

He pulled her over to the sofa and made her sit. Lupe got Luz a glass of water then squeezed onto the other end of the sofa with the girls.

"I'm sorry." Luz drank the water and felt her heart slow. She'd told herself for weeks that Eddo might be dead but the truth was too much to bear. "It was the news. The two men who were killed in Nuevo Laredo. I knew them."

"How did you know them?" Juan Pablo was astonished.

"One was an attorney. The other was police."

"You knew them?"

"The attorney." Luz felt strange and disembodied talking about Eddo being dead. "His name was Eduardo Martín Bernardo Cortez Castillo. I met him last October. He was . . . he was a friend."

"Tía Luz," Martina piped up. "Maybe your friends are in heaven talking to *Abuela* and *Abuelo* and Father Santiago."

Luz blinked at her niece. The little girls had coped well with the loss of their grandmother and Father Santiago, due in part to what she'd told them. The thought steadied her. "Maybe."

Eventually they went into the kitchen and made hot chocolate as Juan Pablo put the remains of the picture into a trash bag. Luz promised Martina and Sophia she'd paint them a new picture of the Madonna.

♦

That night Luz dreamed that she was in the car with her attackers. Eddo was in the car, too, and the noose was around his neck instead of hers. The leather bit into his throat and Luz knew he was wracked with pain.

She was on the verge of saying his name, it was on her lips, and he stared at her in mute appeal, willing her to be silent. Luz woke up just before she said his name, drenched and freezing, her heart pounding and painful.

♦

Chapter 53

Luz pushed open the door and found herself in a small grimy room. A *mestizo* man with wobbly jowls and a cigarette glued to the corner of his mouth looked up from a magazine balanced on his paunch.

"*Buen' dia*," he grunted and looked at her appraisingly.

Luz looked around. There wasn't much else in the room besides the man's scratched and dirty Formica desk, a filing cabinet in a corner, and a wooden chair in front of the desk. Dark blue aluminum blinds covered the single window. Several of the blinds were bent in the middle, giving the window a perpetual smile. The walls were white and bare except for a calendar with a picture of a dolphin on it.

"I was told this was a domestic placement agency," Luz said.

The man pointed to the wooden chair and Luz sat down gingerly.

"*Planta* or day?" he asked.

"*Planta*," Luz said. The word *muchacha* was obviously stamped on her forehead. "I was in Mexico City but I need something in Veracruz now."

"How long you worked?" he asked.

"Nearly 14 years," Luz said.

"Whatcha got?" He held out a pudgy hand. Luz took her letters of recommendation out of her backpack and handed them over.

As the man read the cigarette in the corner of his mouth turned into a thin cylinder of ash. When he finished reading he dropped the letters on his desk, took the cigarette out of his mouth, and lit a new one from the glowing end of the old.

"Your name's Luz de Maria Alba Mora?"

"Yes."

"High class sounding name." It wasn't a compliment.

Luz said nothing.

He looked through the letters again, turned them over, shuffled them a bit. "So where's the rest?"

"That's all I've got."

"Not 14 years worth here, *chica*."

"I worked in Mexico City until late last year but I don't have a letter from them," Luz said.

"Fired?"

"I left," Luz said loftily.

"Caught stealing?" The man grinned nastily around the cigarette.

"No."

The man snorted. "Maybe I got something for you. Good pay. Variety."

"Variety?" Luz had never heard a maid's job described that way. He probably meant a family with ten children and only one toilet.

"You look like a smart girl." He lit a third cigarette. "I got some people that need a *planta*. They pay me a finder's fee and I supply a girl. You stay 31 days. Then you quit and come back here and get a little bonus. Next house you do another 31 days."

"These people only want a maid for 31 days?" Luz asked warily.

He sucked hard on the cigarette. Luz watched the ash travel up the paper toward his mouth. "No," he said. "But you leave after 31 days."

"Right," Luz said softly.

The man was pimping *muchachas*. His contract with the people seeking a maid no doubt said that the finder's fee was nonrefundable after 30 days. The maid stayed an extra day to make sure he kept the fee. He shared a bit of it with the girl, but probably pocketed 5000 pesos each time he pulled the scam. Maybe he did some legitimate placements, too, so his reputation wouldn't put him out of business, but the scamming made the real money. For the *muchacha*, the advantages of working the scam instead of maintaining a real job were obvious; why bother to work hard and impress an employer if the job only lasted 31 days?

A world of passion and righteousness.

Luz grabbed her letters and walked out.

♦

Semana Santa, the holy week before Easter, was full of comforting rituals. Luz joined the solemn walk around the church intoning the Stations of the Cross. Then there was the narrative of the Holy Thursday service and the solemn Good Friday clearing of the altar.

Easter Sunday was clear and bright. Father Patricio was young and had progressive ideas so after Mass there was a *norteamericano*-style egg hunt as well as a *piñata.* In the afternoon they ate a special *comida* at the Rosales' house. The talk was about the children and school and jobs for Juan Pablo when he graduated but Carmelita's father-in-law mentioned the resignation of Hugo de la Madrid Acosta and speculation that Lorena Lopez de Betancourt would become Minister of Public Security. Luz had read the news, too, but couldn't bring herself to comment.

Painting helped, especially at night when the nightmare threatened. Luz painted one Madonna wearing a cloak of stars and another with the Virgin in the regional clothes of Veracruz like the painting she'd done long ago for Father Santiago. Neither was any good. She started a third.

It was done in late March, a few days before her birthday. It was long past midnight when she laid all three canvases on the coffee table and curled onto the sofa to look at them. The first two were faceless, the features hidden in shadow. One she named *La Señora de los Angeles.* The other was *La Señora de Sangre* because of Her red cloak.

Luz had sketched the third Madonna furiously one night after having the dream about Eddo again. The colors were cool grays and blues. *El Greco colors,* she thought and closed her eyes tiredly. That one was easy to name. *La Virgen de las Lágrimas.* Madonna of the Tears.

The house was quiet. Lupe and the girls were asleep. Juan Pablo would be home soon from a friend's house. Luz fell asleep on the sofa, her head pillowed on her arm.

A pressure against her lips made her smile. It was him, his mouth on hers. She watched him kiss her, hair cropped short, hazel eyes full of promise of the night to come.

"Eddo?" Luz murmured.

"I'm going to fuck you proper," Tío slurred.

Luz's eyes flew open. Tío was practically lying on top of her.

"Get off!" Luz shouted, squirming beneath his weight.

"Come here, bitch." Tío fumbled at the fly of her jeans, too drunk to find the button. Body odor and cheap tequila curdled the air.

Luz shoved and screamed at the same time. Tío was surprisingly strong and his fumbling turned into a wrestling match.

There was a chunky, ringing sound. Tío blinked in surprise. He rolled off Luz and onto the floor.

Juan Pablo stood over the sofa with a cast iron skillet in his hand, looking like an enraged Montezuma. He pulled her up. "Are you all right?"

"I think so," Luz gasped. Tío was unconscious, a line of drool tracing down his chin. "I fell asleep and then suddenly he was on top of me."

"He left the gate and the front door open," Juan Pablo said furiously. "Anyone could have waltzed in."

"What happened?" Lupe asked from the stairs.

"Tío came in, drunk as a pig," Juan Pablo said without turning around. "Thought he'd help himself to Luz."

Lupe's eyes widened as she came down, hand on her pregnant belly. "Is he dead?"

"No." Juan Pablo found the door key in Tío's pocket. "But he's out of here. I'll haul his stuff out of the shed in the morning."

Luz and Lupe watched as Juan Pablo grabbed Tío's ankles and dragged him out of the living room, the unconscious man's head thumping against the floor. The sad parade went out the front door, across the yard, and through the gate. Lupe started to cry.

"I'm all right. Really I am," Luz said. She put her arms around her sister but Lupe pulled away and went upstairs.

Luz made some tea to quiet her jangling nerves. When she came back into the living room Juan Pablo was on the sofa staring at the three paintings.

"Your pictures are amazing, Luz," Juan Pablo said. "This one is . . ." He trailed off, pointing at the last painting and shaking his head.

"I shouldn't have tried to do a portrait," Luz said, handing him a mug. "I haven't done a face since . . ."

"It's your face," Juan Pablo said.

"I know it's a face," she said then realized what he meant. "*My* face?"

In the painting, Mary wore a sheer *rebozo* shawl over straight dark hair. Her head was tilted to one side. Under the *rebozo*, Luz's face gazed at the child in her arms, looking as if there was no happiness left in the world.

"Take two to that art place in Mexico City on Sunday," Juan Pablo urged. "Give one to the girls and take the others."

"I can't go back there." Luz sat next to him.

"Why not?" Juan Pablo jostled her. "It's open on Sundays, right? Go."

"Sunday's my birthday," Luz reminded him, loath to tell him about her last experience at Jardin del Arte. "The girls will expect us to do something."

"We can celebrate next weekend," Juan Pablo said. "I can't give you much, Luz, but I can handle things for a day."

The tiny house in Soledad de Doblado felt like a coffin. The thought of being away for a whole day, surrounded by artists and clever people, was sorely tempting.

She just wouldn't take any checks.

◆

Chapter 54

Hh23051955: Site 1 shipments not being received.

Hh23051955: Sites 2 and 3 not operational. Advise alternates.

This was the third time Hugo had posted the same messages. Neither **44Gg449M11** nor **CH5299xyz9** had posted a reply.

Hugo poured himself a healthy dose of brandy. Gomez Mazzo had set up a fortune-making machine, using Hugo's plan and real estate investment, and now was apparently keeping it all for himself. Or maybe he and Max Arias had made some sort of separate deal. But if they had, why hadn't they taken the money out of Banco Limitado first? Why leave it for Fonseca to grab?

And why would Gomez Mazzo have willingly forfeited having the future president on his side? Lorena was a serious contender. Gomez Mazzo knew she'd clean up the Zetas for him and leave El Toro a free hand in the north. The deal had been clear: campaign money in exchange for territory as soon as she took the oath of office.

Moreover, if Arias had made a deal with Gomez Mazzo, Lorena would have had to be in on it. Arias would have little to bargain with unless he could hold out the promise of what Lorena could do as president. But that didn't make sense either, because Hugo would know if Lorena was double crossing him.

Fonseca had closed down Site 2 and taken the money, but why hadn't Gomez Mazzo gotten in touch, figured out another way to get the money from Site 1 back to the campaign?

Hugo gulped down the brandy and poured himself another. Graciela hadn't wanted to go to Canada and the trip was delayed. In the meantime, he was trying to work out just how to divert funds from his businesses into Lorena's campaign but had run up against some of his own company accountants who were a bit too smart for their own good. He'd fire them all, for one reason or another, but couldn't make it too obvious.

Time was not his friend. Romero was still holding strong in the polls and more PAN stalwarts were throwing their support to him as Lorena's momentum ebbed. She was nearly hysterical every time Hugo spoke to her. Fernando was shoving the ministry job at her, pressuring her to serve her country like a *maldita* recruiting poster. Someone was stoking the news pundits into speculating that she would become Minister of Public Security, further damaging the campaign.

"Hugo?" Graciela opened the door to the study.

"What?" He belched, a hot bubble of brandy searing his throat.

"Señor Vargas to see you," Graciela said crisply. "I'm going out."

His wife wasn't as pliant and retiring as she used to be. Graciela had bought new clothes and was out of the house more than she'd ever been, fooling around with some charity. When she was home she texted constantly or was on her computer.

The fucking detective he'd hired hadn't found Arias. Hugo threw him out, drank the rest of the bottle of brandy and passed out in his chair.

♦

Chapter 55

Luz sold *La Señora de los Angeles* for 900 pesos an hour after she got to Jardin del Arte. A few minutes later she sold two sketches and a small canvas of Santa Clara she'd done long ago. Cash sales.

The monochromatic seascapes and pictures of girls and donkeys were still there. The regular artists watched her with a mixture of annoyance and admiration. She caught one of the old men looking at her with a set expression. Luz lifted her water bottle to him in a sort of salute. He just pursed his lips but Luz didn't care. *1660, 1660 pesos* sang around and around in her head. She was wearing Juan Pablo's Santa Catalina sweatshirt and the peso notes crackled in the big kangaroo pocket.

Luz sat on the low rock wall with her sketchpad and watched the crowd. She hadn't missed being in Mexico City, with its millions of people, thin air, and stifling *contaminación*. No, she certainly hadn't missed *la sopa*. But there was a vibrancy about the huge dirty city, a sort of stubborn hopefulness that was like a shot of positive energy.

Nearly everyone who passed said something about *La Virgen de las Lágrimas*. One man stood in front of it for a long time. When he asked her how much it was she said "3000 pesos." If he came back Luz was prepared to go as low as 2000 pesos. Maybe 1500.

An hour later she was bent over her sketchpad when something dry and gentle stroked the back of her neck just *there*. Luz flinched at the unexpected touch and sucked in her breath.

She smelled leather and soap and citrus.

◆

Chapter 56

Eddo knew it was her, despite being at least 20 meters away and approaching her from the rear. It was as if he'd memorized the nape of her neck and the shell of her ear and the way her hair looked pulled back into a ponytail. She had on a navy blue sweatshirt that was too big for her. The hood hung down her back and there were some white letters on either side. She was sitting with her sketchpad in her lap, staring at it intently, just like she'd done in front of the Tamayo.

She jerked when he touched her and the chatter of the crowd carried his words away. He ran parallel to the wall, looking for a way to get to the other side. There wasn't a break and so he simply vaulted over the wall, banging into canvases and nearly kicking over an easel with some monstrous ocean on it.

The owner of the easel yelled at him and Eddo had to stop and say a few soothing words of apology and then he took off again, half running, half walking down the sidewalk. He was ready to start pitching people out of his way, when suddenly he was in front of Luz.

It was simple good luck that he was the one to find her. All of his friends who knew what Luz looked like had taken turns prowling around Jardin del Arte and the Tamayo Museum on Sundays since the army raid. Diego, still guilt-ridden at the way Luz had left the hospital right under his cappuccino-loving nose, had been at Jardin del Arte the previous weekend. Ana and Tomás had gone the week before.

"I can't believe I finally found you," Eddo blurted.

Luz looked dumbfounded. Opened her mouth but didn't say a word. She stood up with her left arm clamped against her side and shoulders hunched like a small broken bird. He thought wildly that whatever was wrong, it didn't matter what, he would fix it.

"This one is the best. How much is it?"

Luz's stunned eyes drifted past Eddo's face and he spun around. A man and a woman, both expensively dressed, were looking at the pictures hung on the tree trunk next to Luz. There were two oil paintings on the tree, one of a fish *mercado* done in her unmistakable humorous style, with the red snapper and salmon grinning and swiveling their eyes as they lay on the ice slab. But the other painting was the one that the people were talking about and he immediately saw why.

It was a painting of Luz as a Madonna. The colors were pale, almost frosty. It was much better by far than the sketches and drawings he'd seen in October. Powerful and wrenchingly painful at the same time. It was hard to look away from.

Luz didn't say anything, just slumped back down on the wall as if her legs wouldn't support her. Her eyes were still wide with shock.

Eddo took down the painting. The couple clustered around him and admired it in low voices. There was a card on the back. *La Virgen de las Lágrimas*. The sorrow permeating the self-portrait tore at his gut.

"The asking price is 10,000 pesos," Eddo said.

◆

Chapter 57

He was dead, Luz had known it for weeks. But he wasn't. Eddo was alive and had just sold *La Virgen de las Lágrimas* for a fortune.

They didn't speak as they got into a big boxy tank on wheels, a different SUV from the one he'd had in October. The engine hummed throatily. As Eddo backed the car out of the space Luz started to shake.

He looked the same and yet different. There was the same taut energy, the same self-control. The difference was a thick streak of silver above his left ear. It contrasted sharply with the dark brown of the rest of his hair and Luz thought distractedly that it was good he wore his hair short, it wasn't as noticeable.

He wore khaki pants, a black sweater that clung to his chest, and a simple black leather coat that came halfway to his knees. A white tee shirt showed inside the V neck of the sweater. He looked quietly wealthy and strikingly handsome, even more so than she remembered.

Luz squeezed her hands between her knees and stared out the side window. The tint made the world outside look dark and stormy. She wondered if the windows were bulletproof. There was a huge lump in her throat and Luz blinked to keep her tears in check.

Eddo wove the big vehicle through the small streets around the park. They crossed Reforma and turned up a side street into the Zona Rosa. The Sunday traffic was light in the city's famous touristy web of restaurants and shops. He finally pulled the car up to the curb in front of a fancy antiques shop.

Eddo got the unsold canvas and the remaining sketches out of the back seat and led her to a residential doorway next to the shop. He unlocked it and they went up three flights of stairs before he stopped and unlocked another door. He held it open and Luz walked past him into a large apartment decorated with angular black leather furniture and abstract art.

"This is my friend Vasco's place. I'm using it while he's away." Eddo gestured stiffly toward the living room. "Go on and sit down. Would you like a glass of wine?"

Luz managed to hold it together until she sat down on the black sofa. Then her tears came hard. Her body was wracked by sobs, her shoulders heaved. She cried because she had loved him, she cried because she had killed him, she cried because nothing could ever be the same between them. She cried because she had known he was dead, because she had been so unhappy for so long, because she couldn't believe he was alive.

She wept wildly into her hands, unable to stop, her body bunched and shaking. The constant ache in her ribs flared into heat.

"Luz, Luz, please," Eddo sat down on the bare coffee table and tried to pull her hands away from her face. His voice came from a hollow distance. "Don't do this."

Luz couldn't look at him but wept as she'd never done before, all self-control abandoned, her sorrow flooding around them. She had put him in danger. Her grief and shame were bottomless.

"I'm sorry," Luz sobbed out. "I'm sorry." She repeated it over and over, hysterical with remorse. She was caught in a burning river of tears and couldn't stop crying, couldn't think of anything besides the need to tell him she was sorry. Her chest was on fire, the intensity scraped her throat raw, and soon she was gasping for air.

"Luz." Eddo's voice was coming from farther and farther away. "Stop it. You'll make yourself sick."

As if to prove him right, Luz started to gag, her body rebelling against the wracking sobs. She stood dizzily, her hand to her mouth, and looked around. Eddo jumped up, caught her arm, and together they stumbled into a small bathroom.

Luz slid to her knees in front of the toilet and retched into the bowl, tears streaming down her face. Her stomach was empty and the retching produced nothing except dry heaves. The spasms shook her again and again as she continued to cough and cry. The room cartwheeled and she held onto the cool porcelain, embarrassment piling on top of everything else.

Slowly, slowly, the horrible retching subsided, the room righted, and she found Eddo sitting on the floor beside her, holding out a damp towel.

"I'm sorry," Luz said brokenly. His kindness only made it worse. "It's my fault. I led them right to you. I'm sorry." She pressed the towel to her face and started to cry all over again, her body trembling.

"Stop it, Luz!" Eddo said harshly. "*Stop it!*"

The sobs stilled in her throat as his voice reverberated off the tile walls.

"*I'm* the one who ought to be saying 'I'm sorry.' It's *my* fault, Luz." Eddo grabbed her arm. "It was my job to take care of you."

He had her by the shoulders now, shaking her. Raw emotion filled the small room.

"Do you understand me, Luz? *I should have been there.*"

Luz dropped the towel. Grief contorted the lean handsome lines of his face and tears streamed down his cheeks.

"Don't cry, Eddo," Luz whispered. "Today's my birthday."

"Ah, *mi corazón,*" Eddo said and his voice was suddenly gentle and full of sadness.

He gathered her into his arms. They stayed quietly on the bathroom floor for a long time, Eddo's back braced against the wall, Luz's head against his chest, until neither had any tears left.

◆

Chapter 58

Listening to Luz talk about the attack was the hardest thing Eddo had ever done. The tile was cold but he couldn't move, couldn't let go of her. She told him about being fired and her mother's death and why she'd thought he was dead. The tears flowed again when he told her that he'd settled all her hospital bills--nothing had been paid by the Vegas--and that he'd been looking for her for weeks. He told her about Panama, trading the CD for El Toro's withdrawal of protection from Hugo's *coyote* and drug muling operation, and the odyssey that followed. And about the traitor inside *Los Hierros*. She listened, wiping her eyes from time to time, and he felt guilty as hell at what he'd put her through.

They were both limp with exhaustion and hunger by the time they got off that bathroom floor. The closest place open on a Sunday evening was Vips. They walked there in silence.

Eddo gestured for Luz to precede him as the hostess showed them to a booth in the back. Luz moved slowly, with her left arm clamped to her side, her shoulder tipped a little. As when he'd first seen her at the park, Eddo was reminded of a broken bird.

The restaurant had Formica tables, orange vinyl upholstery, and laminated menus with photographs of salads and *enchiladas suizas*. They ordered chicken sandwiches and bottled water and made stilted small talk about how every Vips was the same.

He could have been eating cardboard for all that Eddo actually tasted the sandwich. He was halfway through when a woman at a nearby table gave them a disapproving smirk. Eddo glared back, letting the old *bruja* know that it was none of her business, even as he realized how incongruous they must look and what conclusions were likely. Luz's eyes were red, and she looked pretty rough in faded jeans, sneakers, and a man's sweatshirt. Luz saw the silent exchange and tears rolled down her face even as she chewed.

"Hey," Eddo said softly. He reached across the table and wiped her cheek. "Doesn't matter."

Luz nodded.

"I have a new job," Eddo said, wanting to distract her. "I'm working for Arturo Romero's campaign. In Oaxaca."

"Oh." Luz attempted a watery smile. "I guess you didn't want to keep your old job."

"No." Eddo returned the smile. "If Arturo wins I'll be his Attorney General. If he loses we'll set up a law practice together."

The tears spilled over again, which was not what Eddo had intended at all.

"I can make a difference, Luz," he said.

She sniffed. "I know."

"I don't ever to see again what I saw that day in the desert." Eddo remembered Miguel's headless body and exhausted people blinking in the sudden light. "That huge warehouse full of kids."

"Children?"

"That's right. I didn't tell you the worst of it. They recruited families to cross the border. Wanted ones with kids about 7 years old. Big enough to be able to gag down a condom full of coke and pass it later, too young to fight real hard when somebody shoved it down their throats. I'd run into one of their recruiters a couple of months before in Anahuac but didn't realize what was going on."

Luz put down the remains of her sandwich. "That's awful," she whispered.

Eddo nodded. "The money was for Lorena's campaign. If she won, El Toro could pretty much run the country. We still don't think Betancourt believed it. He just let Hugo resign. Lorena is technically still a candidate but she doesn't have any money."

"*Dios mio.*" Luz wiped her eyes with her napkin.

"Are you working?" Eddo asked. "A job you need to get to?"

"No."

"Let's get out of here," Eddo said.

"Yes, I'm done." Luz put her napkin on the table.

"No. I mean out of this damn city." Eddo stretched his hand across the table and touched hers. "Let's go to San Miguel de Allende tomorrow. Find a nice hotel. Stay the week."

"What?" Luz blinked at him as if he was crazy, which he probably was with the need to touch her, hold her, make her whole again.

"We'll get up early. Jump in the car. Go see art." Eddo slid his fingers between hers and laced their hands together.

"I can't go to San Miguel for a week," Luz said, staring at their hands. "I have a family."

"Your sister is how old?" Eddo asked. "Your brother's grown. They'll get by for a week."

"I don't have anything with me. No clothes. Nothing."

"We'll go shopping in the morning," Eddo said. He rocked their clasped hands. "I owe you a blouse, remember?"

"It's just . . . not done," Luz said. Her cheeks were red.

"We need some time to figure out where things stand between us, Luz."

She didn't reply, just kept staring at their clasped hands.

Eddo took a deep breath. "You can see stars in San Miguel," he said.

♦

Chapter 59

Luz's emotions swirled as they walked through the Zona Rosa back to the apartment. Her hand was threaded through Eddo's crooked elbow, the same as in October, and his forearm continually rubbed against her scar. By the time they got back to the apartment she knew she couldn't go to San Miguel with him.

"Coffee?" Eddo asked once they were inside.

"Not too strong," Luz said and slipped into the bathroom.

When she came out the television was on. Eddo was in a chair holding a mug. There was another mug on the coffee table. Luz perched on the sofa and took the mug. It contained a thin milky liquid that smelled like bark. "You made tea?"

"It's coffee," Eddo said.

"Oh."

"Give it back." Eddo set his own mug on the coffee table.

"It's fine," Luz said, a little too loudly.

An old episode of *El Chavo del 8* came on. It was a ridiculously funny show, but tonight the antics of the man pretending to be a boy were just foolish.

"I can't go to San Miguel," Luz said into her mug. "You're going to be Attorney General and I'm some *muchacha*."

"I thought we worked that out, Luz," Eddo said. "Nothing's changed for me."

"I've changed." Luz was suddenly fighting tears again. "I've changed a lot."

"Is there someone else?" he asked. "Someone from home?"

"No," Luz said. "Eddo, please."

"Tell me what's changed, Luz."

Luz bit her lip. Eddo waited. *El Chavo del 8* spun another ridiculous plot.

"I have a scar," she said finally.

"A lot of people have scars, Luz."

"Not like this they don't." She shook her head and then, in spite of herself, the words spilled out in a strained croak. "It's horrible. And red. There's an empty space where the rib used to be and when I touch it . . ."

"It's numb," Eddo supplied.

"How do you know?"

In response, Eddo pulled off his sweater and tee shirt then sat on the end of the coffee table.

The muscles of his chest were as hard and smooth as Luz remembered. He raised his left arm and showed her a red scar a third of the way down his side. It was about as big as Luz's thumbprint. He took her hand and ran her fingers over the puckered flesh, then turned so that his side was to her. She saw where the bullet had come out through the wide flare of his lateral muscle.

"It just hit fat and muscle," Eddo said. "Not like yours."

"You haven't any fat on you," Luz murmured.

"I have plenty here although I think the term you used was concrete." Eddo leaned toward her and tapped the line of silver hairs on the side of his head.

Luz ran her fingers along the silver line, parting the hairs. The scar on his scalp was a thick red jag. "Why did all the hair near the scar turn gray?"

"I don't know," Eddo said. He didn't move his head. It was nearly in Luz's lap. "Looks ridiculous, doesn't it."

"No, not ridiculous," she said, suddenly very conscious that she was touching him and that he was shirtless. "I'm glad you showed me."

"And this." Eddo indicated his left collarbone and Luz saw a bump there.

She fingered the bump then slid her hand back to the silver hairs.

That was where she'd held the cold pack when he told her the day they'd spent together had been the best day of his life.

Very slowly, Luz took her hand away from his head, gathered up the edge of her tee shirt and lifted it just high enough for him to see.

Eddo dropped to his knees to be eye level with the scar. He ran his fingertips over its length.

"Well," he said. "That's impressive all right. They didn't do a very good job of sewing you up, did they?"

"They did at first," Luz said, her voice thick with nerves. "In the hospital. But when the doctor at the free clinic took out the stitches it didn't hold together."

She tried to pull down the tee but Eddo began to massage the scar and the skin around it. "Have you been putting anything on it?" he asked.

"No."

"Taking vitamin C?"

"No." She watched with stunned fascination as he rubbed her skin. His biceps flexed and she could see the veins in his arms.

"You're the most beautiful woman I've ever seen, Luz," Eddo said very quietly.

"No." Luz held her breath as his hand came dangerously close to her bra.

"If you don't want to come to San Miguel, I understand." He had both hands on her now, still rubbing gently. "I know I don't deserve five minutes of your time. But don't let it be because of this. *Madre de Dios*, it makes me want you more, not less. Whatever I can do to make things right between us, Luz, I swear to the Virgin that whatever--."

Luz yanked off her shirt.

♦

There was a blurred passage to the bedroom and a wild fumble for a condom. They came together swiftly, almost savagely. Luz dug her fingers into Eddo's back, pulling him to her, leaving her mark on his skin. She wanted to consume him, devour him, swallow him in great gulps. He ran his tongue over her breasts and she cried out.

And then he was inside her, a fire igniting her from the inside out. The mattress keened beneath them as they rolled across the bed, Luz's knees clenched around Eddo's ribs. His arms were like steel around her shoulders, his hands buried in her hair and their mouths locked together.

Luz ended up on top. Eddo pushed her upright and thumbed her just where their bodies were joined. The climax came before her mind was ready for it and she screamed and convulsed in surprise, riding him through the explosion.

Eddo flipped Luz over as the spasms rocked her. He thrust in and out rapidly, panting hoarsely, his body rigid with need. Luz scraped her nails up his sides and he shuddered. When his climax came Eddo's body jerked, nearly lifting her off the bed. He groaned and bowed away from her and snapped his head back. Luz fought for air as she felt him jerk again and again.

The jerking slowed, then stopped. Eddo grabbed her side and rolled them a quarter turn so that he wouldn't collapse on top of her. They lay tangled together, damp with sweat, chests heaving.

"*Madre de Dios*," Eddo said huskily. He kissed her palm. "You okay?"

"Yes."

"Good." Eddo slid out of her, keeping the condom in place. "Don't go anywhere."

Luz watched as he staggered to the bathroom. As she heard the water run she started to cry, tears of relief and joy and emotional exhaustion coursing down her cheeks. She felt the connection around her heart again; the thread she'd thought was gone forever.

"Hey, hey, what's this?" Eddo came back into the bedroom and touched her wet cheek. "Did I hurt you?"

"No." She shook her head.

"Ah, *corazón*, you're exhausted," he said, his voice full of self-reproach.

"No. It's just . . ." Luz gulped around her tears. "I kept telling myself that just knowing you were alive was enough. But it wasn't."

"I know, *corazón*. I know."

Eddo made her get under the covers. He crawled in with her and kissed her tears and called her Kagemusha until Luz laughed and knew she'd cried enough for one day.

◆

Chapter 60

Tuesday morning Luz stood on the porch of the long white ranch house that the hotel manager had somewhat optimistically called a villa, but which probably had been the foreman's house when the hotel property was a working *hacienda*. The mountain air was crisp and cool and smelled like grass and freedom. She wore skinny black jeans, a pink cashmere turtleneck, Camper walking shoes, Ray-Ban sunglasses, a belted black alpaca sweater coat from Peru, and an array of Dior cosmetics. Her hair was pulled back with a beaded Swarovski clip and a pink suede DKNY purse hung from her shoulder.

Beyond the circular drive in front of the house, across a dirt road that turned to paving closer to the main hotel complex, a huge field of cut grass stretched all the way to a rocky hillside that continued in an irregular line to the right and was punctuated by a line of cypress trees standing tall and thin in the sunlight. If Luz squinted, she could just make out the topmost spires of the cathedral called La Parroquia, nearly hidden by a second line of cypress trees on top of the hill.

Monday had been a day of wonder. Eddo had woken her with a cup of gritty slurry he said was coffee and they'd made love gently, easing past the raw emotion of the previous night. At the Liverpool store in Polanco he'd ignored her agitated protests and bought her one of everything, including a new cell phone she used to call Señora Velasquez and leave a message. They'd gotten to San Miguel de Allende in time to check in, wander the town, and find some dinner. She'd fallen asleep in his arms in front of the living room fire.

Eddo came out of the house and kissed the back of her neck. "Almost Valencia, eh, Jimena?"

Luz leaned into him. "It's perfect, Rodrigo. Thank you

again."

It took them ten minutes to walk to the main hotel complex and another ten to climb the hilly, cobbled streets to the paved plaza called El Jardin in the center of San Miguel.

Up close La Parroquia was small, but majestic and Gothic nonetheless. It dominated one side of El Jardin. It was flanked by an ornate museum building. Outdoor cafés did a brisk business along the other sides of the plaza. Women sold flowers from baskets to the café patrons, while street hawkers sold balloons and simple children's pull toys.

They cruised the art galleries and shops and had lunch in an expensive Italian restaurant. Luz reveled in every new sight and taste.

After lunch they found a bench in front of La Parroquia. Luz got out her sketchpad and pencil box while Eddo bought a newspaper and took out a pair of reading glasses. He was soon engrossed in the sports pages.

Luz drew La Parroquia swiftly, feeling the town's happy energy guide her. She elongated the spires, thin lines delineating the stone blocks, the pointed arches reaching to heaven. She placed La Parroquia in a blue sea with a tiny boat in the foreground. A man and a woman rowed toward the church. Luz smiled to herself as she put a tiny heart atop the church's tallest spire.

"A boat." Eddo put down his newspaper and stared at the drawing.

"What?"

Before Eddo could answer, they realized a tall woman was standing nearby, her head cocked to see the sketchpad. The woman was probably in her late fifties, wearing an expensive mauve tweed coat over a matching dress. She had a perfect coif of auburn hair.

"I'm sorry to bother you," the woman said in excellent, albeit accented, Spanish. "But it's very good. Very clever."

"Thank you," Luz said.

"Do you work in oils?"

"Yes."

"Are you represented?"

Luz's eyes flicked to Eddo; she wasn't sure what the woman meant.

"Not yet," Eddo answered. "Is your interest professional or personal?"

The woman's name was Elaine Ralston and she owned art galleries in New York City and Dallas. A third in San Miguel would open in time for the summer tourism season.

"If you could do it in oils," Elaine Ralston said. "I'd like to see it."

They made an appointment to bring Luz's artwork to her on Thursday afternoon. Elaine Ralston gave Eddo her card and walked on.

"Do you think she was serious?" Luz asked.

Eddo grinned. "Let's go get you some paint."

♦

Chapter 61

Something clicked for Eddo when he saw Luz's drawing. The way Gomez Mazzo and his bodyguards were so accustomed to the roll and pitch of a boat at sea. The lights that turned on in the shadowy yacht anchored outside the Amador Causeway marina at just the right time. Why no one ever saw El Toro in Mexico.

The asshole lived on a fucking yacht.

Wednesday morning, while Luz painted in the living room, Eddo went into the bedroom and called Tomás and Vasco. Surely someone would know how to track down a yacht. After a round of texts they agreed that Vasco would talk to Fonseca, then call Panama City and see what type of records they could get.

Damned if he didn't fall asleep after that. Right in the middle of the day. Eddo woke to find his cell phone plugged into the charger, his reading glasses on the bedside table, and a blanket over him. Twilight gilded the trees outside the window and the old ranch house smelled like fresh coffee.

He wandered barefoot into the living room. Luz was working on her canvases at the table. He got a cup of coffee and sat in the big rocking chair to watch her, still amazed that he'd found her and that she was here with him. She'd lost that broken bird look and in its place was the alluring mix of physical presence, creative energy, and shy radiance that had so attracted him in October. Plus her sense of humor. And intelligence. Everything about her.

The three small canvases on the table looked fantastic to him, but Luz rolled her eyes when he said so and continued to dab at one with a tiny brush. The paints had come in a big rosewood box, which she seemed to think was better than gold, and it was open now, with the tubes of paint and brushes arranged in an orderly fashion. Eddo found himself smiling just to see her work, until he wondered if he was making her self-conscious. He put his mug in the kitchen, kissed the back of her neck, and said he'd go find them some dinner.

He drove to the center of town and poked around the shops. There was a great leather place where he found her a small clutch bag and a *serape* fabric suitcase with leather trim. In another shop he picked up a sheer embroidered *rebozo* shawl. A pendant necklace in a jeweler's window caught his eye. A clever twist of silver joined a cherry-sized nugget of turquoise to a polished oval amethyst.

It was dark when he got back with his purchases and *jamón serrano* sandwiches on thick *chupata* rolls and an assortment of salads. Luz had finished painting. They ate on the floor, the table still occupied by wet canvases. As always they talked about everything and anything. Laughter came more easily with Luz than with anyone else.

Eddo waited until she had finished eating then gave her the things he'd bought, saving the jeweler's box for last. "Happy birthday, Jimena," he said.

Luz shook her head. "You've bought me too much already."

"Birthday presents don't count."

She opened the box and gasped.

"Dios mio, dios mio," Luz stammered. "I can't accept this. It's too expensive."

Eddo clasped the pendant around her neck. "Two rules for you, Luz. Number one, don't argue money with me. I'll let you know if we run out. Number two; don't ever steal anything else out of government offices."

She came to him that night naked except for the stones gleaming against her skin, sweet shyness and open desire on her face at the same time. He was mesmerized. Their lovemaking was a complete fusion, demanding everything he had.

Eddo could barely move when it was over. He lay on his side facing her and tangled his fingers in her thick black hair. The silver chain of the necklace twinkled in the moonlight streaming in from the window. Luz's skin looked like bronze.

"Would you ever dye your hair blonde?" he asked sleepily.

She traced his mouth with her fingertips. "No. It would be too fake."

He wanted to say *good, stay just the way you are* but he was too tired. Luz detached his hand from her hair and tucked his fingers under her cheek. Eddo fell asleep to the rhythm of her breathing.

◆

Chapter 62

Luz put on new jeans and a silk sweater then tidied the dresser top while Eddo shaved and took a shower. The appointment with Elaine Ralston was at 2:00 pm, leaving her five hours to vibrate nervously.

Eddo's duffel was open, clothes spilling out of it. More clothes were on the floor, sorted into overlapping piles; "definitely clean," "probably clean," and a damp mash of soccer shorts, sweaty tee shirts, and muddy cleats. He'd worked out every morning, running drills with a ball up and down the field. Agile and fast, he'd probably been a spectacular player in his youth.

She prodded a dirty mound with her toe. After years of making sure everything around her was in its place, the mess gnawed at her. She went over to the clean pile, picked up a tee shirt and started to fold it neatly, just like she'd folded Señor Vega's shirts. Halfway through she stopped, uncomfortably conscious that this was what she'd be doing if she was Eddo's maid.

Luz sat down on the bed, confused and a little afraid. Why had she thought to fold his clothes? Is that how she thought of herself? As his *muchacha* with a few extras?

Eddo walked out of the bathroom naked, toweling his hair. "Do you want to walk into town for breakfast?" he asked. "Or try the hotel restaurant?"

Luz didn't reply.

"What's up?" Eddo wrapped the towel around his hips.

"I was wondering," Luz said, knowing she was starting a conversation she'd regret. "If you would like me to . . . take care of . . . your stuff." She gestured stiffly at the duffel. "Fold your things. And all."

"Ahhh," Eddo said slowly. He sat next to her on the edge of the bed, his shoulder pressing against hers. "I think we're going to have a moment here."

Luz sat very still. "I guess."

"We have to make a third rule for you," Eddo said deliberately, like a teacher. "No, you may not fold my stuff. You're not my maid or my mother. I don't expect you to act like either." He looked at the piles of clothes on the floor. "I'm usually organized. But rarely neat. Especially where clothes are concerned." He shrugged. "I'll admit to being spoiled. There's always been someone around to take care of my laundry. But it's not ever going to be you."

Luz took a deep breath and squeezed her hands between her knees. "Let me get this straight," she said. "I can't fold your clothes. And I can't stop you from spending too much money."

"And you can't steal things out of government offices in the middle of the night."

"All right," Luz said, unable to quit while she was ahead. "What are the rules for you?"

"No rules for me," Eddo said easily. "Just my job taking care of you."

"No." Luz shook her head and looked away. She should shut her mouth, just enjoy his generosity, but it wasn't right. The inequality in their relationship was too great to ignore. "You've given me a wonderful week in San Miguel, you buy me everything you see. I wouldn't have sold that painting on Sunday or be going to see Elaine Ralston and you won't even let me fold your clothes. I'm just *taking*. It doesn't feel right."

"What are you talking about, Luz?" Eddo said.

"You know," Luz said miserably.

"You're saying that you don't contribute?"

"Yes." She had only herself to blame if he said *hey you're right, it's all too one-sided, glad to know where we stand, here's a bus ticket back--*.

"You saved my life twice, *corazón*," Eddo said. "With your sketches of those men. And in October. I'd say that's a pretty big contribution."

"October?" Luz blinked. "What are you talking about?"

Eddo leaned forward, elbows on thighs. "I spent the Saturday night before we met with a bottle of tequila and my gun. I'd respected Hugo, thought he was a good man. But he wasn't and I had to tell the president. I'd never felt so shitty."

Luz couldn't quite see his expression. He was staring straight ahead.

"Sunday morning it was get out or shoot myself. I hadn't meant to go to the Tamayo. I just found a parking place there." Eddo swallowed. "You were sitting . . . so . . . calmly. That pink sweater. It was like seeing a rose in the desert."

The room was oddly quiet. No morning birds or crickets sounded outside the window.

"El Toro is still out there," Eddo went on. "Thinking I'm in his pocket."

"Stop it, Rodrigo," Luz said. She could tell that his dreams were sometimes a heavy burden, but that he could not let them go and watch the country go to pieces. "You'll catch him."

Eddo looked at her curiously. "I don't always have to be strong with you, do I?"

"You're always strong," Luz said. "You just get tired sometimes."

Eddo looked away.

"This is what you give me," he said after a long silence. "Stillness. Or calm. I don't know what it is exactly but I've been feeling like a greedy bastard taking all that I can get out of you."

Luz's heart banged with emotion and surprise.

"I've been like a metal spring wound too tight." Eddo went on. "Always tighter and tighter, not knowing what to do, just sort of waiting for the spring to break. For years." He stared at the messy duffel and the piles of clothes. "But all this week, you've been unwinding it, a little more each day. I even took a nap yesterday. You don't know what that means to me."

Luz was entirely overwhelmed. "Eddo--."

"But right now." His voiced cracked as he cut her off. "I'm scared shitless that you expect to get back the same thing you've given me. I'm going to disappoint you and you're going to walk."

Before Luz could collect her thoughts and say anything, he

stood up and quickly slipped on his clothes; briefs, jeans, and the black sweater that fit over his chest like a second skin.

"Looking at this mess all week has probably been killing you," he said and opened the closet door. He hung all his pants and shirts and sweaters on the hangers. It took him a while; the hangers slid along the rod but did not detach from it. Luz watched silently as Eddo wrestled with the job. She could have done it much more easily and in half the time, but it was something she had to let him do, for his sake as much as for her own.

He left all his clean socks and underwear in the bottom of the duffel, shoved the dirty things into the mesh compartment, and zipped it shut. There was nothing left on the floor except his shoes. He put on one pair and lined up the others next to the duffel. Finally he turned and looked at her, his face inscrutable. "Ready for some breakfast?"

Luz couldn't stand the tension any longer. She ran across the room and wrapped her arms around his neck. He crushed her to him.

"You could *never* disappoint me," Luz said against his chest.

"I worry, Jimena," he said. "I can be a cold sonuvabitch."

Luz thought of the silver hairs, the men who'd tried to kill him, and how they'd tried to kill her. She took a step back so she could see his face. "If you couldn't be that person sometimes, neither one of us would be alive. But that doesn't mean you have a cold *heart*. You don't. I know. I know you."

To her surprise he made a choking sound and his face crumpled. He pulled her hard against him, burying his face in her hair. She held him as his shoulders shook.

It took a long time but eventually the shaking stopped. Luz felt him relax as she rubbed his back and gently kneaded away the knots.

She knew that he was all right when Eddo kissed her neck. He moved away from her and wiped his eyes with the back of his hand like a little kid. They laughed shakily at each other.

Eddo went into the bathroom and blew his nose. As he came out he shook his head at her. "Do you know the last time I cried?"

"Sunday," Luz said ruefully.

"No, I mean before I met you and turned into a faucet." He sat on the end of the bed.

"No, when?" Luz moved over to him and stood between his knees.

Eddo caught up her hands and laced their fingers together. "I was 18. I tried out for Puebla and didn't make the cut. Punched a cement wall and broke my knuckle."

"They're fools in Puebla. Which knuckle?"

"There." He showed her a small scar.

"So I guess we have to have a rule for you, too. No punching walls."

Eddo laughed.

♦

Chapter 63

Luz went into the restaurant with one hand through Eddo's elbow and the other carrying her new leather clutch. Inside was her copy of a probationary contract that said if the four paintings she'd left with Elaine Ralston sold within six months The Ralston Gallery would represent her in both Mexico and the United States. The afternoon had been an experience she'd never forget. Elaine Ralston had treated her like a serious artist and the two women discussed modern art trends and noted contemporary artists while Eddo reviewed the contract.

The restaurant was breathtaking, the perfect place to celebrate. It had once been a colonial mansion, built long ago by a Spanish grandee who had spared no expense. The most prominent feature was a huge vaulted *boveda* ceiling made of thousands of bricks laid in an arching herringbone pattern. Niches for wine bottles were cut into the plaster below the brick. The supporting wall trusses were solid logs. Luz loved the combination of the antique brick and dark wood against stark white tablecloths and gleaming silver.

"Hey," said Eddo after they'd been seated. "When you're famous and your paintings are in the Prado--"

"--And the Guggenheim."

"*And* the Guggenheim, will you still make me coffee?"

"I'll have to," Luz said. "Otherwise you're going to poison us both."

They toasted her success with champagne, a first for Luz. The bubbly drink was wonderfully cold and popped against her tongue. It was like a magic elixir.

"Like it?" Eddo asked.

"I love it." Luz had never been this happy. Eddo wore a black linen shirt, khaki pants, and an alligator belt. His hazel eyes reflected the flame of the candle on the table. They'd learned so much about each other. The week had been full of moments she could live in forever, but this was the best of all. *Let time stop now*, Luz thought. *Let this be the moment for the rest of my life.*

After dinner, they went to a club and danced, their bodies close, kissing when the music was slow. When the band took a break, Luz found the restroom. An elegant lounge area preceded the main bathroom. An old woman in a black uniform dress handed a clean linen towel to each woman who washed her hands.

Luz tipped the attendant 5 pesos, hoping that was enough for such a fancy place and sat in front of a mirror. Her reflection was extremely satisfying. A week of vitamins, expensive cosmetics, mountain air, and raw joy had let her bloom with new life. She wore a burgundy knit wrap dress that made her waist look tiny and her wide shoulders fashionable. She'd protested when Eddo made her try it on in Liverpool but now she was glad he'd insisted. Tall black sandals and a sleek ponytail completed the outfit. The amethyst and turquoise necklace dangled near her cleavage, making her feel very sexy. Besides the contract, the clutch bag held some makeup. She found lipstick and carefully redid her smile.

"Luz de Maria, isn't it?"

It was Señora Portillo standing behind her and speaking to Luz's reflection. The woman was as glamorous as ever in a skinny black dress and layers of jewelry.

The shock of seeing someone from Luz's old life was like a bucket of ice water over her head. Luz stood to face the other woman. "Hello, señora."

"Selena told me she let you go for . . . an indiscretion," Señora Portillo said. She raked her eyes over Luz's outfit. "She never said it was this."

"I'm sorry?" Luz asked in confusion.

"I saw the man you're with, Luz. Your . . . relationship . . . is obvious," Señora Portillo said. "No matter what he's paying you, it's not a good life. No good can come of it."

Her look as she walked out was sad and knowing and

superior all at the same time.

"Señora, *wait*." Luz threw her lipstick into her clutch and headed for the door. "You don't understand--."

"*Puta*."

Luz froze, feeling the jab of the word between her shoulder blades. She turned and looked into the bathroom. The attendant was the only person there. As Luz watched, the old woman wiped her mouth with the back of her hand as if she'd just spit.

♦

Chapter 64

Luz didn't tell Eddo what had happened. But what had she expected? They were in San Miguel to see where things stood between them. At the end of the week things would still be the same. She was an unemployed *muchacha* with a pregnant sister, a brother, and two nieces to support and he was going to be Attorney General. Someone would always assume that he'd bought her by the hour.

She'd thought the same thing, once upon a time.

Friday morning when he suggested that he teach her to drive she welcomed the distraction. She did so well he let her ease the car onto the street beyond the hotel property. They tooled around the countryside and found the church of the Santuario de Atotonilco. They saw the church's famous murals, then ate an early dinner in a roadside restaurant.

In the evening they went back to El Jardin. They found a place to sit at a café, ordered dessert and brandy, and watched the ever-changing scene in the plaza.

La Parroquia was lit up. Vendors sold balloons, toys, and cones of flavored shaved ice. A happy army of children ran around with little balls on a string with shiny streamers that flashed and twirled. El Jardin looked like fairyland.

"I wish you'd let me drive you home tomorrow," Eddo said.

"No," Luz said. "It would take us all day and then you'd have a 15 hour drive to Oaxaca."

"What's the real reason?"

Luz sighed. "I'm going to have a lot of explaining to do." It was going to be bad enough explaining what she had done that week without him standing in the living room while Lupe stared at el señor through a stupid face and Juan Pablo got hot about Eddo besmirching a sister's honor. But more than that, she didn't want him to see just how poor the house was, didn't want his car dismantled on the street outside, didn't want the neighbors talking. Didn't want this night to end.

"Then we'll meet Tomás and the security service in Mexico City and they'll drive you home."

Luz stared miserably at the children running across the plaza. "Thank you."

"Look." Eddo held out a small nosegay of dark purple violets tied with a white ribbon. An old woman with a basket of bouquets pocketed coins and moved on.

"*Oh.*" Luz put out a finger and touched one of the tiny dark petals. "They're lovely."

"I didn't know I could love anyone as much as I love you." Eddo laid the violets on the table in front of her. "Will you marry me, Jimena?"

Luz blinked. "We can't talk about this now."

"Why not?"

"There are too many people here."

Eddo looked around at the crowded plaza and grinned. "Fine. Let them all know," he said. "I love you. Let's get married. Right here."

"Don't be ridiculous," Luz hissed, suddenly irritated that he'd put her in such an awkward position. Discussing a sheer impossibility in such a public place.

Eddo flinched as if she'd slapped him. He paid the bill and stood up.

They walked up the hill without speaking. Luz put the violets into a mug of water in the kitchen. She tried to think of what to say, how to make him see the absurdity of what he'd asked.

She went into the living room. Before she could say anything Eddo shrugged on his coat.

"Go to bed, Luz," he said. "I'm going to take a walk."

He still wasn't back by the time Luz finished crying and fell asleep.

◆

Chapter 65

Luz woke to the sound of a slamming door.

She lurched out of the bed only to sag with relief when she saw Eddo's suitcase on the floor, his shoes still in the tidy row from Thursday morning.

The mug of violets was on the bedside table. The room was chilly. A door slammed again.

Luz hurriedly threw on a tee shirt, yoga pants, and a sweater, then walked through the house. The view through the living room window made her pause.

On the porch, Eddo sat in the big rocking chair from the living room. As she watched, he pulled off a sweaty sweatshirt and a tee and dropped both on the floor of the porch next to a dusty soccer ball. Steam rose from his skin. He tipped up a bottle of water and drank down half in one swallow.

Luz stepped out onto the porch and closed the front door behind her. The cement was cold under her bare feet.

"Been up long?" she asked.

"Awhile." Eddo drank the rest of the water.

"Did you sleep at all?" She folded her arms and shivered in the thin morning air.

"No."

He leaned back and started to rock. The chair creaked rhythmically.

Luz walked to the other side of the porch and perched on the railing. She stared at La Parroquia. The sunrise bathed the Gothic spires in pale pink light.

"I love you so much it hurts," she said.

The rocking chair stopped creaking.

"We were in Santa Fe and you asked me to draw the band," Luz went on. "People came to look and it scared me. You touched me right here." She touched the back of her neck. "And I loved you."

"Jimena--."

Suddenly Eddo was right there, his arms around her.

"I love you." Between kisses Luz said it over and over against his mouth.

He pulled away and before Luz knew what was happening she was in the rocking chair and Eddo was on one knee in front of her.

"Okay, Luz. Last night there were too many people around." He took hold of both her hands. "And maybe I should be doing this on some beach with a diamond ring but we're not there and I don't want to wait. Will you marry me, Luz? Tell me yes."

"I love you," Luz said. She took a deep breath. "Enough not to let you ruin your career and scandalize your family by bringing home some *muchacha*."

"You're an artist, now, Luz. You just signed a contract with a gallery."

Luz shook her head and pulled back her hands. "Your career would be over and one day you'd hate me for it. 'He married beneath him,' they'll say. And laugh. 'Some *puta* from the *barrio*.' At home I'll be the girl who didn't know her place. 'Thought she was too good to stay where she belonged.' I'll have nowhere to go afterwards."

"This is garbage," Eddo exclaimed. "There's not going to be any afterwards."

"*Dios mio*, Eddo. Your family owns half of Puebla. And you drag in some *muchacha*? Do you think they'll want me to add 'de Cortez' to my name? Your parents will spin in their graves."

"Okay. Okay." Eddo flopped onto the cold concrete and pretended to think. "So if all my friends and all my family and everybody I work with get together and say it's okay, you'll marry me?"

"Stop joking," Luz admonished. "You need someone appropriate to be the wife of an Attorney General. With a background that will help you. Not some *muchacha* who won't know the right thing to do and ruin everything."

"Luz!" Eddo jumped up, his *fútbol* cleats clacking against the porch floor. "You don't marry someone because they're *appropriate* for you. If marriage was just that I'd be stuck with the *idiota* who bought me shampoo because she knew me so fucking well and you'd be married to the good provider your mother picked out." Luz opened her mouth but he went on, leaning over the chair like a goalie waiting for the penalty shot. "And we'd both be ready to kill ourselves. You get married to somebody because together you can do things you couldn't without them. Because together you make each other's dreams come true."

"I'd ruin your dreams," Luz said.

"My dreams need your strength," he shot back.

"*Stop it*, Eddo." Suddenly Luz couldn't catch her breath. He had an answer for everything, answers she'd never heard before. She stood up abruptly and the rocker slammed into the doorway. Eddo jerked back in surprise.

Luz twisted around him and bolted off the porch. She ran stumbling across the rutted drive and cold grass and dirt road. Her heart pounded, tears blinded her. Stones and dirt bit her bare feet.

Eddo caught up with her halfway across the field, fast and surefooted in his cleats. He grabbed her arm and spun her around.

"What did you think was going to happen, Luz?" he shouted. "Did you think we'd both just walk away?"

"You were never mine to keep," Luz cried. She snatched her arm out of his grasp and dug a grape-sized piece of milky white quartz out of the ground. She held it out to him. "It's as if someone gave me the most precious jewel I'd ever seen and said I could hold it for just a little while. But today's the day I have to give it back."

"Is that what you want, Luz?" Eddo closed her fingers around the stone. "To give it back?"

"It's not about what I want." Luz shook her head. "It's what I'm allowed to have."

"You can just let me go?"

"It's so hard." Luz started to cry.

"Then marry me," Eddo said, stepping closer. "Don't open your hand. I'll hold onto you and you'll hold onto me. We'll make all our dreams come true together."

Luz fought for control through her fear and confusion. "I don't know."

"Luz, listen." Eddo put his arms around her. "I know this happened fast. Just don't say no. Say you'll think about it."

Luz rested her head against his bare chest and drew a shaky breath, the stone still clenched in her fist. "Give me some time," she gulped. "Until after Juan Pablo graduates."

♦

They were quiet in the car going back to Mexico City.

"Whatever happens," Luz blurted when they were halfway there. "Don't ever get me a diamond engagement ring. It would remind me too much of Lorena."

Eddo didn't reply. Luz fiddled with her new cell phone, which apparently did everything except cook, but kept going back to the countdown feature. Eddo had marked the Saturday after Juan Pablo's graduation.

It was 63 days until MEET EDDO.

♦

Chapter 66

Mexico City looked a lot better than it had a week ago. The security service was the best and Luz promised to text him as soon as she got home. Eddo was tired but optimistic by the time he arrived at the house in San Angel. It was still the warm, inviting space that had so often depressed him, full of Ana and Tomas and their relationship, but this time the atmosphere was like a tonic.

After Eddo, Tomás, and Vasco had eaten every last bite of dinner and complimented Ana, she kissed her husband and said she'd be back downstairs after the cigar smoke cleared.

As Tomás got out the Cohibas, Vasco brought them up to date. The Panamanian authorities had been fast and efficient but their records were sparse. Vasco had taken what they had and dug further, checking out maritime tracking companies and insurers.

"It's called *Sheba*," he said and passed around a color photo of a yacht. Registered in Panama, it had gone through the Panama Canal the day after Luz got snatched and had taken on supplies at the Amador marina the day Eddo and Tomás were there. "The owner of record is one of the names we found connected to Montopa. I got the picture off the website of a maritime broker."

"This thing is huge," Tomás marveled. "Is that a fucking pool?"

"Think about it," Vasco said. "He's tooling around on his yacht while his thugs, working from what Miguel gave them, try and find you. But you're already in Panama checking out Montopa so they're not having much luck. Miguel leads them to Luz. They snatch her and end up talking to Tomás who makes the arrangements for a meet in Panama City."

"So for Gomez Mazzo to do the meet in Panama City," Eddo mused, recalling his geography. Panama City was on the Pacific side of the narrow isthmus. "The *Sheba* had to go through the canal. That meant it was somewhere in the Caribbean."

"So where's the damn boat now?" Tomás demanded. "It's not like a boat that big can hide, right?"

Eddo puffed thoughtfully on his cigar. "If Gomez Mazzo lives on the boat, who's keeping the drugs moving in El Toro territory?"

"A very trusted lieutenant?" Vasco surmised.

"But they have to meet now and then." Eddo leaned forward. "Maybe that's what the references to sites were in the postings."

Tomás looked grim. "I'm almost afraid to ask where you're going with this."

This could work. Gomez Mazzo's pride would be his undoing. Eddo felt a prickle of excitement. He pointed at Tomás, then at Vasco. "We figure out every marina within, say, five days sailing time from Panama City that can handle a yacht that big. And we put somebody we can trust in every location."

"And if we're wrong?" Tomás asked.

"If they don't find the boat," Eddo went on. "We use one of the userids to send a posting calling for a meeting at Site 4. That's where they met before. The website is still there although it looks as if Hugo is the only one posting."

"You think the rest of them are still live?" Tomás asked. "Despite the end of Banco Limitado?"

"So we follow Hugo," Vasco offered.

Tomas shook his head. "He's holed up in Monterrey. If he buys an airline ticket we won't find out where he's going until he checks in for the flight."

Eddo nodded. "We could end up being a day behind him, at least."

"So we're gambling that we'll find the boat," Vasco said.

"Site 4 is someplace he docks it." Eddo stood up and paced the living room, his thoughts racing too fast for him to stay seated. Between this and the plan he'd cooked up driving back from San Miguel his brain was on fire. "Someplace he can show off his shit to Hugo. I bet they've each been trying to be top dog ever since their arrangement started."

"Good point," said Tomás. "Gomez Mazzo wouldn't want to miss the opportunity to rub Hugo's face in it."

"What about Sonia?" Vasco asked. "Would she know where it is?"

"I'll ask her," Eddo said. She was still in San Luis Potosi and he called now and then. She still thought he was Reynoldo.

"If we do it we're on our own," Tomás said. He got out a bottle of brandy and poured them each a measure. "Maybe bring in Ramirez, the army guy who made the raid on Hugo's operation. He's got his shit together. But no Financial crap this time."

"*Madre de Dios*, you're a genius." Eddo said and came back to his seat. How many times had he sat around a table talking to these two men, planning, arguing, strategizing, bouncing ideas off each other, making something happen. "We set up a meeting, the El Toro leadership comes. Army makes a big sweep while the leadership is otherwise occupied."

"Nice." Vasco blew a celebratory smoke ring.

"Thank you, thank you." Tomás made a little seated bow to both colleagues.

"We got enough good guys to send to these places?" Eddo asked. "Everything going okay?"

Vasco and Tomás were handling *Los Hierros* without him now. They'd all known Eddo would have to ease away from the group once he officially joined the Romero presidential campaign.

"One good cop at a time," Vasco said. "We got enough."

"Enough to do this in two months?"

"What happens in two months?"

"When Luz and I were in San Miguel," Eddo said. "I asked her to marry me. But I'd like to have Hugo and that fucker in jail first."

Vasco made a gurgling sound and Tomás nearly swallowed his cigar. Eddo left them both coughing and went upstairs to see if Ana could help him out with the other thing he had in mind.

♦

Chapter 67

Luz got home after Martina and Sophia had gone to bed. Juan Pablo and Lupe had gotten her message and nothing special had happened while she was away. Luz told them everything over cups of *manzanilla* tea at the kitchen table. Juan Pablo especially wanted a lot of explanation, but his expression softened as Luz told how she'd been mistaken in thinking that Eddo was dead. Everyone was excited to hear how much she'd made at Jardin del Arte and about the contract from The Ralston Gallery. News that a security service would be guarding the house was met with raised eyebrows from Juan Pablo.

"I have to go upstairs now, Luz," Lupe said. She made to stand and fell heavily against the edge of the table.

Luz was shocked to see bright red blood streaming down her sister's leg.

"What's the matter?" Juan Pablo asked.

Luz found her voice. "Help me get Lupe to the sofa," she said urgently. "Then get Carmelita and Señor Rosales to come with his truck."

They made Lupe as comfortable as possible. Juan Pablo sprinted out of the house. Luz got some wet cloths and tried to staunch the steady flow of blood.

"Are we going to the hospital, Luz?" Lupe whispered. Her face was paper-white.

"Yes," Luz said, hoping she didn't sound as panicked as she felt.

"Tell Armando."

Luz blinked. *Tío. Of course.*

By the time they got Lupe to the hospital she was unconscious. Luz and Juan Pablo waited for hours until a nurse came to tell them that Lupe's uterus had ruptured. The baby was dead and they'd had to perform an emergency hysterectomy. Lupe would be in the hospital for at least a week. They'd be allowed to see her the next day.

After a few hours of restless sleep Luz went over to the Rosales' house. Carmelita set out coffee at the kitchen table and Luz told her about the week in San Miguel and the night at the hospital.

"I feel awful." Luz wound up her story. "Lupe must have been feeling bad for days. What if I hadn't come back yesterday but stayed another day? She might have died."

"How were you supposed to know?" Carmelita stirred her coffee. Her clothes were old but tasteful and neatly pressed.

"I shouldn't have gone." Luz sipped. The coffee was nice and strong. She'd probably be hysterical with caffeine and remorse by noon.

"Lupe is going to recover, Luz." Carmelita squeezed Luz's arm. "Tell me about this guy."

"I love him," Luz said miserably.

"People in love are usually happier," Carmelita said.

"He asked me to marry him," Luz said. Carmelita's face lit but Luz held up a hand. "I said I'd give him an answer after Juan Pablo's graduation but I don't know what I was thinking. I can't leave Lupe and the girls." *And too many people think I'm his puta.*

"You don't have to decide today," Carmelita said.

Luz shrugged. "Today or tomorrow, it doesn't matter. I can't just dump everything on Juan Pablo. He needs to have a life of his own."

"So does this man have a name?" Carmelita looked at her over the rim of her cup.

Luz took a deep breath. "Eddo is . . . not *mestizo*. His name is Cortez Castillo and he works for Arturo Romero. *That* Arturo Romero."

Carmelita grinned and put down her cup. "Really? This is like a *telenovela*, Luz!"

There was a clatter of footsteps on the tile floor and Martina and Sophia rushed in with Carmelita's daughters. "Tía Luz! Tía Luz!"

"Hey there." She kissed her nieces and was thoroughly strangled with hugs and wet smacks from both girls who'd stayed with the Rosales' overnight.

"Carmelita said there's not going to be a new baby," Sophia murmured.

"I know," Luz said.

"Do you think the new baby is with *Abuela*?" Sophia climbed up into Luz's lap. "And Father Santiago? And your friend?"

"My friend didn't die, Sophia," Luz said. "I made a mistake. But the baby is an angel now." She hugged the little girl as Carmelita put out a dish of cookies. "Did you have a fun time?"

Martina bobbed her head around a cookie. "Carmelita let us watch lots of cartoons. We made dolls out of towels and she said we could take them home."

"We're supposed to have your birthday party today," Sophia said plaintively.

Luz gulped. She'd forgotten about the plan to celebrate her birthday a week late.

"We'll all go to church together," Carmelita said. "Afterwards we'll get a cake and celebrate Tía Luz's birthday."

"What about Mama?" Martina asked.

"We'll save a special piece for her. One with a rose on it," Carmelita said firmly. "When the doctor says she can have it we'll bring it to the hospital and have another party all over again."

"Oooh," Sophia breathed. "A party in a hospital."

"Thank you," Luz mouthed over the girls' heads to Carmelita. Sophia scrambled down and Luz nearly started bawling about Lupe and the baby that was an angel and the fact that she wouldn't ever marry Eduardo Martín Bernardo Cortez Castillo.

◆

Lupe came home the following week, pale and wan and teary. Tío rang the bell the next night. Luz let him in, sick at heart to think her sister had taken up with such a useless man.

When he left Lupe gave Luz a watery smile. The two sisters had an awkward conversation about Tío that lapsed into a silent stalemate.

The wonderful new cell phone became Luz's lifeline. Eddo's days were busy but they texted each other several times a day and he called every night.

They talked about everything except the answer that she would give him when the countdown reached zero. The only awkward moment came when he asked her to go to Maria Elena Romero's wedding before the 63 days were up. Luz immediately refused; the Romero wedding would be the social event of the year and she wasn't ready to confront something that big. Eddo countered with a *despedida*--a farewell party--for some of the campaign staff the same weekend she was to meet him in Mexico City. Luz reluctantly agreed to go, loath to refuse him twice.

She read voraciously to keep up with him, splurging on newspapers and magazines, and finding news and books on her cell phone, too. Eddo was sure that Elaine Ralston was going to want more canvases and so a corner of what Luz still thought of as her mother's bedroom became an art studio with the contract taped to the wall above a makeshift easel. Her latest notebook bulged with interesting art news and at last there was money to buy whatever supplies she wanted.

Eddo told her about PAN politics and developments with Romero's campaign strategy and read her bits of the book he was working on. Luz challenged him to think about new ideas and let him know what people in the streets were saying about Romero. He laughed at her jokes and discussed the things she wanted to paint and the photographs she took with her phone. They never ran out of things to say and Luz's wonderful cell phone never ran out of minutes.

Before Luz realized it, more than a month had flown by.

One afternoon she impulsively dialed Rosa's old cell phone number.

"Rosa? It's me, Luz de Maria."

"Luz?" Rosa sounded flabbergasted. "I can't believe it! Where are you?"

"I'm in Soledad de Doblado. I went home and stayed there."

"Oh, Luz, I'm so glad to hear from you." Rosa was her same bubbly self. "It's been so long."

"I know."

"Are you all right? Hector said you were in rough shape."

"I was, but I'm fine now. What about you?"

"I got fired after you left. Señora Vega kicked me right out of the house." Rosa made it sound like she'd had a fun day at La Feria.

"Why?" Luz asked.

"She caught me with Alejandro." Rosa giggled. "It was funny. He told her to get out and kept on going."

"Rosa!"

"So I'm back in Cholula," Rosa sighed. "It's really boring here."

"Are you working?"

"No. I've got my *finiquito*. And I'm going to have a baby."

Luz closed her eyes. "Alejandro's?"

"I doubt it," Rosa said and giggled again. "Probably Manuel. Or maybe Domingo."

Luz leaned back in her chair and heard all about Rosa's latest boyfriend. He had an even better job than Manuel. Domingo sold lottery tickets on the main street in Cholula, the one with the alabaster sidewalk.

♦

Chapter 68

Eddo stared at the yellow legal pad in front of him. He'd made a column for each userid and copied down their postings and the dates, trying to find a pattern that would reveal their true identities. Of course **Hh23051955** was Hugo. The last posting was his, asking why Site 1 was offline. It was two weeks old. No other userid had posted since then, as if no one was talking to Hugo any more.

Sonia's userid, **BppBB16003,** hadn't posted since the raid in Anahuac.

The remaining three userids had been silent since shortly after the deal with Gomez Mazzo in Panama, suggesting that they all worked for El Toro and that the cartel leader was sticking to the deal. Two used the same password as Sonia: **1612colcol** and **CH5299xyz9.** Logging into the postings page as either of the two userids had revealed nothing more.

Even more so than the identities of the three outstanding userids, Eddo was intrigued by the four sites referred to in the postings. The only one he'd been able to identify was Site 1, which was the drug muling operation they'd shut down in the desert outside Anahuac. The references to "7s" now made grim sense.

Each of the three mystery userids had mentioned Site 2 or 3 at one time or another. **44Gg449M11,** which used an unknown password, had posted that Site 2 was interrupted but then operating again. **CH5299xyz9,** the userid with the fewest number of postings, had mentioned a team going to Site 3. **1612colcol** usually posted about receiving shipments but had posted that the team could not return to Site 3. Sites 2 and 3 could be Banco Limitado and Hermanos Hospitality, but it was hard to tell which was which.

Site 4 was a complete unknown. Only **44Gg449M11** had ever mentioned it, with a posting that announced a meeting at Site 4 in five days. Sonia had claimed she hadn't gone and didn't know where it was, which meant the invitation wasn't for all the userids. Eddo wondered if Hugo had gone.

"Eduardo?"

He jerked up his head to find everyone around the conference table staring at him. "Uh, sorry," he said sheepishly. "Didn't catch that last one."

Matilda Paredes, Arturo Romero's public relations director, passed him a note. "The Elsa Caso show, in two weeks."

Eddo put down his pen. "What?"

"The Elsa Caso Show." Matilda was young, with bouncy brown hair and a degree in something that wasn't even a major when he'd been to college. "You're booked as the serious guest."

"You're sure?" Eddo asked, looking around the conference table at the campaign's inner circle. Arturo grinned. Almost a smirk. Eddo pretended not to see.

"Highest ranked talk show in the country," said Nestor Solis. The campaign manager often complained that corralling Eddo was the reason his hair had all fallen out. Nestor, a noted international labor lawyer, had worked with Arturo for over 20 years and had been bald the entire time. But the joke, with its undertone of truth, always got laughs. "Just keep it simple. The legal reform platform and your book. The manuscript looks fantastic, by the way."

"Thanks," Eddo said with a weak smile. The book had come together fast, with Eddo writing at night in his hotel room, trying to make the concepts simple, gathering together everything he'd ever thought or previously written about the need for an independent judiciary system, open trials, and training for cops and prosecutors on rules of evidence. Luz had been a great sounding board. The manuscript was getting positive reviews from everyone who'd seen the proofs. But, *Madre de Dios*, Elsa's show was the last place he would have picked to launch it.

Arturo moved the meeting to the next agenda item, which was the campaign's move to Mexico City right after his daughter's wedding. They all chuckled when he warned them not to expect much better than what they had. The Romero campaign headquarters in Oaxaca was the short-term rental of a former newspaper office, furniture and all. The space was chopped up into cubicles and even the conference room walls were just fabric partitions. The campaign had brought in computers and whiteboards but that was about it. Eddo liked the way Nestor was carefully spending campaign funds. Glamorous accommodations weren't high on his list.

For the most part, Arturo's team was made up of people who balanced idealism and practicality. They truly believed they could make an impact on the country and had enough experience to make it happen. Eddo felt comfortable in the group, although he missed the deep camaraderie of *Los Hierros*. In addition to himself, Matilda and Nestor, Arturo's inner circle was made up of Felipe Galindo Moya, who was in charge of domestic policy issues; and Salvador Becerra, their foreign policy expert.

Felipe briefed next on the domestic platform and the meeting got down to serious business. It was nearly 7:00 pm before they finalized the plan. Arturo, Nestor, and Matilda were all pleased. Felipe was ecstatic. Eddo was proud of the role he'd played. He'd given credit where credit was due, of course, and that made their reactions all that much better.

Before everyone scattered, Nestor reminded them to keep an eye out for fresh talent. Not all the staff in Oaxaca would move to Mexico City and they'd need to hire some new blood to replace those who weren't going.

◆

Chapter 69

In San Miguel, Eddo had been open about his past relationships. But he hadn't mentioned last names. Neither had Luz when she talked about her old boyfriends. It hadn't seemed important then.

But it felt important now. And a little sickening.

Carmelita was the only person Luz told about Eddo and Elsa Caso. Her eyebrows went up and she agreed to come over on Sunday with her girls to watch the show.

It had been six weeks since Lupe's miscarriage and she was going up and down the stairs again. She helped Luz make an elaborate meal of *huachinango* in tomato sauce with olives and capers in the traditional Veracruz style. The fish was full of tangy flavor, perfectly complimented by potatoes and jalapeño slices. Luz was too edgy to eat much but watched with satisfaction as the food disappeared rapidly.

There was coffee and *arroz con leche* with *canela* and raisins for dessert. Everyone finished in time for the show. The four girls went upstairs to play with dolls. Carmelita, Lupe, Juan Pablo, and Luz settled in front of the television.

Carmelita squeezed Luz's hand as the show came on. Luz was as nervous as if she was going on the show, instead of Eddo.

A wildly applauding studio audience flashed on the screen, the announcer said "Live! It's Elsa *CAAAAAASO*!!" and Mexico's famous talk show siren walked onto the stage, tossing her head so that her blonde hair bounced. She wore a black leather halter dress that skimmed her knees and showed a lot of cleavage. Spike-heeled alligator boots and an armful of glittery bracelets completed the outfit. The camera zoomed in as Elsa smiled and waved to the audience. She sat on a yellow loveseat with her hem hiked up to show white thighs. Her skin looked like milk.

"Isn't she gorgeous?" Lupe sighed.

"Nice," smirked Juan Pablo.

Luz felt like old leather.

Elsa Caso did her usual opening gush about the evening's guests. There was a soap opera star, a fashion show, Eddo, and then a musical group. Elsa rolled her eyes suggestively as she said, "We have a politician tonight, Eduardo Cortez Castillo. But ladies, he's really a treat for you."

The audience howled. Elsa frequently interacted with the audience during the hour; it was a trademark of her show, like the one serious guest and the yellow loveseat.

Elsa flipped her hair and said they'd be right back, live from the Televisa studios in Mexico City. Commercials rolled.

"More coffee anyone?" Luz asked brightly.

Lupe enjoyed the soap star and the fashion show. Carmelita looked pensive. Juan Pablo was bored. Luz drank coffee and got steadily more nervous.

Eddo finally walked onstage as Elsa stood up and applauded with the audience. Luz's heart leaped. Eddo looked like a movie star in a gray suit, white shirt, and blue silk tie.

"*Que lindo*," murmured Carmelita.

"This is your friend, Luz?" Lupe asked fearfully.

"Yes," Luz said, bursting with pride and thrilled that Carmelita thought he was handsome.

Eddo made a courtly gesture to acknowledge the cheering audience and crossed to the yellow loveseat. Elsa greeted him effusively, pressing her breasts against him during the obligatory kiss.

Luz snapped the handle off her cup.

"It's been so long," Elsa Caso trilled as she and Eddo sat down on the yellow loveseat. Elsa turned to the studio audience and twitched up her skirt at the same time, making it appear an accident. "Eduardo and I are old friends." Elsa wiggled her finger at Eddo. "We've got a lot of catching up."

Luz held her breath as Eddo talked about how lucky he was to be involved in the Romero campaign and plans for legal reform. Elsa made reference to the PEMEX scandal, and introduced a film clip of an old press conference with a younger Eddo talking from a podium about illicit finance. When the view shifted back to the live show Elsa asked him some obviously scripted questions.

It's going well, Luz thought and relaxed a little. Eddo was handling it perfectly, smoothly saying what he'd come to say and sounding brilliant. Elsa flirted outrageously, as she often did with attractive male guests, but Eddo deflected everything with humorous comments and appeals to the audience that brought more applause.

At the next commercial break, Luz leaned back against the sofa. "What do you think?" she asked.

"A pretty smart guy, Luz," Juan Pablo said, impressed.

"I can't believe you know him," Lupe said.

"Elsa Caso's falling out of her dress," Carmelita observed and Luz laughed.

Cleanliness is Healthy faded and the show came back on. Eddo was giving some statistics on the link between rising education rates and falling crime rates when Elsa leaned forward and touched the line of silver hair.

"This is new, isn't it?" she warbled. "Can everyone see this?"

The camera zoomed in on Eddo's temple and the television screen filled with brown and silver hair. The view held for a second, then the camera panned over Elsa's straining bosom. When it widened to normal view Elsa still had her hand on Eddo's head.

"Stop that," Luz said indignantly to the television. Those were *her* silver hairs. She'd seen the scar underneath. She'd held the cold pack to Eddo's head.

"I think she wants him back, Luz," Carmelita said.

"What?" Lupe asked.

"She's his old girlfriend," Luz growled, eyes glued to the screen.

Lupe gasped.

"No shit?" Juan Pablo grinned.

On the yellow loveseat, Elsa Caso edged closer to Eddo. "It's very distinguished," she caroled.

"Now as I was saying about the key to education," Eddo said and eased his head away.

Luz watched Eddo get the interview back on track. Although he kept smiling and talking and joking, Luz knew he was seriously annoyed.

But Elsa seemed oblivious. She turned to the audience and fluffed her hair. "Well, we're almost out of time. Thank you, Eduardo, for coming on the show. Wasn't I right, ladies? Smart and gorgeous." She looked straight at the camera. "Don't we think Eduardo should be one of our bachelors in the charity auction next week?"

The audience roared its approval. Luz clapped a hand to her mouth.

The Elsa Caso Show had been advertising an upcoming episode that was to feature a live charity auction of Mexico City's most eligible bachelors. Wealthy women could bid to win 24 hours with the bachelor, to include dinner and dancing and whatever else happened. Most of the men being auctioned were *telenovela* stars or sports figures.

Eddo gestured to quiet the audience. His smile was rigid. "It's a great cause, Elsa. But I'm not a bachelor."

Luz dropped her hand.

"Now, Eduardo, we know you're not married," Elsa said.

"But I am committed," Eddo said.

Luz glowed. *Committed.* He'd said that right on live television.

"That doesn't count," Elsa trilled happily and turned to the audience. "Don't we think he'd be perfect?" The audience applauded.

"No, I really can't, Elsa," Eddo said.

She tossed her blonde curls. "It'll be worth your while," she said archly. The audience caught on and roared its approval. Luz wanted to reach into the television and tear out Elsa's hair by the roots.

"I'd bid on this one," Elsa shouted provocatively.

Eddo pulled out his cell phone. "You know, Elsa, Luz and I make all the big decisions together."

Luz gaped at the television.

"Who's he calling?" Lupe asked.

Luz's brain coughed and shifted into gear. "Me. *Me*." She shot off the sofa and grabbed her cell phone off the bedside table just as it started to ring. She ran back into the living room and hit the talk button. "*Bueno?*"

"*Corazón?*"

"I can't believe you called me." Luz heard him in her ear and from the television at the same time. It was very unreal.

"So do you think I should get auctioned off next week?"

Luz covered the phone with her hand. "Am I coming through on the television?" she hissed.

Carmelita shook her head.

"No," Luz said, uncovering the phone. "I don't think you should get sold off like a bull in a market."

Eddo disguised a laugh with a cough.

"Just tell her," Luz thought hard for a good excuse he could use. "Just say . . . um."

"It's your anniversary," Carmelita supplied.

"It's our anniversary," Luz said into the phone, thanking Carmelita with her eyes.

"Our anniversary," Eddo repeated, sounding as if he'd known all along. "Of course Elsa will understand that's important."

The audience made sympathetic sounds.

Luz stared at his image on the television. His shoulders suddenly weren't quite so bunched.

"I think next weekend will be a lifetime since I fell in love with you," Luz said softly.

Lupe made a hiccupping sound.

On the television, Eddo's free hand rolled into a fist. "For me, too," he said.

Elsa Caso fidgeted on the loveseat next to Eddo. "Stand by," Eddo said to Luz. He turned to the talk show host. "Sorry, Elsa. Our answer is no. But we'll match the highest bid you receive as our way of helping out."

The audience applauded. Luz heard it coming through the phone and grinned. As she watched the television, Carmelita made an *I'm impressed* face.

"Oh, but you didn't really explain," Elsa said expansively. "Let me." She held out her hand for Eddo's cell phone.

The crowd got rowdy again and Elsa played to it, pressuring Eddo to hand over the phone, saying maybe there wasn't anybody on the line after all.

"Her name is Luz de Maria and she's an artist," Eddo said.

"She won't mind talking girl-to-girl," Elsa said to the shouting audience.

"Maybe we should wrap this up," Eddo said.

"What's he hiding?" Elsa caroled to the audience, whipping them up further.

Luz watched in horror as Eddo reluctantly surrendered the phone before the audience rioted. She thought of just breaking the connection, but then Elsa would be proven right and Eddo would be embarrassed.

"*Dios mio*, Luz," Lupe said, her eyes wide with fright.

"Hey, I'll talk to her if you don't want to," Juan Pablo said.

There was a new voice in Luz's ear. "Hello, this is Elsa Caso." On television Elsa sat on the edge of the loveseat, her knee pressed against Eddo's. His face was expressionless but Luz knew he was furious at being manipulated this way.

"Hello, Elsa." Luz's voice came out surprisingly even.

"Eduardo tells me you're not going to let him be in my auction," Elsa pouted. She sounded as if she was talking to a not-too-smart pet. "This is for a good cause."

"You're going to have to say okay, Luz," Lupe urged.

Luz and Carmelita stared at each other until Carmelita gave a *well what are you going to do about it* shrug.

"I'm sorry," Luz said into the phone. "But it's our anniversary."

She watched as Elsa smiled hungrily at Eddo. It didn't seem possible that he had dated Elsa Caso for a year, they seemed so ill-suited.

"I'm sure he'll raise a fortune," Elsa said and gestured at the audience. The cheering swelled again. The camera zoomed in on Elsa's smiling face, cutting out Eddo. "You can't keep him all to yourself."

Luz tried to think of something clever and failed. "As he

said, he's not a bachelor."

"If there isn't a ring, it doesn't count," Elsa twittered. The audience laughed uproariously.

Carmelita raised her eyebrows.

"He asked," Luz heard herself say icily. "Don't hold your breath for an invitation."

"He did what?" On the television, Elsa Caso abruptly stood up and walked to the edge of the stage. The camera followed. Her expression lost a little of its exuberance.

"Eddo made his decision, Elsa," Luz said, out of patience with the absurdity of the situation. She stood up, looming over the woman on the screen. "Probably the night he told me that I knew him better after one day than you ever did after a whole year. And he was right. *You have no idea who he really is and you're not bright enough to ever figure it out.*"

Carmelita snorted. On the television, Elsa Caso froze where she stood on the edge of the stage, the phone to her ear, her face curved into a limp smile. The audience was quiet.

Luz heard her own heart pounding in her ears. She'd yelled at *Elsa Caso.*

The connection was still live. "As Eddo said," Luz murmured into her phone. "We'd be glad to make a donation. After all, it's really about those handicapped children, isn't it?"

Elsa suddenly unfroze. "Well, I certainly understand," she said, the phone still clapped to her ear. "Lovely meeting you. *Mucho gusto.*"

The connection cut off.

Luz watched Elsa Caso click across the stage and hand Eddo's cell phone to him. "Well, I tried," Elsa said to the audience. She didn't look at Eddo or sit down. "But she insisted her man wasn't free. It must be love."

"It is," Eddo said. He smiled directly into the camera as he put the cell phone back in his pocket. A big electric smile.

A detergent ad came on.

"Too bad you're not going to marry this guy," Carmelita said.

◆

Chapter 70

"Kind of ironic," Vasco said. "I mean, this is what Miguel had wanted to do in the first place."

"Shut up," Tomás said. "Let the man think."

"After his stellar performance on Elsa's show last night, you really think we should trust his judgment?" Sitting on the sofa, Vasco opened a couple of bottles of beer. "I'm not sure we should even let him cross the street by himself anymore."

"He was smart enough to get Luz to bail him out," Tomás noted.

"True," Vasco conceded. "We can't ever let him live that down."

Vasco's playboy apartment had turned into their command post. Big sheets of paper were taped to the living room walls to display the profiles they'd made of each userid and the action at each of the marinas where *Los Hierros* officers were prowling.

Hugo's **Hh23051955** userid had posted again the previous day, another complaint that the expected shipment had not been received. They had folks keeping an eye on Hugo, but as far as they could tell he was barricaded in his house in Monterrey and keeping a low profile. The *Sheba* was still at large; neither the boat nor Gomez Mazzo had been seen in Panama or at any of the large marinas closest to Panama.

Eddo puffed on his cigar, feeling time tick away. Luz would come to Mexico City in just 12 days and he was damned if she was coming to see a man the El Toro cartel considered one of their own. "Okay," he said finally, coming to stand in front of the paper profiles of **1612colcol** and **CH5299xyz9**, the two userids which used the same password as Sonia. "What are the chances that both of these userids are Gomez Mazzo's lieutenants?"

Vasco hauled himself off the sofa and came to stand by Eddo, head cocked to one side as if he was in the Danish embassy and studying a new receptionist. "My guess is that they're both El Toro *sicarios*. Always talking about Site 2 or Site 3. Shipments."

"Or one of them is connected to Hermanos Hospitality," Tomás countered, tapping the profile of **CH5299xyz**. "But not posting anymore because they're dead. Caught skimming or snuffed in a fight over the bank."

"Either of them could be dead." Eddo walked backwards to stick his cigar in the ashtray on Vasco's coffee table.

"Or one of them is actually Gomez Mazzo himself," Tomás continued. "If we use his userid he's going to know he didn't call for a meeting."

"You're like a fucking ray of sunshine sometimes," Vasco said.

Eddo turned to Tomás, hands spread wide, his eyebrows raised.

"I don't have anything better." Tomás shook his head and slumped onto the sofa. "I just want to catch this *cabrón* so bad I can taste it. And his skinny friend who dumped my phone."

Eddo nodded and turned back to the wall to study the profile of **CH5299xyz9**. "This one hasn't posted as much as the others.

"All just a few words," Vasco said. "Stiff. Not comfortable with online communications."

"But this guy posted more and sounds sort of shrill." Eddo indicated **1612colcol**. "If he posted a call for a meeting it might be more in keeping with the personality."

"I agree," Vasco said. "Let's pretend to be a shrill nervous *sicario*."

Eddo looked at both of his friends. "Okay, then. This one?"

Tomás looked grimmer than before. "Do it."

Sonia's laptop was on the coffee table and they gathered around as if it was fire and they needed to warm their hands. Vasco logged onto the posting site as **1612colcol,** using the shared password, then slid the laptop across the coffee table to Eddo. "It's your message."

Eddo took a breath and worked the keyboard. He created a posting with the attachment then typed: "New developments. Discussion required." The enter key sent the posting into the ether. A moment later the page blinked and updated, showing the posting by **1612colcol** as the most recent. "Fuck," Eddo said and swallowed hard. "It worked."

"Keep going," Vasco said.

Eddo created another posting. This time he copied the wording from **44Gg449M11**: "Meeting @ Site 4 3pm in 5 days." He felt his scalp sweat and the scar itch as he hit the enter key.

Tomás muttered under his breath as the page blinked and **1612colcol's** meeting announcement appeared at the top of the postings list. "Five days. He'd better turn up in one of those damned marinas."

Eddo felt as if he'd just run a marathon.

Vasco logged off the site. "How about we go find some dinner?"

"Not Vips," Eddo said.

◆

It was still relatively early when they got back to Vasco's apartment. Dinner had been subdued, each of them a little queasy about what the next five days would bring and perpetually checking cell phones for messages from the scouts at the marinas. Vasco logged on again to check the site while Eddo and Tomás took another look at the information taped to the wall.

"So what did Luz say to Elsa Caso last night?" Tomás asked.

Edo shrugged. "She wouldn't tell me." He managed a grin. "But whatever it was, it must have been excellent. Elsa left the stage as soon as the director yelled 'Cut.' I didn't see her again."

"I think Ana's really going to like Luz," Tomás said.

"Fuck!" Vasco exclaimed. Eddo and Tomás both spun around.

Vasco swiveled the laptop. **1612colcol** was no longer listed as the latest posting.

44Gg449M11: Site 4 in 10 days.

"It's got to be Gomez Mazzo himself," Vasco said, sounding stunned.

"Ten days," Tomás gulped. "He's far."

Eddo stared at the screen, silently willing it to be wrong. Ten days was too far away, too close to the end of this damned countdown with Luz.

"Shit," Vasco said. "We've got to cast a wider net." All of his customary humor was gone. He tapped the keyboard, swearing softly as his fingers flew.

"We don't have enough people," Tomás said and pulled out his cell phone.

Eddo went to the large map of the Caribbean taped up next to the profiles. It hid some weird abstract artwork, the kind that had made he and Luz cringe at Jardin del Arte. Tomás joined him, still texting furiously, as Eddo traced a finger from Panama down the coast of South America. "He could be as far west as the coast of Colombia," Eddo said. "Or all the way over to the little islands east of Puerto Rico. *Madre de Dios.* Maybe we were all wrong pegging him to Panama."

"Got about 20 more places the *Sheba* could dock," Vasco said, staring at the laptop screen. He clicked the mouse and his tongue at the same time. "Make that 22."

"Antigua and Barbuda," Eddo said, the map unlocking a detail from his trip to Panama he'd all but forgotten. "Does it have a marina big enough for the *Sheba*?"

"Gimme a minute," Vasco said. Keys clicked.

"Montopa had some connection to a bank there," Eddo said.

"Falmouth Harbor Marina," Vasco said.

"I'll go there," Eddo said.

♦

Chapter 71

Gomez Mazzo drank some rum cooler as he looked at the postings page and the call by Hugo de la Madrid Acosta's bag man for a meeting. Across the cabin, his three grandchildren played a board game on the carpet with Bridget, their Swedish nanny. His daughter and third wife were on deck. In a minute his wife would come into the walnut-paneled cabin and tell him their guests were waiting for him to join them.

He didn't like that **1612colcol** had presumed to call a meeting at Site 4; that was El Toro's prerequisite. But the wording of the posting made it hard to ignore: "New developments."

Had **1612colcol** found out about the deal with Cortez?

"Look, *Abuelo!*" Five-year-old Norberto held up a game piece. "I won!"

Gomez Mazzo jerked his chin at Bridget. "Take the children on deck and let my wife introduce them."

Bridget wasn't the best looking Swedish woman he'd ever seen but she wasn't bad and he'd sleep with her eventually. Her face tightened at his order, however, and he knew she didn't like spending a lot of time on deck. The Colombians always gawked as if they'd never seen a woman with yellow hair before.

She and the children dutifully cleaned up the game and left the main cabin. Gomez Mazzo went to the built-in walnut desk to spread out a nautical chart. The call for a meeting was an opportunity to get rid of loose ends, he reflected. He would clear away the last vestiges of his arrangement with Hugo and get ready for a new partnership with Cortez. Hugo had become a nagging wild card and this bag man was clearly a problem who could get in the way of the deal with Cortez.

Chino was in Anahuac now but could come back on board

and handle both of them.

But the woman and children would have to be deposited somewhere first. Gomez Mazzo ran his finger over the route and decided on Aruba. Good shopping and discreet hotels. He'd stay a few days to make sure they were settled.

The business in Cartagena was nearly done. It was going very well, with the Colombians impressed by the boat and the fabled El Toro in person. The Colombian group would supply his operation with methamphetamines to feed the ever-hungry market in *El Norte*. The deal was a shrewd one. To begin with, it made sure the group didn't align with the Zetas or try to create their own smuggling route across the US-Mexican border. El Toro didn't have to go to the expense or risk of creating meth labs while the volume the Colombians were willing to provide would undercut any other Mexican cartel's expansion into meth.

Yes, the Colombians were another opportunity he'd grabbed with both hands.

The operation would be in place by the time of the Mexican presidential election. After Romero won, Gomez Mazzo would have Cortez squeeze the Zetas and get a few trusted El Toro men out of jail. The El Toro cartel would still eventually control northern Mexico and the meth business would skyrocket.

He'd been surprised but pleased when Cortez used the army to take out Site 1. It meant that Cortez had significant influence over military operations. Hugo had promised that Lorena could do that but had never put on a demonstration the way Cortez had.

Gomez Mazzo calculated the trip to Site 4, went back to the laptop, and created a new posting. When he logged off he went on deck and drank a toast to his new partners.

♦

Chapter 72

"You could still change your mind," Carmelita said.

"I'm not going to that wedding," Luz said. "Could you really see me with those people?" Women like Señora Vega in gowns and all of them sneering at her.

"If you marry him you'll face them someday." Carmelita adjusted the shoulder strap of her purse as they walked.

"I'm not marrying him, Carmelita," Luz reminded her friend. It was getting a little easier to say but it never hurt any less.

The days had flown by in a blur of text messages and phone calls with Eddo, helping Juan Pablo prepare for his final exams, and fretting over Lupe's relationship with Tío. Before Luz had realized it, her phone countdown read 11 days to MEET EDDO and Juan Pablo's graduation was just around the corner.

"So what's the dress for?" Carmelita asked.

"He has to go to a *despedida* the same weekend we're meeting in Mexico City and I said I'd go with him." Luz got a fluttery feeling in her stomach just thinking about it, but a *despedida* was just a farewell party, hardly as fancy as a wedding.

"I thought he was in Oaxaca."

"The Romero campaign is moving to Mexico City," Luz said, adjusting her stride to step over a hole in the rutted sidewalk. "He'll be living there by the time we get together."

They were headed for the used clothing *mercado* a few blocks away. Except for Eddo's buying spree at Liverpool, Luz had always bought her clothes there.

She slowed as they came to Senora Velasquez's *abarrotes* shop. "Let's get a snack first."

Two officers from the ever-present security service were

with them. At first it had felt awkward and embarrassing but Luz was grateful for the rotation of security officers and their dark SUVs in front of the house and the safety they represented. What had happened to her in that scratched sedan wouldn't happen again. The security people were both male and female, which was surprising, and wore black polo shirts and jeans. All of them had badges and were scrupulously polite, never asking why they had to work in such a shabby neighborhood. Carmelita was very impressed.

One of the security officers went into the store and Luz saw him look around before motioning that she and Carmelita could go in.

Señora Velasquez was behind the counter, as usual, her eyes bright with curiosity. Luz knew the neighborhood was buzzing over the security presence but Eddo had advised her to say as little as possible and she was doing just that.

Two of the vendors from the clothing *mercado* were in the store. Rubia Durango, a few years older than Luz and Carmelita, was nicknamed for her dyed blonde hair. She was a chatterbox but she had the best children's clothes and Carmelita and Lupe both frequented her stall. Chula Mendez was a leathery old woman who mostly sold underwear.

"Luz de Maria," Rubia whooped. She indicated the security officer standing by the doorway ignoring the bags of peanuts and cans of soda for sale. "Nobody sees you for so long and now it's like you're the queen of England."

"Just her maid, Rubia," Luz said, making the others laugh. The women in the shop wore polyester dresses that had probably come from the *mercado*. Carmelita had on jeans and a knit top but nothing close to the quality of the designer jeans and shirt from Liverpool that Luz wore with hair pulled back with a sleek clip from the same store.

"Who talked to Elsa Caso, no less," Chula said archly, eyeing the pink DKNY purse. "That was really you on the phone talking to Elsa Caso?"

Luz smiled thinly. "Yes, I talked to her."

"What did you say?" Rubia bubbled with curiosity. "The show ended and she never said."

Luz shrugged, knowing that Carmelita was trying not to giggle. "I just said Señor Cortez wasn't available for her auction."

"Huh," Rubia snorted. "She wanted to buy him, I guess."

Chula wiped at her nose with a thumb and forefinger, then brushed her hand against her skirt. "You think you can compete against Elsa Caso, Luz? That's getting above yourself."

Señora Velasquez leaned over the counter. "Lupe says that man calls you all the time. I guess you don't need no messages no more."

Luz felt her face redden as she looked at the narrow shelves crammed with sweets and snacks, wishing Lupe had kept her mouth shut. "No, I have a new cell phone."

"How'd you meet someone like that, Luz de Maria?" Rubia wasn't satisfied. She settled against the counter and winked at Señora Velasquez.

"At a museum," Luz said.

"Really?" Rubia said. "That's not what Lupe said."

Chula chimed in. "She said you worked for him." She raked her eyes over Luz's outfit. "Guess you had to dress up to work there."

"No," Luz said, taken aback. "We met at the Tamayo Museum in Mexico City."

Chula sniffed, a wealth of disbelief in the sound.

"He's real handsome," Rubia said. "You don't see the likes of him around here."

"Your mother," Señora Velasquez sighed. "I don't know what she would make of all this, Luz de Maria. He's not your kind."

Luz fished around in the barrel of ice for sports drinks, hating being the object of gossip, hating Lupe's wagging tongue. Hated the reminder of that last conversation with her mother.

Carmelita gathered up some bags of chips.

Luz paid for the drinks and the chips without saying anything else. Señora Velasquez put their snacks into a plastic bag, exchanging glances with Rubia and Chula the entire time.

Once outside with the security guards, Luz turned back toward the house, nearly running with the need to get away.

"Let's not go to the market now," she said.

"Luz de Maria Alba Mora." Carmelita grabbed Luz by the arm and yanked her to a stop. "Have you ever in your entire life told somebody *chingate*?"

The security officers took up positions around Luz and Carmelita.

Luz was startled by Carmelita's intensity and bad language. *Chingate* meant *fuck you* in the most vulgar and literal way possible. "What are you talking about?" she asked.

"Don't let those old crones make you feel bad about Eddo," Carmelita said, gesturing at the store. "I can't believe you didn't say anything. Don't you know how to stand up for yourself?"

"Of course I do," Luz protested. "I hit a man with a broken bottle once."

"You should have hit Rubia and wiped that look off her face."

"But then he shot me."

"You didn't die," Carmelita pointed out.

Luz realized that Rubia and Chula were watching from the doorway of the *abarrotes* store.

She swallowed hard and steered Carmelita back to the SUV in front of the Alba house. "Can you take us to the Liverpool department store?" she asked the security officer. He opened the rear door for them.

"You didn't want to go to a party in Mexico City in a secondhand dress, anyway," Carmelita said triumphantly as she climbed into the vehicle.

"I'll get shoes, too," Luz said.

◆

Chapter 73

Yolanda, one of the administrative assistants, squeezed by the pile of packing boxes in the hallway and tugged on Eddo's sleeve. "Eduardo, can you come to the front for a moment? We need your signature."

Eddo walked into the main reception area of the campaign suite and signed his name on the digital pad held by a courier from an overnight delivery service. He walked back to his own cubicle, opened the envelope, and pulled out a single sheet of paper with the Montopa logo at the top. Below was a color photo of him and Elsa Caso on the yellow sofa. In the photo Eddo had his cell phone to his ear and Elsa was tossing her hair, clearly impatient. The caption read "already bought."

He dropped the paper on his desk, and sprinted back to the reception area. "That delivery guy?" he nearly shouted. "Where did he go?"

"He left," Yolanda said. "What's the matter?"

Eddo didn't answer but shot out the door and down the service stairway. He made it to the front door of the building in time to see a scooter zip down the dark street.

He bolted back up the stairs. The younger staff was still milling around, talking about going to a nearby restaurant for dinner. His face must have looked like thunder because the conversation stopped. Yolanda, a motherly type who always had a pad of paper in her hand, frowned at him. "What's going on?"

"Where's Arturo?" he asked.

"He left early," Yolanda said. "It's the wedding rehearsal tonight, remember?"

"First thing tomorrow, please," Eddo said. "Find out how the delivery company got the envelope. Where it got picked up. How long they took to get it here."

Yolanda wrote it all down, then looked up. "Okay, anything else?"

Eddo took a deep breath and collected his thoughts. "I'll be out of town after the wedding," he reminded her. "Off the grid with some buddies before the move. Just remind Matilda and Nestor. I've already arranged to send all my personal stuff to Mexico City. You have the address there."

"I made sure everyone has it," Yolanda said.

"And you have the other important date on everyone's calendar?" Eddo asked.

"Yes." Yolanda shook her head. "Your schedule is crazy. Do you ever sleep?"

"Not if I can help it," Eddo said. "You've still got Luz's number, right? And her security?"

"Yes and yes."

"Thanks, Yolanda."

Eddo went into his cubicle, logged off his computer, jammed the picture into his briefcase, and left the campaign headquarters for the apartment hotel where he'd been living.

The small apartment was as sterile as the other places he'd lived in over the past few years. It was too late to run but he got on the treadmill anyway, needing to burn off the tension and pure rage he felt at seeing himself described as *bought*. By the third mile he admitted to himself that the investigation had never been just about Hugo. In the back of his mind he'd always planned to shut down the El Toro cartel and if he was right about Site 4, they'd do it.

They still needed to find *Sheba*, however, and let the yacht lead them to the meeting.

He ran five miles, the photo still bothering him. Eddo wiped his face with a forearm. It wasn't by chance that the photo was of him talking on the phone. The message was that if Eddo got out of line, Luz could be a target. And Eddo was not going to let that happen. Again.

Then there was the fact that the photo had been sent to campaign headquarters. Was that a not-so-subtle way of letting Eddo know that Gomez Mazzo regarded Arturo as bought, too?

Eddo showered, found some dinner, and called Luz. He got

his second shock of the day when a man answered her cell phone. Eddo was about to head for his car when he realized it was Luz's brother.

Juan Pablo sounded very mature. "Luz is indisposed."

"Indisposed?" Eddo asked. "As in, she's in the bathroom?"

"Well, yes."

"She's okay? She's not sick?"

"She's taking a bath," Juan Pablo said. A little humor crept into his voice, as if he'd heard his own tone and realized it was overkill.

"So how's everything going?" Eddo asked. "Security car parked in front?"

"Yes," Juan Pablo said. "Tonight just like every night. Or is tonight special?"

It was clear not much got past this kid and Eddo liked that. "There might be some developments," Eddo admitted. "It would be good if you had your own way of getting in touch with me. Just in case."

♦

Chapter 74

Hugo slid his hands over the keyboard but didn't type anything. Max Arias had his nerve, coolly disappearing for months with millions of Lorena's campaign money and then posting a cryptic message like "New developments." The developments were probably that some El Toro goons were on to him and the little fucker suddenly wanted to negotiate and save his skin. Well, Hugo would give **1612colcol** some new developments to think about. Hugo was going to wring his fucking neck and get the money back. That would be a new development.

Apart from being a thief, Max had totally steered him wrong with that crap about the stoolie from the fictional *Los Hierros*. That kid had been hot air with his shit story about Cortez being head of *Los Hierros,* having a girlfriend in Lomas Virreyes, and being barely scratched by the attempted carjacking on the Periferico. The truth was that *Los Hierros* was a media fabrication, the girlfriend had turned out to be some anonymous maid, and the local Puebla newspapers had covered Cortez's slow recovery. Maybe Cortez had been part of Fonesca's investigation which had led to Luis' arrest and Hugo's resignation but he hadn't played a major role. Now, sporting a decent scar, Cortez was working for Arturo Romero, just as Hugo had assumed last year that he would.

The study was quiet. The whole house was quiet. Even the flatfooted maid who clumped through the house on planks had gone quiet. They were all tiptoeing around him. Family. Friends. Business associates. More like former friends. Former business associates. Monterrey was like a cemetery.

They'd sent Reynoldo to boarding school. Graciela was gone most of the time. Talking to Lorena was a complaint session. She still hadn't caved in to Fernando's pressure to become the next Minister of Public Security but he hadn't yet been able to duplicate a financial scheme as good as Hermanos Hospitality.

He was close, however. The plan was to use an ailing subsidiary that imported pulp paper for his print media outlets as a substitute. The company was being "sold" with the help of a clever accountant. When it was under new ownership, he'd start to funnel funds from his other business interests into it, wash them through the import paperwork and then use cash for Lorena's campaign. As much as he hated to admit it, he was basing his moves on Max Arias' blueprint. Hermanos Hospitality had been the perfect setup, just far away enough not to be connected with anything Hugo owned and he was sure that Fonseca's people had never known about it.

The new company would be handled the same way. And of course, he needed a way to get Site 1 restarted.

The scheme with the kids had been pure gold.

Max had done him a favor, Hugo reflected as he poured himself a brandy. Gomez Mazzo had responded to Max's posting, giving Hugo a chance to talk to his former partner for the first time in months.

Los Pinos was still within his grasp.

◆

Chapter 75

He wasn't sure why, but Eddo blabbed his guts out to his sister Pilar at Maria Elena Romero's wedding.

There were cocktails and dinner, toasts and dancing and more dancing. He'd mangled a couple of duty dances and spoke to the people he'd needed to speak with and then somehow ended up in a corner with Pilar telling her all about Luz. How they'd met. The investigation into Hugo's mess and what had happened to her. Finding her again and the week in San Miguel. Everything he was planning.

"Let me get this straight," Pilar said, looking at his cell phone display. "In a little over a week you're expecting Luz de Maria to give you an answer to your proposal."

"Yes."

"And this is how you want to handle it."

"Yes."

"And guilt has nothing to do with it."

Eddo said, "I knew she was the one before anything happened."

Pilar pursed her lips. They had the same light eyes and wide jaw but the family resemblance ended there. Pilar was a suburban housewife now, but she'd managed to combine Mexican elegance with a *norteamericano* sense of style. The striking combination was on display tonight in a simple black gown, with dark hair wound into a sleek bun and her trademark pearls at her throat.

"Well, she's not in it for the money," Pilar said. "If she was she would have jumped at the chance to marry you."

Eddo felt a spurt of anger. "Be a snob if you want, Pilar," he said. "If she says yes, we'll get married, whether or not you approve."

"I'm happy for you," Pilar protested. "But this just seems like too much."

"You know me," Eddo said. "Nothing halfway."

"I know." Pilar rolled her eyes at him, making Eddo laugh. She reached out and squeezed his hand. "Hard to believe my little brother finally wants to get married."

They touched champagne glasses and drank. Eddo looked around the hotel ballroom, trying to see the reception through Luz's eyes. Tuxedos and evening gowns. Full orchestra, ice sculptures, rose topiaries, gifts for 500 guests. The cream of the PAN political machine was there, talking, dancing, and paying homage to Arturo and Imelda. The only missing luminaries were the Betancourts who had attended very few social events lately.

"Did you invite her to come tonight?" Pilar asked, as if reading his mind.

Eddo nodded glumly. "She's afraid of all this."

"If she's as smart as you say she is," Pilar said. "She understands the rules. People know each other's place in society and can be very cruel to anyone who tries to move up."

"Rules can be broken," Eddo said. Pilar's husband and daughter were dancing together. His niece waved over her father's shoulder and Eddo waved back.

"She's having a wonderful time." Pilar's gaze followed Eddo's. "Thanks for having Imelda and Arturo invite us. This really is the party of the century."

Eddo nodded. "So are you going to help me?"

"Just tell me one thing, Eduardito. Is this supposed to be compensation for all the times you're going to scare her to death? Getting shot or rushing off to save the country?"

Eddo's cell phone rang.

"Got a lead," Vasco said as soon as Eddo answered. "*Sheba* was in Aruba."

"*Madre de Dios*," Eddo swore.

The rest of the conversation was brief. Eddo disconnected and kissed Pilar, barely conscious of the wedding reception still swirling around them. "I've got to go. There's a plane waiting for me. Tell Bill and the kid bye from me."

"I rest my case," Pilar said.

"What?"

"Nothing," Pilar shook her head. "Go."

On the way out of the reception hall Eddo called Luz to tell her he'd be out of touch for awhile.

◆

Chapter 76

Two days after Eddo's last call, in a silky nightgown she'd worn only briefly in San Miguel, Luz plunked herself on the sofa with a glass of wine and some newspapers. It was long after midnight and the summer rain had stopped. She'd had the dreadful nightmare again, the one in which the noose was around Eddo's neck instead of her own, and she couldn't go back to sleep.

Only the lamp next to the sofa was lit. The living room was warm and muggy. Juan Pablo would graduate in just a few days. After that, presuming Eddo survived the hunt for El Toro and reestablished contact, she'd go to Mexico City and tell Eddo that she couldn't marry him. They'd have a few days together and that would be it. Arturo Romero would win the election and Eddo would become Attorney General. She'd take care of Lupe and the girls and keep Juan Pablo from having the sort of wasted life she had. Maybe by the time she was old and gray the gossip would have died down.

Luz sipped some wine and opened a newspaper. She was soaking up more news than ever since Eddo had gone wherever he'd gone, always looking for credible information related to drug violence but afraid that she'd find something awful at the same time.

The Veracruz newspaper had a bright blue masthead and a color photo of a bus accident on the front page. Another article reported that 15 male bodies had been found in an abandoned hotel. The violence in the north of the country was spreading as cartel-affiliated gangs rounded up migrants to move drugs up from the southern border with Guatemala and then killed them when the job was done.

Reforma was a taste of Mexico City. Luz found the June

review of the Tamayo Museum exhibits and savored every word. Next came the international news and the national news. She turned another page and there was Eddo, staring out at her in living color from the *La Gente* society section. He was obscenely handsome in a black tuxedo with a crisp bow tie, dancing with a beautiful woman in a strapless blue gown. One hand was placed possessively on her bare back. The other hand clasped hers. The woman was small and fine-boned. Her head barely came up to Eddo's wide shoulder. She had a heart-shaped face, creamy skin, and sleek chocolate hair piled in loose curls like a Hollywood starlet. She looked to be in her early twenties, all innocence and upper class femininity. Her head was thrown back so she could see him and the look on her face was one of utter adoration. Eddo gazed down at her with real warmth and affection.

The caption read: *PAN attorney Eduardo Cortez Castillo of Puebla accompanied heiress Carolina Porterfield.*

The back door grated open and the kitchen light went on and Luz flinched so hard she nearly fell off the sofa.

Lupe and Tío walked out of the kitchen and into the living room. They must have been in Tío's old shed by the forge. What they had been doing was obvious. Lupe's frizzy hair was matted on one side, she was barefoot, and the buttons of her old housedress were misaligned. Tío's shirt hung outside his pants. He looked greasy and sloppy as he leered at Luz's thinly-covered breasts.

"We didn't think anyone was still up." Lupe murmured something to Tío and edged him to the front door. Tío grunted and raised his head over Lupe's shoulder to look at Luz again. They walked out the door. The front gate squeaked open.

Lupe reappeared. She closed the front door, fussed with her hair, and perched on the arm of the sofa. Her eye fell on the *La Gente* section. "Is that him?"

Luz reached for the newspaper but Lupe snatched it up first. "They sort of match," she said.

"What?"

"Both so shiny."

Luz grabbed the newspaper out of Lupe's hands and folded it, hiding the picture, sick at heart. "What's going on with Tío,

Lupe?"

"Armando needs a place to live." Lupe slid off the arm of the sofa and onto the cushions.

Luz drew up her legs to make room. "What happened to the place where he was living?"

"Esteban was letting him stay at the shop."

"So?"

"But Esteban said Armando had to come to work every day," Lupe said, as if Esteban had perpetrated a grave injustice. "I thought Armando could move back here."

"Absolutely not," Luz said swiftly. She sat up straight. "Tío loses his place to stay because he's too lazy to hold down a real job?"

"He wants to restart the forge," Lupe pleaded.

"No." Luz felt her whole body tense. "If his living arrangements were contingent upon his job, maybe Tío should have approached things a little more seriously."

"Don't try and fool me with your big words, Luz," Lupe said. "You're not being fair."

"Listen to me, Lupe." Luz reached for her sister's hand. "How can you forget why he got kicked out of the house?"

"That was a misunderstanding," Lupe said, pulling her hand away.

Luz rubbed her eyes. Her sister was mired in the tiny world of the *barrio*, tolerating and abetting the worst behavior of men who liked to drink much and work less. She viewed change with suspicion and was content to live like a martyr, using gossip as her release.

"What are you doing with him, Lupe?" Luz asked tiredly. "What kind of life can he give you?"

"The real kind," Lupe flung back. "You think you're so above it all with your señora hair and fancy clothes. But at least Armando is here with me." Lupe poked the folded copy of *Reforma*. "Your fancy man isn't going to keep promises to some flat-haired *muchacha* because she can draw pretty pictures. You were tricked and everybody but you knows it."

Luz leaped up. "Lupe!"

"You're making a fool of yourself." Lupe stood up to face

Luz. "It's embarrassing. Everybody has been talking about you since that show."

"Mostly you," Luz said hotly. "Why on earth have you been telling people I worked for Eddo?"

"I was trying to protect you," Lupe exclaimed.

"How about protect yourself?" Luz shot back. "Tío can't hold down a job but you come running every time he unzips his--."

"Hey!"

Luz and Lupe both turned to see Juan Pablo on the stairs, textbook in hand. "I've got my physics final tomorrow," he said. "Unless there's some quiet around here, one of you is going to have to take it for me."

Juan Pablo looked pointedly from one sister to the other then stalked back up the stairs and slammed his bedroom door. The air in the house rippled.

"Look, Lupe," Luz said stiffly. "If Armando wants to restart the forge, I can live with that. But he doesn't move back in."

Sophia started calling. Lupe went upstairs.

Luz picked up the newspaper and went into her room.

Maybe Lupe was right. The thought squeezed Luz's heart. Eddo was having a torrid relationship with this Carolina Porterfield woman, who was probably 20 years younger than he was, because she was the sort of woman he should be with. Young, rich, upper class, flaxen and lovely in all the ways Luz was not. And the woman clearly adored him, it had been written all over her face. Eddo loved this woman because she didn't argue and was tiny and perfect. She didn't have *indio* hair or shoulders like an oil rig worker.

She was appropriate.

♦

Chapter 77

The Minister of National Security of Antigua and Barbuda, Dr. Evan Wibley, was a dick.

Eddo watched the clock on Wibley's wall tick for eight minutes as the minister alternately studied Fonseca's letter, handled the Mexican warrant for the arrest of Gustavo Gomez Mazzo, and made slight lip-smacking sounds. From time to time a saliva bubble formed at the corner of his mouth and lasted until the next soft smack.

It was Eddo's second day on the island of Antigua and so far he'd found out that the Falmouth Harbor Marina was expensive, picturesque, and private as hell. Eddo had gone on a scouting mission the previous day and figured out that the yachts were huge, their owners were rich, one entrance controlled access to the slips, and tourists weren't allowed. The road past the marina entrance was lined on the town side with upscale shops, restaurants, and maritime supply companies, none of which looked like the sort of place Gomez Mazzo frequented.

Eventually Wibley put down the letter, which had been formatted in both Spanish and English. "I'm sure you realize that this documentation does not give you arrest powers under Antigua and Barbuda law," he said.

It didn't give him arrest powers in Mexico, either, but Eddo wasn't about to say that. "Of course," he replied. "I can only request your help in the event that Gomez Mazzo docks here."

Wibley frowned. "And you say your government has credible evidence to suggest this, uh, criminal is coming here."

"Yes." Eddo came as close to grinding his teeth as he'd ever done. They'd gone over this three times already. Eddo's English was getting the most practice since he'd left college but he was having a tough time with the British accent, a legacy of Antigua and Barbuda's former Commonwealth affiliation. "We have reason to believe he docked at Falmouth Harbor Marina at least once before."

Wibley nodded. Touched the copy of the warrant again with a fingertip. Eddo had a powerful memory of Bernal Paz recoiling from the warrant for Hugo's banking records.

"Yachts from all over the world enjoy the security and beauty of Antigua's facilities," Wibley said. He was a handsome, dark-skinned man in his mid forties with short graying hair. Classic fashion was obviously a secondary consideration in paradise; the minister's outfit of blue polyester sport shirt, yellow tie, and checkered sports coat reminded Eddo of a *Sabado Gigante* game show host.

"I would appreciate your assistance in getting the docking records from the marina authorities," Eddo said. "And have your defense forces ready to detain and turn him over to Mexican authorities should he come to Antigua."

"Antigua and Barbuda is known for its discretion," Wibley said. "We have to be careful not to violate the trust our guests place in our institutions."

"I'm sure your institutions possess the professionalism and discretion that this situation calls for," Eddo countered.

Wibley smiled, revealing saliva-coated white teeth. "Violation of privacy is at issue."

Eddo stood and walked to the wall opposite Wibley's desk. It was covered with pictures of Wibley and various celebrities on boats showing off the man-sized fish they'd caught. Most of the celebrities were male Hollywood action stars accompanied by busty blondes. As Eddo studied the pictures with his back to Wibley he could feel the man's attitude change from confidence to consternation. Maybe he wasn't used to people turning their back on him or maybe there was something else going on. "This is a request from one nation to another," Eddo said, examining a young sci-fi star gloating over an enormous swordfish. "I'm sure Antigua would not like to cause a diplomatic incident. Should this criminal dock here, after this official request has been made, with a warrant that shows that Gustavo Gomez Mazzo has been a wanted man in Mexico for more than six years, and Antigua does not render assistance . . ."

Eddo turned and smiled at Wibley.

The minister stood and set Fonseca's paperwork on the edge of the desk, clearly wanting Eddo to take it back. "I'll have to consult with my government to see if your request for the docking records is in keeping with the law. Could you stop by tomorrow at this time?"

It was the Antigua and Barbuda equivalent of *come back in 15 minutes*. Eddo got the same reception in the office of the commandant of the Antigua and Barbuda Defense Force. From the way the major who deigned to talk to him mouthed platitudes like *privacy for our guests* and *trust in our institutions*, it was clear that Wibley had been on the phone as soon as Eddo had left his office. The major threw in a nice twist, however, claiming that the Defense Forces only had jurisdiction if a crime had actually been committed in Antigua and Barbuda.

It was mid afternoon and the sun was smiling down as Eddo got out of his rental car. It was just breezy enough for him to be comfortable in khakis and a short-sleeved shirt and sunny enough to need his Ray-Bans. Antigua was pristine and panoramic and across the straits Barbuda was probably pretty much the same. The scene was beautiful wherever he looked, with a cobalt sky and beaches that made him want to see Luz stretched out naked, her skin caramel against the white sand, her hair wet and tangled like *la sirena*.

No wonder Gomez Mazzo came here. Nice change from stuffing kids with cocaine and murdering Zetas on dusty streets.

Eddo walked up the steps to the small building housing the commanding officer of the Antigua and Barbuda Coast Guard. It was close to the Falmouth Harbor Marina, on the southeast side of the island, in an area known as English Harbor. A gray patrol boat was pulled up to a long dock. The boat was gleaming and shipshape, which was a good indication of the professionalism of our institutions.

The first thing Eddo saw inside the building was a long glass trophy case crammed with photographs of soccer teams, ribbons, gold and silver trophies, signed game balls, and other mementos from years of inter-island defense force competition.

He bent to read the inscription on a particularly old trophy. *1944 Caribbean Watchstander Finals.*

"You a fan?"

Eddo straightened up. The speaker was an athletic black man in his early thirties wearing a lightweight but crisply pressed uniform with impressive epaulets. His hair was as short as Eddo's. "Always," Eddo said. "Nice collection in your showcase."

"You look as if you could do some serious damage yourself."

"On a good day," Eddo said.

"We play on Saturdays," the officer said. "Always happy to accommodate a visitor."

"Thanks," Eddo replied. "I'm looking for the commanding officer."

"You found him." The man held out his hand. "Ian Crispell."

Eddo shook hands. "Eduardo Cortez."

"I gather you're not from around here, Mr. Cortez."

"Mexico."

Crispell nodded. "Please don't tell me your wife lost a diamond ring while water-skiing and you'd like the Coast Guard to go look for it."

"You get a lot of Mexicans here with that kind of money?"

"A few." Crispell nodded again as if he had taken Eddo's measure and liked what he saw. "Come on into my office and tell me what brings you to our humble shores."

Crispell's office had a large Antigua and Barbuda Defense Forces seal on the wall and a recruiting poster for the Coast Guard but otherwise it was plain and sterile. The window looked out over the dock and the shiny patrol boat.

The Coast Guard commander indicated the chair across from the desk. Eddo sat, smiling at the lack of décor. "Looks a lot like my office at home," he said.

"And what is it that you do at home, Mr. Cortez?" Crispell sat in the swivel chair behind the desk. He was a neat worker with only a few files on the desk, their edges aligned. The surface of the desk gleamed with polish.

"I close down drug cartels," Eddo said. "And I need your help."

Crispell got up and closed the door. When he sat back down he leaned forward. "I'm almost afraid to ask, but how can the Antigua and Barbuda Coast Guard help?"

"I have reason to believe that the head of the El Toro cartel, Gustavo Gomez Mazzo, occasionally docks his yacht called *Sheba* at the Falmouth Harbor Marina and that he'll be back soon for a meeting with some associates."

Crispell's jaw dropped. *Madre de Dios* but the guy should never play poker with Tomás.

"Here's the warrant for his arrest and a letter from Attorney General Fonseca." Eddo put the documents on the desk.

Crispell read both the letter and the warrant. "The Coast Guard will do whatever we can, Mr. Cortez, keeping in mind we're a force of less than 30 people and only four patrol boats." He started scribbling on a piece of paper. "But frankly, this is above my pay grade. You need to go see the Minister of National Security, Dr. Wibley. Here are directions to his office in St. John's."

"Wibley said he has to consult with his government to determine if it's legal to tell me if the *Sheba* has ever docked at Falmouth."

Crispell put down his pen. "You've seen Wibley, then?"

"This morning."

"He gave you the hand?" Crispell asked.

"Sorry?" Eddo hadn't heard that English expression before.

Crispell held up a hand as if stopping traffic. "The hand."

"Well put," Eddo said. "You want to tell me why?"

"He's my chain of command," Crispell said. "So, uh. No."

Eddo folded his arms. "Part of the Coast Guard's mandate is the prevention of drug smuggling. It's right on your website."

Crispell rubbed his chin and squinted at Eddo. "Do you have reasonable suspicion that--." He checked the letter. "This *Sheba* will be bringing drugs into Antigua and Barbuda?"

"The owner of the *Sheba* is a known drug smuggler," Eddo said.

The phone on Crispell's desk rang. He rolled his eyes as if

in apology and picked up the receiver. "Crispell."

Eddo watched as Crispell's face displayed concern, then dismay, and finally anger. Crispell said, "Yes, sir," and "No, sir," and a last "I'll let you know if I hear anything, sir." He hung up and rubbed his chin again. "You're pretty popular here, Mr. Cortez."

"Just a small circle of admirers," Eddo said.

"Too bad I never met you."

"You can stop and board the *Sheba* on suspicion of bringing drugs into your country," Eddo said, swinging the conversation back to where he needed it to be. "Detain Gomez Mazzo long enough for Mexico to request extradition and get some cops here to pick him up."

Crispell cocked his head at the phone. "You're asking more than my career can afford."

Eddo didn't reply, just used the tried and true method of letting an uncomfortable silence test the other man's nerve.

He was a decent guy and Crispell cracked fast. "Listen," he said. "The American consul will be in town tomorrow. Go talk to him. Maybe he can twist Wibley's arm or something." He sighed and wrote down a number. "Here's my cell. In case of an emergency."

"Thanks."

Crispell handed Eddo the paper. "I like this job, Mr. Cortez," he warned.

♦

Chapter 78

Graduation day was bittersweet.

Luz sat in the big church of Santa Catalina during the graduation mass and watched Juan Pablo in his new suit sitting with his classmates in the front pew. She'd worked so hard for this day but had always imagined it differently.

Maria would be there, pleased and weepy that her baby was graduating from high school. Luz and Lupe would be happy and excited and still close.

After the Mass, the graduates filed out of the church, through the school garden and into the school's gymnasium. Guests followed and sat on folding chairs. The bishop made the keynote speech then handed out the diplomas and awards.

Juan Pablo graduated fourth in his class, won the language medal for the highest grade point average in English and French, and was awarded the Athlete of the Year trophy. Luz nearly burst with pride as he walked up to the podium again and again. Seated between Luz and Lupe, Martina and Sophia swung their legs and bounced each time they heard Tío Juan Pablo's name. Luz stole a glance at Lupe. Her sister's eyes were teary.

Luz reached out her hand. Lupe took it and squeezed gently. For a little while things were all right again.

♦

Juan Pablo left on the all-stars *fútbol* tour the day after graduation. Tío came and worked the forge that afternoon. Luz kept an eye on him, drifting between the forge and the house on the pretext of doing laundry and hanging it in the yard. After *la cena* she carried some clean tee shirts upstairs to Juan Pablo's room.

As Luz put away his things she saw that his dresser drawers were nearly empty. He'd asked to borrow the big rolling suitcase she'd been given by Hector and Luz had not given the request much thought. Now as she looked around, she saw that his new suit, all of his shirts and pants, his *fútbol* equipment, and his sports bag were gone. The desk was stripped of his diploma, the fourth place certificate, the language medal, the trophy, and all the other academic ribbons and awards he'd won in high school. Gone too were his few prized books, including his Tolkien paperbacks and the copy of *El Cantar de Mio Cid* Luz had given him for graduation.

♦

Chapter 79

Eddo introduced himself to Alan Dowd as the latter was winding up dinner with a stout local gentleman. The American consul looked surprised when Eddo handed over an old business card proclaiming his importance as the Director of the Office of Special Investigations and asked if Dowd would join him for a drink at the bar at his convenience.

The restaurant was fish-themed, with strands of dark blue netting strung across the ceiling, punctuated by cork floats and recycled glass orbs. Battered tin lanterns on every table added an authentic touch. Enormous stuffed swordfish hung on the side walls, arched to look as though they were leaping out of the ocean. The back of the place was open to the beach. Diners who didn't mind bugs sat out on the deck.

A big sign over the bar read "The Blue Marlin" and specialty drinks were served in margarita glasses with blue glass seahorse stems. The soundtrack was all steel drum, played soft enough to hear conversation and the waves lapping the beach below the deck. The bartender charged Eddo the equivalent of 200 pesos for a tall glass of tonic water with a wedge of lime. Eddo slid onto a bar stool, a vantage point from where he could see Dowd and his dinner companion in the main dining area, and thought about what Luz would have to say about the decor. It would be something acidic and then there'd be that *I shouldn't have said that* look that always made him laugh. *Madre de Dios* but he missed her.

Dowd appeared after 30 minutes of fish-gazing. "So Mr. Cortez, what can I do for you?"

"Let me buy you a drink."

Dowd ordered a *Cuba libre*, which made Eddo's stomach wince, and they moved to a booth in the back of the bar.

"I have an unusual problem," Eddo said. "And I hope you have sufficient influence here in Antigua to help me."

The waitress brought Dowd's drink and he raised it in a salute to Eddo before taking a long, appreciative swallow. "I probably can't help your immigration situation, Mr. Cortez," Dowd said.

"Not every Mexican has an immigration problem," Eddo said. He took out Fonseca's letter and the warrant and passed them across the table. "I have reasonable suspicion that the head of the El Toro cartel will be in Antigua in two days."

"The El Toro cartel?" Dowd asked. "What the hell's that?"

"Responsible for nearly half of the cocaine and marijuana flowing over the border into the United States," Eddo said, trying not to let his astonishment show. How was it possible that a *norteamericano* diplomat in the region hadn't heard of the El Toro cartel? "El Toro has killed more than 20,000 people over the last three years, including two US immigration agents last year. Head of the cartel has been on our wanted list for years."

Dowd drank some more *Cuba libre*. "Why tell me?"

In his early fifties, Eddo guessed, with blondish-grayish thinning hair, a long morose face, and a paunch. Dowd wore a blue striped button-down shirt without a tie and a beige suit that had seen better days.

"The head of the cartel might be coming to Antigua," Eddo said again. "The locals don't seem all that interested."

"Wibley." Dowd finished his drink in a gulp.

"Yes," Eddo said and signaled for the waitress to bring Dowd another.

Dowd nodded his thanks. "Dr. Wibley doesn't want problems like yours."

"So he just pretends they don't happen?"

"Worked for him so far," Dowd said. "When was the last time Antigua made the news for anything but a touristy good time?"

Eddo indicated the papers. "If you could just take a look."

"Sure." Dowd read the letter, stopping only when the second *Cuba libre* came. His hands on the paper were soft and unhealthy-looking. No wedding ring. Probably divorced. Paying alimony. No girlfriend, either.

"This is a sorry situation, but I can't help you," Dowd said. He drank down half of his new drink, folded the papers, and gave them back.

"I hear you have some pull with Wibley," Eddo said. "Maybe you can suggest that he allow the local Coast Guard to search the *Sheba*. Suspected drug dealing."

Dowd sighed and polished off the rest of his latest drink. "Mr. Cortez, I'm not the ambassador. Just some mid-level bureaucrat who passes through two, maybe three days a month to process visas, eat lunch with the Chamber of Commerce and dedicate a school."

"Your government has a warrant out for Gomez Mazzo's arrest, too," Eddo pointed out.

"Maybe." Dowd licked his lips. "I've never seen it."

"Call your FBI. Or DEA."

Dowd played with his empty glass. "So how do you win?"

"I don't care who takes this guy out of circulation, just as long as he's gone."

"Wibley's the government here," Dowd said with a shrug.

Dowd wasn't signing up to help but he wasn't jockeying to leave as long as the drinks were coming. Eddo caught the waitress's eye. She said something to the bartender who reached for the rum.

"You have a pretty nice deal here," Eddo observed to Dowd. "Fly in, schmooze a bit. Make a couple of speeches. Go back to your embassy."

"In St. Kitts," Dowd supplied.

"I can see how you wouldn't want to mess it up," Eddo said.

Dowd nodded. "It's not a bad gig."

"Good career move?"

Dowd eyed Eddo with the first real spark of personality the consul had shown so far. "Fucking career backwater," he said.

"So how'd you end up here?" Eddo probed.

"The usual," Dowd said. The waitress brought his third *Cuba libre*. He didn't immediately drink but shook it so that the ice cubes clattered together. "Didn't keep my pecker at home."

"Hooker?" Eddo asked.

"Ambassador's wife." Dowd inhaled a mouthful.

"Worth it?" Eddo indicated the restaurant, the island, the whole fucking career backwater.

"Nah." Dowd gave a funny little laugh.

The man was a *borracho* but probably the kind that always stayed just this side of drunk.

"So," Eddo said. "You want to be the famous guy in the newspaper who caught El Toro and got the million dollar bounty? Or the guy whose diplomatic career peaked in Antigua?"

"You asshole," Dowd said and Eddo knew he had him.

◆

Chapter 80

The day **44Gg449M11** had designated was the first overcast day since Eddo had arrived in Antigua. Tropical Storm Alice was blowing through the Gulf, according to the news, and Antigua expected to feel the fringes.

Eddo wasted away the morning cruising the shops on the street that ran parallel to the Falmouth Harbor Marina, feeling as if time was running through his fingers like sand. He was almost certain that Antigua was Site 4 and that Wibley was in Gomez Mazzo's pocket. But if he was right, had Wibley warned off Gomez Mazzo? Had the meeting been canceled in a way that bypassed the postings website? Was Eddo spinning his wheels while there were a dozen things he could be doing in Mexico City to get ready for Luz coming in just two days? His frustration level hit a record high as he loitered in an over-priced trinket shop.

Several people came and went from the marina gate. It was run like a *privada* housing development. Those coming in had to show some sort of identification or were met at the gate and signed in as a guest. Beyond the gate, only a few enormous yachts could be seen. The rest were masked by a tall privacy fence. Falmouth had been built for discretion.

The sky darkened as Eddo whiled away the time within sight of the marina gate. If *Sheba* was there Eddo was sure the meeting would be held on board; Gomez Mazzo would want to show off. Hugo would have to present himself at the gate and be met. On the off chance that the meeting was somewhere else in Antigua, Gomez Mazzo would have to leave the marina.

Tropical Storm Alice hit with a vengeance right after noon. Rain slashed down like the last judgment and Eddo took refuge in the sandwich shop where Dowd was supposed to meet him at

2:00 pm.

The place was decorated in a style Eddo thought of as British plantation, with fake palm frond fans turning overhead and a lot of mahogany and rattan. He stretched out lunch with dessert and coffee that he didn't want. Just as he checked his watch for the tenth time in as many minutes, two burly uniformed Antiguan cops walked into the restaurant, looked around the place and made for his table.

"Identification, please," one of them said.

Eddo stood and handed over his passport.

The found the picture page, studied it and then glared at Eddo. "Eduardo Cortez?"

"Yes," Eddo said. The two cops hadn't so much as looked at anyone else in the restaurant.

The cop flipped through the passport some more, then coolly pocketed it. "Your passport doesn't have the proper entry visa," the cop said.

The other cop yanked Eddo around by one arm and slapped handcuffs around Eddo's left wrist.

"Hey, wait a minute--."

The cop was built like a mountain. Eddo's right arm joined the left behind his back and the handcuffs clicked shut. The old collarbone injury throbbed.

"Resisting arrest," the cop said. "Passport fraud. Illegal entry."

With a hand under each of his arms, the cops manhandled Eddo out the door of the restaurant as the patrons and servers gawked. "Send his bill to the ministry," one of the cops said and then they were outside in the rain.

"Listen, look at the passport," Eddo said as they shoved him down the sidewalk toward a small white police van parked a block from the marina gate. The rain poured out of a drab gray sky. Water sluiced down the back of Eddo's neck and soaked his shirt. He stepped in a puddle as the cops barreled along and his shoes squelched noisily. "There's been no fraud. Got my passport stamped at the airport."

"Yeah, sure." The cop on Eddo's left grinned and yanked upward, nearly pulling Eddo out of his wet shoes. "And it's not raining."

As if to underscore his words, lightning streaked across the sky and thunder boomed in the distance. His collarbone protested vigorously and Eddo shut up.

As they reached the van a long black town car rolled up to the marina gate, wipers batting from side to side. Ignoring the pain in his shoulder, Eddo twisted to catch a glimpse of a familiar thin man carrying a large umbrella walk out of the marina gate.

Metal clanged as the cops opened the rear doors of the white van. "Get in."

"Wait a minute." Eddo put his foot on the floor of the deck as if to step up but stalled, watching the scene at the marina gate. Hugo de la Madrid Acosta got out of the town car, ducked under the umbrella, and walked through the entrance with the thin man.

"You deaf? Get in."

Eddo felt himself lifted bodily, his collarbone screeching now. He was thrown into the rear of the van. There weren't any seats, just a smooth metal floor, slick with the rain spraying in. Eddo slid across the small space on his face, his hands still bound behind him. His head banged against a metal panel dividing the holding area from the rest of the vehicle. Shadowy daylight cut to black.

♦

Chapter 81

Luz sat on the bench in the cemetery, trying to sketch under the warm afternoon sun but her attention kept wandering. Eddo still hadn't called or texted and Luz was supposed to fly to Mexico City the day after tomorrow.

The image of Eddo dancing with Carolina Porterfield wouldn't go away. Maybe he wasn't out hunting El Toro, maybe he'd run away with Carolina Porterfield. Maybe Luz would miss having to tell him there would be no wedding because she'd never see him again. She'd know for sure that it was over when the security guards left and her phone stopped working.

The sketch reflected her mood. Headstones slumped mournfully and branches of the big tree at the far end drooped as if to comfort. She switched to a soft lead to smudge in the thick summer leaves when she heard footsteps on the gravel path.

Young Father Patricio, in paint-stained jeans and a cheap white tee, walked rapidly over the gravel. His head was down and he obviously wasn't looking where he was going because he nearly tripped over Luz's feet.

"Father?" Luz asked as she made a gesture of reassurance to the security guard by the church gate.

The priest halted in mid-stride and ran a forearm over his eyes, leaving a streak of white paint across his cheek. He was obviously nonplussed at encountering someone in the normally deserted cemetery. "Uh, hello," he said uncertainly.

"I'm Luz de Maria," Luz said. "Lupe's sister."

"Of course," Father Patricio said.

"You left a smudge, Father." Luz touched her own cheek. "Have you been painting?"

"No." Father Patricio collapsed onto the end of the bench like a sack of onions.

Luz put her drawing pencil back in the case. She'd never seen him in anything but a long black cassock and the combination of jeans and sadness made him look younger than Juan Pablo. "Are you all right, Father?"

Father Patricio leaned forward to rest his elbows on his knees and buried his head in his hands. He couldn't be more than 25, Luz guessed. He was her height and sturdily built, with a plain round *mestizo* face and dark hair that he combed straight back. If he hadn't been a priest he could have been any one of the young men she'd seen in the bus station in Mexico City with a backpack full of resignation.

"I wasn't painting," he said into his hands. "I was making a mess of the sacristy. Just like I've made a mess of everything else."

Luz felt herself torn between concern and chagrin. The last thing she wanted to deal with was this needy young man who was never going to take Father Santiago's place.

But the priest looked miserable and she could neither draw while he was there, nor just rudely leave. "Show me," Luz said.

She hadn't been in the sacristy since her last confession with Father Santiago and she hardly recognized the room. The curling posters and threadbare curtains were gone. The table and cabinet, both pushed to the center of the room, had been sanded and refinished in a dark gloss.

One wall was streaked with white paint. Fat gouts dribbled down to puddle on the brown baseboard. The taupe color of the original wall color showed through the white. Newspaper on the floor was marked by paint footprints.

Father Patricio waved an arm. "Another crazy idea."

Luz smiled. "The kids loved the egg hunt."

"Father Santiago never wanted new holy water fonts," Father Patricio said, mimicking the older ladies of the parish. He sounded like Chula. "Father Santiago organized the craft afternoons differently. Father Santiago's sermons weren't so long. Father Santiago understood Santa Clara."

Luz cranked open the window to let in fresh air. The abandoned paint supplies were in a corner. The roller was sticky with paint but still in the manufacturer's plastic wrap. The young priest had bought the right supplies but apparently just smushed the paint onto the wall without first unwrapping the roller. No wonder the wall was a drippy mess.

"Father Santiago was here for more than 30 years," Luz said as she gingerly worked off the wrapping. "And then suddenly he was gone. People were upset. Even a little angry to see someone new." *Including me.*

"I was ordained last December," Father Patricio said. "I put a bigger lock on the door and that's the only thing nobody's complained about."

Luz dropped the paint-smeared plastic wrapping on the newspaper with the wet shoe print then wadded up the paper and stuffed it into a trash bag. "We all still miss Father Santiago," she said. "As a friend. And a priest. We'd all gotten used to the way he did things. It'll just take a little time to get used to new ways."

Father Patricio just stood there and Luz knew her words sounded lame. She busied herself with the task at hand. She found an old can, poured some paint into it, handed Father Patricio a narrow paintbrush and showed him how to cut in the edges of the walls while she filled in with the roller. They worked in silence, Father Patricio carefully following her directions while Luz redid the mussed wall until it was a pristine sheet of white.

"That looks great," Father Patricio said. "You're really good at this."

Luz moved to the next wall. The white paint was so much cleaner looking than the nondescript taupe. "I usually paint smaller surfaces," she said.

Father Patricio sat on the floor to edge above the brown baseboard. "You did the Madonna I put in the vestibule, didn't you?"

"Yes."

"So how come you never come to the crafts afternoon with your sister?"

Luz moved the small stepladder to get at the top of the wall. "That's Lupe's time to talk to her friends."

"They're not your friends?"

"Not really."

Father Patricio dipped his brush in the can. "I watch the Elsa Caso Show." He grinned for the first time that afternoon. "For the fashion."

Luz clambered down the ladder to reload the roller with paint. "You listen to the gossip, too?"

"Hard not to." Father Patricio stopped moving his little brush along the edge of the wall. "You're pretty famous around here."

Luz got back on the ladder and worked the roller against the wall.

Father Patricio came to stand by the ladder, paint can in one hand, brush in the other. "Are you going to marry him?"

Luz sat on the top rung, irritated at his blunt manner. "No. I have to take care of my sister and her girls."

"You think your sister needs a babysitter? What about Armando?"

"Father, you shouldn't be gossiping about your parishioners," Luz said.

"It's only gossip if you talk about somebody else and we're talking about you."

It was like arguing with Martina and Sophia. Luz shoved the roller against the wall again. "Look, I'm not marrying him for a lot of reasons."

"Such as?"

Worse than Martina and Sophia.

"There was a picture of him in the newspaper with someone else," Luz said. "He's been traveling so I haven't been able to ask him about it."

"So you don't trust him."

He'd left 200 pesos for a taxi. The Vegas hadn't paid her hospital bills; he'd taken care of everything. "He's the most honorable man I know," Luz said.

"Then there's another explanation." Father Patricio went back to the baseboard.

Luz loaded the roller again and started on the third wall, not sure how she'd ended up talking to a boyish priest she hardly knew and whose manner was a sledgehammer compared to

Father Santiago's soft voice and infinite patience. "It doesn't matter, Father," she said. "He's going to be the Attorney General."

"You don't like Attorney Generals?"

"I used to be a *muchacha,*" Luz explained.

"So?" Father Patricio stopped moving his brush to look at her.

"Don't get paint on the baseboard," Luz said.

Father Patricio carefully wiped the drips. "I don't understand."

"Look." Luz took a deep breath of latex fumes. "His world is rich and wealthy and I'd embarrass him and ruin his career."

"Says who?"

Luz shook her head. Father Santiago would never have said *Says who*? "I just know," she said.

"Really?" Father Patricio asked. "You went someplace with him and it ruined his career? What was he going to be before he got demoted to Attorney General?"

"No, that's not what I meant. I just know what will happen."

"Well, that's a handy excuse."

"An excuse for what?"

Father Patricio moved to the window and filled in around the opening. "So you can avoid facing anything too hard. Like leaving home and mixing with people you don't know. Learning how to be a politician's wife. If you stay here you'll never have to do anything like that."

"I told you," Luz said. "I'll ruin his career."

"You still haven't given me any proof."

Stung, Luz dropped the roller into the paint tray. "Some people say there isn't any proof that God exists," she said.

"That's why God invented faith," Father Patricio said.

Luz started on the last wall, simmering with anger.

But by the time she was halfway done, she had to concede that this boy priest had a point. Her concern for Lupe and the girls didn't need to be the determining factor. The decision to tell Eddo no didn't have to be set in stone.

Maybe there could be a test, some way of proving if she was right. Maybe, just maybe, she wouldn't be so out of place in

Eddo's world. After all, she knew where to place salad forks and what drinks to serve business associates and even how to drive a car.

The upcoming *despedida*, if Eddo was back by then, could be the proof. Arturo Romero and all of Eddo's PAN colleagues would be there with their wives. The women would be clones of Señora Vega and Señora Portillo.

If the event was a humiliating disaster, Luz would tell Eddo no. He'd probably be relieved after seeing firsthand that she didn't fit in. But on the slim chance she got through it without anything dreadful happening, she would tell him yes. *Yes.*

Yes. The despedida would decide. Luz couldn't wait to tell Carmelita. It was a tidy, scientific solution and the thread wrapped around the notion as if it was an extension of her heart.

Luz clambered off the ladder with the nearly-dry roller. They'd used all the white paint and the sacristy glowed. The little room looked bright and spacious and a little like Elaine Ralston's art gallery. Luz didn't know why Father Santiago had never thought to paint the room.

"Thank you." Father Patricio's plain face lit with satisfaction. "I never could have done this by myself."

"I think you're going to be just what Santa Clara needs," said Luz.

♦

Chapter 82

The boat was a beauty, all right, and Hugo couldn't help but admire the workmanship. But the cabin décor was garish and loud, with too much red and a painted mural of a giant black bull snorting and pawing the ground. The painting was a crude reminder of who Hugo was dealing with and it turned the yacht from a beautiful woman into a lap dance whore.

Gomez Mazzo's creepy bodyguard with the slitty eyes was there again. Chino, Gomez Mazzo called him and the name was apt, although Hugo had never seen such a skinny bastard of a chink. Like the other time they'd met on board the yacht, Gomez Mazzo's other keepers were heard but not seen.

As rain pounded the upper deck, the yacht rolled a little. Hugo dropped into one of the swiveling captain's chairs and Gomez Mazzo sat in the other. Chino lounged against the wall. Below the hideous mural, the walls were discreetly divided into burled wood cabinets. Indentations substituted for door handles.

"So we wait for your friend," Gomez Mazzo said.

"He moved money, that's all," Hugo said. "Not a friend."

"His developments?"

"Whatever they are, it doesn't matter," Hugo asserted. The chink guy had a flat, unblinking stare and it was giving Hugo the creeps. For the first time since this whole scheme started he felt exposed, even more exposed than when he'd been in Betancourt's office with Fonseca. The unspoken rules that had protected Hugo then were not the rules that Gomez Mazzo and his hired dog played by. Their rules weren't steeped in tradition, just money and a twisted sense of loyalty to whomever was the most cruel.

"No?" As Gomez Mazzo spoke, the chink guy moved closer to him. Rain drummed on the roof of the cabin and the deck rocked gently.

"He walked away with my money."

"Did he?" Gomez Mazzo smiled in genuine mirth. "He handled your money and just walked away with it? It sounds as if you were not very careful, my friend."

"I mean to get it back today," Hugo said. He pointed to the chink. "With or without your help."

Gomez Mazzo shrugged noncommittally. "He took your money but he spoiled my arrangements."

Hugo crossed one ankle over the other knee and affected complete composure. "These arrangements can be made over again, but even better this time, because I'll be in charge of every detail. But first let's talk about what happened to the operation and where the money from all my ideas has gone."

"The operation was no longer in El Toro's interest," Gomez Mazzo said. "Some business interests become liabilities. Others become more important."

Hugo slammed both feet on the hideous shag carpet and his finger punched the air at the same time. "We had a deal, Gustavo. I put my name on the line with that land and those bank accounts."

"You were supposed to keep the *federales* away from the bank," Gomez Mazzo snapped. "Twice you did not do what you promised. Maybe one time El Toro can fix it. But the second time the promise is as good as dirt."

"I lost everything," Hugo reminded him. "You already had your cut in your pocket."

Gomez Mazzo didn't reply.

"Look," Hugo said. "So we start again. We get the money that Max took and start again. I have a plan to restart Lorena's campaign. You'll still get what you want after the elections."

"That's all you have to negotiate with?" Chino spoke for the first time since meeting Hugo at the marina gate with an umbrella. His voice was a thready rasp. "Money someone stole from you?"

"When Lorena is president," Hugo argued. "She can be your partner or someone else's."

The threat hung in the air.

Gomez Mazzo waved his hand at Chino. The chink moved. For a moment Hugo felt a shiver of fear. He relaxed when the thin man opened a tall cabinet, revealing a well-stocked refrigerator, and took out two bottles. He popped the tops and handed a bottle to Gomez Mazzo and to Hugo.

Hugo looked at the bottle. It was a cooler drink. A fucking rum cooler.

♦

Chapter 83

Eddo woke up face down on cool concrete. He pulled himself to a sitting position and nearly passed out again. All the blood in his body seemed to have pooled in his head and it pulsed like an angry drumbeat.

The handcuffs were off and he gingerly touched his face. A swelling under his right eye hurt like hell and caused his eye to squint. Pain seared across his face as he found his cheekbone. Probably something in there was broken but at least none of his teeth felt loose. Dried blood flaked off his forehead and he traced it to a scrape near his hairline. It hurt, too, but didn't seem serious.

As things came into focus, he realized he was in a jail cell. White walls, stainless steel toilet, narrow cot, no blanket, strong smell of disinfectant. He was barefoot and his pockets were empty. No cell phone, watch, belt, or wallet. His backpack, containing not only his essentials but the warrant and Fonseca's letter, was probably still in the restaurant.

Eddo stepped to the bars. They were painted white and very clean. Not even any fingerprints. Our institutions got more professional every day.

"Hey," he shouted, nearly sending the pain in his face into overdrive.

After an eternity, a heavyset cop ambled through a doorway. "Sleep off your drunk, eh?"

"I'd like to make a phone call," Eddo said.

The cop shrugged and walked away.

"Wait a minute," Eddo called. "What time is it?"

The cop didn't come back and Eddo allowed himself a string of Spanish invective. He stood by the bars for a couple of minutes then sat on the cot and closed his eyes.

The guard ambled back, as if there was all the time in the world. He unlocked the cell and rolled the bars to the side. "One call."

He led Eddo to a clean white hallway and handed him a token for a pay phone. "Three minutes." The guard sat down in a chair about ten feet away.

Crispell answered his cell phone on the second ring but the connection buzzed with static.

"This is Cortez. I'm in jail."

"What? Cortez?"

"Can you hear me? The cartel meet is going down now."

"Now?"

"I saw my guy go into the marina and I recognized the man who met him."

"Look," Crispell said and then static cut him out. Just as Eddo was wondering if he'd lost the connection for good, the voice came back. "--the storm. I'm about two miles from shore."

"You're at sea?"

The connection buzzed and reestablished. "--search and rescue. Is Dowd there?"

A dozen Spanish words came to Eddo's lips and none of them were good. "I'm in jail. Local cops picked me up as I was waiting for him."

The guard walked over to the phone and broke the connection. "Three minutes are up."

Eddo was escorted back to the cell and the bars clanged back into place. Eddo furiously paced the small space, and then flung himself on the cot.

He was just reflecting that he had to be the stupidest bastard alive when there was a commotion in the hall and three men charged into the holding area. Eddo recognized Dowd, his thinning hair plastered to his scalp and the shoulders of his navy windbreaker beaded with rain. The guard looked annoyed as he unlocked the cell.

"Nice to see you," Eddo said.

"Crispell called. What the hell happened to you?" Dowd exclaimed. He looked more clear-eyed than when he'd been downing *Cuba libres* and Eddo hoped he stayed that way for the next few hours.

"Cops escorted me to their van and I landed on my face," Eddo replied.

"Let me introduce Jack Stemmer," Dowd said. "DEA. From Miami. Last flight in before the storm closed the airport."

Stemmer looked like the stereotypical *norteamericano* cop: brush cut gray hair, granite jaw, sharp blue eyes. He was taller than Eddo and probably weighed 30 pounds more, all of it from serious weightlifting.

"Thanks for coming," Eddo said and shook hands with Stemmer.

"And this is Ronald Tenpenny," Dowd went on. "He's your lawyer."

Tenpenny was the portly Antiguan that Dowd had been dining with the night Eddo had approached him in the restaurant. They briefly shook hands as the group moved into the main part of the police station and Eddo collected his belongings. He checked the time and he strapped on his watch: 4:30 pm.

They emerged from the police station into a dark downpour. The palm trees around the building drooped as if they were made of cooked *nopales* and the parking lot was littered with debris. The station was on a coastal road and they could see waves spume against the seawall. The din of the rough surf competed with the rain and thunder. If Crispell was still at sea he was having a hell of a time.

Tenpenny led the way to a large SUV. He and Dowd got into the front and Eddo got in back with Stemmer. As Tenpenny drove out of the lot the wipers beat furiously and the rain drummed on the roof. "We got your pack from the restaurant," Dowd said to Eddo.

"Thanks." It was on the seat. Eddo reassured himself that the warrant and Fonseca's letter were still there.

Stemmer looked at his own watch. "Dowd says you told the local coastie that the guy you're tracking went into the marina a little before two."

Eddo nodded. "Hugo de la Madrid Acosta."

"I met him once," Tenpenny said from the front seat. His British accent was smooth and educated.

"Ronald was Wibley's predecessor," Dowd supplied.

Eddo briefly outlined the months of investigation into Hugo's land deal near Anahuac, the Banco Limitado accounts, the userid scheme, how they'd tracked the money and found the password used by some of the userids and set up the fake meeting.

"What about the original smuggling operation?" Stemmer asked.

The SUV took a turn at high speed and the tires squealed on wet pavement. Oncoming traffic moved considerably slower, headlights straining to pick out the road in the slashing rain.

"The army shut it down," Eddo said, omitting details of how they'd found the location. "Hugo and El Toro were mostly using kids to mule across the border."

"And the business with the boat?"

"We pieced it together," Eddo said. "El Toro's got a front company in Panama that cropped up when we looked at the money trail. On paper, *Sheba*'s owner is the company treasurer."

"Shit," Stemmer said. "This is big."

"I'm hoping we can roll up both de la Madrid Acosta and Gomez Mazzo." Eddo rubbed the side of his face. It was still swollen but he didn't think that the cheekbone was broken after all. "Can you arrest Gomez Mazzo?" he asked. "Do you have that sort of authority here?"

"No," Stemmer replied. "But I can make a hell of a stink until the coastie shows up."

Tenpenny said something and the SUV slowed. The road ahead was flooded on one side. A barrier had been erected, creating a one lane road. A cop in an ankle-length yellow rain slicker was directing traffic. The SUV came to a halt as the cop motioned for the oncoming traffic to go ahead.

"That yacht's not going anywhere in this storm," Dowd said.

♦

Chapter 84

After three hours Gomez Mazzo was out of patience.

"We are done," he announced. "Unless you know something El Toro doesn't."

"I told you," Hugo said. "I don't know where Max went. I've had a detective looking for him."

"Not even Lorena knows where he went?"

"I keep telling you." Hugo narrowed his eyes. "The fucker ran off with her money. Do you think we'd be here if she knew where he'd gone?"

Gomez Mazzo leaned forward. "Why are we here, my friend?"

"What do you mean?"

"Is this man really coming? Or was this all just a trick? A trick to catch the great El Toro? Surely you didn't come all this way just to convince me that Lorena can still be president." Gomez Mazzo snapped his fingers. "Her campaign is gone, just like that, and Arturo Romero will take the nomination."

Hugo's face darkened. "Lorena will be president."

Gomez Mazzo laughed. "She's fucked your brain away."

"We had an agreement," Hugo said. "You owe me."

"El Toro owes you?" Gomez Mazzo laughed harder.

The cabin door opened and Chino slipped in, shutting the door against the rain and wind before much came in. Gomez Mazzo went to him. "Anything out there?"

"Nothing," Chino said. He slipped off the hood of his black rain jacket. "Everyone is inside."

"This was a mistake." Gomez Mazzo didn't know what game had been played on him but El Toro hadn't lasted this long by being tricked by others. Maybe the message from **1612colcol** had been a fake, maybe the bag man had been killed before the meeting, or maybe Hugo was playing some sort of game. With so many questions, *Sheba* couldn't stay. "Tell the crew to be ready to go as soon as the rain lets up," he said to Chino.

"Listen." Hugo made his way across the cabin to confront Gomez Mazzo. "There haven't been any back room deals. Lorena will take her orders from me when she's president. Do you want me telling her to leave El Toro alone?" He paused. "Or maybe you didn't hear me say that maybe the army walks away from some other friends."

"I heard that," Gomez Mazzo blazed. "You think you can blackmail me?"

"I'm saying you'd better know who you're dealing with."

Gomez Mazzo suddenly shoved Hugo against the wood paneling hard enough to make the man's head ring and the big yacht rock. Hugo's eyes clouded with the impact and he started to slide down the wall. Chino caught him. The thin man nailed Hugo in the groin with a knee, then shifted his weight and snapped Hugo's head around. Bones crunched noisily.

Chino let go and the body of Hugo de la Madrid Acosta slumped to the carpet.

Gomez Mazzo prodded the stomach with the toe of his shoe. Hugo had been just another *estupido* who thought he could get what he wanted because he was *criollo*. He'd never really had a fire in his belly. Cortez would make a much better partner. "Do something with it fast," he said. "Before it shits and stinks."

Chino nodded. "We'll dump it when we're out to sea."

"Stow it and then tell the crew to get us out of here."

As Gomez Mazzo left the cabin Chino started taking rum coolers out of the refrigerator.

◆

Chapter 85

Tenpenny skidded the SUV to a stop in front of the marina and they all spilled out into the driving rain. Cold needles of water glittered in the light of the marina gate. The uniformed security officer behind the desk held up his hands as they rushed into the guardhouse but put them down as Tenpenny stepped to the front.

"Ah, my good man," Tenpenny said. "Tell me where a yacht called the *Sheba* is parked."

"Mr. Tenpenny," the guard protested. He was a dark-skinned man in a green uniform bearing the Falmouth Harbor Marina logo. "I'm not allowed to do that."

Tenpenny winked at him and reached for a set of keys on the counter next to the guard's computer. "Then we will just wander about and find it ourselves."

The guard looked sick as Tenpenny handled the keys. "Mr. Tenpenny, you don't want to go out there in all this rain."

Tenpenny nodded soothingly at the guard, full of sympathy but unspoken authority as well. "Now, you know I'll take care of you."

The guard sighed and flipped through a binder. "Slip 42, first row past the fire station."

"Which is the key to the row?" Tenpenny pressed.

The guard took the keys from Tenpenny and led the way out the back door of the guardhouse, into the driving rain.

The marina was a vast city of maritime skyscrapers. The place was well lit by fancy wrought iron street lights and their wet shadows stretched as they approached each one, and then shrank as they passed out of the circle of light. Parked parallel to piers so wide and solid they looked like streets, the yachts loomed above the water, ghostly in the dirty sky, punished by the storm for their arrogance and opulence. From what Eddo could see, there had to be at least six street-like piers branching off from the boardwalk. Yachts were parked on either side of each street.

The entrance to the pier with the sign for slips 40-49 was opposite a small office with a firefighting symbol on it. The guard unlocked the gate and they all passed through, Eddo and Stemmer in the lead.

The first slip's marker read "40," meaning that the *Sheba* in slip 42 would be the third yacht in the row, a distance of more than a Mexico City block. A red light winked on in the distance and movement disrupted the straight lines of rain. The radar dish on top of *Sheba's* cabin was revolving.

"Fuck," Eddo and Stemmer said at the same time. Eddo broke into a run and felt, rather than saw, the DEA man keep pace.

Two men met them on the pier in front of *Sheba* as the yacht's engines ground out a soft growl and the big boat began to vibrate out of the slip. Both were armed, but neither had a weapon in their hand and Eddo knew Gomez Mazzo wouldn't want to bring that sort of attention to himself in Antigua.

Like Tomás, Stemmer was the best kind of brawler, the kind who liked a no-holds-barred kind of fight. A couple of punches and then Stemmer got a hand around each guard, clanked their heads together, and dumped them on the pier.

"Nice job," Eddo said as he bent over the unconscious men and scrabbled for the still-holstered guns. He handed one to Stemmer. Dowd and Tenpenny, both puffing heavily, drew up just as the small drawbridge linking *Sheba* to the pier fell into the water.

"She's going," Dowd gasped.

Eddo sprinted hard for the edge of the pier, Stemmer moving nearly as fast. Both made a flying leap for the narrow break in Sheba's railing where the drawbridge had been attached and fell heavily, half on the boat and half sliding down toward the water as the yacht vibrated from the labor of the engines at low throttle. Eddo grabbed desperately at the left side of the railing, and heard Stemmer grunt as the other man hooked an arm over the railing on the right and started pulling himself forward.

"Cortez!" Dowd called from the pier and Eddo looked up from the wet deck just in time to see another of Gomez Mazzo's goons loom out of the yacht's dark interior. Eddo rolled onto his side and raised the gun taken off the other guard but it was whipped away with a force that left his hand stinging as the weapon plopped into the water below. Two shots rang out, close enough to Eddo's head that he nearly lost his tenuous purchase on the slick deck. The guard crumpled, dropping a crowbar as he fell. Blood pooled under him, quickly diluted by the rain.

"I guess they know we're here now," Stemmer said, gun in hand, as both he and Eddo got to their feet.

Sheba was still moving slowly away from the pier, the wet deck humming and the engines groaning, as if to unused to maneuvering in such a tight space. The boat was dark, however, except for a few small red running lights. Eddo picked up the crowbar. The metal was slick.

"Let's go find your guy," Stemmer said.

Eddo wiped cold rain from his face. "What do you think? Make our way up?"

"They're not outside in this weather," Stemmer said.

The yacht was the size of a floating mansion, but Eddo had seen a picture of the interior layout, thanks to the maritime broker's website that Vasco had found. He led Stemmer around the side of the yacht to the stairs leading to the main deck. They were thrown against the railing twice as the pitch of the engines changed and *Sheba* abruptly stopped then reversed. Whoever was at the controls was trying to maneuver the yacht like a car out of the tight space against the pier. Eddo wondered if a tug boat usually took the yachts out of their slips and towed them to the harbor entrance. He glanced at his watch, the dial luminous in the darkness. Only a few minutes had passed since Tenpenny had braked the SUV in front of the marina gate.

The main deck was painted white, a ghostly effect in the darkness. The swimming pool took up about a third of the deck area and was shuttered for the night by an aqua-colored fabric cover. The cabin roof extended over one end of the pool, a sleek slice of fiberglass. A door was centered under the roof and presumably led into the main cabin of the boat.

"I'll take the lead," Stemmer said, his voice low.

They edged around the side of the pool, rain drumming noisily on the part of the cover that wasn't protected by the roof overhang, the rain puddling and weighing down the fabric. Standing under the overhang was a welcome relief from the slashing rain. Both men were soaked. Eddo wiped water out of his eyes again, feeling it trickle through his hair and down his back. His linen shirt felt like wet armor and his khaki pants were water-logged from the knees down. He hadn't bothered to put his socks back on after getting his personal items back from the jail guard and his feet felt cold and small inside his loafers.

Stemmer reached out and turned the latch on the door. To their surprise the door swung inward. Stemmer used his free hand to gently open it all the way so that it rested against the inside wall. They could see an empty corridor. Holding himself sideways, Stemmer started to ease through the doorway.

A burst of gunfire cartwheeled him backwards. The bigger man slammed into Eddo and both of them went down.

The engines changed pitch again, settling to a throaty purr and *Sheba* picked up speed. The deck tilted. Eddo felt himself careen backwards, weighted down by Stemmer's inert form. The deck railing stopped their slide.

The cabin door swung awkwardly on its hinges, the fiberglass shattered in a starburst pattern on the latch side. There was neither sound nor movement on the cabin side of the portal.

Stemmer was out but he wasn't dead. Eddo hauled himself out from under the larger man. He felt around for Stemmer's gun but only found the crowbar, sticky with blood.

Snatches of a Spanish language conversation competed with the rain drumming on the fabric pool cover. On his hands and knees and exposed as hell, eyes straining in the dark, Eddo plastered himself against the wall by the shattered door just as a figure emerged.

It was the thin-faced Asian man who'd given Eddo and Tomás the cell phone with the Site 1 coordinates. He was armed with a long gun, an attached safety strap wrapped around his arm. The muzzle of the weapon nosed out of the doorway first, trained on Stemmer stretched out on the deck.

Eddo swung the crowbar in an arc, smashing into the stock. The Asian pulled the trigger as the force of the crowbar blow sent him off balance, and the weapon erupted on full automatic, spraying metal across the side of the yacht and ripping into the pool cover. Eddo struck again with the crowbar and the weapon flew out of the shooter's hands. The *brrrp* of its firing was replaced by the skitter of metal and plastic as the long gun snaked across the deck, still tethered to the man by the safety strap.

Eddo threw himself after the weapon, managing to stay on top of the Asian's arm as they fought for control of the long gun. The man was smaller than Eddo, but had the wiry build and gutter instincts of someone who knew how to fight against the odds. They rolled violently across the deck, each clawing for the upper position. Eddo managed to get the safety strap unwound from the Asian's arm and forced the weapon against the other man. He pulled the trigger but got an empty click. Hands closed in on Eddo's throat, coming together like an iron noose.

Eddo used both hands to ram the stock of the weapon into the man's head. He felt himself choke and used the last of his strength to strike again and again, holding the weapon in both hands.

The fingers relaxed and Eddo sucked in rain and air and got to one knee. The Asian's head was a bloody mess and his eyes were closed.

"Fuck." Stemmer was coming around. His eyes fluttered and then registered surprise.

Eddo jerked to the side just as the crowbar sliced through the air, brushing his cheek.

He parried the next blow with the long gun and the crowbar clattered away. Eddo jumped to his feet and the Asian came upright with a long thin blade in his hand.

As the knife sliced close, Eddo stepped back. In the dark it was hard to see anything beyond his opponent's hands and Eddo didn't realize how close they were to the edge of the pool until both fell through the torn fabric cover.

The fabric closed over them as they exploded into the inky water. The total immersion into the drumming blackness was both astonishing and disorienting. Eddo felt himself touch bottom and the disorientation partially lifted. He kicked upwards, losing his shoes, only to hit his head against a portion of the pool cover that was still holding fast against the thundering rain. There were only a few inches between the level of the water and the straining fabric and he desperately gulped moist air. Then as the crown of the Asian's head broke the water Eddo lunged for the knife hand and pulled the man back to the bottom.

They twisted and wrestled under the water, the knife's silver flash and the Asian's bared teeth the only things to be clearly seen in the murk. Eddo managed to get a foot against the Asian's chest and bore down. The other man hadn't been able to get a lungful of air and Eddo hadn't run eight miles a day for nothing. His lungs burned like halftime at La Marchesa and his eyes stung from the chlorine but he kept his hand clamped around the Asian's wrist as he stomped the Asian to the bottom of the pool. When the knife arm slackened, Eddo forced the knife hand toward its owner's chest and drove it in up to the hilt. The water bubbled thickly around the shaft and the Asian went limp.

Eddo found the tear in the pool cover and hauled himself out of the water and onto the deck. For a moment all he could do was lie there and gulp air, the rain rinsing his face.

"Cortez."

Stemmer was sitting by the railing, looking chalky but defiant, the gun he'd taken off the guard on the pier back in his right hand. There was a black clad body in a heap by the door and the deck beneath was bloody. "Was that El Toro?"

"His enforcer," Eddo managed. He sat up, feeling the sting of a cut by his left ear. His chest ached and his teeth started to chatter.

"Maybe he's run out of guards."

♦

Eddo and Stemmer found Gomez Mazzo alone in the main cabin, an overly decorated space with a symbolic red and black mural that wasn't anything anyone would have ever called art. The room was the sort of space expected of a yacht, lots of built-ins and nothing out except two large trays stacked with bottles of rum coolers sweaty with condensation.

"We weren't expecting company," Gomez Mazzo said from behind his pistol as Stemmer and Eddo dripped on the carpet.

Stemmer's side was stained with blood from the slug in his shoulder but his hand was steady enough as he pointed his own gun at Gomez Mazzo.

"Where's Hugo de la Madrid Acosta?" Eddo asked.

Gomez Mazzo shrugged. "Why should I know?"

"That's right," Eddo said. "You're just a simple businessman from Panama. On vacation here in Antigua."

"Whose new business partner has paid him a visit?" Gomez Mazzo's lip curled as he took in Eddo's bare feet and wet clothes.

"Business partner?" Stemmer asked.

"So now you think you have tricked El Toro?"

"What the fuck's going on here, Cortez?" Stemmer growled.

"We made a trade awhile ago," Eddo said, still staring at Gomez Mazzo. "So the army could shut down de la Madrid Acosta's operation. He thought that meant he'd bought me, too."

A foghorn blared out of the night and a voice ordered the *Sheba* to halt and prepare to be boarded. The yacht shuddered violently, the engines suddenly screaming. The tray of rum coolers tumbled onto the carpeted floor with a clatter of glass. Eddo and Stemmer were thrown against the wall. Stemmer grunted in pain and staggered, smearing the paneling with blood.

Gomez Mazzo, seated in a chair that was bolted to the deck, was merely jolted to the side.

Time slowed as Eddo watched Gomez Mazzo right himself and take aim at Stemmer and then Eddo was falling across the DEA man, grabbing the gun as they both went down and he fired with Stemmer's hand still wrapped around the stock. He fired again and again as the yacht rolled with the engines at fever pitch. The shots still echoed as the *Sheba* stopped with a tremendous crash like a train coming off the rails.

Eddo spilled to the opposite side of the cabin, tangled up with Stemmer and dozens of bottles. The *Sheba* wallowed heavily and Eddo managed to pull himself up in time to see Gomez Mazzo, a look of surprise in his face and one scarred hand over his stomach, pitch forward onto the carpet.

The *Sheba* rolled again. Cabinet doors damaged by Eddo's wild shots began to pop their latches. A tall door by Gomez Mazzo's chair creaked open, the wood splintered at the top. As *Sheba* rolled to the other side, sending the rum cooler bottles tumbling across the carpet in the other direction, the door swung wide and the body of Hugo de la Madrid Acosta fell out.

◆

Chapter 86

Luz was in the car with her attackers. Eddo was in the car, too, and the noose was around his neck instead of hers. The leather bit into his throat, breaking open the veins, and blood gushed down his white knit shirt. Luz screamed and struggled to fight, to save him, but she was pinned down and the men were a dead weight on top of her. She kept screaming as the car sped and the men laughed as Eddo's eyes rolled back and there was a bell in her ear, a bell that was drowning out--.

Luz woke up with a gasp, drenched in sweat and tangled in her bed sheets. Her cell phone was on the pillow next to her face and it was ringing.

She sat up dizzily. "*Bueno*?"

"Turn on the news, *corazón*!"

"Eddo?"

"Did you forget what my voice sounded like?"

"Yes," she choked out. "Where have you been?"

"I just got back to Mexico City," Eddo said. There was a lot of background noise.

"Are you at a party?"

"We got him, Luz." Eddo replied. "Gomez Mazzo. Yesterday. Go turn on your television."

The phone still clamped to her ear, Luz stumbled to the living room and turned on the television. Cartoons. She found a morning news show and stared at the screen in disbelief. Gustavo Gomez Mazzo, aka El Toro, had been killed on his yacht off the island of Antigua during a sting operation conducted jointly by the local Coast Guard and a *norteamericano* drug enforcement agency.

"*Por Dios*," Luz breathed, eyes glued to the television. "He lived on a boat?"

"I didn't make the connection until you drew that picture in San Miguel," Eddo said.

"I can't believe it," Luz said. She was dizzy with excitement and relief. "I mean, I knew you'd get him. I just--. I don't know what I thought! I'm so proud of you!"

"I'm a little banged up," he said.

Luz felt her heartbeat surge. "How banged up?"

"Nothing that's going to keep me from celebrating," he said. "We're all at Tomás and Ana's house. Everybody's pretty wound."

"I can hear."

"Wait, let me close the door."

Luz went back to her room and climbed onto the bed as she heard a door close on his end of the connection.

"I know we said tomorrow but I can't wait one more day to see you," Eddo said, his voice coming through clearly now. "When can you be ready? The security team can drive you today."

Last week's *La Gente* section was on the bedside table. Carolina Porterfield still gazed reverently at Eddo; they still danced like movie stars. "There was a picture of you in the newspaper," Luz blurted.

"Because of El Toro?" Eddo asked sharply.

"No, from Arturo Romero's daughter's wedding." Luz fought to keep her voice steady. "You and a lovely woman in a blue dress."

"It was a color picture?" Eddo said, as if that mattered. There was a gurgling sound as he drank something.

"Yes," Luz said. "Front page of *Reforma's La Gente* section."

"Can you save it?"

Luz's phone slid through nerveless fingers and landed on the bed.

"Luz? Luz? Are you there?"

Luz picked up the phone. "You want me to save this picture for you?"

"Why? Does it look bad? Am I using the wrong fork?"

"No. You both look . . . stunning."

"Then could you? I mean, I'm just her old uncle, but I'm sure Pilar would want to have it. She keeps everything. Carolina's school pictures, ticket stubs, report cards."

The bed tilted like a ride at La Feria. Luz closed her eyes and teetered helplessly. *Carolina Porterfield was his niece. The daughter of his sister Pilar who married a gringo and lived in Atlanta.*

"Is there still going to be a *despedida*?" Luz asked. The *despedida* would decide. She drew her knees to her chest, hugged her ribs, and mentally gabbled a prayer to the Virgin.

"Absolutely," Eddo said.

"I can be ready by noon," Luz said.

♦

Luz walked out of her room carrying her pink purse, the suitcase Eddo had bought her in San Miguel, and the dress for the *despedida* in the garment bag from Liverpool. She wore her best jeans, a simple black top, and black flats.

Tío, Lupe and the girls were at the kitchen table. Tío looked vaguely hung over.

Luz fought down anger. She hadn't heard the front door open. Tío hadn't just come in. No, he and Lupe had probably spent the night together in the shed. He was slipping back into the house by degrees.

"How's this?" Martina slid a drawing across the table to Tío.

"Make this part smaller." Tío moved his finger around a line. "Otherwise it'll fall over. The top will be too heavy." He slid the paper back to her and guzzled some coffee.

Martina had drawn a candleholder for Tío to make in the forge.

◆

Chapter 87

Eddo looked around the hotel suite. It was decorated in shades of cream, coral, and gold, which struck him as a little feminine, but the hotel had a pool and a spa and a gym and all the other amenities he'd wanted. It was also close to the new campaign headquarters in Polanco.

The living room contained a plush chenille loveseat, matching armchairs, a flat screen television, and an elegant dark wood dining set. A small kitchenette was fully stocked with china, crystal, and an ice maker.

He set his laptop and an armload of newspapers on the desk and walked through the French doors to the bedroom. Besides a king-sized bed and gilt bedside tables, another armchair could accommodate someone sitting at a mirrored vanity table. A second flat screen television was angled to be seen from the bed.

"This is the suite you specified, Senor Cortez," the concierge said from the doorway. "You're all unpacked.

"Thank you," Eddo said. Yolanda had managed his move to Mexico City. Pilar and Ana had managed everything else. The concierge withdrew, reminding him to call when he wanted the dinner and flowers sent up.

Eddo sank into a chair. All he had to do was relax and wait for Luz.

He'd landed in Mexico City before dawn, his system still humming with adrenaline. His nerves were so taut and raw that his hands were shaking.

They hurt like hell, too, a reminder of the fight with the Asian guy. His face was still a mess, although the swelling had gone down. The cut by his ear had bled like crazy but a small butterfly bandage had taken care of it. He and Stemmer, who'd been amazed when told the full story of the deal with Gomez

Mazzo to shut down Site 1, had been treated at the hospital. Stemmer would be fine. Dowd was a new man and Crispell was a national hero.

The room phone rang. Totally startled, Eddo shot out of the chair. The phone rang again. Eddo took a breath and answered it.

"Señor Cortez, your guests are here."

"Please send them up."

He opened the door and waited in the entrance. He heard the elevator swish open and a security guy stepped out, followed by Luz carrying that pink purse and a garment bag. She was flanked by another security guy. A third carried her suitcase.

Edo smiled, feeling his face twinge. Luz's eyes widened at the bruises. "Hello," she said softly.

"Come on in." Eddo stepped aside so the whole retinue could walk into the suite. He waved a hand at the French doors. "The closet is through there."

Luz looked at him a little uncertainly, but she went through to the bedroom and Eddo heard her gasp. "This is beautiful," she called.

"I'll be right there," Eddo replied. He took a moment to talk to the security team. There hadn't been any problems during the trip or in Soledad de Doblado. The team would stay in Mexico City while Luz was there and he gave them instructions for meeting up with the rest of the detail and handling the *despedida* before thanking them and seeing them out of the suite.

Luz must have heard the door close. She walked back into the living room and Eddo got his first real look at her.

"You look great," he heard himself say.

She touched his face, taking stock of the black eye, the purpled cheekbone, the bandage by his ear. Her fingers lingered on his jaw under the bruise. "Always the head," she said.

"Concrete," Eddo said. "No lasting damage."

She gave him a watery smile and slid her arms around him. Eddo held her close, his face in her hair, fighting for air around the tightness in his throat.

"I want you to tell me everything," Luz said into his shoulder and he knew she was crying. "But not when I'm so shaky."

"Later," Eddo said with a gruffness he hadn't intended.

"It's all right to be tired now, Rodrigo," Luz whispered.

It seeped away, then, the fear and the adrenaline and the violence. The spring inside him unwound, one turn at a time, and Eddo closed his eyes and let it happen.

◆

Chapter 88

"So who is the *despedida* for?" Luz asked as the big black SUV pulled away from the hotel. The event that would determine the rest of her life was about to begin. Luz hoped she wouldn't have a stroke first.

The last three days had passed too quickly. The hotel had been an oasis where they'd talked and made love and eaten food that was delivered to the room on a skirted table. By mutual agreement, discussion of her decision was put off until after the weekend. Luz wondered if Eddo also secretly knew that the *despedida* would decide it all.

At least she looked nice, the product of a visit to the spa in the hotel that Eddo had arranged. Fully expecting to be asked to leave, she was instead there for hours, emerging as shiny as she was ever going to be, with flawless skin and subtle mauve nails. Her hair gleamed in a French knot.

The turquoise silk Marina Rinaldi dress had narrow shoulder straps, a figure-hugging bodice, and a full skirt. Luz's birthday necklace was centered in the plunging V of the neckline. Eddo had complimented her 20 times already.

The beaded purse she'd bought to match the dress was in her lap. The chain handle gave her nervous hands something to toy with. The white stone was in her dress pocket. For luck. Or something.

"Who?" Eddo kept his eyes on the road as the car turned west on Reforma. The bruises on his face had faded to yellow. "Oh. Arturo's former personal assistant. He's going back to Oaxaca."

"Oh." Luz admired her shiny toenails in an effort to distract herself. The tall Bruno Magli turquoise suede slides made her ankles slim and her calves shapely. "Did Arturo get a new assistant?"

"Yes." Eddo's eyes flickered to her and then back to the road. "Great guy. Real asset to the team."

The team. The team she'd meet in just a few minutes. The people who would decide her future. "So what have you told them about me?" she asked as her stomach churned. "Anything I should know?"

"Well," Eddo considered. "They know your name is Luz de Maria. That you're an artist. Think you're amazing from Elsa's show."

"Did you tell them you proposed?"

"Oh yes." Eddo started drumming on the steering wheel, an uncharacteristic nervous motion. "Everyone you meet tonight will know I've asked you to marry me."

Eddo was wearing a white shirt, an impeccably tailored tan suit, and a Pineda Covalin silk tie that had probably cost 700 pesos. Luz had picked it up while he was in the shower, intrigued by the design of tiny purple flowers on a yellow background. Below the tag reading *Pineda Covalin, Mexico,* a second tag said *Edición Especial, Violetas.*

Luz thought about the conversations to come. *How did you two meet?* In front of the Tamayo Museum. *Have you been seeing each other long?* We met in October. *Didn't I see you once at Selena de Vega's house, wearing a gray dress and serving cocktails?*

They were still in the Chapultepec Park area, cruising the northern fringe of Lomas Virreyes. Most of the houses were embassies or ambassadorial residences.

At the end of Alpes Eddo turned right onto Montes Auvernia. They continued a little way then he turned right again, this time into a wide driveway. Huge black double doors, each centered by a brass knocker as big as Luz's head, were set into a tall salmon-colored stucco wall. The wall was topped with iron spikes. Eddo tapped the horn. The doors slowly swung inward.

Luz was nearly panting with the effort to stay calm. She thought wildly of shouting that he had to take her back to the hotel. She was ill. Leprosy. Having a heart attack.

The big SUV crunched over gravel. A man in a snappy

security uniform stepped out of a guard house set into the stucco wall. He threw Eddo a crisp salute. Eddo nodded and the SUV rolled forward.

"*Dios mio*," Luz gasped suddenly. "We didn't bring a gift." Upper class people always brought hostess gifts. She'd blundered horribly before she even got to the *despedida*.

Eddo looked at her. "I . . . uh . . . sent champagne ahead."

"Champagne?"

"The hostess enjoys champagne." Eddo swung the SUV into a circular drive, parked behind two other big vehicles, and helped Luz out. Several chauffeurs and bodyguards were standing by the other vehicles. They all nodded at Eddo.

The circular drive bordered a flagstone courtyard. The focal point was a stone fountain nearly six feet in diameter. It was dry, which wasn't surprising given Mexico City's perennial water shortage, and the huge basin was filled with pots of red geraniums.

"This is lovely," Luz said, looking around. A large two-story stucco house surrounded the courtyard on three sides. It had been built a long time ago in the massive Spanish colonial style, with a clay tile roof, gray stone sills, and tall narrow windows. More pots of red geraniums abounded, along with lemon trees and flame-flowered *corona de Cristo*. Clematis and bougainvillea softened the corners of the house. The salmon stucco, gray stone, and bright flowers made a striking combination.

"I like it, too." Eddo led her past the fountain, through a stone archway in the left wing of the house, to a covered loggia supported by massive stone columns.

"Look." Luz pointed up. Several multi-pointed Moravian star lanterns glowed overhead. "We saw those everywhere in San Miguel."

"So we did," Eddo said.

The carved front door was open. They walked into a wide hallway with a high ceiling. Another Moravian star lantern hung down like a chandelier. A maid appeared and extended a tray with two champagne flutes. Eddo took both glasses and handed one to Luz.

"Thank you," Luz said. She smiled at the maid. The girl was wearing a white blouse, black jeans, and a salmon-colored chef's apron. Her short permed hair was pulled off her face with a salmon-colored hairband. Not only was the maid unusually dressed, but she matched the house.

"*Por nada*, señora." The maid blinked at Luz, the tray vibrating in her hands.

It felt odd to be addressed as señora by a maid. Luz smiled again, wishing the poor girl didn't look so petrified.

"Thank you," Eddo said and the girl left the room.

Luz sipped her champagne and looked around nervously. They were alone in the *sala*. It was a huge living room, with a bank of arched windows on a long wall. Opposite the windows, a wide staircase with an iron handrail curved up to the second floor. The stair risers were inset with traditional blue and white *azulejo* tiles. The size of the room was magnified by high ceilings, exposed beams, and a stucco fireplace that ran the length of the far wall.

The architecture was old-fashioned and magnificent, but the room was stark and bare. The walls were white and completely undecorated. The floor was made of polished gray stones laid in a herringbone pattern. The room was sparsely lit by two crystal and wrought iron ceiling fixtures, insufficient for such a large space. The need for table lamps was apparent but the only things in the room were three furniture-sized lumps hidden under bubble wrap and brown paper. Two wrapped packages the sizes of framed pictures were propped against a wall.

"Have these people just moved in?" Luz asked.

"I guess so," Eddo said.

"And they're hosting a party?" Señora Vega would have died rather than host a party in a less than perfect house.

"Let's look around," Eddo said.

"Yes," Luz said. It was better to just get the *despedida* over with. "Let's go find this party."

They walked across the big *sala* to a set of white painted French doors. Eddo opened the doors and flicked a switch.

Luz gasped.

The room on the other side of the French doors was a

formal dining room, a true *comedor*, with a vaulted *boveda* ceiling. The bricks were old and narrow, making the room appear even higher and wider than it was. Below the soaring brickwork, the two long walls were golden. The wall at the end of the room was made of old stonework into which was set another pair of French doors.

"Like it?" Eddo asked.

"*Dios mio*, it's gorgeous," Luz breathed, staring upwards. "Doesn't this remind you of the restaurant in San Miguel?" She walked to the nearest long wall and ran her hand over it. The stucco had been gold leafed by a master craftsman. The effect was luminous. Luz had never seen such a room.

"But do you like it?"

"I love it. Can't you just imagine sitting at this table for hours and hours? Nobody would ever want dinner to end."

There was a long rectangular pine table in the center of the *comedor*, large enough to comfortably seat two dozen people. It was dark with age, with legs as thick as Luz's waist. A matching sideboard at least eight feet long was pushed against one gilded wall. Luz ran her fingers along the edge of the table, the beaded evening bag dangling from her wrist by its chain. "If this was my party, I'd keep the doors open and use the *sala* and the *comedor* at the same time. You could do a buffet for 200."

"Really?" Eddo said. He steered her through an archway in the gold leaf and they found themselves in a breakfast room full of large wooden crates and cardboard boxes. On the far side of that room there was a door with an inset window so the help could see if el señor and la señora were finished with the meal.

They walked through it into a large kitchen with dark wood cupboards and stainless steel appliances. The maid who'd brought the champagne was there, along with two other maids similarly dressed. All three immediately bobbed curtsies.

"Señor, do you need something?"

Eddo shook his head. "Just showing la señora around." He turned to Luz. "This is the kitchen," he said unnecessarily.

Luz took his hand and pulled him back into the *sala*. He seemed more nervous about the party than she was.

"Let's check out upstairs," Eddo said and trotted up the

wide staircase.

"Eddo!" Luz hissed. He didn't turn around. Luz had no choice but to follow him upstairs, cursing whoever had hosted this *maldita despedida* and then hid it.

The landing at the top of the stairs was bigger than the living room in Veracruz. Four doors opened off it.

"Three bedrooms, each with their own bathroom," Eddo said, suddenly sounding like a salesman.

"That's nice--," Luz started to say.

"This is the master bedroom." Eddo opened a door.

Luz pursed her lips, unable to believe his audacity, but the room was sensational with another enormous vaulted brick *boveda* ceiling. Like the *sala*, the room had no furniture in it although a large pewter chandelier hung from the center of the vault. The walls below the vault were creamy white stucco. There was a fireplace at one end of the room, which struck Luz as an unbelievable luxury.

"Ever sleep in a bedroom with a fireplace?" Eddo asked.

"Rodrigo." Luz touched his arm. His muscles were like iron under the fluid wool of his jacket. "We shouldn't be up here. We should ask where to go for the party."

"Right," Eddo said. He walked to the hallway, opened another door, and flipped a switch. Light illuminated a flight of narrow stone stairs.

He started up the stairs, turned at a landing, and disappeared. His footsteps echoed against the stone as he climbed.

"Eddo!" Luz exclaimed.

Above her, Eddo's footsteps stopped. "Are you coming?" he called.

Luz reluctantly mounted the stairs, her high heels clicking on the stone. The stairs turned twice before she walked through an open door.

Eddo was standing in the middle of the most beautiful sunroom she'd ever seen. It was a perfect half circle of floor-to-ceiling palladium windows. The stairway entrance was centered in the one flat wall so that the windows curved around it. Another brick ceiling rose and arched above the windows and the plank wood floor. The faded red *boveda* brickwork continued down the walls but the windows were set close together so that only 18 inches or so of brick showed between the white painted window moldings. The thick walls caused the windows to be recessed into niches and there was a seat built into each niche below the glass. The windows reflected the light from two wrought iron chandeliers, obscuring the milky darkness outside and emphasizing the fact that the room was completely empty.

"This is incredible," Luz murmured. Despite her misgivings about wandering through a strange house, she drifted to the center of the room and looked around. One window was wider than the others and she realized it was a set of French doors. There was probably a rooftop patio.

"Wouldn't this make a great studio?" Eddo asked. His voice almost echoed in the vast space.

Luz revolved, taking in the complicated masonry, the dramatic window seats, and the dark wood floor. "What, to paint in?"

"Yes."

"It would be fabulous." The room was large enough to accommodate any number of huge canvases. The windows would let in as much light as *la sopa* allowed. Luz swept her gaze around the room once more and sighed. "Let's go. The *despedida* has to be somewhere."

"Wait," Eddo said.

Luz suddenly wondered if he was ill. A cord in his neck throbbed above the collar of his shirt. His hands were rolled into fists and his knuckles were white. "What's the matter?" she asked in alarm.

"I lied to you, Luz," Eddo said. He turned away from her. "Knew I was lying when I said it. Said I would to wait until Monday to talk about us, but I lied."

"You want to talk now?" Luz dug her fingernails into her palm.

"I thought I could bribe you, but I was fooling myself," Eddo went on. "We'd both always wonder."

"I don't understand."

"I need to know right now, Luz, before we go any further."

Eddo spun around. His hazel eyes blazed. "Yes or no. Are you going to marry me or not? You've had two months. If you haven't decided by now, you never will."

"Now?" Luz asked faintly.

"Right now." Eddo crossed the space between them, took her hand, and sank onto one knee. "For the third time, Luz de Maria Alba Mora, will you marry me?"

Luz's eyes slid away from his, unable to deal with the emotion and the immediacy she saw there. He wasn't supposed to be asking now. The *despedida* was supposed to decide.

The despedida was supposed to decide. Her brain did acrobatics as Eddo knelt in front of her. These floors needed polishing. His pants were getting dirty. People had just moved in. They didn't even have furniture yet.

Her cell phone rang.

◆

Chapter 89

To Eddo's amazement Luz jerked her hand out of his grasp.

"My phone," she said breathlessly. "Maybe it's Juan Pablo. He's in Guadalajara." Eddo went to say something then shut his mouth as Luz fumbled for her evening bag. She got the phone out but the bag slipped away from her and fell with a beaded chime onto the floor.

Eddo got to his feet and walked away. He stood facing one of the windows, his back to her. He watched her reflection in the window, phone pressed to her ear. Her mouth moved but he had no idea what she was saying. Her bag was still on the floor. He wondered if another man had called her.

The room was warm. Eddo took off his jacket and laid it on one of the window seats with exaggerated care. He loosened his tie and sat down, refusing to face the truth but knowing that he couldn't avoid it much longer. He hunched over with his elbows on his knees, hands clasped together, and stared at the floor. He'd killed two men and survived a fight for his life without flinching. But right now he wasn't sure he could hold it together.

"Thank you very much," Eddo heard Luz say into the phone. "I'll call you back on Monday."

She broke the connection and came over to him. She stopped when the full skirt of her dress brushed his clasped hands.

He didn't move or speak.

Luz reached out and touched his head where the hair had turned gray over the scar. He couldn't help reacting then, turning his head slightly so that her hand brushed his cheek.

"I'm sorry," Luz said. "I said in San Miguel that I needed time to think. But I just wasted all that time worrying. We'll never get those months back. If you want to be mad at me I'll understand."

Eddo closed his eyes. There was nothing to say. Maybe she'd loved him once or maybe she'd confused it with an emotional rush from what had happened to both of them. Maybe San Miguel had been some forbidden fun for her, but when she got back home she realized that she didn't love him. Or like Pilar had implied, Luz was smart enough to know he was no bargain, that his lifestyle was a chance she wasn't ready to take. Whatever it was, he'd been too caught up in Arturo's campaign and the hunt for Gomez Mazzo to see it.

"That's not all I'm sorry for." Luz's voice was as shaky as he felt. Good, so this was hard for her. "I'm sorry, too," she said. "Because I don't know how to be a politician's wife."

Eddo still didn't speak. He didn't trust his voice.

"I don't know how to do a lot of things you need a wife to do," Luz continued. "It would be different if you were the type who wanted to count plates in Puebla. But I probably wouldn't feel the same if that's the sort of person you were."

She stepped closer, between his knees now and again Eddo couldn't help himself. He slid his arms around her and pressed his cheek into the waist of her dress. Luz stroked his head and he felt himself shudder.

"I'm sorry," Luz said. "I love you, but I don't know to do those things."

"Yes, you do," Eddo said against her dress.

Luz kissed the top of his head, then pulled his hands away, forcing him to him sit up. Eddo felt her press something into his palm and saw the white quartz stone from San Miguel.

"Just don't open your hand," Luz said. She curled his fingers around the stone. "I'll hold onto you and you'll hold onto me. You can teach me the things a politician's wife is supposed to do. Like driving the car. We'll make all our dreams come true together."

She moved back a step.

Eddo slowly uncurled his fist. He stared at the stone, reconciling her words with what he'd been so sure of two minutes ago, then pushed himself off the window seat and walked past her. He put the stone in his pants pocket and picked up her beaded evening bag. He came back to the window seat and placed it carefully on top of his suit coat.

"Nice purse," he said.

Luz blinked at him. "Thank you."

"So." Eddo moved away from her. "Let's get this issue cleared up once and for all. Are you going to marry me or not, Luz de Maria Alba Mora?"

"Yes," Luz said. "I'm going to marry you, Eduardo Martín Bernardo Cortez Castillo."

"Are you sure?" He paced slowly across the wooden floor without looking at her.

"Positive," Luz said. She paced in opposition to him. "I hope that coincides with your plans."

"What about the high class bitches and gossips?" Eddo clasped his hands behind his back.

"I've learned a new phrase," Luz said. She stopped pacing to make a dismissive gesture. "It goes like this. '*Chingate.*'"

"I see." Eddo tried to keep from grinning. He paced to the right. "Will you take de Cortez as your name?"

"If my future husband so desires." Luz paced to the left.

Eddo inclined his head. "He does."

"Then I shall be proud to practice saying Alba de Cortez."

Eddo stopped pacing and turned around to face her. He folded his arms across his chest. "When?"

"Whenever you like," Luz replied evenly.

"Tomorrow," he said. It was a challenge.

Luz raised her eyebrows. "As it happens I'm free tomorrow. I had an important conversation on the agenda but it appears to have been overtaken by events. And it was with some crazy liar so it probably wasn't important."

"Good," Eddo said.

"Good," Luz said.

They stared at each other from opposite sides of the space, light from the chandeliers reflecting off the windows.

"*FINALLY!*" Eddo shouted. He charged across the room and swept up Luz in his arms. She shrieked with laughter as he swung her around the huge half circle. When Eddo stopped he sank his mouth onto hers. They kissed again and again, laughing and clutching at each other.

Footsteps scraped up the stairway.

"*Wow*, Luz," Juan Pablo blurted. "You look like a movie star."

♦

Chapter 90

I'm hallucinating, Luz thought. Overexcitement and too much kissing. Or maybe the spa stylist had twisted her hair too tightly.

But it was Juan Pablo, wearing his graduation suit and a Pineda Covalin tie exactly like Eddo's. He was holding hands with the girl from the newspaper. Carolina Porterfield looked much younger in a pink flowered sundress and flat sandals. Her hair fell in soft waves over bare shoulders.

"She said *yes*," Eddo said, grinning broadly. "*Yes*. Just now."

"*This is so great, Luz!*" Luz found herself enveloped in a bear hug. Juan Pablo squeezed until she couldn't breathe, much less think. When he let go Carolina hugged Luz.

"I'm Carolina." Her Spanish was heavily accented. "I think it's wonderful that you're going to marry Tío Eduardo."

"This is so great. This is so great." Juan Pablo hugged Eddo as if congratulating a good friend.

"I know you're Carolina," Luz said.

"Was it the house?" Carolina grabbed Luz's hands. Her accented words tumbled out happily. "It *must* have convinced you, *right*? I just *knew* it would."

"*This is so great.* Isn't this a great house?" Juan Pablo grabbed Luz again and kissed her cheek. "It made you decide, didn't it?"

Eddo grabbed Luz from behind and pulled her away from Juan Pablo. "Hold on, everybody," he said. "We didn't get to the house yet."

"You didn't tell her?" Juan Pablo asked in surprise. Carolina reattached herself to him.

Tell me what? Luz wanted to say but her brain had turned

into *masa* dough.

"No." Eddo grinned at Juan Pablo and Carolina. "She said yes first."

"All *right*," Juan Pablo said happily. He and Eddo exchanged knowing glances then Juan Pablo grabbed Luz from Eddo and hugged her all over again. "Luz, *this is even better.* Congratulations. This is great."

They were handing her around like a rag doll. It was too surreal. Luz grabbed Eddo's arm. "How do you know my brother?"

"He's . . . uh." Eddo looked at Juan Pablo. They both grinned guiltily. "Let me do this right," Eddo said. He shifted Luz to face Juan Pablo and Carolina. "Luz de Maria, may I introduce you to Juan Pablo Alba, Arturo Romero's personal assistant?"

"His assistant?" Luz repeated.

Juan Pablo beamed.

"Señor Alba is escorting my niece Carolina Porterfield." Eddo turned to the young couple and made a courtly gesture. "Juan Pablo, Carolina. May I introduce my *prometida*, the noted artist Luz de Maria Alba Mora."

"But you can't be here," Luz said to Juan Pablo. "You're in Guadalajara playing *fútbol*."

"I didn't go to Guadalajara, Luz." Juan Pablo shrugged sheepishly.

"Please don't be mad, Luz de Maria," Carolina pleaded.

"Let me explain, *corazón*," Eddo said.

"Yes, you explain," Luz said.

"I called one night and he answered your phone," Eddo said hastily. "We talked about security at the house. Juan Pablo and I kept in touch and I was impressed. He's a good communicator and a clear thinker. Gets things done. So when Arturo said he needed another pair of hands, I suggested we get Juan Pablo up here and see how it went." Eddo kissed Luz's cheek. "Well, the first day Juan Pablo fixed grammar mistakes in a press statement, unclogged Arturo's schedule, found his keys, and made about half a dozen other problems go away. Arturo was pretty happy."

"So . . . wait." Luz blinked, trying to take it all in.

"We've got an arrangement," Eddo said. "He's living in the chauffeur's quarters out back. Rent is one college course per semester. He already registered at UNAM."

"College? Chauffeur's quarters?" Luz was more bewildered than ever. "What are you talking about?"

Eddo's arm tightened around her. "Luz, remember you told me never to buy you a diamond engagement ring?"

"Yes."

"I listened." He paused. "I bought you this house instead."

"You did not," Luz said.

"Not an engagement ring. An engagement house."

"No."

"Yes."

"No."

"Yes."

"To live in?

"I think she's getting it," Eddo said as Juan Pablo and Carolina grinned. "Yes, that's pretty much the plan. We'll live in the main house. You can use this room as your studio. My office is in the other wing. Juan Pablo is in the chauffeur's quarters. I thought we could call it Casa Valencia."

Suddenly Luz was sitting in a window seat. Eddo pressed her head down between her knees.

"I'm not passing out," Luz gasped to a blurry floor. "I'm too dressed up."

"Keep breathing," Eddo said.

"You just want to look down the front of my dress."

Eddo laughed and let her sit up. Luz gulped air as the room regained its lines.

"You knew about this all along?" she said to Juan Pablo.

"Time for us to go," Juan Pablo said. He and Carolina vanished down the stairs.

"Now what?" They'd left so fast Luz felt a stiff breeze.

"Do you remember in San Miguel when we were arguing on the porch?" Eddo eased onto the window seat next to her. "I asked you if all my friends and all my family and everybody I work with got together and told you it was okay, would it convince you to marry me."

"Eduardo Martín Bernardo Cortez Castillo," Luz said slowly. "What have you done?"

"You're the only one coming to a *despedida*," Eddo said. "Everybody else is here to convince you to marry me."

"*Dios*," Luz choked.

"The plan was for you to succumb to either family pressure or the house bribe," Eddo admitted. "But after last week, I didn't want that between us. Nothing lasts unless it's built on honesty."

Luz stared at him in wonder. Life with this man would never be boring.

Eddo pulled Luz to her feet. "I have one last surprise for you. Stay right here." He walked her over to the French doors and made her face them. Luz could see herself in the window, backlit by the chandelier.

"Okay." Luz smoothed her dress in the glass and then Eddo turned out the lights.

He came back to stand beside her. As Luz's eyes adjusted she could see outside. It was a standard Mexico City night. The sky was milky dark. But as Luz looked out the windows, it seemed as if she was seeing a thousand twinkling stars below her. The sky was blank but the ground was scattered with silver flickers.

"It's a *barranca* down there," Eddo said. "Cuts across the entire back of the property. Pilar and Carolina stuck about a thousand candles into the walls this morning." He kissed the back of her neck, just there. "I tried to find stars but there aren't any in this whole damn city. Will these do?"

Tears pricked the back of Luz's eyes. "They'll do very well."

◆

They stepped onto a wide flagstone patio. It was surrounded by a low stone wall and lit by candles. Several people started applauding. The cheering spread to the people standing on a second patio a few steps below the first.

"She said *yes*," Eddo shouted exultantly. Luz blushed.

A woman detached herself from the crowd. She was wearing a slate gray silk dress, a rope of pearls, high-heeled sandals, and familiar hazel eyes.

"Welcome to the family, Luz de Maria," the woman said.

"Thank you, Pilar," Luz said.

The crowd shifted and the noise swelled. Luz was engulfed by *Los Hierros*. Diego was the first to kiss her. He was shouldered out of the way by Vasco. Then others she didn't know but who wanted to congratulate *el jefe's* lady. And she finally met Ana, Tomás's wife.

"I suppose you know what a *pendejo* you're getting, Luz de Maria," Tomás said jokingly.

"Hey, you're here to talk her into it, not make her change her mind," Eddo protested.

Someone near them tapped on a glass for quiet and Luz realized it was Arturo Romero. The former judge and now presidential candidate was tall and thin, with a quiet dignity that was more forceful in person than on television. His wife Imelda stood next to him.

Luz blinked. Romero was wearing the same tie as Eddo. And Juan Pablo. And Tomás. She looked around the crowd. Every man was wearing the same tie.

A maid came by with a tray of champagne flutes. Eddo took two off the tray and handed one to Luz. There was a purple paper flower wired to the stem of each flute.

"Ladies and Gentlemen, may I have your attention." Romero's voice was deep and strong. "I've been asked to propose a toast to my very dear friend and colleague Eduardo, and to Luz de Maria, the bravest woman in the world." He got a big round of laughter and applause for that one. Luz saw Diego hooting on the upper patio and raised her glass to him. He was wearing the expensive Pineda Covalin tie with a black shirt and jeans; the sort of rogue who'd get a lot of attention in rave clubs in Colonia Roma.

"Now please," Romero said as the applause subsided. "I've known Eduardo for a good many years. He's a man of action, someone who doesn't sit still for very long. The woman who will be by his side in good times and bad must have courage and fortitude and a generous heart."

Eddo put his arm around Luz's waist.

Romero held up his glass. "He has had the incredible good luck to find just that person." He bowed to Luz and met her eyes. There was nothing but warmth and respect in his gaze. "But Eduardo is not the only beneficiary of this incredible woman's talent. For it was her concept that will launch the Violet Revolution. Eduardo may be getting a wife, but the rest of us are getting a genius!" There was more applause and cheering.

"Come the fall, these little paper violets are going to be all over the country," Eddo murmured into Luz's ear. "They're going to be the symbol of the education campaign. The Violet Revolution."

"So raise your glasses with me," Arturo Romero said. "To Eduardo and Luz de Maria. Long life and happiness forever. *Salud.*"

"*SALUD,*" everyone chorused.

Luz met them all. The Romeros and Eddo's PAN colleagues seemed to regard her as a wizard for having unwittingly given the campaign a theme. The Cortez family treated her like royalty, the older aunts and uncles welcoming her with an enthusiasm she never expected. They obviously loved Eddo and respected his work, but clearly considered him the black sheep of the family, the one who wasn't content to stay in Puebla but instead did disreputable things like become a cop and go into politics. At least now he was getting married.

There was little talk of Luz's family or background, although she got questions about her artwork. One of the younger uncles was disappointed that she did not paint nudes.

It was a magical night. There were big buffet tables laid out on the lower patio, groaning under huge copper pans of *paella*, roast chicken, salads, and desserts. Tubs of ice chilled bottles of beer and an endless supply of champagne, while a waiter made *mojitos* from cold rum and fresh limes and mint.

The *barranca* was a long narrow cut in the earth, about 12 feet deep, 40 feet long, and 20 feet at the widest point. Flagstone steps led down into it from the lower patio. The bottom was flat and grassy. A *mariachi* band set up at the far end. After people ate they danced in the *barranca* as the candles twinkled all around them.

Luz ate *paella* and drank champagne with Eddo, Ana and Tomás, and Vasco and a tiny woman named Conchita who had once worked for Eddo. Juan Pablo moved easily through the crowd, Carolina attached to him like a limpet. He knew everybody and seemed quite at ease. Later, Luz danced with Arturo Romero. It was similar to dancing with a flagpole. Eddo danced with Imelda and Luz knew he was having the same experience. After that *Los Hierros* claimed her and Luz danced with half a dozen men, and then with Eddo's Tío Bernardo who ran Marca Cortez. She danced with Pilar's husband Bill who made her try out her English with him. His Spanish was excellent so they ended up speaking a mix of languages. When their dance ended Pilar intervened.

"I thought you might like a break before your feet wear out."

"I'd love to," said Luz. "Thank you."

They found a quiet table on the upper patio.

"Let's just sit for a minute and chat," Pilar said.

There was something in the older woman's tone. Luz folded her hands on the table, sure she knew what was coming.

"Eduardito didn't do you justice, Luz de Maria," Pilar began. "You're much more glamorous than he described."

Luz smiled thinly, waiting for the punchline.

"I know you love my brother," Pilar said. She twisted her pearls into a knot. Luz wondered if they were real. "But he's a difficult person. He bulls through life with his head down, pitching obstacles out of his path. He and Arturo play in the big leagues. Against some tough opponents. It's an ugly game in this country and they play to win."

"I know," Luz said.

"But are you sure you can live with it?" Pilar asked. "That's really what I have to know. Eduardito is as tough as they come. Life with him will be messy."

"I'm pretty tough, too," Luz said. She met Pilar's eyes.

Pilar nodded. "I expect you are." She slid an envelope across the table to Luz. "Here. It's not much but I hope you take it."

Luz touched the envelope. The Cortez family had been kind to her all night, probably because Arturo Romero was there. But now the real message had arrived. The envelope was thick. Cash, no doubt. How much was a pure *castellano* bloodline worth these days?

"Does Eddo know you're doing this?" Luz asked.

"Oh, dear, no." Pilar rolled her eyes. "Don't show him either. We don't need his temper going off in all directions."

"No," Luz said. "We wouldn't want that."

"Go ahead," Pilar urged. "Open it before he comes up here."

Chingate. Luz knew she'd say it to Pilar if she had to. She opened the envelope and pulled out a handful of old photographs.

"What's this?" she asked blankly.

"I thought you should have them," Pilar said. "To start a family album."

Luz spread the photos on the table, flushed with relief and shame. "Thank you," she murmured.

There was Eddo around age three; a scowling, chunky fellow, wearing a miniature *mariachi* outfit complete with spangled and embroidered jacket and a wide *sombrero*. Eddo about age ten, with Pilar and their parents. He'd lost the baby fat but not the scowl. Eddo playing *fútbol* at four, at six, at 12, at 17.

"Check out the hair." Pilar pointed to one picture of him running with the ball. He was in his late teens. His hair was long and pulled back into a ponytail.

Luz chuckled. "I'll bet he was wild."

"He was hell," Pilar said. "My mother never told him no."

The other pictures were of his high school graduation, his college graduation, and his graduation from law school. Eddo in his Highway Patrol uniform.

"That was when he made lieutenant," Pilar said.

Luz put down the photo. "Pilar, can I ask you a question?"

"Of course."

"What were your parents like?" Luz swallowed hard. "Would they be happy? You know, about me marrying Eddo?"

"Hmmm." Pilar sat back in her chair and considered.

"It's no, right?"

"Twenty years ago, you would have been right." Pilar nodded. "The Cortez name meant a lot to my father. My parents saw Eddo as the one who would carry it on."

"But he'd carry on the name with the appropriate woman," Luz offered.

"The appropriate woman is the one who knows him and still loves him." Pilar pointed a manicured finger at Luz. "That's you, Luz de Maria. And if it's any consolation all my aunts and uncles seem pleased. You've made a very good impression."

"Nobody's mentioned my background at all," Luz said, giving Pilar another opening. "Everyone's been . . . discreet."

"Look, Luz de Maria." Pilar leaned forward and her voice got hard. "Twenty-seven years ago I married a *gringo* and moved away and I didn't do it because I needed a job in *El Norte*. Know what I mean? You don't think that raised eyebrows in this family? You don't think that was a hard thing to do? Bill worked for a big department store back then. He came to Puebla on a buying trip and that was it for me. Six months later I was living in a strange country, and *everything* was strange. I'd gone from being a rich pampered girl living in a *hacienda* to being a nobody, just Bill's *spic* wife in a tiny apartment. I didn't know English very well. I couldn't cook. I didn't even know how to do my own laundry. I put Bill's ties in the washing machine and they came out like shoelaces."

"Oh," Luz said, nonplussed.

"And get this." Pilar gave a knowing half smile. "Bill's not Catholic."

Luz stifled a gasp as the enormity of what Pilar had done hit her.

"Mama called every week for years," Pilar said. "Wanted to know when I was moving back to Mexico. I'd cry and cry every time I hung up. She sent money, too, said Bill couldn't give me a nice lifestyle. Bill would get furious and send it all back. He thought I was going to leave him. It's why we didn't have Carolina until so very late." She sat back in her chair. "So now Eduardito is marrying a *mestizo*. It's not the end of the world for the Cortez family and everybody knows it."

"What does everybody know?"

Eddo was right behind Luz. She and Pilar had been so engrossed in their conversation they hadn't seen him come up.

"I've been looking for you two." He pulled up a chair and dropped into it with easy grace. His tie was loose, the suit coat gone, and he held a half-smoked cigar. He grinned at Luz and the emotion sparked between them.

"This is a private conversation," Pilar said. "I'm telling her all your bad habits."

"She already knows." Eddo gestured with the cigar at the photos spread out on the table. "What have you got there?" His eye fell on the photograph of himself in the police uniform. "You're kidding me."

"These are mine," Luz said and scooped up the picture before he could do anything. "Pilar gave them to me."

"Ah, *Madre de Dios*," Eddo groaned as he caught sight of the chubby *mariachi*. "How could you do this to me, Pilar?"

"Paying you back for that arrow in my head." Pilar stood up. "Have you seen Bill?"

"He's playing some tequila drinking game with Diego and the guys." Eddo indicated the lower patio. "Hard to tell who's winning."

"Your friends are degenerates." Pilar rushed down the steps.

"Come dance with me, *corazón*," Eddo said. "I'll even get rid of this cigar."

They left the photos with her purse and his suit coat on the lower level of the patio and walked down the steps into the *barranca*. The *mariachis* were playing a slow guitar serenade. Eddo put his arm around Luz's waist and caught up her right hand. The candles glittered as the couples turned slowly on the grass. The night air in the *barranca* was pleasant and fresh as if *la sopa* didn't settle that low.

Arturo gave them a knowing smile as he and Imelda swayed by. Luz thought that there must still be a lot of romance in their relationship. Carolina and Juan Pablo didn't notice anyone else as they danced pressed together.

"They're dancing awfully close," Luz murmured.

"Don't worry," Eddo said. "I talked to him. Man to man."

"Thank you."

"You did a good job with that kid."

Luz sighed in contentment. "This like being in a bowl of stars."

"And the ball is never out of play," Eddo said.

"The ball?"

"Juan Pablo and I kicked the ball around in here. *Madre de Dios* that kid can run."

It had been a long day and the surprises and shocks had taken their toll. Luz took off her shoes but held onto them as she and Eddo danced. She rested her head against his shoulder and the guitar music lulled her.

"You know, *corazón*," Eddo said. "I was serious about getting married tomorrow but I don't think it can be done that fast."

"I know. But let's just do it as soon as we can."

"What about Lupe?"

"She's making a life with Tío and I need to accept it."

"The way she'll have to accept that you're making a life with me." They moved gently in time to the music.

"I'd like to send the girls to Santa Catalina," Luz said. "If Tío's there, he can do the rest."

"Whatever you want to do is fine with me."

"You're a good man, Rodrigo," Luz said against his shoulder.

"Thought about a honeymoon?" Eddo asked.

Luz was almost afraid to say it. "New York?"

"The Guggenheim."

"But I don't have a visa."

"My wife can get a visa." Eddo swayed her as the guitars strummed a slightly faster riff. "So, first New York for the Guggenheim, then how about Madrid? We should go to the Prado and then the Museo del Ejército."

"Museo del Ejército?" That was Spain's Museum of the Army.

"I hear Tizona is on display there," Eddo said.

"Tizona," Luz murmured. "I'd like that, Rodrigo."

"I love you, Jimena," Eddo said into her hair.

"I love you, too." Luz felt the thread around her heart like the ribbon on a gift. Eddo would always have the other end and it would always stretch.

The grass was cool and soft under her bare feet. Her head was in the right place against Eddo's shoulder with the bump in the bone. Everyone else drifted out of the *barranca*. The party was winding down. Tío Bernardo was asleep in a chaise, Diego and the rest of the *Los Hierros* group were playing dominoes on the upper patio, aunts and uncles were picking over the desserts, the PAN contingent was having cognac, and Pilar was filling Bill with coffee.

"Hey," Eddo said. "You never told me who called you."

"What?" Luz yawned.

"Upstairs. When we were talking. I was on one knee, if you recall, and your phone rang. Who was it?"

"*Oh.*" Luz raised her head to look at him. So much had happened that night she'd all but forgotten the call. "It was Elaine Ralston. Guess how many of my paintings sold the first week the gallery was open?"

Eddo stopped dancing and looked as if he'd been struck by lightning. "Four."

"Yes. All four."

"*I knew it!*" Eddo shouted, startling the *mariachis.*

He lifted Luz off the ground and she tipped her head back and laughed. The sound echoed against the walls of the *barranca* and rippled past a thousand stars. Eddo's hazel eyes sparkled silver at her and Luz was so ecstatically light that she was flying in his arms and time stopped because *this was it.*

This was the moment she was supposed to have for the rest of her life.

◆

Epilogue

The space was a paean to Mexican history, with an enormous framed antique Mexican flag stretched across one wall and vintage photographs of Mexican government landmarks on the other side of the room. The dark wood conference table could seat 40 and was half filled with the ministry's top executives.

The monthly event was equal parts status check and social gathering. A late lunch was always served; this time it was chicken broth with rice and egg followed by *albóndigas en chipotle quemado*. Monte Xanic merlot from Hugo's favorite local winery accompanied the meal. Waiters took away the plates and set out a buffet of coffee and assorted *postres*, then discreetly left.

Lorena carried her coffee to the head of the table and the meeting officially came to order. She said a few words about how happy she was to be there as the new Minister of Public Security and how welcome everyone had made her feel. She'd given up her presidential campaign to serve her country in its time of need, she stressed, implying that she really belonged at a higher level.

She wound up her remarks to the group, with her wise yet sincere smile hiding the uncomfortable awareness that her audience appeared to be made of stone. Placards had been made with the name and office of each person and behind the placards all but one of the executives seated at the big table were men. All wore the same flinty expression. The lone woman was a tiny thing who at least had a small smile on her face. Lorena decided the woman would be her ally. *Lorena's your sister.* She'd ask her to stay afterwards, be interested in whatever the Office of Special Investigations did, imply it could have a bigger budget.

Lorena finished her remarks and gestured to the man on her immediate left. He was the head of the legislative liaison office and discussed some new law having to do with police retention and recruitment. There was a bit of discussion around the table that Lorena didn't quite follow, and then the next man started talking about his office and what was going on there.

When it was Conchita Félix Pacheco's turn she mentioned that a new attorney had joined the office and they were at full strength for the first time since November. She didn't say anything else, just turned to the next person around the table.

The tiny woman was no doubt intimidated by being in a room of men. "Just a minute," Lorena said magnanimously. "We'd all like to hear more about what your office is doing."

To Lorena's surprise Conchita just smiled. "That's all I have today," she said.

"Really, I must insist," Lorena said.

"Let's keep going," Ernesto Silvio said from his seat at Lorena's right.

The meeting continued as Lorena seethed that once again Ernesto Silvio appeared to be managing her affairs. She hadn't wanted him to come to the ministry with her but Fernando had insisted that she'd need a new Chief of Staff. That had turned out to be a big job, with everybody except Lorena herself reporting to him.

When all the discussion ended and Lorena adjourned the meeting, she asked Conchita to remain. To her chagrin, Silvio stayed in the room as well, chatting to the executives as they filed out the door. They all laughed at insider jokes Lorena didn't understand.

At last it was only the two women and Ernesto Silvio. The Chief of Staff puttered over to the dessert table. Lorena took advantage of his preoccupation and fixed Conchita with her wise, older sister look. "Please understand that I will be your patron here in the ministry," Lorena said. "You can compete with these men, don't let them intimidate you."

"Señora, I appreciate your consideration," Conchita said. Her smile was cold when it should have been grateful. "I'm perfectly comfortable with my ministry colleagues."

"Of course you are," Lorena said soothingly. "But it was obvious you didn't want to say very much in front of them." She patted the other woman's forearm in a gesture of female solidarity. "I want you to know I think women have to speak up, demand to be treated as equals."

Conchita's smile stayed in place but her eyes flickered over to Silvio and back before she spoke. "Most of the activity in my office is restricted and cannot be discussed in an open meeting like this."

"Well," Lorena said, disguising the fact that she hadn't known that some things would be classified. "You'll have to brief me separately."

"Certain permissions are necessary and not everyone has them," Silvio said. He had a plate of chocolate cake in one hand and a fork in the other as he came over to where the two women were standing by the head of the conference table. "Another dessert, Conchita?"

"No, Ernesto." Conchita's smile for Silvio was genuine. "You know I don't eat sweets."

He actually chuckled. "You spent too much time working for Cortez."

"I'll see you next week, Ernesto," Conchita said. She looked at Lorena, that coolness on her face once more. "Good afternoon, señora." She picked up her purse, a very nice French leather bag, and left the conference room.

Lorena turned on Silvio. "How dare you presume to dictate who is briefed and on what issues?" she snapped.

"Authorization to access certain information is the law," Silvio said and took a bite of cake.

"Do you mean to say," Lorena said, realization dawning. "That I do not have the proper authorization?"

"The President has instructed that you will not be authorized to see restricted information," Silvio said. He put his cake plate on the table and moved to the conference room door. "So please do not press Conchita or any other department head for information you are not authorized to see."

He left.

Lorena went into her office. It was a grand space and she'd filled it with framed pictures of her public appearances. She sat in Hugo's chair, at Hugo's desk, and thought about how confused everything had become. Once upon a time she was going to be president of Mexico.

But now she was in jail and her own husband had provided the warden.

El Fin

From the author

Thank you for reading THE HIDDEN LIGHT OF MEXICO CITY, the novel I wrote after living in Mexico for several years. It is based on many of the people I met and the experiences I had there. No matter what else I write or where I go, HIDDEN LIGHT and Mexico will always have a special place in my heart.

Keep reading. There are extra goodies ahead!
- Glossary of Spanish words, and
- An excerpt from CLIFF DIVER, the first Detective Emilia Cruz novel.

All the best, Carmen

About Carmen Amato

Carmen Amato writes mystery and suspense, including the Detective Emilia Cruz police series set in Acapulco and optioned for television. Emilia Cruz is the first female detective on the Acapulco police force, confronting Mexico's drug cartels and legendary government corruption.

Originally from New York, Carmen was educated there as well as in Virginia and Paris, France, while her experiences in Mexico and Central America inspire many of her books. Visit her website at carmenamato.net to get a free copy of the Detective Emilia Cruz Starter Library.

Glossary of Spanish Terms

Abarrotes: snacks
Barranca: canyon
Cazuela: clay oven dish used for baking casserole-style recipes
Cena: dinner
Chica: girl
Chilaquiles: breakfast hash made with leftover tortillas
El Norte: the United States
El teniente: lieutenant
Federales: Mexican federal police
Fútbol: soccer
Halcone: word meaning falcon used by drug gangs to mean a person acting as a lookout
Jefe: chief, person in charge
Madre de Dios: Mother of God, used as exclamation
Maldita: damn, damned
Mercado: market
Norteamericano: North American
Oferta: altar
Pendejo: asshole, jerk
Placas: license plates
Pistolero: gunfighter
Pollo: chicken
Posada: Christmas pageant in which children act out the story of the birth of Jesus
Rayos: exclamation, similar to "oh hell"
Sicario: cartel henchman or assassin
Sitio: taxi service operating from a fixed stand
Talavera: hand painted pottery from the Puebla region

CLIFF DIVER
Detective Emilia Cruz Book 1

Chapter 1

"It's against Mexican law," Emilia said.

"Driving a car?" the *gringo* asked skeptically.

"Just what is your relationship to the owners of this car and their driver?" Emilia asked. The man sitting next to her desk had yellow hair and a starched blue shirt and the impatient confidence all *norteamericanos* seemed to have.

"The Hudsons come to Acapulco every few months." He pulled out a business card. "I manage the hotel where they stay."

Emilia took the card. *Kurt Rucker, General Manager, Palacio Réal Hotel, Punta Diamante, Acapulco.* The Palacio Réal was one of the most exclusive and luxurious hotels in Acapulco, an architectural marvel clinging to the cliffs above the Punta Diamante bay on the southeastern edge of the city. Even the card was rich, with embossed printing and the hotel logo in the corner.

"Let me explain," Emilia said. She carefully laid the card next to the arrest file on her desk and tried to look unimpressed as she settled back in her desk chair. "A Mexican citizen may not drive a vehicle that carries a foreign license plate without the foreign owners of the vehicle being in it."

"So the problem was that the owners weren't in the car," Rucker said.

"Yes," Emilia said. "Señor Ruiz was alone in the vehicle."

"The Hudsons drive down to Mexico several times a year." Rucker leaned toward her and one immaculate sleeve bumped the nameplate reading *Detective Emilia Cruz Encinos*. There were initials embroidered on his shirt cuff. KHR. Emilia resisted a sudden silly urge to run a finger over the stitching.

"They always hire Ruiz when they come," he went on.

"They travel all over and he does errands alone. There's never been any trouble before. Monterrey, Mexico City, Guadalajara."

"Well, señor." Emilia moved her nameplate. "Here in Acapulco we enforce the law."

"Of course." His Spanish was excellent. "I fully understand. But how do the Hudsons get their car back?"

From across the squad room, Emilia saw Lt. Inocente watching her from the doorway to his office. *El teniente* nodded curtly at her then started talking to another detective. It was late afternoon and almost all the detectives were there making calls, writing up reports, joking and arguing.

Emilia opened the file and scanned the report of the arrest of Alejandro Ruiz Garcia, charged with illegally operating a vehicle with foreign *placas*. Three days ago he'd been arrested in front of the main branch of Banamex Bank. Bailed out by a cousin the next day. Ruiz had been driving a white Suburban owned by Harry and Lois Hudson of Flagstaff, Arizona. The vehicle was now sitting in the impound yard behind the police station. The keys were in Emilia's shoulder bag.

"Why are you here instead of the Hudsons?" she asked.

"They returned to the United States," Rucker said. "Before they left they asked me to help get the car back."

"They left Mexico?" Emilia didn't know why she should be so surprised. What was one car more or less to rich *norteamericanos*?

"They flew. Said it was a family emergency."

Emilia closed the file. "Señor, in order for the Hudsons to regain possession of their car they must present proof of ownership."

"Of course." Rucker passed a paper across the desk. "Here is their title to the vehicle."

It was a copy of an official-looking document. Emilia knew enough English to pick out words like *name* and *number* and *address* but it didn't matter. The document was meaningless under Mexican law. She handed it back with a sigh. "Señor, they need to provide the history of the vehicle, including all sales transactions and verification of taxes paid every year of the car's life."

"What?" His eyes widened in disbelief.

They were the color of the ocean far beyond the cliffs at La Quebrada.

Emilia had never seen eyes like that and it took her a moment to realize he expected an answer and another moment to untangle her tongue. "After six months, if they have not produced the necessary documentation, the vehicle becomes the property of the state."

The disbelief drained out of Rucker's face as he realized she wasn't joking. He exhaled sharply, as if he had the lungs of a swimmer, and his gaze traveled around the squad room, taking in the gray metal desks, ancient filing cabinets, and walls covered in posters, notices, and photographs from ongoing investigations. Most of the detectives were in casual clothes; those who'd been outside much of the day had shirts stained with sweat at the neck and underarms. All of them wore weapons in hip or shoulder holsters. Emilia wondered if he realized that she was the only woman there.

El teniente went into his office and closed the door.

"There's a complicating factor," Rucker said to Emilia. "The Hudsons' cell phone is out of service. I was hoping that you could give me the contact information for their driver. He might have another number for them."

"I would have to check with my superior before giving out that sort of information," Emilia said primly.

"I'd appreciate it if you would and then call me." Rucker stood and held out his hand. "Thank you very much, Detective Cruz."

"You're welcome." Emilia stood up, too, and shook his hand. His grip was dry and strong.

Rucker smiled at her, a wide smile that lit his face and made the blue-green eyes. His teeth were perfectly straight and white.

Emilia smiled back, caught, knowing this was the wrong place and the wrong time and the wrong man but unable to stop smiling at this *gringo* whose world of wealth and leisure was light years away from the *barrio* she came from. She wished she was wearing something nicer than her work uniform of jeans, tee shirt and the Spanish walking sandals that had cost two months' salary. Her gun was in a belt holster and her straight black hair was scraped back into its usual ponytail.

"Oye!"

Emilia gave a start and dropped Rucker's hand. Her partner Rico loomed over her desk.

"You're done here," Rico said to Rucker, jerking his chin in Emilia's direction, his leather jacket falling open to reveal his gun. "She's got a man."

Emilia felt her face flush with embarrassment and anger, but before she could say a word, Rucker held out his hand to Rico. "Kurt Rucker. Nice to meet you."

The bustling squad room was suddenly silent. Lt. Inocente opened the door to his office and stood in the entrance again.

Disconcerted, Rico shook hands. The handshake held for a fraction too long. Emilia watched Rico's round face tighten. He let go first.

Kurt Rucker nodded at Emilia and walked out of the squad room. The noise level went back to normal.

"Ricardo Portillo, you're a *pendejo*," Emilia hissed at Rico.

"That *gringo* has a grip like the bite of a horse," Rico said in surprise, flexing his hand painfully.

"Don't be lying and saying I've got a man unless I ask you to," Emilia whispered hotly and slammed herself into her chair.

"Stay with your own kind, *chica*," Rico warned. There was an edge to his voice.

"You're not my mother." Emilia jerked her chair around to face her computer, effectively ending the conversation. Rico made a snorting noise as he went back to his own desk.

Emilia typed in her password and checked her inbox. A review by the Secretariat de Gobernación of drug cartel activities across Mexico. A report of a robbery in Acapulco's poorest *barrio* neighborhood that would probably never be investigated. Notice of a reward for a child kidnapped in the nearby town of Ixtapa who was almost certainly dead by now.

Emilia turned away from the computer and scanned the room. Silently she counted the detectives in the room. Including herself and Rico, eight of Acapulco's ten detectives were there. Silvio, the most senior detective, was at his desk, as was his partner Fuentes. Gomez and Castro, the two most raucous men, were joking by the coffee maker. Macias was at the murder board wall copying something into a notebook about the latest set of virtually unsolvable cartel killings. Sandor was swearing quietly by the decrepit copier as he fooled with the paper trays. She knew that Loyola and Ibarra were out on a call that had come in after lunch. They were all accounted for.

She took a roll of toilet paper out of her desk drawer and walked out of the squadroom.

Maybe she shouldn't care and just use the public women's bathroom behind the holding cells but they weren't going to scare her out of what she'd earned. As a detective she had the right to use the detectives-only bathroom. It was down the hall from the squadroom, quieter and brighter than any other facility in the building. The stalls had long since lost their doors and there was rarely any toilet paper but it was reserved for the elite of the police force and that included her.

Emilia went in. The space was long and narrow with the three doorless toilet stalls along one wall. On the opposite wall a row of urinals hung below a mirror running the width of the space. A single sink was located between the last urinal and the door. The cement floor was cracked and spotted with yellow stains. This late in the day the place smelled of piss and stale cigarettes but Emilia was alone.

She went into a stall, slid down her jeans, sat down on the cool porcelain and let nature take its course.

The bathroom door opened and Lt. Inocente came in.

As Emilia watched helplessly, he glanced at the mirror above the urinals. *El teniente's* face was expressionless as he saw Emilia's reflection as she sat on the toilet with her jeans around her knees and the toilet paper in her hands. Emilia pulled her gaze down before her eyes could meet his in the mirror.

There was the soft sound of a zipper being pulled and then Emilia heard a stream tinkle into the urinal. She hastily used the toilet paper and fastened her jeans. Lt. Inocente probably watched her every move but she wasn't going to give him the satisfaction of letting him know she was bothered. Emilia didn't look at him or say a word as she tucked the toilet paper roll under one arm and washed her hands at the sink. When she left, Lt. Inocente was still standing motionless in front of the urinal with his pants unzipped. The stream had ended.

Emilia walked back to her desk and flipped the roll back into the drawer.

When she'd first started to use the detectives' bathroom the men had often followed her in. They'd do what *el teniente* had done, but loudly and joking about it, making sure she saw their equipment. Emilia had ignored them, until the day five walked in and stood around the doorless cubicle. As soon as she started to pull up her pants Castro had opened his own pants and announced he was going to give her what she'd been looking for. He'd shoved his hand between her legs, with his own pants around his thighs and Emilia had grabbed his balls and dug in her fingernails and head butted his chest at the same time. Castro had screamed like a stuck pig as Emilia charged hard, driving him backwards through the surprised onlookers until the back of his head connected with the rim of a urinal. The porcelain had cracked as Castro's eyes rolled back in his head and the episode was over.

Since then, by silent agreement, none of the detectives ever went into the bathroom when they saw Emilia head out of the squadroom with her roll of white toilet paper.

Except for *el teniente*. It wasn't frequent, maybe only every few months, and he never said a word but it was still unnerving. Emilia didn't know if it was an accident--his door was usually closed so he probably didn't realize she'd walked out with the toilet paper--or deliberate. She didn't really want to know as long as he didn't bother her.

Her phone rang. It was the desk sergeant saying that a Señor *Rooker* wished to see her. Emilia avoided Rico's eye as she said, yes, the sergeant could let el señor pass into the detectives' area.

A minute later Rucker was standing by her desk, sweat beaded on his forehead. The starched collar of his shirt was damp.

"There's a head," he gulped. "Someone's head in a bucket on the hood of my car."

One last thing . . .

If you enjoyed THE HIDDEN LIGHT OF MEXICO CITY and think others will, too, your input would be greatly appreciated. Please leave a book review on Amazon.com.

Thank you and happy reading.

All the best, Carmen

www.carmenamato.net

Made in the USA
Middletown, DE
24 October 2022